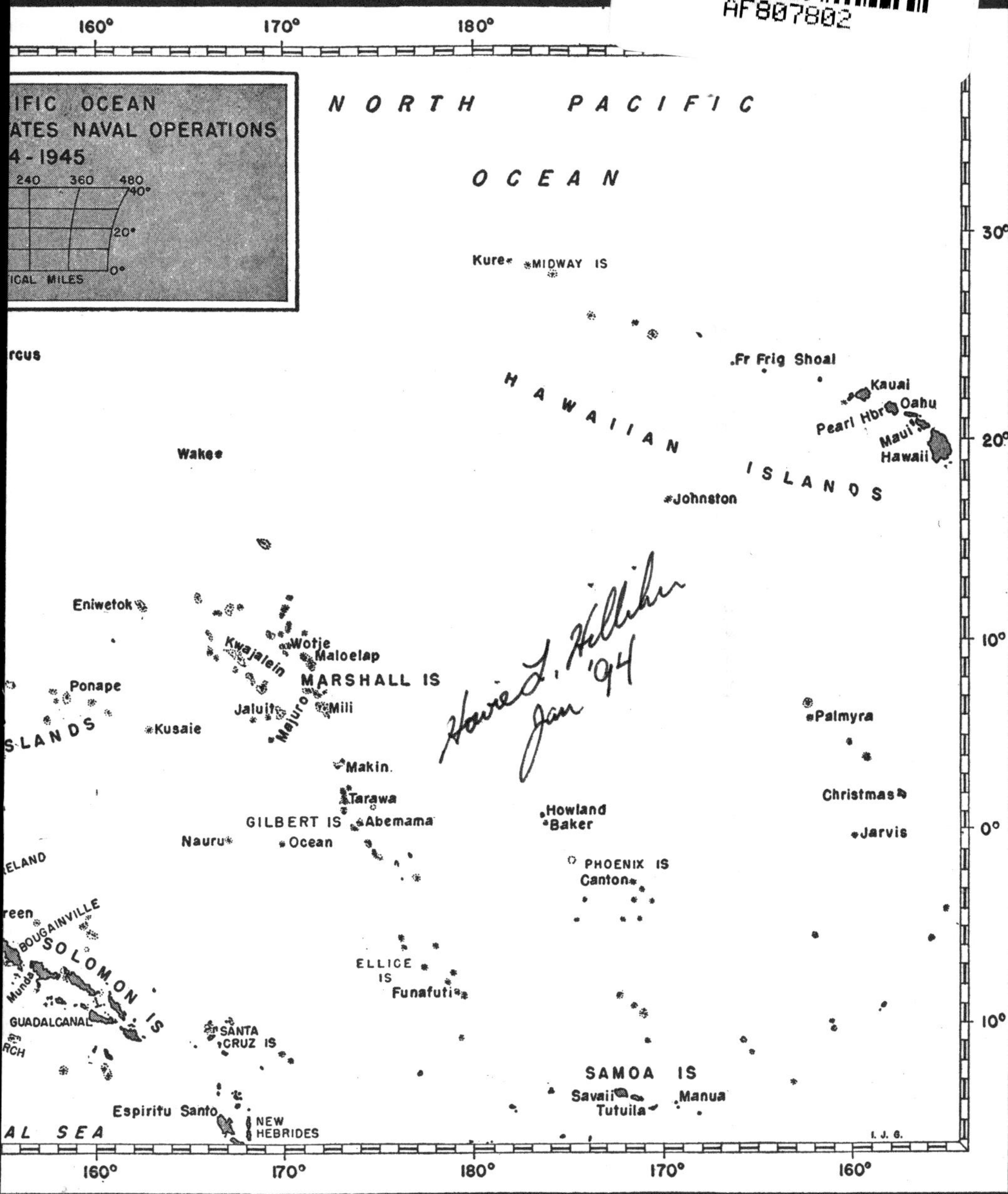

IFIC OCEAN
ATES NAVAL OPERATIONS
4 - 1945
240 360 480
40°
20°
0°
ICAL MILES
NORTH PACIFIC OCEAN
160°
170°
180°
30°
20°
10°
0°
10°
Kure
MIDWAY IS
Fr Frig Shoal
HAWAIIAN ISLANDS
Kauai
Oahu
Pearl Hbr
Maui
Hawaii
Johnston
Wake
rcus
Eniwetok
Kwajalein
Wotje
Maloelap
MARSHALL IS
Jaluit
Majuro
Mili
Ponape
Kusaie
SLANDS
Makin
Tarawa
GILBERT IS
Abemama
Nauru
Ocean
Howland
Baker
Palmyra
Christmas
Jarvis
PHOENIX IS
Canton
ELAND
reen
BOUGAINVILLE
SOLOMON IS
Munda
GUADALCANAL
RCH
SANTA CRUZ IS
ELLICE IS
Funafuti
SAMOA IS
Savaii
Tutuila
Manua
Espiritu Santo
NEW HEBRIDES
AL SEA
I. J. G.

New Guinea

A NOVEL BY

WILLIAM P. MACK

Vice Admiral, U.S.Navy (Ret.)

N&A

The Nautical & Aviation Publishing Company of America
Baltimore, Maryland

Library of Congress Catalog Card Number : 93-26229

ISBN : 1-877853-28-3

Printed in the United States of America
Library of Congress Cataloging-in-Publication Data

Mack, William P., 1915
New Guinea: a novel / by William P. Mack.

p. cm.
ISBN 1-877853-28-3
1. World War, 1939-1945—Naval operations, American—Fiction
2. World War, 1939-1945—Campaign—New Guinea—Fiction.
3. United States—History, Naval—20th century—Fiction.
I. Title
PS3563.A3132C48 1993 93-26229
813' .54—dc20 cip

CHAPTER ONE

Lieutenant Junior Grade Richard Auerbach cranked up the wheels on his F4F Wildcat fighter and glanced astern as the deck of the carrier Enterprise receded behind his tail. His wingman was struggling to catch up with him. Auerbach, as section leader, had to locate and concentrate on the other section of two Wildcats ahead. Farther out were several other four-aircraft divisions gaining altitude and heading northwest toward the Central Solomon Islands. Somewhere astern was Rennell Island.

He had a few seconds to check his cockpit and his personal gear. At just under six feet, his one hundred and eighty pounds seemed to be stuffed into his flight suit. The survival gear he was wearing further crowded the small cockpit. He pulled the helmet closer over his sandy hair and adjusted his goggles over his blue eyes. He sat forward against his shoulder straps to test their adjustment and could feel them restraining his chest. He felt that he was ready, and he looked ahead as far as the limits of his cockpit would allow.

The last intelligence his flight had been given in the stuffy ready room was that the heavy cruiser *Chicago*, now some 50 miles ahead, had been torpedoed by Japanese aircraft. The mission of the *Enterprise* fighters was to keep any more Japanese aircraft flying from bases in the Solomons from attacking the stricken cruiser. Auerbach hoped the Japanese would show up. So far he had made several attacks on fleeing Zeros but had not shot any down.

Soon the flight leader spotted the *Chicago* and her screen of half a dozen destroyers. ''There she is,'' the flight leader said over his radio. ''A helluva sad sight.''

Auerbach took his eyes off the fighter ahead for a few seconds and looked down. The crippled cruiser was barely making way behind a straining fleet tug.

He took a quick look at his watch. It was 1600, only a half hour since they had taken off, but it seemed like hours had passed. He shifted his buttocks on the hard parachute pack and tried to find a more comfortable position. He resigned himself to the discomfort and hoped the Japanese aircraft would show up soon.

On the fifth orbit around the task group, the flight leader said, ''The ships below report many radar contacts approaching from the northwest.''

Then the destroyer with the air control duty below ordered them to ''Vector three zero zero buster.''

The aircraft ahead turned to the course, and Auerbach eased his throttle ahead to match the increasing speed of the flight leader. ''Torpedo planes ahead,'' The flight leader said. ''Intend to attack toward the west. Follow me.''

The flight leader's F4F nosed over, and the other aircraft followed. Auerbach was nervous. This was too easy. There must be Japanese Zero fighters ahead somewhere. He tried to shield his eyes from the setting sun, but it was hard to see toward the sun. All he could see was a rainbow colored ring on his windshield.

Then he saw them through the reflection. A swarm of black spots was coming right at them, growing in size by the seconds. ''Zeros at ten o'clock,'' he shouted.

But the flight leader was intent on the Japanese Betty torpedo aircraft now only hundreds of yards ahead, and he continued to lead the flight in.

Auerbach gave a hand signal to his wingman and broke off to meet the incoming Zeros. In seconds he was in the middle of a swirling mass of aircraft, all wearing the red ball of Nippon on their sides and wings. He managed to dodge the first bursts fired at him by the nearest Zero and turned to try to gain position on the tail of another Zero. For a few fleeting seconds a Zero crossed his sights, and he got off a short burst. The bucking of his aircraft felt good, but he knew he had not hit the Zero. Then a second Zero flashed across his vision, and he banked to follow it at full throttle. The Zero was too maneuverable for him to stay with it, and he was only able to get off three quick bursts. Then he sensed trouble from the rear, and he looked over his shoulder for his wingman. There was nothing there but the whirling propeller of a Zero closing in behind him. As he watched it, small puffs of smoke grew from it and were swept aft. He tried to pull up, but it was too late. The Zero poured a stream of bullets into his after section. He smelled escaping fuel and hydraulic fluid, and the bullets hitting the armor plate behind him jarred his body. The armor plate saved him, but he soon realized the aircraft was a goner. He fought the crippled aircraft as it spiraled downward and finally got it level a few hundred feet from the water.

When he looked at his compass he realized he was headed north, away from the *Enterprise*. He started to turn to the southeast, but then he looked at his gauges. The gasoline gauge was rapidly winding down toward zero, and the oil gauge was keeping it company. He knew he would never reach the carrier, so he looked at the chart strapped to his thigh. Guadalcanal Island was up ahead, but he would never reach it, either. He looked over the side. The seas were moderate, and he began to go over in his mind the procedures for ditching in the water. He remembered the advice of one of his instructors that when it became inevitable, go in before you ran out of gas, so that you could have positive control of the aircraft in its final minutes. He looked around for friendly aircraft, but the sky was empty. He pushed down his radio transmitter button and said, "This is Bulldog two ditching fifty miles east of Savo."

The gas gauge was now almost at empty, and he decided to ditch as soon as possible. He opened the cockpit canopy, ran through the check list for ditching, and started down, nose high and just above stalling speed.

The landing on the calm sea was surprisingly gentle, and the aircraft made one small bounce and settled, almost level. He heaved himself out of the cramped cockpit, inflated the small rubber raft, and threw it over the side. He inflated his rubber life preserver and jumped over the side, wresting control of the rubber raft before it floated away.

With one hand on the side of the raft, he heaved himself awkwardly into the yellow rubber elongated doughnut, wishing he had paid more attention to the escape drills he had suffered through in flight training. Darkness now would be less than an hour away, and he hurried to inventory the equipment in the raft and secure it in case a wind came up.

He watched his upended Wildcat slowly float downwind, and in a few minutes it lost its remaining buoyancy and slipped below the surface with a final gurgle. He was alone in his small raft.

There were no ships in sight as he scanned the horizon, but he was hopeful that one would pass by the next day. As far as he could remember he was on the direct line from Noumea to Guadalcanal. He covered himself with a rubberized poncho he found in the raft and settled in for the night, trying to find a comfortable position.

He slept fitfully, dreaming of sharks, and the dawn came slowly. His watch was soaked, and he had to estimate time. He was stiff and sore from the cramped position he had been in all night in the small raft, and he stretched his arms and legs to restore circulation. He reached over the side and splashed salt water in his face.

Just as he had completed rubbing his face, he heard a strange hum, and he searched the water surface and the horizon. There was a small spot just above the horizon and slightly to the left of the rising sun. He watched it carefully, and it grew in size. When he was sure, he said aloud, "Jesus! It's an aircraft, but whose?"

He hoped it was American, but he knew it probably wasn't. Maybe a lone Jap coming back from a night harassment of Henderson Field. One of the lone night bombers the *Enterprise* pilots who had landed on Guadalcanal had complained about.

As it got closer, Auerbach became surer that it was Japanese, and he pulled his small poncho over him with the blue side up. When the aircraft was a thousand yards away, he knew he couldn't survive in the raft, and he slid over the side, took a deep breath, and submerged as far as he could go, fighting the rubber life jacket that was trying to keep him up.

In seconds he could hear the steady roar of machine guns, and the raft above him jumped and quivered as projectiles tore through it. One spent projectile tumbled end over end down through the blue water.

When Auerbach could no longer hold his breath, he surfaced and grabbed a handhold on the raft. He looked toward the west and could see the Japanese aircraft headed away. He was probably safe from another attack, but he had other problems. Air was hissing from a dozen holes in the raft, and he knew he had only a few minutes to salvage its contents. He was still wearing his inflated rubber life jacket and a webbed belt with a pistol and small first aid kit. He shoved a tin of malted milk tablets and a pint-sized container of water in his pockets, and checked to see if he had his signalling mirror and whistle. He put one of the celluloid oars over the side, and it floated. He put a second over and covered the pair with his poncho. Just as he was securing the poncho, the raft spluttered and sank. He was on his own. He looked to the west and shook his fist at the direction he had last seen the Japanes aircraft. "So much for Bushido, you Bastard!" he shouted.

He floated for hours in his life jacket, trying to keep the blue side of the poncho under him so that his brown flight suit would not attract sharks, but none appeared. When the sun was almost overhead, he thought he saw a gray shape to the south. He watched it grow until he was sure it was a ship. The ship came almost directly at him, zigzagging periodically, and he began to wonder if it might run him down. He rigged the poncho to an oar and waved it awkwardly. In half an hour he could see that it was a destroyer, and when it turned away on a zigzag course he could see it had a single stack. Soon it was close enough for him to use the signalling mirror, and he flashed the SOS signal.

The destroyer steadied on a course directly for him, and he knew they had seen him. When the ship was closer he could see the small white numerals on the bow. They read 452.

Soon it stopped alongside, and several men climbed down a cargo net to help him up. Once he was on deck, a dark-haired lieutenant commander met him and said, "I'm Lieutenant Commander Forrest Dubose, the Executive Officer of the *Carson*. Welcome aboard. I'll turn you over to our Doctor here."

The Doctor, standing next to Dubose, said, "Are you injured?"

Auerbach said, "I don't think so. I feel pretty stiff, but I think that's from spending the night trying to sleep on a small raft."

The Doctor grinned. "Come down below. We have a standard treatment for downed aviators."

When he handed Auerbach a small bottle of brandy, Auerbach said, "This was worth the trip. By the way, where are you bound?"

"Guadalcanal," the Doctor said.

"Damn! Maybe I need another of these."

Auerbach was landed at Guadalcanal the next day, still in his flight suit, which had been dried in the ship's laundry, and carrying a small bag of spare underwear and shaving gear donated by the supply officer.

The doctor saw him off because the ship was at general quarters waiting for the usual noon air raid. Dubose waved from the bridge.

Auerbach walked up from the beach and soon caught a ride on a passing jeep to the Henderson Field flight headquarters. On the bumpy ride he passed dozens of junked aircraft, some pushed into puddles of water-filled craters beside the runway. The tired-eyed Marine driver described the recent battles for control of the island. "Pretty bloody and gettin' worse," he said finally. "We need more help."

The jeep driver dropped him at the operations office, and he walked in the open doorway and looked around. No one paid any attention to him. "Anybody home?" he asked.

A thin lieutenant commander glanced at him. "Sit down, son, we've got a war on. Be with you in a minute when these bastards leave."

Then a wispy siren began to wail, and in a minute bombs began to fall on the air strip outside. Auerbach started for the door to find a trench, but all the officers and men inside the operations office stayed there, so he came back from the door and sat down on a box of rations.

After about fifteen minutes and another salvo of bombs, the siren sounded again twice, and the lieutenant commander turned around and came over to Auerbach. He held out his hand. "Finley here. What can I do for you?"

"I was shot down yesterday south of here, and I'd like to get back to the *Enterprise.*"

Finley laughed. "So would about a dozen other guys from the *Enterprise.*"

"What's the trouble. Was she sunk?"

Finley wiped the perspiration off of his face with a rag. "No, but she high-tailed it for Pearl Harbor. All of you guys are supposed to stay here and fly missions out of Henderson Field until she comes back.''

''How long will that be?''

''Maybe two weeks,'' Finley said.

''So what do I do now?''

Finley took him over to the door and pointed across the battered runway. ''See that tent under those bare palm trees over by those F4Fs? That's the *Enterprise* group. The senior pilot will be glad to see you. He needs pilots. They all landed here yesterday because they didn't have enough fuel to get back to the carrier. They've been flying three missions a day since, and we need twice as many.''

Auerbach picked up his small bag and trudged around the edge of the steel-matted runway toward the tent. He kicked aside many spent shell casings of all sizes, empty ration cans, and even an empty beer botle with a Japanese label.

When Auerbach reached the tent, he pulled back the entrance flap and went inside. Five pilots in flight suits were lying in cots around the periphery of the tent. Flight gear, life jackets, and belted pistols were stuffed in the corners and a few personal items hung from the ridge pole at the tent top. Auerbach said, ''Anybody home?''

One pilot lifted his head and said, ''Who the hell wants to know? And it's not my turn to fly.''

''Dick Auerbach, and you can go back to sleep.''

Two other pilots sat up. One said, ''I'll be damned. We thought you were gone.''

''No. I got a ride here on a destroyer. Some can named the *Carson*.''

''Oh, yeah. I've heard of her. She's working around here and up the slot. How was she?''

''I was only there a few hours. Nice guys. Good food. Great brandy.''

''You should have stayed aboard. The boss over there will work your tail off.'' He pointed to a sleeping lump in a pilot's suit that had not stirred.

Another pilot said, "You'd better head for the hills before he wakes up, or you'll be going on the next mission. We've got more aircraft than we have pilots."

"How come?"

"A lot of wounded pilots waiting to leave and a good bunch of Marine aircraft maintenance guys."

The senior *Enterprise* pilot stirred, groaned, and sat up. "What's all the noise? How can I get any sleep?"

One of the pilots said, "We've got new meat. Dick Auerbach just walked in."

"Good." The senior pilot looked at Auerbach with a wicked grin. "You fly at 1600. Second section leader. Joe is your wingman. Bomb load two five-hundreds. Your call sign is blue one and your wingman's is blue two. Mine's eagle."

"Bomb load? I'm a fighter pilot."

"Sure you are, but only after you drop your bombs. We're going after a bunch of Japanese destroyers that are expected to land troops just before dark. Then we get to stay around and fight off the Zeros looking for us. You'd better get some sleep."

Auerbach said, "Why are you guys sleeping in the daytime?"

"When you've been here a couple of days you'll find out. Every night a couple of Jap bombers come over and try to keep us awake."

Another pilot spoke up. "They do, but it's so damned hot I can't sleep anyway."

At 1600 Auerbach was in a dusty Wildcat with the engine tuning up. A Marine mechanic leaned over him and checked his harness and equipment. "Everything okay, sir?"

"I guess so. This is a pretty rapid operation."

The Marine grinned. "The whole damned place is rapid. If you don't hurry or if you stop to look back, the Japs will get you. Good luck."

The Marine hopped down, and Auerbach taxied out behind the first section of Wildcats ahead. He looked over his shoulder to make sure his wingman was following. Then they were at the end of the runway, and in a few minutes they had run up their engines, let the brakes off, and were off down the runway in formation.

Auerbach had never seen Guadalcanal from the air. After take-off he turned and looked back at the groves of coconut palms ranged along the shore of the northern part of the island. Many were shattered and drooping, victims of the furious exchange over the past months of naval gunfire, artillery fire, and bombs. Behind the beach on the top of the hills were patches of brown grass and the long brown zigzags of entrenchments, and well beyond that the dark green of jungle.

Then Auerbach concentrated on the aircraft ahead. The formation was climbing rapidly because the intended targets were not very far ahead. The flight leader hoped to intercept the incoming troop-laden destroyers about fifty miles north. When the formation was at altitude, it began to orbit in lazy circles. There was not much daylight left, and Auerbach knew that if they did not see the enemy in the next half hour the flight would have to return to Guadalcanal.

But on the third orbit the flight leader came on the radio. ''Eight ships bearing three zero zero. Targets: first section, lead ship; second section, second ship; join up five miles south. Go!''

The first section leader did a wing-over to port and his wingman followed. Auerbach delayed three seconds and then followed in the same maneuver, separated enough so he could see the target. The destroyer grew in his windshield as he dove at it. He pushed his goggles up off of his face so he could see better. As he got closer, he recognized the raked stacks and the banks of torpedo tubes. Running men and equipment cluttered the decks, and huge white wakes followed the speeding ships.

Then his wingman shouted, ''Zeros behind us!''

Auerbach was too busy lining up the destroyer in his sights to acknowledge the transmission or to push his goggles down over his eyes. In seconds he was at his drop point and he pickled off his bombs. He could feel the Wildcat lighten as the bombs left, and the pickup in speed as the drag decreased. He pulled up hard, and gravity began to draw blood from his upper body. He looked around over both shoulders for Zeros. He knew he could not pull any more g's, and he could feel his insides compressing downward.

His wingman yelled, "Look out! Zero on your tail. I can't get to him!"

Then he saw the Zero coming in behind him. He pulled the Wildcat to the right with all his strength, but it was too late. He felt projectiles hitting the armor plate behind him. He tried to pull his arms and legs in alignment with the plate. Some of the projectiles that missed the plate hit the windshield from the inside, and Auerbach could feel the small pieces of his windshield peppering his face where his goggles should have been. Another projectile hit the windshield itself, and it exploded in a cloud of small pieces of plastic. Auerbach's eyes seemed to turn red, and most of his vision disappeared.

Auerbach reached for his eyes and tried to rub the red away, but the pain was intense, and he knew he was in trouble. He held down the radio transmitter button on the stick. "Blue two! This is blue one! Can you see me? I can't see anything much. Just a faint horizon."

"I can see you. I'm behind you, and the Zeros have left. Don't know where the first section is, but we're roughly pointed for Guadalcanal. Can you fly the bucket?"

"It seems to fly okay. I don't smell anything burning, but I can't see to land the aircraft because of the fuzzy horizon. I think I'm about level."

"Just about. Your left wing is down a hair, and you're descending a little. Do you think I can talk you down to a landing at the airfield?"

"Not on that damned field. Too much trouble at both ends."

''Then you'll have to use your parachute or make a water landing. I think I can talk you down all right. I see the wake of a ship off toward Guadalcanal, but it's too far away to make out if it's one of ours. Come left about ten degrees and we'll head for it.''

Auerbach said, ''I'll try the water landing.'' He knew the Wildcat was stable enough to fly itself in a straight line if he didn't interfere with it too much. He tried to use minimum controls, fighting off the urge to make corrections that he thought might be necessary from the feel of the seat.

His wingman said, ''This is blue two. Nose over until I tell you to stop.''

Auerbach pushed the stick forward gently until he heard his wingman say, ''Hold that. You're headed for a landing just ahead of that ship. Cut your throttle until I tell you to stop.''

''I see a small dot on the fuzzy horizon,'' Auerbach said. He eased the throttle back slowly, and he could feel the aircraft lose speed. ''Is that ship friendly?''

''I can't see it too well because it's headed away from us, but I think it has a single stack. Anyway, it's your only choice now.''

''Damn!'' Auerbach said. ''I may spend the rest of the war in a Jap prison camp.''

''Don't think so. If it's a Jap it probably won't stop for you.''

Auerbach sighed. ''I'm committed now. How am I doing?''

''Level off. You're at two hundred feet. Good course and attitude. I'm sure you can stay level, and you won't need to bail out.''

Auerbach took a deep breath. The crisis was only seconds off.

''This is blue two. This will be my last transmission. Good luck. You are at fifty feet. Pull back gently on the stick until I tell you to stop. At the same time cut the throttle all the way and pray.''

Auerbach went over the check list in his mind for a water landing, but he didn't see how he could do much of it when he couldn't see the gauges.

"This is blue two. Stop!"

Auerbach eased his backward pressure on the stick and cut the throttle. There was an ominous quiet in the cockpit, and then the aircraft hit the water. The impact threw him forward against his restraining harness, and the force pushed the air out of his lungs. He felt the aircraft bounce at least twice, and then the Wildcat mushed down into the water. In the sudden stillness he could hear water lapping around the aircraft. He felt for the catch, pushed the canopy back, and crawled out of the cockpit. He could sense that the aircraft was slighty nose down. He climbed to the edge of the wing, pushed off, and jumped.

The water was as warm as he remembered it from a few days before. When he was afloat, he tried to use the salt water to clear the blood from his eyes, but the movement of his hands hurt his eyes, and he knew he could not do much more. He tripped the toggles on his inflatable life jacket and heard the welcome hiss of carbon dioxide filling the jacket. He settled back to await rescue, hoping the ship his wingman had pointed him toward had seen him and was friendly.

Time was hard to estimate, but he thought that at least half an hour had passed before he detected what he hoped was the faint rush of water by the bow of a ship. Then he could hear the whine of blowers and the whoosh of stack gases, and he guessed that the ship was backing down. Auerbach crossed his fingers and held his breath.

From somewhere above came the sound of voices. "He's not looking at us. He's either unconscious or he can't see. We'll have to go down the net and get him."

Auerbach let out his breath and uncrossed his fingers. The voices were American.

There were two soft splashes and soon Auerbach could feel the hands of two men grabbing his arms.

"Can't see much," he said.

"That's what we figured," said a gruff voice. "Just take it easy, and we'll get you aboard."

Auerbach relaxed and felt himself being dragged backward. After a few seconds the hands turned him around.

"Can you feel the net?" the gruff voice asked.

He reached out and could feel the hairy rungs of rope in a cargo net. "I've got it," he said. He pulled himself in and began to climb. When he reached the top, strong hands lifted him over what he thought were the lifelines and laid him on deck.

A familiar voice said, "I'll be damned! His face is bloody as hell, but I think it's Auerbach again. What the hell do you think we are? A taxi?"

"Is that you, Doctor?" Auerbach asked.

"Yes, you're on the *Carson* again. We'll take you below and see what we can do. You're going to hear the sound of machine guns in a minute. We're going to sink your aircraft before we leave."

He could hear another familiar voice. It said, "Dubose here. One more trip with us and we're going to charge you a mess bill."

An hour later, after the doctor had examined his eyes, Auerbach felt a large bandage being put across his eyes. "What's the verdict, Doc?"

"I think you'll be all right after an expert gets through with you. The only trouble is that the best eye experts are all back in the States."

"What will you do with me?"

"We'll be in Guadalcanal tomorrow morning and put you ashore. I'm sure they'll fly you on a hospital aircraft back to the States."

Four days later Auerbach reached the States and was transferred to the naval hospital in Oakland. In an operating room, the bandage was removed from his eyes, and he was aware that at least two doctors were examining him. There were low murmurs as they pulled back his eyelids and seemed to be shining lights in his eyes.

"Can you see the light?" one voice asked.

"Hell, yes, and it hurts. It's the first real light I've seen in days."

The doctor behind the voice laughed. "That's a good sign. I think we'll be able to clean out all the pieces of windshield, do a little fancy sewing, and have you back in shape in a couple of weeks."

"Can I fly again?"

"There is some doubt. You'll have some scarring on your eyeball surfaces. You may spend the rest of the war on a ship."

A month later Auerbach sat in the office of the Commanding Officer of the hospital. The Captain finished examining his record and questioned the eye surgeon and flight surgeon sitting across the room.

He turned to Auerbach. "I'm afraid your flying days are over, but you can see well enough to go to sea in a surface ship. Have you ever had any time in them?"

"Yes, sir, some in my summer cruises at the Naval Academy and a year before I went to Pensacola."

"I don't know what plans you have for a naval career, but you can have a perfectly normal one at sea."

Auerbach sighed deeply. "I don't know about that. Flying was what I've always wanted to do."

The Captain nodded sympathetically. "I can see how you feel, but I recommend you do your best to adapt. You will feel better about it with time."

"I guess it's the only alternative I have."

"I'll call the surface detailer in the Bureau of Naval Personnel for you and we'll see what we can do." He rang the bell for his secretary and instructed her to place the telephone call. In seconds, Auerbach was talking to a pleasant-voiced commander who asked what he could do for him. Auerbach outlined his problem, and asked if he could be assigned to a destroyer.

The commander said, "I'll get the destroyer detail officer on the intercom."

After a few minutes, the commander came back on the phone. "It's all arranged. You'll have to go to school for about six months at damage control, fire fighting, and sonar schools and will be ready to board your ship in December. We'll give you a couple of weeks leave after your schools."

Auerbach asked, "Any chance of being assigned to the *Carson*?"

"Why do you want her?"

"I have a personal attachment to her. She picked me up twice at sea."

"I think we can arrange it. She was one of the ships the destroyer detail officer gave me. She'll be getting out of the yard in Vallejo in December. I'll write your orders today. Good luck."

CHAPTER TWO

Commander Alden Sorenson sat at a small table in a room of the Mark Hopkins Hotel in San Francisco. On the table was a a scattering of road maps, travel brochures, and books on San Francisco and the south seas. He pushed aside a book on New Guinea and picked up a brochure on the Vallejo Hotel. The next day he and his wife would check in there.

Sorenson, usually known as Tex, pushed back his chair, stood up, stretched his wounded leg to ease its stiffness, and limped over to the large window in the east side of the hotel room. It faced the bay side of the city, and Sorenson could see over the low bank of fog covering downtown San Francisco and extending to Treasure Island out in the bay.

The morning fog was dissipating, and as he stood there, the tower of the Ferry Building at the foot of Market Street emerged from the white blanket. He couldn't see it yet, but he knew Market Street ran from the Ferry Building to a tunnel at the western end of the long street. The day before, He and his wife Ferren had taken a trolley through the tunnel at the end of Market Street and had walked around the beautiful suburban area on the other side of the tunnel and through Golden Gate Park.

The wartime shortage of gasoline had limited their travels around San Francisco to bus and taxi trips. The food in the restaurants had been varied and good, and the night clubs had been excellent, featuring well-known dance bands. Still, Sorenson had liked best their trip to the beach where they had walked on the sand and rocks, listening to the barking seals sunning themselves on the tops of large piles of rocks. The Sutro hot-baths and swimming pools behind the beach had given them a touch of the tropics in the dead of winter.

Their recent marriage had begun a honeymoon that was about to end in two days when he was due to report to his new ship in the Navy yard in Vallejo. He stretched his arms and remembered the wonderful days he and Ferren had spent, first at the Sorenson ranch in Texas, and then in San Francisco. Gasoline rationing had required them to make an almost direct trip from Norfolk to San Francisco. Only some black market gasoline and a free tankful he had picked up at his Texas ranch had made it possible to go out of the direct line and stop in Texas. He was grateful that he had been able to talk Ferren into marrying him in spite of her desire to postpone the marriage until after the war. Ferren had lost her first husband on a destroyer in the Atlantic, and she did not want the tragedy to be repeated.

Sorenson was tall and slim, and slighty bowlegged, a legacy of years in the saddle during his youth on his parents' ranch. His short, blond hair topped a rugged and almost handsome face. A long scar ran from the hairline of his right sideburn to his chin. He rubbed his cheek slowly, remembering the day he had been pitched into a barbed wire fence by a frightened horse. He could feel the slim smoothness of the thin scar, and his expression was pensive as he thought about the days on the ranch. He knew he could go back there after the war and enjoy an easy life, but something about the Navy might just hold him in it after the war.

So far his only taste of command had come when he had taken over command of the USS *O'Leary*, an old four-stacker, in battle with submarines in the Atlantic. He had commanded her briefly when the captain was wounded and had almost gone down with her. Her quarry, a German Sea Wolf class submarine, had torpedoed the *O'Leary* with a new acoustic torpedo. But he had sunk the Sea Wolf first, and it had been considered a moral victory. At least the Navy had thought so when it had awarded him the Navy Cross.

Now he was waiting for his wife to return from shopping at the big department stores on Market Street so he could take her to lunch. He realized that his stomach was grumbling, and looked at his watch. It said 1200, and he walked into the bathroom to clean up before Ferren arrived.

Lieutenant Junior Grade Richard Auerbach sat in the lobby of the Mark Hopkins Hotel, idly watching the women walking around the lobby. He had spent the first few days of his leave staying at the Commodore Hotel in downtown San Francisco. Someone had told him the most beautiful girls in the world lived in San Francisco. The girls he had seen there were either hurrying suburban housewives trying to shop in the depleted stores around Market Street, or the shop girls themselves. The housewives had been too busy to respond to his advances, and the shop girls had been too tired at the end of the day to want to go out with him.

On the spur of the moment he had decided to spend the last few days of his leave somewhere else. A bartender had recommended the Mark Hopkins Hotel lobby. On the basis of that recommendation, he had checked in at the Mark. Now he was down to one last day, and he had not been able to establish a relationship with any of the dozen girls he had approached. True, the girls were all attractive, but they all seemed to be wearing wedding rings, or they looked at his uniform and politely thanked him for his interest.

Then he was sure his vigil had been rewarded. Across the lobby came what he had been waiting for. She wore a saucy hat perched on a short haircut. Her hair, where he could see it, was very dark and shining. Her face was not quite classically beautiful, but it was open, serene, and very attractive. She walked with a graceful gait, her pleated skirt swaying around her slim, well-muscled legs, encased in nylon stockings. She stopped in front of the hotel desk.

Auerbach whistled silently, idly wondering where she had gotten the scarce nylon stockings, and sprang to his feet. By the time she was at the desk, he was at her side. ''Pardon me,'' he said. ''I have an emergency. Can you help me?''

She turned and looked at him, obviously taking in his uniform and his general appearance. ''What can I do for you?'' she asked.

''Ah, this is a little public. Can we sit down over there?''

She followed him to a group of chairs, and they sat down. She looked at him inquiringly. ''Yes?''

He squirmed a little. ''Ah, I'm not much good at this. My emergency is that I've only got one day of leave left, and I can't find anyone to share it with me. Would you have dinner with me tonight?''

The girl sighed, and Auerbach knew he had lost. He tried another tack. ''How about lunch?''

She shook her head. ''Lieutenant, I'm sure there are a dozen girls who would like to join you.'' She began to take off her gloves.

Auerbach said, ''But that's just the trouble. None of them will. You are my last chance.''

Now her gloves were off, and he could see a large diamond ring on her ring finger. He shook his head. ''Sorry. I hope I haven't offended you.''

She grinned. ''You haven't. What ship are you assigned to?''

''I'm on leave, and tomorrow I report to the *Carson* in Vallejo.''

She appeared to be strangling. Auerbach reached over and patted her on the back. She waved him off, and then he realized she was trying to keep from laughing.

She said, "I'm all right, but I'm afraid you're in for a surprise."

"What's the trouble?"

"I don't think I'll tell you today. Enjoy your last day of leave."

She got up and walked back to the desk. Auerbach watched her walk away. My God, what legs! It was worth the try, he thought. To hell with tomorrow.

Ferren got out of the elevator and walked down the corridor to her room, still laughing quietly. She put her key in the lock and walked into the room. There were sounds of splashing coming from the bathroom.

"Hello!" She shouted. "I'm back."

Sorenson came out of the bathroom holding a towel around bis waist. "How was your trip?"

She threw her arms around him. "Who cares about a shopping trip when I'm here with you?"

He kissed her deeply and then let her go. "I take it you're trying to tell me the honeymoon isn't over. Would you like to skip lunch?"

She laughed. "I wouldn't go that far. I'm hungry. Besides, I have a funny story to tell you."

"All right. I'll get dressed and then let's go to lunch. You can go on one last shopping spree this afternoon. We have to check out tomorrow morning and then drive up to Vallejo."

"Isn't this a day early?" She asked.

"Yes. I want to get there in time to make a surprise visit to the ship late tomorrow afternoon. I don't have to report officially until the day after that, but I'd like to see the ship when they aren't expecting me and to talk to some of the officers I had sent there."

"Isn't that a little unfair?"

"All's fair in love and war, and this is getting ready for war."

CHAPTER THREE

The next morning Alden and Ferren Sorenson checked out of the Mark Hopkins Hotel and loaded their baggage into a four-doored green Buick. After a leisurely drive north along the side of San Francisco Bay, they arrived at the Hotel Vallejo in time for lunch.

Over lunch, Sorenson said, "I'm going down to the ship late this afternoon as I'd planned. I want to take a look at her from the pier. If I feel the urge, I may go aboard and pick up my mail. In any case, I'll be back for dinner."

Ferren grinned. "If you see a nice blue-eyed, brown-haired young man named Auerbach, you might bring him back for dinner."

Sorenson laughed wickedly. "I don't think so. When he finds out you're his Captain's wife he's going to hit the silk."

"Promise not to tell him you know about what happened?"

"I promise, but when he finds out he's still going to feel like the deck dropped out from under him."

Ferren bit her lip. ''I think he can take anything as long as he thinks you don't know.''

Sorenson drove slowly down the pier and parked his car well away from the foot of the brow so he could observe the ship without being recognized.

His first impression of the Carson was favorable. He knew she was a Sims class destroyer, but he had never seen one of that class in the Atlantic. Through the maze of electrical power lines and hoses festooned across her, he could see the general shape of the ship. She was sleek and powerful looking, and he knew he would be proud to command her.

At her bow the small hull numbers 452 were painted in white. Her forecastle deck swept gracefully back to just aft of the bridge level. Then the deck dropped down a level and ran all the way aft to a narrow stern. A large single stack rose and raked back at a graceful angle aft of the bridge. He could see the uptakes of four boilers coming up through the deck and melding into the bottom of the stack.

Forward on the forecastle was a single 5-inch gun mount, the gun barrel protruding from a protective box-like steel structure. Aft of the gun mount was a raised deck house running aft to the break of the forecastle deck. On it was a second 5-inch gun mount and aft of that was a heavy steel gun tub containing two single 20-millimeter machine guns.

The bridge structure rose three levels from the forecastle deck, and Sorenson could recognize a Mark-37 gun director with the latest fire control radar on top used for the control of the 5-inch gun battery. Two torpedo directors occupied corners of the bridge.

On the foremast were a flat bedspring-shaped antenna for an air search radar and a new smaller parabolic antenna that he reasoned must be for the new surface search radar, called an SG.

Aft of the stack ran a raised narrow deck carrying one quadruple torpedo tube mount. Then came an after deck-house carrying a third 5-inch gun mount. Slightly above it and forward were two 40-millimeter twin mounts flanked by two single 20-millimeter mounts.

On the fantail was a fourth 5-inch gun mount and two depth charge racks. There were four K-guns, two on either side, mounted on the main deck below mount 53. A depth charge rested on each K-gun, and a rack next to it carried three extra depth charges for easy reloading.

Sorenson took a deep breath. She was far more powerful than the ship he had just left, the *O'Leary*, an old four-stacker, and he could hardly wait to command her. He wanted to stroke her, to feel her respond, and to possess her. Then he laughed. What the hell, I've already got the most beautiful woman in the world. Why would I want anything more?

The desire to board her became stronger, and he picked up his brief case, left the car, walked toward the ship, and strode briskly up the brow. He stopped at the top of the brow, faced aft, and saluted.

A deep voice shouted, "Attention on deck."

Sorenson could see all the crew in sight freezing at attention. He turned toward the source of the voice. "Steele!" Sorenson said. "Aren't you here early?"

A short, mild-looking Lieutenant looked up at him through his steel-rimmed glasses. "You're early, too, sir. I couldn't stay away."

Sorenson stepped off the brow and grasped Steele's hand warmly. "I'm glad to see you."

"A lot of the *O'Leary* sailors are already here and more are coming." Steele said. "Are you reporting aboard today? The Executive Officer, who is also Acting Commanding Officer, is ashore and is expecting you tomorrow."

"I know. I just came aboard to pick up my mail and I'll be off again. Officially I'll report at 0800 tomorrow."

"I think most of your mail is up in your cabin. Let's go see, and I'll send for Carmody. He's a chief yeoman now."

"Glad to hear it. I'll follow you. Please tell the crew to carry on. We're losing working time."

"Sorry, sir." Steele turned and ordered, "Carry on."

In his new cabin Sorenson found a stack of mail. He opened his briefcase and started to put it in. Then he realized that he had little room and he took out a dozen medal boxes and a sheaf of citations.

"What are those, sir?" Steele asked.

"Medals and citations I picked up at the Twelfth Naval District when I reported in on the way here. There are two for you, a Silver Star and a Bronze Star. The others are for members of the crew of the *O'Leary* who have reported to the *Carson*. I want to present them after I take over."

Steele said, "I see from your ribbons that you were awarded the Navy Cross, a Bronze Star, and a Purple Heart."

Sorenson shook his head. "I don't feel right wearing them. The *O'Leary* crew should have gotten get them, not me."

Steele said, "I don't think they'll feel that way. We all owe our lives to you."

Sorenson frowned. "But it's the ones I couldn't save that bother me."

"You did the best you could. It was a tough fight against a helluvan opponent."

There was a knock on he door. Sorenson turned and said, "Come in."

The door opened and Chief Yeoman Carmody entered. He was of medium height and build with a ruddy complexion. His beaming face was topped by a thatch of reddish brown hair. "Captain! Am I glad to see you! It's been too long." He came over to Sorenson and gripped his hand.

Sorenson returned the firm grip and took the chief's elbow in his other hand. "Just long enough for both of us to get married and go on honeymoons. I hope yours was as wonderful as mine. Sit down and tell me about it."

Carmody eased his wiry frame onto the bunk. "It was great. My wife and I enjoyed the car your wife gave us for a wedding present. That little red Ford could really go. Good mileage, too. Otherwise we wouldn't have been able to stop in Texas."

"I take it you did a little prospecting for 'awl' there." Sorenson drawled the word.

Carmody laughed. "Aw, come on, Captain. Now that I'm a chief I've learned to say 'oil' like all these non-Texans aboard this ship."

Sorenson leaned over and put the mail in his briefcase. "Where did you go in Texas?"

"Home, and then we stopped to visit your brother on your ranch. He showed us a great time." Carmody beamed. "I spent a day going over some of your property. I told him I thought I found at least one location where I was sure there was oil."

"What did he say?"

"He said there might be, but he was making more money running cattle on the property now."

Sorenson laughed. "Sounds just like brother Ed. He doesn't care much about making money. He loves the land and really doesn't want those unsightly oil rigs cluttering it up."

Carmody scratched his head. "Maybe you and me can change his mind after the war is over."

Sorenson became somber, and he glanced at Steele, sitting in a nearby chair. "Maybe, but we have to win it first, and I hope this ship can help. I'm going to leave in about fifteen minutes. Can you meet me at the brow with a list of the crew and a roster of the officers?"

"Of course, sir. I knew you'd want that the first thing. I've got them ready, and I've listed the home towns of all the crew. For the officers I've made excerpts from their biographies. When you have time, I'll give you the service records of all the crew, a few at a time."

"Thanks," Sorenson said. "I'll see you in a few minutes, and I'll be aboard at 0800 tomorrow." Carmody left.

"Let's talk for just a few minutes," Sorenson said to Steele. "I think you know how much I value your opinion. Tell me how this ship is doing and what's wrong with it, if anything."

Steele squirmed in his chair slightly and thought for a minute, the overhead light reflecting off his glasses. "Well, Captain," he began. "As you would expect after a good overhaul and a lot of alterations, we have the latest in weapons and radars and I think a good engineering plant, although I'm no expert in engineering. All I know about it is that the engineering officer is the same one who ran the plant for the last two years and the engineers never missed a bell. He says it's in good shape, and I believe him.

"Chuck Steiner has been aboard for a week and seems to have a handle on the gunnery department, although it's new to him. He has a few pieces of equipment that aren't yet up to par. He'll want to talk to you."

"But didn't he go to 5-inch gunnery school?"

"Oh, yes, sir. I'm sure he knows all about the gun batteries in theory, but he hasn't actually fired these particular batteries. Finlay MacIntosh has been here for two weeks and says the torpedo battery is ready." Steele took off his glasses and wiped off an invisible spot. "I'll never forget how he saved us by firing the last load of our fish at that Sea Wolf submarine. If he could do that, he can fire any of these torpedoes."

Sorenson nodded in agreement. "It sounds like the ship and her equipment will be ready. How about the officers and crew?"

"Well, you know some of the officers. In addition to the ones we've talked about, Doctor Fineman has reported as medical Officer and Lieutenant Junior Grade Renard is deep in the supply department inventories. He says they'll be up to allowance when we leave. Lieutenant Junior Grade Jablonski is here as Navigator." Steele cleared his throat. "I know your opinion about him."

"Yes. An excellent navigator and a first rate officer. I notice that you haven't said anything about the Executive Officer. Is that intentional?"

Steele hesitated briefly and looked down at his finger nails.

Sorenson said ''This isn't like you. You never hesitated to express an opinion before.''

Steele took a deep breath. ''Sir, you put me in a bad spot. Right now he's my Executive Officer and also my Commanding Officer. I feel I have to be one hundred percent loyal to him as long as this relationship exists. Tomorrow you will be my Commanding Officer and I'll be glad to answer that question more frankly. But then again, when you meet him and take command, I won't need to express an opinion.''

Sorenson sighed. ''Point taken. I should not have asked that question, and, as usual, you've done the right thing. But I think I smell a problem coming on. Please tell the Executive Officer I'll be here at 0800 tomorrow, and will be at his disposal all day long for inventorying publications and doing whatever is necessary to be ready for a brief change of command ceremony the next morning.'' Sorenson picked up his briefcase. ''What time does the yard start work?''

''Eight o'clock, sir.''

''We'll have the ceremony at 0730 the day after I report. It will be over early enough so as not to interfere with the start of work.''

Steele shook his head and smiled. ''I'll deliver the message, but you may have some convincing to do.''

Sorenson's lips moved into a straight line. ''Don't worry. I'm good at that. By the way, has a new officer named Auerbach reported yet?''

''Yes, sir. He's in the wardroom. Would you like to see him?''

''Not right now. Would you tell him Mrs. Sorenson and I would like to have him join us for dinner at the Vallejo Hotel at 1800.''

''Glad to. He'll be there. He'll enjoy meeting Mrs. Sorenson.''

Sorenson tried to suppress a smile, but the corners of his mouth twitched. ''Oh, I'm sure he will. Let's go down below and see if Carmody is ready.''

Carmody was waiting at the brow. "Here you are, sir. This will make a good night's reading."

"Thank you, Chief, you look great in your new uniform."

Sorenson saluted the petty officer of the watch and asked for permission to leave the ship. It felt good to be with his old shipmates. Then he saluted the colors aft and walked down the brow. As he got into his car, he felt the weight of the papers Carmody had given him under his arm. He took them in his other hand and slid them gently across the seat. He thought about how many lives were represented by the listings and how much they would depend on him in the future. He would have to make hard decisions that might send some of them to their deaths, but he knew if he commanded them well they would do whatever he called upon them to do well. They were the life blood of the *Carson*, and he would have to do his best to take care of them.

On the signal bridge, Chief Signalman Simon Brophy stirred his coffee with half a doughnut. He knew he was twenty pounds over-weight, mostly because of the inaction in the yard. He had exhausted the potential of all the bars and cafes within 50 miles of Vallejo and found them wanting. Now he looked forward to getting back to sea. He had an Irish twinkle in his gray eyes, and his animated face showed the scars of a dozen bar room encounters.

He leaned heavily on the flag bag and looked down at the quarterdeck. Then he punched the man next to him. "Hey, who's that commander leaving the ship?"

The man next to him wore the uniform insignia of a chief steward's mate. His skin was a light brown, not much darker than Brophy's deep tan. "It's a day early for the new skipper, but that must be who it is," Williams said.

Brophy finished his doughnut. "You're probably right. Looks lean and mean."

"Carmody used to serve with him. Says he's a great skipper and a helluva guy."

Williams took the top off a small pan. "Another doughnut?"

Brophy shook his head. "I'm already too fat. I eat too many of those things."

Williams regularly brought doughnuts and pastries up to the signal bridge. Brophy knew it was his way of repaying him and the signal gang because Brophy let him send and receive messages. Brophy knew Williams liked signalling, and he could send and receive flashing light and semaphore as well as any of Brophy's signalmen.

Brophy thought Williams could pass the test for at least first class signalman, but the Navy would not let a Negro try for any rate except steward. He had heard that there were a few exceptions, but he had never seen a colored deck or engineering petty officer. Brophy knew that Williams was wasting his time, but he wanted to help him be prepared in case the Navy ever saw the light and opened up other rates to Negroes.

Williams put the remaining doughnuts on the counter of the signal bridge desk and started below. "Time to cook up all that garbage for evening chow."

Brophy laughed. "That's not what I hear. All the officers say you're a great cook. See you tomorrow after the change of command."

Sorenson drove back to the hotel thinking over his feelings about the crew so deeply that he forgot to tell Ferren about their dinner guest.

Ferren met him at the door. "How did you like your new ship?" she asked.

"Beautiful! Almost as beautiful and just as graceful as you are."

"That kind of flattery won't make me any more willing to share you with her. I still don't like the idea of your leaving. When you were in the Atlantic you got home every month or two. Now I understand you might be out there in the Pacific as much as two years.''

''Possible, but not probable. This is 1943, and the war might end before the two years are up when we would normally come back for overhaul. Then there are other ways we could get back earlier.''

Ferren's face became somber, and her shoulders drooped. She said slowly, ''I don't want to hear about them, but I guess I should.''

''Well, we could be damaged enough so that we couldn't be repaired by a tender in the forward area. Then we'd be sent back here for repairs. We could also be sunk.''

Ferren sighed ''I don't want either. See if you can find a better way.''

Sorenson looked at his watch. ''Damn! I forgot to tell you we're having a dinner guest tonight at 1800.''

Ferren said, ''Thanks a heap. That gives me just an hour to get ready.''

''You look good enough to eat just as you are.''

''Who is this guest?''

''Lieutenant Junior Grade Richard Auerbach, United States Navy.''

''Oh, no, you wouldn't do that to him! I was just kidding this afternoon. You promised not to tell him about me.''

''I haven't met him yet, and I haven't told him anything. I just want to meet a young officer with all that initiative and with the good judgement to pick you.''

Ferren giggled. ''Actually, I can hardly wait to see his face when he sees me.''

''I'm going to meet him in the lobby at 1800. I'll seat him so he's facing the elevators. You can wait a few minutes to come down, and then make any kind of entrance you want to. How this young man handles the situation will be a graduation examination in diplomacy for him. If he does okay, I'll push him along as fast as I can. Now while you get ready, I'll read the biography about him that Carmody gave me.''

"How is Carmody, and did he like my car?"

"Rave notices on both counts. He and his wife are very grateful to you."

Ferren retreated to the bathroom, and Sorenson sat down to read Auerbach's biography. He had hardly completed the first page when he shouted to Ferren. "He can't be all bad. He's a busted out aviator!"

She poked her head around the bathroom door. "Just like you."

"No, he wasn't thrown out of flight training like I was. He was a fighter pilot flying off the *Enterprise* near Guadalcanal. He got zapped by a Zero twice and wounded in the eyes the second time. He's no longer physically qualified to fly."

"But qualified to go to sea on a destroyer."

"Yes, I know it sounds like we're the second team, but in reality we are. Many good officers can't fly but can do all the things required at sea and make fine destroyer officers."

"Like you," she said firmly.

"Thanks. Now finish getting ready."

"I'm through with the bathroom. You get five minutes in it."

Promptly at 1755 Sorenson strode off the elevator to a group of seats in the lobby. He had hoped to get there before Auerbach arrived, but Auerbach beat him to it. As Sorenson approached the chairs, an officer in blues, carrying his cap under his arm, rose and smiled at him. Sorenson liked what he saw and hoped he would like him more later. Auerbach was almost as blond as he was himself and like him, had several new scars running down his left cheek. He was at least two inches shorter than Sorenson's six feet, but probably ten pounds heavier. His face was angular, but reasonably handsome, and his best feature, next to his blue eyes, was a set of flashing white teeth, which Sorenson admired as he made his way over to the chairs.

He grinned in return and said, ''Lieutenant Auerbach?''

''Yes, sir, but have you got me mixed up with somebody else? I've never had the honor of meeting you.''

''Oh, no, you're the right one. Please sit down. Mrs. Sorenson will be down in a few minutes. You know how the ladies are. She wants to make a good impression.''

''Sir, I understand you're taking over command tomorrow. There are a lot of officers and men from your old ship aboard who speak very highly of you.''

''Thanks. They'll carry the ship until I can get my feet on the deck. I suppose the Executive Officer is doing well.''

''Uh, I don't know about that. I haven't met him yet.''

''How long have you been aboard?''

''Just two days.''

''And you haven't met him?''

''Well, that's not much time and he's been busy. Some of the other new guys haven't met him either.''

Sorenson said, ''I think we'll change that. I understand you're a physically disqualified aviator.''

''Yes, sir. My eyes were damaged by an exploding windshield off Guadalcanal and I had to ditch. The *Carson* picked me up. She also picked me up two days before that when I was shot down.''

You couldn't see when you ditched?''

''Not much. My wingman talked me down.''

You're lucky to be here. That's a tough thing to do. I hope your luck holds. We may need it.''

Suddenly Auerbach blanched. Sorenson had seated him so he was facing the elevators, and Sorenson didn't need to turn around to see what was happening. He could read in Auerbach's face Ferren's slow approach. He knew Ferren was smiling at Auerbach, and Auerbach rose from his chair. Sorenson watched him closely. Auerbach's face was frozen at first, but when Ferren said in her lilting voice, ''Ah, Mister Auerbach, nice to see you again,'' Sorenson could see a faint smile spreading across

Auerbach's face. But his eyes were still wary and troubled.

Sorenson grinned, wondering how he would handle the rest of the crisis.

Auerbach said in a tremulous voice, "Could you be Mrs. Sorenson?"

Ferren said, "Yes. Please sit down. Perhaps my husband can find us some drinks."

Sorenson said, "But we can have some in the dining room in a few minutes."

"Yes, dear, but I'd like one now. Wouldn't you, Lieutenant?"

"Ah, yes, ma'm. I'd like one very much. A double scotch, please, sir."

Soernson grinned. He thought Auerbach was dong well so far.

When Soernson left to find a waiter, Auerbach leaned forward and said quietly, "Mrs. Sorenson, I didn't know who you were. Can I apologize?"

Fereren giggled. "What for? I was flattered. By the way, did you have any luck for the evening?"

No, ma'm. I finally have up and went to the opera."

Do you like classical music?"

"Oh, yes, very much."

"Then you have something in common with my husband. He likes it, too."

Auerbach shook his head. "I'm afraid this will be a short tour of duty for me. If you tell him, he'll have me transferred to Iceland."

"I don't think so. Why don't you be the one to tell him?"

Auerbach sat back and shook his head. "I guess I'd better take my medicine."

Soernson came back and said, "The waiter is on the way. What were you two talking about so intently?"

"Nothing of any importance. I think Mister Auerbach has something to tell you."

Auerbach sat upright and cleared his throat. "Sir, this is the hardest thing I've ever done."

"Harder than landing a Wildcat in the water when you couldn't see very well?"

"Ten times as hard. There isn't way to do this easily. Sir, I tried to pick your wife up in the Mark Hopkins Hotel lobby."

Ferren was struggling to keep from laughing.

Sorenson frowned. "Well, I don't blame you. She's a pretty nice package. I picked her up in the supply depot in Norfolk"

Ferren gagged and spilled her drink. Auerbach looked at her wide-eyed.

Sorenson said, "See, she does have some faults. She can't hold her liquor very well."

Auerbach said, "Sir, I suppose this means you'll have me transferred."

"Not at all," Sorenson said. "I'm gong to put you in charge of teaching the younger officers how to conduct themselves socially."

Auerbach saw his chance. "Sir, if you're really going to keep me, would you reconsider my assignment?"

"Why do you want to change? Aren't you going to be the first lieutenant?"

"Yes, sir. But I want to take the offensive. That's why I went into flying. As far as I can figure out, a first lieutenant doesn't really do anything interesting at all. All I'll drop is the anchor instead of bombs. I'll shoot paint at the bulkheads instead of bullets at Zeros, and I'll chase the hell out of guys who drop cigarette butts on the decks.

Sorenson laughed. "I see what you mean. I'll put you in training for the relief of both the gunnery officer and the torpedo officer. They're the heart of our offensive capability."

Auerbach beamed. "This won't be like flying, but I think I'm going to like destroyer duty."

Ferren shook her head. "I don't understand men. He likes classical music, too. You might put him in charge of the wardroom phonograph record collection."

CHAPTER FOUR

Early the next morning Sorenson put on his best blue uniform, and Ferren helped him brush it off carefully.

"When will you be back?" she asked.

"About six."

"Any surprise guests for dinner?"

He laughed. "No. Unless I can pick up someone in the hotel lobby."

She poked him in the chest. "I'll be down there waiting."

Sorenson drove to the pier and parked in a space near the ship. He took out his briefcase and walked over to the brow. As he walked up it, he could see a lieutenant commander standing near the top of the brow. He guessed that the officer was just short of six feet and about one hundred and ninety pounds. Some of it looked like fat, but maybe he was just muscular. His hair, where Sorenson could see it under his cap, was black, and his face was darker than usual for that time of year. As he got closer, he could see that the officer's lips were full and his jaw firmly set. There was a hint of stubbornness in his face.

Sorenson stopped at the top of the brow and went through the ceremony of coming aboard. After the last salute, he stepped down off the end of the brow and looked at the lieutenant commander waiting there. His face was unsmiling, and Sorenson tried to put him at his ease with a broad smile of his own.

The officer put out his hand and said, ''Sir, Lieutenant Commander Bedford Forest Dubose, Executive Officer and temporary Commanding Officer. Welcome aboard the *Carson*.''

Sorenson blinked. Dubose had a heavy southern accent. ''Glad to be here,'' Sorenson said. ''Can we sit down and talk somewhere?''

''Yes, sir. Your cabin is waiting for you. I understand you saw it yesterday. Your steward is named Vila. I'm sorry I didn't know you were coming. It would have been in better shape. I think you'll find it in satisfactory condition now.''

''It was fine.''

Sorenson followed Dubose to the cabin.

Dubose opened the door and stood back while Sorenson entered.

Sorenson said ''Please join me, and let's send for some coffee.''

Dubose pushed a call bell, and in a few seconds a Filipino with a cheerful brown face poked his head in the open door.''

''Vila, Steward's Mate Second Class, sir.''

Sorenson returned his smile, stood up, extended his hand, and said, ''Commander Sorenson here. I'm about to be your new Captain. Thank you for the excellent job you did preparing this cabin for me. I understand you were serving in the *John D. Ford* in the Asiatic Fleet and you are from a small barrio in Cebu.''

''Yes, sir. I am. The *Ford* was a wonderful ship. I hope to go back to the Philippines on the *Carson* some day soon.''

Sorenson said grimly, ''I think we all want to get there, too. Will you bring us some coffee, please?''

Vila said. "Right away, sir."

Sorenson turned to Dubose. "Let's sit down and get to the business of the day."

Dubose sat down, still unsmiling, and, Sorenson felt, a little stiff.

Sorenson said, "First, let's get to know each other a little better. I'm from Sorenville, Texas, and I'm basically a cattle hand. After I did that for a few years, I went to the Naval Academy. I washed out of flight training in my final week for something I'd just as soon not talk about. Then I was sent to a destroyer in the Atlantic Fleet as gunnery officer. She was rammed and sunk by a merchantman in the North Atlantic. I managed to swim away. Next I was sent to a four-stack destroyer, also in the Atlantic. We escorted a lot of convoys and put up a hell of a fight against the wolfpacks, but the *O'Leary* was finally sunk in a fight with a new submarine of the Sea Wolf class, or rather we sank each other. After a short leave and a recent marriage, I was ordered here."

Dubose nodded. "That seems like a long and arduous tour."

"It was," Sorenson said, "And I'm glad it's over. I look forward to beginning a good relationship with you, and I'll do all I can to see that you have a chance to qualify for your own command as soon as possible."

Dubose's eyes brightened a little, but he still hadn't smiled.

Sorenson said, "I'd like to know more about you. I've read your official biography, but that didn't tell me much. I'd like to know more details. I see from your biography that your full name is Nathaniel Bedford Forrest Dubose. Was General Forrest an ancestor?"

"Yes, sir. I'm a direct descendant."

"And you prefer to be called Forrest instead of Nathaniel?"

For the first time Dubose's lips began to lift in a smile, but he controlled them, and they returned to a straight line. "Yes, sir, Nathaniel is a bit much. So is Bedford."

Sorenson nodded. ''Many southerners use their middle names. I don't have one. My name is Alden, but I'm called 'Tex.'' '

This time Dubose did smile slightly. ''I don't know which is worse, Alden or Nathaniel.''

''I agree. Tell me more about your background.''

Dubose raised his heavy black eyebrows. ''From my biography you will know that I completed a degree in animal husbandry at the University of Alabama and also completed the Naval ROTC course and was commissioned ensign in 1939. I've served in destroyers ever since. This is my third. I'm hoping to command one soon.''

''I take it you've lived in Alabama all your life.''

''Oh, yes. I'm a sixth generation Alabama boy, and my ancestors before that came from French Canada. They settled in Selma County and began to raise cotton. At one time they had the biggest plantation in the county, but the war between the States almost broke my granddaddy, General Forrest. His daughter married my father, who was a Dubose from a neighboring plantation. Since then cotton has fallen on hard times, and most of us in the black soil belt have taken to raising cattle. We make out, but we don't give you much competition in Texas. I suppose you've got a big ranch there.''

''Well, big enough to take care of all the steers we run on it.''

''How many?''

''I don't rightly know. My brother runs it. He says he has enough cattle to fill up all the grazing land on the ranch. When he gets too many, he sells some and buys more land. Right now he's selling a lot to the government because of the war. Why did you decide to leave the ranch, uh, plantation, and join the Navy?''

I'm one of four brothers and two sisters. I'm the youngest, and the plantation wouldn't support all of us. I've decided to make the Navy my career.''

''Who works on your spread? Ah, plantation?''

"Mostly black field hands. The rest of us just supervise."

"Can you handle a rope?"

Dubose looked like he smelled something unpleasant. "Certainly not. We use eastern saddles without pommels. The field hands mostly ride big mules and use western saddles. They do the roping."

Sorenson sighed. "You've missed a lot if you haven't handled a rope and personally worked cattle. But to each his own. Tell me, what do you think of the officers and men of the *Carson*?"

"Many of the enlisted men I know and served with during the time we were operating in the Solomons. Most of these are very competent at their jobs and were well-trained under the previous commanding officer. Socially not so good, and the new ones are worse. The officers are mostly new. I presume you had something to do with that. I don't know them well yet."

"Seems to me you don't know the new ones at all. Some of them say they haven't even met you."

Dubose colored slightly under his dark complexion. "I'll meet them in due time. As for individuals, I've seen something of some of them. Steele, for instance. He looks like a weak sister, and I doubt if he knows much about sonar."

Sorenson's jaw dropped. "That's what I mean about not getting to know your officers. As sonar officer on the *O'Leary* he was given credit for sinking three and a half German U-boats. I'd say that shows he knows something about sonar. As for his appearance," Sorenson continued, "he may be short and mild looking, but I don't think you'd want to get into a boxing ring with him. He was the eastern inter-collegiate champion for two years when he was at Yale. He weighed 135 pounds then, and I'd guess him at 140 now. Frankly, he's as strong as his voice, which he got from three years as coxswain of the Yale varsity crew. I wouldn't want to tangle with him. Who else do you have doubts about?"

Dubose paled slightly, but recovered. "Well, there's Steiner. He does have some gunnery background, but he's never served with a 5-inch gun battery. Besides I think he's Jewish, and I wonder if he'll hold up when the going gets tough."

Sorenson snorted. "What! I don't believe what I've just heard. Steiner happens to be German and has been a gunnery officer in battle for a good many months. I've trusted my life to him, and he's always come through. As for your remark about his being Jewish, I wish he were. The Jews have always been great fighters."

Dubose remained silent.

Sorenson said, "I think we have a case of bigotry here. I can't tolerate prejudice in any man and especially not in my Executive Officer. We've got to straighten that out and soon. By the way, in case you were about to make a similar remark about Doctor Fineman, he happens to be an Episcopalian of English descent. His paternal grandfather was Jewish, but under Jewish law, Fineman isn't Jewish because his mother wasn't Jewish. It doesn't make any damned difference one way or the other either to me or to him. He's a fine man, a close friend, and a very good doctor."

Dubose said, "But you must admit he has Jewish blood. You're the cattle rancher. Don't you believe in breeding and blood lines?"

"Of course, for animals."

"Why not for people?"

"We're not animals."

Dubose shook his head. "Some of the enlisted men who joined us recently act like animals."

"I'll straighten them out, but if you want to talk about blood lines, Fineman has in his veins and genes the traits of hundreds of doctors, philosophers, professors, and industrialists. He has far more latent talent than either of us. I don't see how anyone can look down on him."

Dubose was silent for a few minutes while Sorenson was cooling down. Then he said, "I see your point. I'll do my best to change my attitude, but please remember it's going to be difficult for me. I've been raised differently all my life, and I'll have to make a fundamental change in my outlook."

Sorenson shook his head. "Maybe I shouldn't be so rough on you. The Navy is wrong, too. It legally discriminates against Negroes."

"That's right. We only have three aboard, and they're all stewards. The chief steward is named Williams, and he's not allowed to shift to any other rate, although he could qualify for any of a dozen."

Sorenson said, "We've got to talk about this more when we have time. Some day the Navy will see the light and change their policy. Now what did the last Captain do that I should continue?"

For the first time Dubose smiled. "Everything. He was a fine skipper, and we miss him. He was a very srict disciplinarian, and I liked that. He could really handle this ship, and he knew how to fight her. You'll have a difficult time replacing him."

"I'm glad you feel that way. I hope in time to have you feel that way about me. Perhaps I should just give you my philosophy of command. I don't think you will find it difficult. I believe in doing everything possible to make a ship able to fight. That's our job, and in the end it saves lives. When that's done, I believe in enjoying life and that goes for the officers and men. That, in a nut shell, is what I believe."

Dubose cleared his throat, obviously not impressed. "Sir, I understand you want to take over command tomorrow morning. That's not much time. We're supposed to run through all the general drills, make an inventory of the confidential publications, inventory the narcotics, and do a lot of other important items." Dubose looked at his watch. "It's already 0900."

"All right, let's get at the inventories. We should complete them by 1600. The only general drill I want to see is fire drill. The others will be meaningless if we can't even train our weapons."

Sorenson shifted in his chair to ease his leg. "In the yard, preventing a fire or fighting it is all important. At 1630 today I want to see a fire drill. After that, we'll have one at 1630 every day just after the yard crews have left the ship and our crew has gone ashore. That way the duty officer will know for sure who is on the fire detail and can make sure they all know their duties. Also, either you or I will inspect the ship for places where fires might start.

"As for the changing of command ceremony, I'm not big on ceremonies as such. I think this should be an occasion where all the crew can see me and and I can see them. I'll talk to them later. We can have it at 0730 tomorrow and complete it before 0800. That way we won't lose any working time for the yard force. Do you agree?"

Dubose was silent. Then he said with very little enthusiasm, "Yes, sir."

Sorenson sent for another cup of coffee and word for the communication officer that they were ready to inventory the confidential publications. "While we're waiting," he said, stirring his coffee, "there's one more point I want to make. You know I'm from Texas, and you also can tell I don't have much accent left. At the Naval Academy they try to remove most local accents. There's a reason for it. They think it best that those who are to give orders all use the same basic English and have little accent. That way in the heat of battle or even in a peace time emergency orders won't be misunderstood. When I go back to Texas, I speak Texan with the best of them. You are still speaking with a very deep Alabama accent aboard ship after all these years in the Navy."

"Yes, sir, and I probably always will."

"I don't mean you should not be proud of your southern heritage and manner of speech. Personally I find it very pleasant, but many of the crew may not understand you well. I feel that what you and I have to do is learn a second language. Our own local language for personal and home use, and a neutral English for use aboard ship."

Dubose shook his head, but there was a slight smile around his mouth. "Captain, you're going to be a hard man to satisfy, but I'll do my best."

"That's all I ask. Now let's go to work."

Down in the wardroom pantry Chief Steward's Mate Charles Williams pulled his white apron straight over his Khaki uniform to avoid soiling it. He always dressed neatly, and his khaki shirts had been altered to accommodate his large shoulders and to fit tightly around his narrow waist. He kept his curly black hair neatly and closely trimmed. It framed a rugged face, a little less black than the two other steward's mates at work in the pantry.

Both men were named Jackson, and called Big Jackson and Little Jackson to distinguish one from the other. Little Jackson, like Williams, was from Detroit. Little Jackson had joined the Navy to avoid further entanglement with the tough Detroit police force, but Williams had joined because he disliked the noise and grease of the automobile assembly line.

For Williams, the recruiting chief had painted a rosy picture of opportunity, travel, and fresh air, but Williams had soon found out that the opportunities were not for everybody. Not even the fresh air. The pantry was stifling at times. For Negroes, opportunity was still being a steward, and he had given his all to make the best of it, studying hard at cooking school. Now, even though Vila was supposed to be the cook, Williams still did most of the cooking and let Vila take care of the Captain.

Big Jackson, polishing the silver, held up an oyster fork. "What's dis for?" he asked.

Williams rolled his eyes. "How many times have I told you to say 'this,' and not 'dis?'"

Little Jackson laughed. "You tell him every day. He still sounds like a field hand."

Williams said, ''He was a field hand. From Selma, Alabama, near the Exec's home town, but he's got to learn to speak good English if he wants to get promoted.''

Big Jackson said, ''You big city guys think you own da place. Let up.''

Vila came in the pantry door, his bright Filipino face beaming and his black eyes twinkling.

Little Jackson said, ''Well, how was he?''

Vila spoke very good English, but occasionally, like many Filipinos, slipping and pronouncing 'the' as 'de.' Vila said, ''Seems like a nice guy. Stood up and shook hands with me. He's from Texas.''

Williams said, ''I've got a good recipe for chili.''

Vila shook his head. ''Carmody told me he hates it. Had to eat too much of it as a kid.''

Little Jackson said, ''What was he? A cowboy?''

Williams snorted. ''Not even cowhands like to be called 'boy.' He was a cowhand.''

''Little Jackson asked, ''Is he bowlegged?''

Vila said, ''Well, a little. He's about six feet tall. Light brown hair. Has a scar on the right side of his face. If he was a Filipino, I'd say he'd been in a knife fight, but I don't think he was. Doesn't seem to be that kind of guy.''

Williams said, ''I take it you liked him.''

Vila shrugged, ''I don't know him that well yet.''

Big Jackson said, ''Dem Texans are pretty good honkies.''

Williams shook his head. '' 'Them,' not 'dem.'' '

Big Jackson said, ''Whatever.''

Vila said, ''When I was taking more coffee up to the Captain's cabin, I heard him and the Exec going at it pretty good.''

Chief Williams glared. ''Vila, don't ever repeat anything you hear up there, not even to me. If you do, I'll have you back here cooking again.''

Big Jackson grinned and shook his head. ''Hee! Hee! Back to Filipino chicken and rice. Can't stand it! Vila, keep yo' big mouf shut.''

Chief Williams sighed, '' 'Mouth,' not 'mouf.' Keep your big mouth shut.''

CHAPTER FIVE

The next morning, after an early breakfast, Sorenson drove down to the ship with Ferren, who wanted to keep the car to run errands.

As they drove out on the pier, Sorenson stopped where they could see the *Carson*.

Sorenson said, ''Well, what do you think of her?''

Ferren shook her head pensively. ''So that's my rival. I don't like her for that reason, but I must admit she has fine lines like some of your Texas quarter horses.''

''That's what I think, too.''

''What time will you be home tonight?''

''About five. I want to set a good example by getting off the ship early, but not too early.''

''You're taking over command right away?''

''At 0730 this morning, about ten minutes from now.''

Ferren looked at her watch. ''May I pull over into that parking space and watch?''

''Sure.''

He kissed her goodbye and walked up the pier to the brow.

Dubose greeted him on the quarterdeck, and they went up to the cabin while the crew was being assembled on the forecastle.

Vila brought them coffee and left, carefully closing the door.

Dubose cleared his throat nervously. Sorenson noticed his unease and asked, "There's something on your mind?"

"Yes, Captain, I've had a night to think about our meeting yesterday. It seems I don't please you. I'd like to request reassignment."

Sorenson laughed and shook his head. "Hell, no. We had a private conversation. I wasn't your Commanding Officer then. Now we forget everything in the past and start over. I don't believe in having officers relieved just because they don't please their commanding officer. I think it's up to the commanding officer to convince an officer he differs with to change his ways, and I think I can convince you in time. If we can't reach a meeting of the minds, then we can reconsider. All I ask is that you try to make the changes I have suggested. If you do, I see no reason why we shouldn't get along together. I promise you if you do well you'll end up better off than on any other ship in the Navy. Are you willing to take a chance?"

Dubose smiled. "Well, my family has always been a gambling group. We lost a little money from time to time, but we won a lot, too. Those sound like good odds. I'll take a chance."

At 0730, when Steiner, as acting Executive Officer, had reported the crew assembled on the forecastle, Sorenson and Dubose walked out and stood on the upper deck in front of gun mount 52.

Dubose made a few brief remarks commenting on the fine job the crew had done in the yard, and then said, "Since I am remaining on the ship, I have no orders to read. I now introduce your new Commanding Officer, Commander Alden Sorenson."

Dubose moved back and Sorenson stepped forward. He read his orders. When he had finished, he turned to Dubose, saluted, and said, "I relieve you, sir."

On the signal bridge, the chief signalman broke a new commission pennant and hauled down the one flying from the mast.

Sorenson turned to the crew grouped below on the forecastle deck and began to speak. "I am honored to take command of this fine ship, and I pledge to maintain her reputation. I will do every thing in my power to make her ready to fight again after a long period in the yard. We will leave the yard in a week. It will be a very busy period, and all of us will have to work hard to make sure we are ready to go to sea and to fight. Then we will sail to San Diego for two weeks of refresher training. After that I am sure we will go back to the far Pacific."

Sorenson turned to Dubose. "Commander, please dismiss the crew."

The ceremony was over, and it was as short and simple as Sorenson had promised.

While the change of command ceremony was in progress on the forecastle and on the small deck in front of gun mount 52, First Class Quartermaster Jerald Wencey was stationed on the bridge to supervise the breaking of a new commission pennant at the mast head and the hauling down of the old one. A seaman designated as a signalman striker was assigned to assist him. All the other quartermasters and signalmen were down on the forecastle.

Wencey had stood at attention as the new commanding officer came out on the small deck around gun mount 52. His assistant,Seaman and signalman striker Pete Caruso, stood next to him, lounging against the bulkhead.

"Stand at attention!" Wencey said out of the corner of his mouth.

"What for?" Caruso said. "They can't see us up here."

"Doesn't matter. We can see ourselves. Stand at attention."

Caruso reluctantly straightened up.

When the new Captain began to read his orders, Wencey said to Caruso, ''Stand by the commission pennant halyards.''

When the new Captain said, ''I relieve you,'' Wencey nodded at Caruso.

Caruso pulled down on the part of the halyard, called a tail line attached to the bottom of the new commission pennant. The pull broke a small string in which Wencey had wrapped the new commission pennant, and it fluttered free in the freshening breeze.

Wencey nodded again, and Caruso slacked the halyard holding up the old commission pennant, and it began to descend. When it reached the top of the flag bag, Caruso caught it, cast it free of the halyards, and brought it to Wencey.

Wencey said, ''Good job. Next time do it better.''

Caruso muttered. ''Always do it better. You think I'm a machine. By the way, what's the good of this switch anyway? This pennant has a lot of good time on it yet.''

''In a few minutes I'm going to present it to the Executive Officer.''

''A souvenir, eh?''

''Yes. A small reminder of his two months in command.''

''Big deal.''

''Maybe not to you, but it will be for him.''

After the ceremony, Sorenson went back to his cabin. As he entered it, he turned to Dubose. ''Please have all the officers come up to see me in order of seniority. I'd like to have you here with me when they come in. They can wait in the wardroom until we call for them. This will take a little time, but I think it's important that I meet each one as early as possible.''

Dubose left to make the arrangments, and Sorenson walked over to a port. He looked up the pier at the automobile parking places. He could see Ferren driving away, and although he knew she couldn't see him, he waved. He knew what a lonely life she would have when he left to go to sea. He hoped she would not have to lose him like she had lost her first husband, on a sinking destroyer.

Soon Dubose returned with Lieutenant Steiner, the gunnery officer. Sorenson greeted him warmly and asked him to sit down.

Sorenson noticed that Steiner had added a few pounds to his square frame. "A little too much homecooking?"

Sorenson noticed that Dubose seemed surprised. Steiner laughed and patted his stomach. "Yes, sir, just storing up a little extra. I'll have it off in the first month at sea."

Sorenson thought that Steiner's earnest face and deep-set eyes were unchanged, and he remembered the careful performance of duty he had grown to expect from Steiner from their months together. Steiner's brown hair was neatly trimmed in a crew cut, and as usual, his uniform was clean and well-pressed.

Sorenson had known Steiner from the *O'Leary*, so he talked about old times for a few minutes in order to give Dubose a chance to observe Steiner in a relaxed setting.

Then he said, "How do you like the 5-inch battery on this ship?"

Steiner grinned. "Great. This is a lot easier than trying to keep a 4-inch battery operating."

Sorenson noticed that Dubose seemed surprised.

Sorenson said, "I hope to see more of you soon. This is just a chance to say hello again."

Steiner left, and Sorenson said, "That wasn't much exposure to Chuck Steiner, but I think you'll find we couldn't have a better gunnery officer. He's really been through the mill. Now let's talk to Steele for a few minutes. We've already talked about his personal characteristics, so it won't take long."

Steele came in and sat down, his bright eyes sparkling behind the rimless glasses covering his penetrating gray eyes. Sorenson said "I had a chance to say hello to you yesterday, but I wanted to say hello officially and to ask you if you see anything in the sonar area or in any other part of the ship we need to take care of before we sail."

Steele shook his head and said in his deep voice, "No, sir. The sonar checks out all right at the pier here, but we won't know all the facts until we get to sea. It has some new features that were added in the yard, but basically it's like the one on the *O'Leary*. Terrill, our head sonarman, was with us in the *O'Leary*, and you know he's top rate. I won't know how the other sonarmen perform until I see them operate at sea aginst a submarine."

Dubose straightened in his chair when Steele began to speak and followed what he said closely. When Steele departed, Dubose whistled, "What a voice! He shook the bulkheads."

Sorenson grinned. "Maybe you see one of my points. It's important to get to know your officers and petty officers as soon as possible. Now let's say hello to Doctor Fineman."

Fineman came in, his handsome, open face showing his affection for Sorenson. He clasped Sorenson's hand warmly. "Good to see you, Captain. I hope you took my advice about the honeymoon."

Sorenson laughed and turned to Dubose. "David was my best man at our wedding a couple of weeks ago. He gives pretty good advice."

Dubose said, "I could use some. My wife left a week ago for our plantation. Said she had to get back because it was almost calving time."

Fineman said, "Sorry. I don't know much about calving. The Captain ought to be able to help you, though. He's a big horse and cattle man."

Sorenson said, "I don't know much. Those Texas cows are tough. They just go away and hide in the brush and come back with a calf."

Sorenson noticed that Dubose was assessing Fineman carefully, and he hoped he was noticing Fineman's intelligent face, aristocratic nose, and good manners. Fineman did have a very black beard which required careful shaving, but Sorenson suspected that Dubose had the same problem with his dark black hair.

When Fineman departed, Sorenson asked. "What did you think of him?"

Dubose didn't hesitate. "Since I talked to you, I've gone over all the officers records, and if you hadn't scheduled these meetings today, I'd have done the same thing. To answer your question, I'm impressed. I notice he had trained in psychiatry, but I'm sure he's had enough experience by now to take care of any kind of medical problem that might come up."

"Good. I agree." Sorenson continued. "I doubt if you've seen much of the next officer. He's a real pistol. He's probably spent most of his time up in the yard supply depot stripping them of everything he can carry."

"Is he dishonest, or will he be exceeding our quarterly allottment?"

"Oh, no. You can bet he won't spend any extra money. He just knows how to get what he needs. Maybe a trade or two, or finding a sympathetic friend in one of the issue offices. His name is John Renard, and the Supply Corps has never been the same since he joined it. Let's call him in."

Dubose opened the door and called Renard in. Sorenson got up and shook his hand warmly. "Glad to see you. I hear you've been busy."

Renard came in and eyed the Executive Officer warily. He looked remarkably like Sorenson, except that his hair was slightly red and his face was unscarred.

He sat down at Sorenson's invitation and said, "Captain, the old gang has been waiting for you."

Dubose looked straight ahead. Renard looked at him out of the corner of his eye. "I mean we missed you. As for the Supply Department, everything is fine. Luckily we don't need any cold weather clothing where we're going."

Sorenson remembered the times in Norfolk when he had sent Renard off to get special cold weather clothing to help fight the bitter cold in the Atlantic. "No, but we may need other things. How about beer?"

Dubose's eyes widened, and Renard asked, "Do you mean it?"

"Certainly. It's entirely legal, and it's encouraged. We can buy it here and store it away under lock until we reach some remote atoll or island where we can take it ashore with us."

Renard thought for a moment. "Well, I can rearrange a storage locker for it."

Dubose broke in. "I don't think we have any money in the recreation fund. I've tried to spend it down on things we could use at sea."

Sorenson said, "I approve of that, but I think the beer will be important, too. I'll advance the recreation fund whatever you need to buy the beer."

Renard grinned. "I thought you would."

When Renard left, Dubose said, "I know you must have had a close personal relationship with the officers who served with you, but wasn't he a little off base with that last remark? All the officers and enlisted men you brought with you seem to be lax and undisciplined, and they're bringing down the overall tone of the ship the previous commanding officer worked so hard to maintain."

Sorenson sighed. "You may as well know, but keep it to yourself. I have spare cash for things like that. Renard and Fineman and Chief Carmody know, but I'd prefer that the others not find out. As for the discipline, my style is more relaxed than you've been accustomed to. I promise you we won't go 'Asiatic,' but we'll enjoy life more."

Sorenson consulted the list of officers. "I've already met young Auerbach, and I think you know him by now. We'll skip him. Let's shift to some of the officers who were already with the ship. I'd like to see the Chief Engineer next. Before he comes in, tell me something about him."

''His name is Reifel, and he's a full Lieutenant. He's a mustang, fleeted up from a chief machinist's mate. I think he knows all there is to know about this type of engineering plant, and he kept it running under some difficult circumstances off Guadalcanal.''

''Such as?''

''We had a shell hit in the forward engine room. He and some others were overcome by low-pressure steam and had to be carried out. He was back down there in five minutes and stayed there until the plant was running full speed again.''

''Is he all right now?''

''I'm not sure. He's never gained back the weight he lost out there, as you'll see. He spends most of his time in the forward engine room. Only eats about one meal a day in the wardroom and then at second sitting.''

Sorenson said, ''Let's have him in.''

Reifel came in and looked at Dubose tentatively. Dubose introduced him to the Captain. Sorenson smiled and said, ''I'm glad to meet you. I hear you're a fine engineering officer.''

Reifel was a half foot shorter than Sorenson and weighed no more than one hundred and twenty pounds. His cheeks were gaunt and pinched, but he looked healthy. Sorenson made a mental note to ask Doctor Fineman to take a look at him, both physically and mentally.

Reifel grinned slightly and nodded his head but said nothing.

Sorenson said, ''Please sit down and let's talk a bit. Are you married?''

Reifel's voice was a surprise. It was smooth and low, almost like a crooner's. ''Not now. My wife died some years ago.''

''Sorry,'' Sorenson said.

Sorenson had not expected the resonant voice and looked at Dubose.

Dubose tried to ease the tension. ''Reifel leads the church services when we have them. He's the whole choir by himself.''

Sorenson said. ''I'll remember that when we have the opportunity to have services.''

''Thank you, sir,'' Reifel said.

Sorenson said, ''Do you think we will have any trouble in the engineering department being ready to get under way at the end of this week?''

''A few small problems. We're almost ready now. We're tuning up.''

After Reifel departed, Sorenson sat silently for a few minutes, toying with his coffee cup. Then he said, ''What do you make of Reifel? He's obviously competent, but he seems scared of something.''

Dubose shook his head slowly. ''I didn't want to have to bring this up, but you've been straight with me. I've told you how much I admired the last Commanding Officer. But he was also a tyrant in some ways. He always talked shop at the wardroom table. Poor Reifel, good as he was, just reached the point where he didn't want to eat when the Captain was at the table.''

Sorenson nodded understandingly. ''I appreciate your frankness, and I'll guard your confidence. Please tell Reifel to be at lunch, and I think he'll be surprised.''

Lieutenant Junior Grade Sydney Scorse was the next to enter. Sorenson noticed that he was short and a little overweight. Black eyes peered out from a slightly rounded face, but somehow Sorenson suspected there was a harder and leaner face beneath the extra fat. His nose was slightly Roman in shape, and his hair was black, in tightly curled ringlets.

Dubose introduced him and said, ''Scorse is the Communication Officer. He's had a lot of experience at it, and I think he'll continue to do a good job.''

Sorenson said, ''Yes, I remember you from the publications inventory yesterday. They were in excellent shape. You've done a good job with them.''

After some general conversation, Sorenson said, ''Do you foresee any problems in your department?''

''Well, sir, I'd like to ask if you would consider having the Doctor and the Supply Officer help with the decoding.''

''Of course. They're quite good at it, and they'll volunteer.''

There was a smile on Scorse's face as he went out the door.

''What was that all about?'' Sorenson asked.

The last Commanding Officer wouldn't let anyone but the Communications Officer decode. He thought it was inappropriate for any one else to help because of the Geneva Convention. Poor Scorse almost worked himself to death. He's one of the most conscientious officers I've ever seen.''

Sorenson grinned. ''He doesn't look overworked.''

''You should have seen him when we entered the yard. He was thinner than Reifel.''

Sorenson looked down the roster of officers. ''I see John Jablonski is still on leave. I know him well, and there isn't a better navigator in the fleet.''

Dubose grinned. ''I was hoping you'd say that. I've been navigating until we entered the yard.''

''Don't you like it?''

''I like it fine, but it interfered with my duties as Executive Officer. As you know, taking sights at dawn and dusk and at noon uses a lot of the time I'd like to devote to supervising the ship's routine.''

Sorenson nodded. ''You've taken your last sight for a while.''

Dubose grinned. ''Thank you, sir.''

Sorenson went back to the roster. ''I see that Lieutenant Junior Grade Finlay MacIntosh, the new torpedo officer, is also still on leave. We won't have to worry about him, either. He'll be a fine torpedo officer.''

Dubose said, ''He seems to be well qualified.''

Sorenson grinned. ''The only thing wrong with him is that he's a damned Scottish sheep herder.''

Dubose frowned. ''Are you serious?''

''Yes and no. He's a Scot all right, and he was studying sheep husbandry when he entered the Navy. I'm trying to talk him into shifting over to cattle.''

Dubose said, ''We don't have any radar officer yet. I hope we'll get orders for one soon.''

Sorenson said, ''We will. A young ex-radarman first class is now completing advanced radar school. As soon as he graduates he'll be ordered to us.''

''I take it he's good.''

''Superb. Bronte was an expert at operating and repairing radars, and now he will know the theory as well, and he'll use the results in CIC.''

Dubose said, ''That's all of the officers, and it's time for lunch. If you'll excuse me now, I'll see you there at 1200.''

Sorenson stopped in the wardroom pantry on the way to lunch and introduced himself to the wardroom stewards. When he left, Williams, the black chief steward, whistled softly and said in his Detroit accent to Vila, ''That's the first time I've ever had a Captain come into my pantry except for Saturday inspection in all the years I've been in the Navy.''

Vila grinned. ''Nice guy, but don't fool around with him.''

''Don't intend to,'' Williams said.

Sorenson sat down at the head of the wardroom table with the officers ranged on either side according to rank. Dubose was on his right and Reifel on his left. The officers had lost no time in electing Fineman as mess treasurer, and he sat at the other end of the table.

Sorenson looked at Reifel and smiled. ''Reifel, I understand you've been too busy to join the wardroom for lunch.''

Reifel slowly looked up from the plate of soup he hadn't touched. Before he could say anything Dubose said, ''I'm glad to see he could make it today.''

Sorenson hit the side of his water glass with a knife. When conversation had stopped, he said, ''Gentlemen, I hate to make a speech at our first meal together, but I thought it wise to set a few ground rules. You all know that it is not customary in a wardroom to discuss politics, religion, or women. I'd like to add that we won't indulge in shop talk here either. I know there will be times out in the forward area where that rule will have to be violated, but still it's my general policy. I want the wardroom to be a home away from home for you all and a place where you can relax and laugh a little. End of speech.''

Sorenson picked up his soup spoon and noticed out of the corner of his eye that Reifel was eating his soup. He turned to him and said, ''This isn't shop talk. I really want to know the answer. How's the coffee in the forward engine room?''

Reifel looked at him for a few seconds, and then a smile broke out on his gaunt face. ''Best in the fleet, Captain, I hope you'll come down and try it.''

Sorenson grinned broadly, ''On the first day out of port'' he said.

The ice was broken, and the volume of conversation soared.

Dubose, listening, said, ''Most noise I've heard outside of a 'Bama fraternity house on a Saturday night.''

After lunch Sorenson called Renard to his cabin and asked him to sit down. ''John, I'd like you to call the Mark Hopkins Hotel in San Francisco and make reservations for dinner for six for Saturday night at six o'clock. And then reserve six tickets for the concert at the San Francisco Opera House at eight o'clock.''

Renard beamed. ''Certainly, sir. Sounds like a big night.''

Sorenson said, ''I hate to tell you, but you're not invited.''

Renard's face fell. ''Am I too young?''

''It's not only that. You don't sing well enough.''

''May I ask who your guests are?''

''You shouldn't ask, but I'll tell you anyway. Mrs. Sorenson, Lieutenant Commander Dubose, Lieutenant Reifel, Doctor Fineman, and Lieutenant Junior Grade Auerbach.''

''Can Auerbach sing?''

''I don't know, but he likes classical music. Stop pouting. I'll include you in the next party. It'll be a livelier group.''

Saturday afternoon about 1500, Ferren drove the green Buick down to the pier and they picked up the four officers waiting at the end of the brow.

Sorenson pointed to Ferren. ''We've got a driver who doesn't drink. She's a little heavy on the throttle sometimes, but very safe. Dubose, you get in the back with Reifel and Fineman, and Auerbach can sit in the middle up front, but not too close to the driver.''

Ferren giggled, and Auerbach reddened.

Ferren said, ''Sit as close as you want to.''

The trip down was pleasant and quick, with Fineman telling stories of his travels from the back seat. Whenever Fineman lagged, Sorenson chimed in with memories of their cruise on the *O'Leary*.

Promptly at six o'clock Ferren barreled into the curving driveway of the Mark Hopkins Hotel, scattering bell boys and arriving guests.

Sorenson said, ''Easy, dear, these westerners aren't used to your low approaches.''

Auerbach turned to Ferren ''Can you fly?''

''Sure. I've got a license and everything.''

Auerbach shook his head. ''Don't think I want to go up with you.''

Dinner was excellent, and Sorenson spent most of his time plying Reifel with fattening foods. Reifel began to emerge from his shell, and soon was telling stories of his boyhood in Kansas. They lingered so long over coffee that Ferren had to make up time on the way down the steep hill from the Mark Hopkins to the concert. Auerbach held his breath and exhaled it audibly on one occasion.

Sorenson said, ''Would you like to take over the care and feeding of this young daredevil?''

Auerbach's voice was unsteady. ''You ought to send her out to the Pacific to take on some of those Zeros.''

Ferren said, ''I'd go if they'd let me. Maybe some day the country will recognize that women can do anything men can do. Flying isn't all that hard.''

Auerbach sighed. ''Maybe not in a straight line, but gyrating around with those Zeros is hard on your insides. I don't think it's for girls.''

After the concert by the San Francisco Philharmonic Orchestra featuring semi-classical selections, Sorenson took them to an Italian restaurant the Maitre'd at the Mark Hopkins had recommended. ''He said they had something called pizza that was very good. I never heard of it.''

Fineman said, ''Obviously it's an Italian dish. Very popular in Italy, but not known at all in the States except in San Francisco. I had it here on one of my trips. Those who have had it at this restaurant lately say it's so good it ought to spread throughout the States some day.''

Pizza turned out to be a round piece of pastry flattened and twirled in the air by a chef and finally put down in a large pan and filled with cheese, tomatoes, mushrooms, and a variety of spices. After a quick bake on a board with a long handle in a very hot oven, it was placed in front of Sorenson to carve.

''Smells like the real Italian thing I remember,'' Fineman said.

The first one merely whetted their appetites, and a second and third quickly disappeared.

The trip back might have been long, but Fineman started to sing the arias from the selections the orchestra had played that night. Soon Reifel joined in with his deep base voice, and Dubose added a surprisingly good baritone.Sorenson's and Auerbach's voices were in between range, and soon Fineman said, "This sounds pretty good except for those unnamed amateurs in the front seat who don't exactly fit in. Ferren, I know you can sing. We need your soprano, but it would be better if the other two just listened."

Auerbach said, "Ah, doesn't she need to keep her attention on her driving?"

"She's never better than when she's doing two things at once," Sorenson said.

Ferren's voice was just right, and the quartet became better as the miles rolled quickly by.

At the brow, the group piled out of the car and leaned over the driver's side to say good night to Ferren.

Reifel's smile was genuine. "Best night I ever had," he said.

Dubose was almost sad. "Wonderful night, but I wish my wife could have been here, too."

Ferren said, "I understand you said she had to go back to the plantation for calving. Couldn't someone else have helped?"

Dubose sighed. "She doesn't think so. I met her at the University when she was studying to be a veterinarian. She hasn't practiced since we were married, but she thinks no calf can be born on the plantation without her. My sisters are away at the University, and my brothers, all except the oldest, are in the services. My oldest brother likes to have her there. That's all it takes. Just one please from him, and she's gone."

"I hope we can meet your wife some time," Sorenson said. "She sounds like an interesting person. If you don't want her to help, we can use her in Texas."

Dubose straightened up and said wistfully, "No, you can't have her." Then he looked at the others and said,

"Let's go. We've got tomorrow to rest and then Monday is our big day to get ready to sail."

Sorenson said, "I'll see you all Monday morning."

Ferren waved goodbye and let out the clutch. Sand and dirt flew up from the rapidly spinning tires, and the big Buick was off in a typical Ferren take-off.

Auerbach moved out of the way of the flying dirt and watched the red tail light move down the pier. When the car rounded a warehouse building and the tail light suddenly winked out, he closed his half-opened mouth. Then he shook his head. "She certainly would burn up a runway."

Fineman, standing nearby, said, "Actually she's a pretty safe pilot. Automobiles seem to set her off."

"Who taught her to fly?"

"The Captain."

"Where did he learn?"

"At Pensacola. He was within a week of graduating when he got involved in a flat-hatting incident and was washed out."

"Didn't the Navy ever take him back? They needed pilots desperately a year ago."

"They gave him a chance, but he turned it down."

"What? I'd give my right arm for another chance. Why didn't he take the offer?"

"He had a better one. Command of a destroyer."

"And that's why he's here?"

"It's a longer story than just that. He had to prove himself to the Navy as an executive officer first, just as you will have to work your way up. By the way, how is your hearing?"

"All right, I guess, but I have some trouble with high pitched sounds lately."

"Since your last accident?"

"Yes. A projectile exploded in my cockpit and seemed to affect my hearing."

"Did you sing in a choir as a boy?"

"Sure. I was pretty good."

"But tonight you didn't sing very well. You seemed to hesitate when we got into the high notes."

Auerbach leaned back against a big steel bollard. "You're right. I first noticed it at the opera the other night. When the soprano was supposed to sing the high notes I thought she had stopped singing."

Auerbach could see Fineman shake his head in the partial light from the overhead light up on the quarterdeck. Fineman said, "We've got to test you tomorrow."

Auerbach groaned. "Don't tell me the Navy is going to kick me off this ship. too."

Fineman shook his head. "I doubt it. I hope your hearing loss is temporary and that your hearing will come back. We'll test you tomorrow and then again when we get to Pearl Harbor in about ten days."

"If you turn me over to the ear mechanics at the hospital, I'm done."

Fineman grinned. "I'll test you in my own laboratory first. If that's successful, maybe the hospital bit won't be necessary."

Fineman turned and started up the brow, Auerbach following him. They saluted the quarterdeck and then saluted Chief Carmody, who had the petty officer of the watch duty.

Carmody said, "Welcome back, gentlemen. Did you have a big musical night? Any good western stuff?"

Fineman said, "Nothing from west of Vienna."

After they had stepped down off the brow to the quarterdeck, Auerbach said, "Where does the Captain get all this money to teach his wife to fly and to take us out on the town?"

Carmody heard him and grinned. "He has a few extra cattle down in Texas."

Fineman cleared his throat loudly. Auerbach could see Carmody redden slightly.

Carmody's voice was faint. "Well, just a few old steers scattered around the place."

Fineman looked at Auerbach. ''If you really want to know you should ask the Captain.''

Auerbach shook his head, ''I don't have to have a steer fall on me. I'll just keep quiet.''

Fineman looked carefully at Carmody. ''A good idea all around.''

CHAPTER SIX

Sorenson and Ferren spent a leisurely Sunday, having a late breakfast, and wandering around Vallejo in the winter winds of Northern California. When they got back to the hotel, Ferren had decided to leave for San Diego Monday morning, a day before the ship was due to sail.

"If I don't leave a day early, I'll get to San Diego a day after you arrive," she said.

"Makes sense to me. I'll help you pack, and you can drop me off at the ship tomorrow morning."

"I'll call Maria Steiner and tell her about my plans. She's going to drive down with me. The Steiners don't have a car."

Dinner was somber. Ferren said, "I liked our little home in the hotel. I hope I can get a place in San Diego as nice."

"Fineman has been to Coronado before. He says it's smaller but better than San Diego and closer to the fleet landing."

"I've talked to him. I'm all set at a small hotel, and The El Cordova can handle us by Friday at the latest. Here's the address of the small hotel he recommended. I'll be there early Thursday."

The next morning Ferren dropped Steiner and Sorenson off at the ship. She waved at Auerbach, who had the day's duty, and was off in a squeal of tires and rubber smoke.

Sorenson grinned as he saluted Auerbach. ''You'll get used to it in time. I have.''

Monday was frantic. Yard workmen bustled about making last minute repairs. Barges came alongside to load ammunition, stores, and supplies on the ship, and long lines of men carried them below.

Renard dashed around the decks, supervising the loading of fresh provisions and supplies, and Steiner worried about inventorying the ammunition coming aboard.

Sorenson sat calmly in his bridge chair, watching the activity below and signing papers Carmody brought up to him. By lunch he had had all he could take, and he retreated to his lower cabin to get it ready for sea. Vila came in and helped him, and soon all the furniture was lashed down and the contents of his locker secured so that the motion of the ship would not fray his uniforms.

Sorenson turned in early. About 0200 he was aware of a slight regular movement of the ship. In his cabin, he couldn't hear anything but the whirr of the ventilators, but he was uneasy. He put on his trousers and a parka and went up to the bridge. The wind was blowing about 20 knots and the sky was overcast. There was no one on the bridge, because they were in port, but he could see the quarterdeck watch below. He went down to the quarterdeck where the duty officer and the petty officer of the watch were bent over under a light reading a dispatch.

''Good morning,'' Sorenson siad. ''What's going on?''

Steele, who had the duty, said, ''Captain, I was just about to call you. This weather report says we'll have winds as high as 30 knots tomorrow morning. Do you want to ask for a delay in departure?''

''No. Just take a look at the mooring lines and the large fenders from time to time. We should be able to ride out 30 knots okay. Call me if it gets over that.''

Sorenson went back below to his cabin and set his alarm for 0500.

Sorenson was on the bridge shortly after daylight. Early as he was, Jablonski was there before him with the harbor chart secured to the chart desk.

When Sorenson appeared, Jablonski saluted and grinned. ''I knew you'd be up here early. Can I send down for some coffee?''

''Please, sugar and cream, and then let's take a look at the charts.''

Sorenson looked closely at the clouds overhead and then at the surface of the water. When the coffee arrived, he bent over the chart with Jablonki.

''We've got at least a thousand yards of good water off the pier,'' Jablonski said. ''Your problem is the large tender astern and the two ships outboard of it. That means you'll have a tough time getting the ship far enough off the pier to turn around and pass them before the wind blows you down on them.''

Sorenson walked out on the port bridge wing, which was the wing toward the channel. He watched the wind lines on the water in the growing dawn and said, ''The wind is about 10 degrees on our outboard bow at 30 knots.''

Dubose came up to the bridge, and Sorenson brought him up to date.

Dubose said, ''Captain, I recommend you ask for a postponement in our departure time or at least that you ask for two tugs.''

''Thanks for the recommendation, but I don't think we'll need either.''

Dubose was very agitated. ''But, Captain, If you go out astern as almost all ships do, the wind may carry the high forecastle we have down on the pier edge, or maybe into the ships astern. You'll be taking a big chance."

Sorenson grinned. "We'll use an old aircraft trick. We'll use the wind as a tug."

Dubose wasn't convinced, but he followed Sorenson down to breakfast. Sorenson ate a huge breakfast, but Dubose picked at his food, obviously concerned.

At 0730, Sorenson said, "Let's go."

On the bridge, Steele, who had the deck during getting underway, said, "Captain, I've never handled this type of ship before, but I think the high bow will give you trouble. We don't want to scrape off all that paint we just put on it."

Sorenson grinned. "We won't." He looked down on the forecastle. "Isn't that Chief Boatswain's Mate Shaky Bellows down there?"

"Yes, sir. He came aboard off leave last night. So did Ensign Bronte."

"I see Chief Bellows is already in charge. I guess Auerbach is relieved to have some experienced help up there. This will be his first time getting the ship underway as first lieutenant."

Dubose folowed the direction of Sorenson's eyes. "My God. He must be 60 years old!"

Down below Bellows took off his cap to secure it more firmly in the wind.

Dubose said, "Look at that. He's almost completely gray."

Sorenson nodded. "Also, he's Polish and he has a heavy accent. Your Bama drawl and his accent are going to have to compromise."

Dubose said, "I think I'll have to use Auerbach as an interpreter. Captain, can I get him off the ship in San Diego?"

"Hell no. He knows more about seamanship and how to motivate the young seaman down there than any other chief in the Navy. After a week, you'll agree that we're lucky to have him."

''Sir,'' Steele interrupted ''the ship is ready for getting underway.''

Dubose tried one last time. ''Captain, won't you reconsider?''

''No, thank you. I have the conn. Steele, you take the deck. Dubose, normally I would have you handle the lines, but this is going to be a little tricky, so I'll handle them myself.''

Sorenson walked over to the starboard wing of the bridge and looked at the stretching mooring lines. ''Main Control, stand by to answer all bells. Single up all lines!'' he ordered.

The six mooring lines were numbered from the bow aft. Numbers one and six went straight across to the pier. Two and three crossed as they spread from the forecastle to the pier. Aft, four and five did the same.

When the report came up that all lines were singled up, Sorenson ordered, ''Slack one, two, and three. Take in four and six.''

He could see Dubose shudder, but remain quiet.

Almost miraculously the bow began to swing slowly to port against the wind. Soon it was pointing directly into the wind, and Sorenson said, ''Port ahead one-third.''

When the bow was clearly across the wind, Sorenson said quietly to the talker, ''Tell the forecastle to take in all the forward lines.''

The ship, which had begun to drift slightly aft, moved slowly forward, and the bow began to swing rapidly to port.

Sorenson said to the talker, ''Ease five.'' He looked aft. The after line was holding the stern toward the pier and preventing it from drifting into the ships astern. Then he looked forward again. The bow was swinging to port even more rapidly.

Dubose was speechless. Sorenson said, ''Looks like magic, but it isn't. The wind gets down between the bow and the pier and actually pushes the bow out against the wind, instead of in, which you would expect.''

Soon the ship was almost perpendicular to the pier, headed across the channel. Sorenson ordered, ''Take in five. Starboard ahead two-thirds. Port back one-third. Left full rudder.''

The *Carson* moved away from the pier and still swung to port, the wind now blowing her high bow around like a sail. Her stern was soon clear of the ships astern.

Jablonski, watching, said, ''I recommend course two zero zero down the channel.''

Sorenson turned to Wencey, who was steering, ''Come to two zero zero. All engines ahead two-thirds. Steele, take the conn.''

Sorenson walked over to his chair and sat down. Dubose followed him. Before Dubose could say anything, Sorenson said,''How about some coffee?''

Dubose said, ''Yes, sir, I'll send for it. I guess I owe you an apology.''

''What for? You gave me sound advice. I was lucky. There's an amount of wind that you can't exceed for this method to work.''

''What would have happened if you'd misjudged it?''

''Nothing much. The bow wouldn't have moved out, and I'd have had to give up and stay there until the next day or call for tugs. We'd have been a day or several hours late getting to San Diego.''

Dubose grinned. ''And Ferren wouldn't have liked it.''

Sorenson sighed, ''Neither would the commanding officer of the Underway Training Unit who's waiting to put us through hell. We'd have loused up his schedule.''

The trip south started in the high winds of the early morning, but by the time the *Carson* reached the lower bay they had moderated. At the turn into the main San Francisco Bay Channel, the winds were down to 10 knots, and the overcast had lifted to reveal a brilliant blue-skyed day with soft white clouds scudding in from the Golden Gate.

At 15 knots the bow cut through the small whitecaps, and Sorenson strode up and down the bridge, breathing in the cool air. He quietly caressed the recently varnished wooden rail around the top of the bridge bulwark.

The turbines below pushed the *Carson* through the shimmering seas without effort or vibration, and Sorenson knew he was fortunate to have been ordered to command such a beautiful ship.

The huge red form of the graceful Golden Gate Bridge loomed ahead, and Jablonski gave the officer of the deck a course to steer for the middle of the center span. When Macintosh, the officer of the deck, looked inquiringly at Sorenson, he nodded and said, "Make it so."

Sorenson walked over to his bridge chair and sat down. He looked at the quiet navigation bridge with the members of the watch studying the dials and controls before them. He was content. Ahead lay San Diego, and he hoped Ferren's trip south in the green Buick would be quick and safe.

On the port wing of the bridge, Caruso stood next to Wencey watching the Golden Gate Bridge become larger. He shook his head and pulled his hat down against the brisk breeze. "Damnedest pile of red lead I ever saw."

"That isn't red lead," Wencey said, "It's just painted red."

"You could have fooled me. In the navy yard we had the ship painted with red lead half the time. Why couldn't we just paint the ship red like that bridge?"

Wencey shook his head and went off to find the Chief Signalman.

They steamed under the Golden Gate and almost to the Farallone Islands before heading south for San Diego.

The next morning after breakfast, Sorenson headed down to the forward engine room. Reifel was standing on the steel grating and met him at the bottom of the ladder. He grinned. "I knew you were coming. Welcome to the engineering plant. How would you like your coffee?"

"If it's as good as you say it is, black."

Reifel sent the engine room messenger off to get the coffee and introduced Sorenson to the Engineering Department chiefs. "This is the senior chief, Chief Machinist Mate Lloyd. He's been aboard since the ship was commissioned. Then there's Chief Watertender McKinley. He came over from a tender last year. Chief Electrician's Mate Kilcline is also an old hand."

Sorenson shook hands with the three chiefs and took his cup of coffee from the grinning messenger. "Any problems yet?" he asked.

Reifel said, "I'd like to crank her up to full speed for an hour or two. Then we'll know."

"Light off the extra boilers and let me know on the bridge when you're ready. The weather is right."

Sorenson drained the last drops from his white coffee mug and handed it back to the messenger. "Best cup of coffee I've ever had. Thanks."

The chiefs left to get ready for the full power run, and Sorenson went back to the bridge, leaving a happy Reifel at the bottom of the ladder.

Within the hour the *Carson* was making 36 knots and hardly trying. Dubose said. "She might do more, but this is all we ever needed off Guadalcanal."

That afternoon Sorenson ordered the guns to be test-fired. Steiner had fired a 5-inch battery at gunnery school, but he wanted to fire his own battery. One gun had a misfire, but it was quickly corrected. The 40-millimeter and 20-millimeter batteries cranked out streams of tracers at red helium-filled balloons. Back on the torpedo deck, the torpedomen filled the red rubber balloons from steel helium-filled tanks, tied them off, and released them on order of the gunnery officer. They lifted like red roses, seeking the upper air. Sorenson, watching, thought they were losers either way. They would be destroyed by gunfire, or, if they escaped that, they would explode in the thin upper air. He took a deep breath of salt air and walked to the other side of the bridge, resolved that the *Carson* would not be a loser.

Twenty-four hours later, Point Loma, at the entrance to San Diego Bay, loomed out of the early morning fog, and Jablonski navigated them safely into the anchorage off the Sonar School. They were no sooner anchored when a big motor launch full of officers and petty officers, each carrying a clip board, came alongside. A rangy lieutenant commander loped up the hastily rigged accommodation ladder. The officers and petty officers in the motor launch followed him at an even faster pace.

Dubose, meeting the officer at the top of the ladder, said, "You guys look like a bunch of locusts."

The lieutenant commander smiled and said, "I'm Lieutenant Commander Phillips from the Underway Training Unit, and I'm to be in charge of your underway training. Today we give you an inspection in port and tomorrow we get underway for every drill and exercise in the book. Now I suggest we go down to see the Captain, and that I turn my locusts loose on you right away to save time."

Dubose took a deep breath and said. "Let them have at it, and follow me."

The day was a hazy fog of rapid activity for Sorenson and Dubose and even worse for the officers and crew being harried by the various inspectors.

At 1600 the training team left the ship as fast as they had come; Sorenson immediately started liberty. Dubose volunteered to stay aboard and get the plan of the day ready for the next morning's early sailing and exercises, and Sorenson left by boat for the Coronado landing.

A friend he met at the landing gave him a ride to the address of the small hotel where Ferren had told him she would be staying. The friend talked about the latest news from the Pacific war all the way to the hotel. Sorenson knocked on the door of the room number Ferren had given him, and the door flew open. He started to take her in his arms, but the girl standing there beside the open door wasn't Ferren.

"Sorry," he said. "I thought you were my wife."

An attractive young girl looked at him carefully and said, "Well, if you don't find her, please come back."

Sorenson grinned back at her, "Could you tell me where a Ferren Sorenson went? She was supposed to be here."

The young girl picked up a slip of paper. "Oh, yes, she moved to the El Cordova up the street this morning. Apartment 202."

Sorenson thanked her and walked up the street to an attractive, low-lying set of apartments across Ocean Boulevard from the large and imposing Hotel Del Coronado. He located apartment 202, knocked on the door, and stood well back.

The door opened. It was Ferren. She noticed that he was standing away from the door. "Come on in. I won't hurt you. At least not until after dinner."

He explained the reason for his caution as he took Ferren into his arms. Then he let her go. "What do I smell cooking?"

"Just like a well broken-in husband. Always thinking of eating."

Sorenson said, "All that sea air made me hungry."

After dinner, they walked down the edge of the sea wall fronting the ocean. The houses were beautiful, a mixture of California ranch style and two-storied brick, all surrounded by vari-colored Martha Washington geraniums. At the end of the street they chose to go down to the beach and walk back in the sand toward the hotel.

"This reminds me a little of Virginia Beach," Sorenson said."

''Where we had our first date.''

They walked almost back to the start of the sea wall, and then sat on a large boulder. Ferren stirred the sand with her shoe. ''Tex, I've thought a lot about the time when you'll be gone. I don't think I can just sit in the hotel. First, I've got to find an apartment.''

''Good idea. I'll help you hunt.''

''Then I've decided to teach school. They are so desperate for school teachers here that I can start right away. My Virginia license will be accepted. I love kids, and it would make the time pass faster.''

''How about trying for one of our own?''

''I've thought about that, too, but I want to wait until after the war. I'd like to have you around when it's born and when it grows up. If you don't come back, we'd both be lonely. If I stick to school children, I can always turn them back to their mothers.''

Sorenson said, ''That sounds fine to me. Let's get back to the apartment. I've got to leave at five o'clock tomorrow morning.''

''Will you be home every night?''

''All except two. The inspectors who ride us like to get home, too.''

She looked at him pensively. ''How long will this last?''

''We're scheduled for two weeks, but anything can happen. The war out west is heating up.''

Ferren scuffed her shoe deeper into the sand. ''Just what I was afraid of.''

''Sorenson said, ''Are you sorry you agreed to marry me even if the war wasn't over?''

She threw herself in his arms and sobbed. ''Oh, no. The last month has been wonderful. If it's all we have, I'll never forget it.''

He held her closely, stroking her dark hair and wondering if he had done the right thing in marrying her before the war was over. Then he held her even closer, and he knew even the short time thay had been together was worth it, no matter what happened.

The next week was a blur of firings, drills, exercise, and inspections conducted both day and night. On Saturday, as they were headed back to port, Dubose dragged himself up to the bridge. Sorenson was almost too tired to smile, but he managed a weak grin.

Dubose said, ''This is almost worse than war.''

''I agree, but nobody is being killed.''

When they coasted slowly up to the anchorage off the Sonar School, Sorenson noticed a new light carrier moored at one of the piers at the Air Station. There was an unusual amount of activity around it. Loaded barges were moored to its outboard side, and aircraft were being hoisted aboard on the land side.

Dubose noticed it, too. ''Looks like they're about to go west soon.''

Dubose had been a good prophet, but he failed to guess that the *Carson* would go with her. After Sorenson had left the ship, a message came in terminating the *Carson's* underway training and assigning the *Carson*, a heavy cruiser, and another destroyer as escorts for the carrier on the voyage to Pearl Harbor.

Dubose reluctantly sent Scorse ashore with a copy of the message to give to Sorenson at the hotel with the information that they were to get underway at noon the next day. Then he requested fuel delivery by barge and enough ammunition to replace the ammuntion they had fired in underway training.

Renard frantically ordered enough fresh provisions to carry them to Pearl for delivery the next morning.

Sorenson heard the knock on the door and felt uneasy. No one knew them in Coronado, so he suspected the knock came from someone from the *Carson*. He opened the door and discovered Scorse's unsmiling face. ''Come in,'' he said.

''I don't think you'll want me to come in when you see what I've brought you,'' Scorse said.

Ferren heard him. ''How about a drink?''

Scorse brightened. ''Maybe we all need one.''

Sorenson read the message and said, ''Right. A double for me.''

At noon the next day Ferren sat on the huge boulder she had shared with her husband a few days before. She could see the San Diego Harbor entrance and the buoys stretching out to sea from the entrance.

Half an hour later the bow of the *Carson* poked out of the harbor entrance, followed by a sister destroyer and a few minutes later by a carrier. Astern of her steamed a new heavy cruiser.

Ferren watched the destroyers fan out into a screen ahead of the larger ships and begin what she knew was a search for submarines.

In half an hour the carrier had cleared the entrance buoys and a large bulge of white water grew under her stern as she increased speed.

The destroyers formed a screen ahead of the carrier, and the formation began zigzagging.

Ferren watched the ships as they passed slowly over the horizon. When she could see nothing but a cloud of haze, she burst into tears. For half an hour she sat crying. Then suddenly she straightened up and wiped her eyes. ''Enough of that,'' she said aloud. ''Now to the Board of Education to volunteer to teach the little devils. May they all be Navy Juniors and have my troubles.''

CHAPTER SEVEN

Sorenson knew from the dispatch he had received the day before that the carrier he would escort was the light carrier *Cabot,* a recently constructed ship. The heavy cruiser was the *Boston,* also new. The other destroyer was a sister ship named the *Ransome.* Sorenson was senior to the commanding officer of the *Ransome* and therefore the screen commander.

Both destroyers got under way at 1130 to precede the heavier ships out the channel. Once past the outer buoys, the destroyers spread in search of submarines. When the carrier and the cruiser came out shortly afterward, Sorenson ordered the destroyers to form an antisubmarine screen in front of the heavy ships.

As they settled into station, Sorenson walked aft on the bridge and looked toward the huge white mass of the Hotel Del Coronado on the Coronado beach front. He knew Ferren would be on the beach looking out to sea. When he had left her before in Norfolk, he had always returned in a month or two. Now he didn't know when he would be back. Instead of months, it might be years.

Last night he had held Ferren in his arms all night long while she cried softly. Just before dawn he had made gentle love to her for the last time, and she had dried her tears and gotten up to fix breakfast while he dressed.

Then Ferren had said a very controlled goodbye at the Coronado boat landing, and he had looked back and watched her standing on the landing as the ship's boat rumbled across the Harbor.

Now he realized for the first time the enormity of what he was doing. A year, or maybe two, would be a long time for him, but he would be caught up in the war. For Ferren it might seem an eternity, and he hoped she would carry out her plan to teach school.

Dubose's voice broke into his reverie. "Excuse me, Captain, I have the plan of exercises the carrier commander has formulated. As expected, launching and recovering aircraft are the main part of it, but there is also ample time for gunnery, shooting against towed sleeves, and for radar tracking drills."

Sorenson examined it. For the first time in Sorenson's knowledge, there were aircraft interception drills, where attack aircraft were sent out on random bearings, told to make simulated attacks on the formation, and defensive fighters were given commands by radio to follow directions to intercept the incoming aircraft, known as bogies. Sorenson had heard that the *Enterprise* had a fighter director group and that a school had been established in Pearl Harbor, but he had never seen it in practice.

Sorenson and Dubose looked at the schedules for these exercises. " 'Fighter direction,' this is being called," Sorenson said, "and we need to qualify some of our officers for controlling the direction of fighters."

Dubose said, "Young Bronte, our new radar officer, was talking about that at breakfast. He says he was qualified at radar school as a fighter director. Only he called it 'as an air controller.' "

"I think that's the new name," Sorenson said. "How did you like Bronte?"

"He's very mature, and he has a nice personality. I take it he's a good man with the radars, but I haven't had any personal experience with him yet."

"You'll find he's excellent. He's not only technically well-qualified, but he has fine personal characteristics."

Within the hour the *Carson* was assigned as plane guard, and Sorenson brought her around smartly astern of the carrier. Then they turned into the wind, which was only twenty degrees off the course they were trying to make good, and flight operations started.

Auerbach came up to stand officer of the deck instructional watches, and Sorenson noticed that he was watching the aircraft intensely, giving body English as each one labored into the air.

Sorenson walked over beside him. "That's all over now. You'll have to forget flying and concentrate on learning to conn this ship. It's as hard as piloting. The only difference is if you make a mistake here you may kill three hundred men instead of just yourself."

Auerbach colored slightly. "Sorry, Captain, I'll do my best."

On the second day the wind increased to 30 knots from the south and the rain in the heavy squalls pelted the *Carson*. They were making 22 knots, and Sorenson conferred with Reifel to calculate whether or not they could reach Pearl Harbor without fueling. They reached the reluctant conclusion that they would need fuel if the carrier kept up the diversions from course for flight operations, zigzagging, and radar tracking drills.

Sorenson sent off a visual dispatch requesting fueling once before arrival at Pearl Harbor.

Back came the answer, "Can you fuel now?"

Dubose shook his head. "That's a hell of a note. It's too rough to fly, so we fuel the destroyers. Why do you flyboys think like that?"

Sorenson grinned. "I guess I'm truly an ex-aviator, because I don't like it either, but we can do it."

He sat in his bridge chair and wrote an answer saying the *Carson* was ready now. Brophy took the message blank and transmitted it by flashing light to the *Ransome* and the carrier captain.

In an hour the signal was hoisted to commence fueling, and the *Carson* was designated first fueling ship.

Sorenson said, ''Apparently the *Ransome's* commanding officer didn't like it either and wanted to wait and see how we would do before he volunteered.''

Dubose said, ''The forecastle will be mighty wet. Can I keep the fueling crew under cover until we've come alongside?''

''Sure. Bellows is used to fighting the weather on the forecastle of a four-stacker. The low deck height on one of those old ships is awful. He's gotten soaked in icy water many a time in the Atlantic. He'll have the fueling crew ready on a minute's notice.''

When the signal was made by the carrier commander to commence fueling, Sorenson took the conn and came around to take station astern. The carrier maintained course, which brought the wind about forty degrees on her port side. The carriers were all rigged to fuel from the starboard side because of the various overhanging parts of the carrier on the port side.

Sorenson increased speed temporarily while they were going down wind.

''We'll give them a thrill,'' he said to Dubose.

He rounded up under the carrier's stern and slowed to 15 knots. The carrier had slowed to 12 knots for fueling and seemed to be crawling.

As he made the approach parallel to the carrier, Sorenson over-shot by a few feet, but the building swells were blanked off by the bulk of the carrier, and the *Carson* began to settle down. Sorenson ordered the forecastle fueling crew to take station, and Chief Bellows, followed by his men, trotted up the ladder from the main deck and out on to the forecastle. Swells were breaking against the side of the *Carson*, but only light spray came over the deck.

Soon Sorenson eased into 50 feet, and the carrier sent over a light messenger line with a weighted 'monkey fist' at the end of it. The men sprang forward, retrieving the end of the line, and began to heave in. A larger line followed, and then the large black hose began to emerge from the opening in the side of the carrier.

On the forecastle, Bellows shouted, ''Ah-hiv in ona haline!''

Dubose, listening above said, ''What was that!''

Sorenson grinned. ''He has his own language. English laced with a Polish accent and modified by how his dentures feel that day.''

Steele, who had the deck, said, ''Basically you ignore the Hs and subtract the accent. He said, 'Heave in on the line.' ''

Dubose looked at Sorenson. ''I remember what you said about accents. What do we do with him?''

''We keep him supplied with good fitting dentures. He's one of a kind. He's too old to change much, but you've got lots of years yet in which to change. He gives only one group of simple commands and the men know what he wants. You and I have to cover a larger range of orders in our business.''

Soon the hoses were lashed in the fueling trunks, and the carrier began to pump.

Sorenson found the *Carson* surprisingly easy to keep in position after his experience with the *O'Leary*. He relaxed and sent for a cup of coffee.

Dubose said, ''I thought this would be tougher than it is.''

Sorenson laughed. ''We'll see much worse than this when we get in typhoon country. Steiner has been out there in the Asiatic Fleet, and he says in a typhoon it's worse than the Atlantic.''

In less than an hour the Chief Engineer reported all tanks full, and Sorenson directed that fuel hoses be returned. As they began to ease back, Sorenson said to Dubose, ''Take her back to position.''

Dubose said, ''I have the conn.''

Sorenson grinned. ''First time I've heard you speak without a heavy accent.''

Dubose's expression was neutral. "I'm trying."

The next morning the weather moderated, and the exercises resumed. Bronte came up to the bridge to say hello to the Captain. Sorenson grinned when he saw him and shook hands warmly. "Your ensign's stripes look great. I'm sorry I didn't get to say hello sooner."

Bronte said, "I came aboard late the night before we sailed, and you were very busy early the next morning."

Sorenson noted Bronte's tan had faded. "I see you officers didn't get in much sunbathing at radar school."

Bronte shook his head. "Almost made me want to turn in my officer's stripes."

"You'll have a chance to catch up this week."

Bronte nodded. "Yes, sir, I met a few nice nurses over there when I was at school."

Dubose came over and said hello to Bronte. Sorenson said, "You've met Ensign Bronte?"

"Oh, yes. I met him the night he came aboard."

Bronte said, "Our next exercise is air control. They're going to give us a chance to control fighters. Would you like to come down to the Combat Information Center?"

Sorenson said, "I hope it's bigger than the one we put together on the *O'Leary*."

Bronte said, "It's big enough to hold a dance. You and the Executive Offier can both fit in easily."

Sorenson said, "Good. Can you fit in Lieutenant Auerbach? He's an ex-pilot and should be able to help with our air-control problems."

Bronte beamed. "Sure. I'd like to see one of those fighter jocks face to face."

They went down to the CIC and leaned over Bronte's shoulder as he watched little circular arcs indicating aircraft move across the screen and gave orders on the radio to the pilots of the various groups.

"Can't make head nor tail of it," Sorenson said.

Bronte said, "It isn't as easy as you would think. You have to learn where the center of these arcs actually is and on what range line it's located. That's what takes the schooling and the practice."

Auerbach said, "I never knew I looked like that up there. No wonder some of the orders were approximate."

Bronte said, "Yes, there's some guessing, but there's a lot of space up there to play with."

Bronte gave a final order to the section of two fighters he was controlling and they acknowledged. In a few seconds the section leader could be heard over the loudpeaker saying, "Tally ho! One bogey angels nine. Course one six five. Am attacking."

Bronte said. "See. We did it. Now maybe those carrier hot shots will let us join their team."

Sorenson said, "Do they give you trouble?"

"Yes, sir. Right now out in Task Force 58 only aviator air controllers are allowed to handle aircraft intercepts."

Sorenson shook his head. "I'll see what I can do. In the meantine I want Mister Auerbach to begin training under you as an air controller. I can see that if we get in the business, we'll need more than one controller."

The remaining days of the short transit were busy and productive, and when they rounded the distinctive shape of Koko Head on the Island of Oahu, Sorenson was confident they were as ready as they could get except for firing at surface targets at night and firing torpedoes.

Soon Diamond Head came into view, and the bridge crew trained all their binoculars and telescopes on Waikiki Beach as it slid by.

Brophy, who had been to Hawaii before, said, "You guys are wasting your time. The beach is too far away. Wait until liberty and go down there."

Caruso asked, "Is it all the picture magazines say that it is?"

Brophy said, "I don't know what picture magazines you read, but it isn't much any more. Lots of coral in the water and not many women tourists. At least not many under thirty."

The destroyers patrolled in the bright tropical sun while the big ships entered the net off the entrance to Pearl Harbor. When they were in, the *Carson* was ordered to moor outboard of two other destroyers at Tenten Pier, and Sorenson brought her in smoothly next to an outboard destroyer. After they were moored to the other ships, the sea breezes were suddenly cut off, and Sorenson noticed the heat for the first time.

When they were secured, Sorenson dressed in his best uniform and went to headquarters to call on Admiral Nimitz and then on the Commander of the Destroyer Force.

When he came back, Dubose met him on the quarterdck. Sorenson said, "Come to my cabin."

Dubose followed him in, and Vila brought in two glasses of iced coffee.

Dubose mopped his brow, "I hope this is all right, Captain."

Sorenson, opened his tie and shirt. "Wow! It certainly is. I'm not used to this heat."

Dubose laughed. "Wait until you get out farther west. This is mild compared to Guadalcanal."

When Vila had left, Sorenson said, "Where we're going it will be worse than Guadalcanal. We're scheduled to operate with the carrier group, Task Force 58, for about two months and then to go to the New Guinea area to join the Seventh Fleet."

Dubose picked up an atlas from Sorenson's desk and opened it to New Guinea. He whistled. "It's just below the equator."

Sorenson said, "That means we've got to make all prepartions for the real tropics. We'll need to clean out the ventilation systems and make sure all the electric fans work.''

Dubose nodded. ''I'll get on with it. How long do we have?''

Sorenson went on. ''We go out west with the same group we brought here. Let's start liberty as soon as we can today for half the crew at a time. I won't go ashore at all. You stood by a lot of time at Vallejo and San Diego, and I want you to get ashore. Take Reifel and some others with you and have a good time.''

CHAPTER EIGHT

Doctor Fineman stopped by to see Auerbach in his stateroom as soon as the ship had moored. When he knocked on Auerbach's door, Auerbach said in a resigned voice, "Come in."

Fineman went in. "You don't sound very happy. What's the matter?"

"I'm worried about my hearing."

"Why so?"

I can't seem to understand my new Chief Boatswain's Mate. I'm afraid my hearing is getting worse."

Fineman laughed. "Understanding Chief Bellows will come with time. Nobody understands him at first. Let's go ashore tonight and give your hearing the Fineman test."

Auerbach shook his head and rubbed his hands over the scars around his eyes. "I don't feel much like it."

"No choice. It's me or the hospital. We have reservations at a place I know. The Exec and Reifel are joining us for dinner and the evening. I think you'll enjoy it."

Auerbach sighed. "If I'm going to flunk your test, they might as well be there."

About 1800 Fineman found a taxi, and Dubose, Reifel, and Auerbach piled into the back seat with Fineman in the front seat with the driver.

Fineman directed the driver along the road to Honolulu and then to a suburb to the east of the city. After a couple of false turns, Fineman said, "I see a landmark, that bent palm tree. Now I remember where it is. Take the next turn to the right."

Dubose asked, "How long has it been since you were here?"

"About seven years. It's changed a lot since the war started. Most of the buildings around here are new."

In a few minutes Fineman spotted the entrance, tucked away among some coconut palms and banana trees, and they drove up to it and got out.

Auerbach said, "It looks like a haystack."

"That's fake thatch on the roof," Fineman said. "Just atmosphere."

A table was waiting for them, reserved by Fineman by telephone, and dinner was very good. A few highballs before dinner and a lot of wine made them all a little noisy by dessert time. Fineman began to hum one of the arias from the program they had heard in San Francisco, and the others joined in.

When they finished, Fineman said, "Dick, you didn't hesitate on the high notes then. Come with me and we'll give you the Fineman final auditory capability test. This is just the right time for it. The band is taking a long break."

Fineman got up and strolled over to the bandstand with Auerbach close behind. A very large Hawaiian was sitting at the edge of the raised structure tuning the steel guitar resting on his lap.

Fineman said, "Good evening, Duke."

The large Hawaiian looked at him in surprise. "How you know my nickname is Duke?"

"Easy," Fineman said. "Fifty percent of kane Hawaiians born after 1930 are called Duke."

"What's this kane stuff?" Auerbach asked, looking warily at the guitar player.

"Kane is Hawaiian for man, or male."

The Hawaiian said, ''My name is Duke Kalana, but you no answer my question, Buddy.''

''See that,'' Fineman said. ''Fifty percent of the haoles born at that time were named Buster or Buddy, and Hawaiians called all white guys Buster.''

Auerbach said, ''And what's a haole?''

''A white person.''

Auerbach said, ''I understand that now, but I'd like an explanation of the names.''

Fineman said, ''In the 1930s, Duke Kahanamoku, a Hawaiian, and Buster and Buddy Crabbe, two haole brothers, were Olympic champion swimmers swimming for Hawaii. This was the golden age of swimming out here, and naturally Hawaiian families named their boys Duke and the white women named their boys Buster or Buddy.''

The large Hawaiian said, ''Thanks. What can I do for you, Buddy?''

Fineman pointed to Auerbach standing next to him. ''My friend here has had a hearing problem, and I'd like to see if it's getting better. Would you play a succession of high notes on your high string, ending with the highest note you can play?''

''Sure. I got some high notes only my dog can hear.''

Kalana tightened the high string even further, put the steel rod on the neck of the guitar, and began to pick the notes with the other hand, moving the steel down the neck after each note.

Fineman said to Auerbach, ''Raise your hand when you stop hearing the notes.''

Auerbach raised his hand about three notes from the end.

Kalana said, ''You damned near good as my dog.''

Fineman said, ''I think he's okay now, but let's do at again. This time, Dick, turn around so you can't see the guitar.''

Auerbach turned around, and confidently raised his hand on the same note.

"Great!" Fineman said. "That proves it. You're as good as the rest of us."

Kalana shifted his heavy bulk. "All you guys was pretty good. I heard you singing. Would you come up here and sing a coupla pieces?"

Fineman said, "We'd like to, but we aren't much good yet."

Kalana laughed, "You ain't heard what goes for singing in here later. You guys good. Take this piece of music and go over it at the table. Anybody sing this, they gonna get applause. I send four pitchers beer over to your table while you learn it."

Fineman sighed with pleasure. "I'll see what the others say."

He and Auerbach went back to the table and sat down.

Dubose said, "How did he do?"

"Fine, but the hearing test is going to cost us something."

Reifel patted his pocket. "That's all right. We've got plenty of money with us."

"Not that," Fineman said. "They want us to sing this piece."

Dubose looked at the sheet of music, his black eyes concentrating on the words and notes. "The melody is simple, but half the words are in Hawaiian."

Fineman said, "Hawaiian is easy. All the vowels are long."

Reifel started to hum it. "Easy," he said. "I'm willing to try."

Auerbach looked at the bar. "The big guy is going to send over four pitchers of beer."

Dubose licked his full lips. "Then we'd better do it before we drink all that beer."

They hummed through the piece, and when they thought they were ready, Fineman nodded ot Kalana.

Kalana put down his guitar, got up, and went to the microphone. "Wahines and Kanes, tonight Duke Kalana brings you a first. A quartet of Buddies and Busters just in from the States singing Aloha Oe."

Fineman led the group up in front of the bandstand to the microphone, and they turned to face the noisy audience. Dubose said under his breath to Fineman, ''I hope the orchestra knows this piece.''

Fineman tried to keep from laughing. ''It's their national song,'' he said. ''It was written by one of their ancient Queens, Liliuokalani.''

Kalana started the introduction with the orchestra, and the words began to pour out of the apprehensive quartet. They were rough when they started, but grew better as they warmed up.

They ended with the chorus. ''Aloha Oe. Aloha Oe. Eke ona ona noho ika lipo. A fond embrace. A hoi ae au. Until we meet again--.''

The crowd quieted when they began singing, and at the end, there was rousing applause.

The four bowed and went back to their table to take care of the beer.

Reifel toasted his shipmates with a full glass. ''Not bad. They liked it.''

Fineman shook his head. ''Kalana's dog could sing that song, and they'd like it.''

The remainder of the beer soon disappeared, and Auerbach said, ''Why don't we volunteer to sing a couple of other pieces for some more beer?''

Dubose, now feeling quite relaxed and happy, said, ''Good idea, but what?''

Reifel said, ''How about Danny Boy? It sounds Hawaiian. Maybe they won't know the difference.''

Fineman nodded. ''Let's try it.''

They hummed it quietly twice, and then Fineman went up to see Duke Kalana with a request to sing again for more pitchers of beer.

Kalana grinned. ''You guys can try. If you get no boos, I throw in a palm leaf hat for each of you. Good souvenirs.''

They earned the palm leaf hats with a surprisingly smooth rendition of Danny Boy.

''Dat's a good song.'' Kalana said. ''What you say the name was? Kane Boy?''

''Oh, yes,'' Fineman said. ''Close enough.''

The rest of the evening was devoted to celebrating Auerbach's successful hearing test and trying out a few more songs for free. When the Moana Palace closed, Kalana volunteered to take them back to the ship. They sang all the way back, with Kalana adding a high Hawaiian tenor to the group.

The next morning Renard began to take aboard the provisions and supplies he had ordered on their arrival. Tropical fruit of several kinds arrived by truck and was carried across the inboard ship by hungry sailors who ate their fill before it arrived aboard. Several stalks of bananas were hung aft of the quarterdeck and soon disappeared. A fuel oil barge filled them from the outboard side and an ammunition barge replaced the ammunition they had expended enroute.

After lunch Sorenson went topside to watch the parade of sweating men. Then he left for the *Cabot* to be briefed on the next leg of their trip.

When he returned, he told Dubose to have all the officers except Renard, who was still hard at work, gather in the wardroom. In fifteen minutes the last one straggled in, and Sorenson began.

''First, we get underway at 0800 tomorrow preceding the *Cabot* and *Boston*. We will go off the coast far enough to fire our guns about 1300. Then we'll meet eight oilers and two ammuntion ships coming from the States. They won't go into port, but will continue on out to the forward area.''

Dubose asked, ''We'll be in their screen?''

''No. They have their own screen of the new destroyer escorts. We'll remain a separate group maneuvering ahead of them to search for submarines and then when we get closer to the forward area we'll take station to the southwest to protect them from Japanese aircraft coming from the Marshall and Gilbert Islands.''

Steiner asked, rubbing his crew cut head, ''Will we go that close to those islands?''

''Not necessarily. We go wherever the carrier task force is at the time we join up with it. Also, the Japanese have been running some very long attack missions from those islands.''

Steiner said. ''We can sure use the surface firings. We missed out on some at San Diego. How about night firings?''

Sorenson shook his head. ''There won't be time. We're supposed to simulate night conditions when we fire.''

Auerbach said, ''You mean we know they're there, but we don't peek.''

Sorenson laughed. ''That's it. We use radar from start to finish. Spotting and everything.''

Dubose said, ''The surface ships in the Solomons were beginning to get good results from radar control about the time we left. As far as I know the Japanese still don't have surface radar.''

Sorenson stirred his coffee. ''Right. But they still have tremendous torpedoes.''

MacIntosh shook his head doubtfully and said in a faint Scottish burr, ''We thought the German torpedoes were good. These are longer range, and the war-head is half again as powerful.''

''How about our torpedoes?'' Dubose asked.

Sorenson rubbed the scar on his cheek and said. ''Unfortunately, the firing we had at San Diego is the only one we're going to get.''

MacIntosh shook his head. ''These torpedoes are better than the ones we had on the *O'Leary*, but not much. The guys over on the tender say they're still not reliable as to depth control, and many of them don't explode even when they're sure hits. The submarine boys are going nuts. The skippers have decided to disable the magnetic exploder, and the results are getting better. If we fire, we should set them to run shallow and disable the magnetic exploders. Then we might get some hits.''

Sorenson nodded. ''Let's do that. I guess that's it. Everybody come back early tonight. We've got a big day tomorrow.''

After dinner, Sorenson went to the officer's club to telephone Ferren. The connection was noisy, but he did find out that she was teaching school and looking for an apartment. He reminded her of his fleet post office address and asked her to write every day.

Her voice faded at the end, but he thought he heard her promise to write frequently. He decided to walk back to the ship. The exercise in the tropical night tired him so that he was able to sleep fitfully, thinking about Ferren and the months before he would see her again.

CHAPTER NINE

Early the next morning the *Cabot* and her escorts got underway, departed Pearl Harbor, and steamed off to the east. Early as they were, a long-suffering fleet tug towing a target was earlier, and the *Cabot* reported it on radar.

The surface gun firings were elementary because the raft-like barge on a long tow wire limited the tug's speed and maneuverability. The raft had a large canvas target suspended between two masts.

The destroyers were allowed to fire first because the *Boston*'s large guns might destroy it before the smaller ships with smaller guns could fire at it.

The *Carson* was designated to fire first. Dubose and Jablonski formed a team to navigate the ship visually so that the tug would be safe and within the proper range and bearing limits.

Steiner and his director crew were required to use radar, first for acquiring the target from the surface search radar, and second for determining the course and speed of the target and taking it under fire. After the initial salvo, only radar could be used to spot the fall of shot and to make corrections to the range and deflection to bring the salvos on target.

Sorenson watched the exercise on the bridge PPI, also simulating what he would do normally in a night action. He was not allowed to look directly at the target.

When Dubose had the *Carson* in position, he announced, ''Surface action, port!'' and the surface search radar began looking for thetarget. When Bronte found it on his radar, he passed the word over the telephone circuit, ''Surface target. Single ship. Bearing one five six. Range one three oh double oh.''

After a few minutes of plotting the range and bearing, a process known as tracking, CIC reported ''Target course, three four zero. Target speed zero five.''

Dubose would normally have been in the CIC, but in his place Bronte passed this information up to the 5-inch battery director, and soon Steiner reported, ''On target. Solution. Request permission to open fire.''

On the bridge at the surface search PPI, Sorenson had been following the sequence of actions, treating the radar target as if it were an enemy ship. At the navigational plot on the bridge chart, Dubose checked the data to make sure the guns would be trained on the target and away from the tug. ''Range clear,'' he announced.

Sorenson took a deep breath, thinking that they would soon be doing this in actual combat. ''Commence firing,'' he shouted.

In seconds the first salvo boomed out. Sorenson resisted the impulse to look up to see where the salvo landed, and kept his head down.

Second and third salvos went out as Steiner fired a spotting ladder with the first salvo deliberately a little over and the third deliberately under. Up in the director with him, his fire control radar operator watched his radar display anxiously. Then Steiner, looking at a duplicate display, saw the salvos on the radar landing.

''Down two,'' Shouted the radar operator.

Steiner applied the spot to the fire control system, and another salvo went out.

The radar operator reported, ''No change! No change!''

Steiner ordered, ''Rapid fire!'' The guns boomed out almost continuously.

At the end of ten salvos, Steiner ordered, "Cease firing! Cease firing!"

He called down to the bridge, "How did it look?"

Dubose, the only one on the bridge allowed to watch the fall of shot, said, "Damned good. Your fourth salvo and all after it appeared to be hits, just as you planned."

Steiner grinned and said to his director crew, "Nice work. We won't know just how good we are until we get the results from the camera crew."

Bentley, the young ensign who had just come aboard in Pearl Harbor from the gunnery school there, said, "They'll take a couple of weeks. Before we get the results we may already be firing at the enemy."

Steiner nodded. "I'll go with the Executive Officer's evaluation. I think we're ready."

The other ships moved to the firing range, and Sorenson and Dubose idly watched as the other ships moved into position and conducted their firings. When the crusier *Boston* began to fire, they watched in amazement. First the *Boston*'s 8-inch battery raised towering geysers around the target raft, and on some salvos the whole raft was obscured. By the time the *Boston* fired her 5-inch battery, most of the target was in tatters.

Sorenson said, "That's a magnificent ship. I'd like to command a cruiser some day."

Dubose, watching next to him, said, "Are you going to stay in the Navy that long?"

"I don't know. I'm beginning to like the Navy more and more, but I'm not sure I want to keep on leaving my wife for such long periods."

The target was now completely torn from the masts, and the *Cabot* and her escorts moved off to find the tanker group.

Before dusk they found the plodding tankers, and the commanding officer of the *Cabot* moved his group to a position 10 miles in front of the tanker group and commenced flying antisubmarine searches.

The trip west was filled with drills and searches, first for submarines, and then when they reached the vicinity of the Marshall Islands, for Japanese aircraft.

Sorenson and Dubose spent hours leaning on the bridge rail watching flight operations. Auerbach, when he had the watch, joined them, and Sorenson and Auerbach commented on the ability, or lack of it, of the pilots.

One day Dubose had had enough of the kibitzing and started below. He passed by the signal bridge desk and looked down. ''Doughnuts! The crew's menu didn't have doughnuts on it today.''

Brophy coughed. ''Ah, no sir. Those are some Chief Williams made for the signal gang.''

Dubose shook his head and his lips compressed. ''He's not supposed to do that.''

Sorenson heard the exhange of remarks and said to Auerbach. ''There's going to be trouble there. Talk to Chief Williams and tell him to see me if he gets too much of a hassle from the Exec.''

Auerbach said, ''Aye, aye, sir. I see what you mean.''

Before Auerbach left, Sorenson said, ''You're making good progress qualifying as officer of the deck. I predict you'll qualify by the time we reach the Western Pacific and Task Force 58.''

Auerbach said, ''Captain, have you ever steamed in formation with a large carrier group?''

''No, but with some large formations going to the Casablanca operation in the Atlantic.''

''I stood a few indoctrination watches on the Enterprise. It looked pretty tough to me over on the screening destroyers. I'll understand if you want me to stand a few more indoctrination watches after we arrive.''

Sorenson smiled. ''Maybe I'll need some help, too.''

Two days later they were given a geographical position in which to rendezvous with Task Force 58. Sorenson held a quick meeting in the wardroom, leaving Dubose in charge on the bridge.

When all the officers were present, he told them about the rendezvous. ''There isn't any one on board who has ever steamed in a screen with a task force this big. Does anyone know what to expect?''

Auerbach said, ''I've seen a small formation from a carrier bridge. I hear with Task Force 58 each of the four task groups has about four carriers, four cruisers or battleships, and about sixteen destroyers. Each task group steams in a circular formation.''

''Who's at the center?'' Jablonski asked.

''No one.''

Jablonski laughed, his eyes sparkling behind his rimless glasses. ''Unbelievable. How do we keep station?''

''The large ships will be about on circle three, evenly spaced with a cruiser between each carrier. We just plot them all on a circular maneuvering board and calculate the distance and bearing to us from whichever ship is designated the guide.''

Sorenson said, ''How about the screen?''

''Almost always a circular screen. If a destroyer leaves station for any reason, such as to become a plane guard, the other destroyers move up to fill the station. The screen is usually out on circle eight, or at eight thousand yards from the center of the formation, but this varies with the number of destroyers and the sonar conditions.''

''Where will the other three task Groups be?''

''I think the Task Force Commander usually stations them about ten miles from him in a number of formations depending on which direction he expects the enemy forces to come from.''

''Then sometimes we can't even see some of the ships in the Task Group?''

''My friends I talked to said there were lots of times they couldn't see anybody,'' Auerbach said, ''But don't worry. After we join, we'll be called over to the flagship to get an operation order. The one I saw was about two inches thick and gives us all the standing orders about what we're to do in almost any eventuality."

Sorenson said, "That's a lot of studying to do in a short time."

Auerbach grinned. "That's only the start. Then you get another thick operation order and set of instructions from the screen commander. My friend said they're worse."

Sorenson groaned. "This Navy gets more complicated every month."

Auerbach said, "I don't think it will be as bad as you think. The guys I talked to weren't all that smart and they made it without running anybody down. It's comforting to know what you are supposed to do without waiting for a bunch of signals."

Scorse bristled. "Don't they ever use signals?"

"Sure, but the ships are not very close together. They use flag hoists when they can, but mostly they use TBS radio. You'd better make sure Bronte has ours well tuned up."

Bronte rolled his eyes. "I hate that damned radio set. It's more trouble than all the radars put together."

Bentley said, "What does TBS mean? Talk between ships?"

Scorse grinned knowingly. "Hell, no. T is for transmitter. B is for the second series, and S is for the S modification of that series.

Sorenson said, "I trust you've got enough spare parts for it."

"Yes, sir. Spare parts aren't the trouble. The damned thing just won't stay in tune well."

Sorenson said, "You'll have to make it your first priority. A missed signal could kill us all."

As they steamed toward the rendezvous, in the wardroom pantry Chief Steward Williams held a large aluminum pan close against his stomach, beating cake batter for dessert that night. Vila and Big Jackson watched him. Williams said, ''The key to good flavor is to warm the ingredients before you mix them.''

Vila laughed. ''That's the only kind of ingredients we had in the Philippines. Everything was hot.''

The door of the pantry was pushed open. Lieutenant Commander Dubose stepped inside. His face was grim. ''Chief Williams, did you furnish doughnuts made in the wardroom pantry to the signal bridge?''

''Ah, yes, sir, ah—.''

''And don't mock my accent. You can say 'I' perfectly well.''

''But, sir—.''

''Don't interrupt. You know perfectly well the general mess and the wardroom accounts are to be kept separately. Also the food.''

''Sir, I—.''

Dubose turned on his heel and left.

Chief Williams said, ''Damn! He wouldn't even give me a chance to tell him I pay for those doughnuts myself.''

Big Jackson whistled softly. ''My, he was mad.''

Vila said, ''Not really. Something's eating him.''

Williams sighed. ''Anything black eats him.''

Vila shook his head. ''If it gets too bad, you ought to go to the Captain.''

Big Jackson said doubtfully, ''Why? He cain't help.''

Williams eyes gleamed. ''Oh, yes he can. Some day he'll make it right for me.''

The next day the *Cabot* group fueled one last time before joining Task Force 58. One ship at a time left the *Cabot* group and joined the tanker group. Sorenson said to Dubose. ''You take the conn for this fueling.''

Dubose grinned. ''Thank you very much, Captain. I was never allowed to conn the ship for fueling under the last skipper.''

Sorenson said confidently, ''You won't have any trouble. As soon as you're checked out, I'll start on the other officers.''

The fueling course was almost into the wind, and the seas were light. Sorenson noted a slight nervousness in Dubose as he took the conn and made the approach, but soon Dubose calmed down and brought the ship into fueling position smartly.

After the approach, Chief Bellows shouted, ''Ha-beara haand ona dat ha-line!''

Dubose laughed. ''I got that. Bear a hand with that line.''

Sorenson sat back in his chair and allowed his thoughts to wander about his relationship with Dubose. He thought Dubose was making an effort to do the little things he had suggested. His accent, at least on board ship, was lessening. He listened as Dubose gave orders to the helm, and they semed to be much more understandable. He was beginning to overcome his initial doubts about Dubose in most areas, but there remained one last hurdle, and Sorenson wasn't sure Dubose would be able to get over it. Dubose was prejudiced. Prejudiced against other races and colors, and maybe more. Sorenson thought no ship could run efficiently and happily for very long with such a major fault in one of its top officers.

Then he wondered if such a fault was correctible. Dubose was motivated toward the Navy and toward the ship, but Sorenson couldn't see much change. He knew he would have to watch him carefully.

He was brought back from his reverie by Dubose. ''Captain, we've finished fueling. Request permission to break away.''

''Permission granted. God job. Let Auerbach take us back to station.''

As the Carson steamed under tropical skies, she was in readiness condition III, with one 5-inch gun mount completely manned and ready to fire at all times. Above the bridge, the Mark 37 5-inch gun director was manned with a crew capable of training the director on any air or surface target, generating a fire control solution, and automatically controlling and firing the 5-inch gun mount on watch.

Just forward of 5-inch mount 53, rotating crews, augmented by the crew of mount 54, stood watch on the 40-millimeter machine gun platform, ready to man either 40-millimeter twin machine gun.

That afternoon, 5-inch mount 53 was the mount fully manned. The mount captain, wearing a set of telephones, now dangling on his neck, sat on a small platform near the top of the mount structure. The platform was designed so that his head could stick out of a small hatch and he could see forward above the mount. His head was protected from the blast of the adjacent guns by a small round shield.

Smith, the mount captain, stared at the marching waves in the distance and tried to keep awake. He rubbed his eyes with his oil-soaked knuckles. The smarting from the oil awakened him, but he was still bored by the lack of action.

Down in the mount, Seaman First Class Donald Kittredge sat next to one of the two open doors in the sides of the mount. As the mount trainer, he also wore a telephone head set with one ear piece over one ear. When required, he could get up in a hurry and make his way forward to the metal seat and brass hand wheels where he could train the mount.

Now he sat on the hard steel deck. The second ear piece was pulled back so that he could talk to Big Jackson, who sat next to the door.

Kittredge stood all of his watches in the mount and his cleaning station was in the lower magazines of the mount. Consequently he saw little sun, and his white skin, light brown hair, and gray eyes were in startling contrast to Big Jackson's dark hair, eyes, and skin.

The mount was trained in just the right direction so that the breeze generated by the ship's motion would sweep through the mount doors, and Kittredge and Jackson were enjoying its cooling effects.

Farther forward in the mount, Kittredge could see the pointer and the spademan playing Acey-Deucey on a worn canvas game board. Copper pennies and steel washers clinked as the players moved them on the board. The other two members of the loading crew watched, now and then offering comments.

Suddenly Kittredge clamped the single earpiece to his ear and listened intently. Then he pushed the button on the transmitter down and said, "Mount 53, Aye, aye."

He lifted his head toward the mount captain above him and said, "Smitty, the director says to train and elevate the gun in the direction of the sun."

Smith groaned. "There goes the ventilation. Do it."

Kittredge said, "We should have been trained in the most probable direction of air attack all the time."

Smith sighed. "Take care of your own problems."

Kittredge started to get up, but Big Jackson put out a hand. "Lemme do it. Ah always lak to train dis sucker."

Big Jackson and the pointer got up and made their way past the Acey-Deucey board to the mount control positions at the front of the mount and sat in the metal seats. As they turned on the large hydraulic pumps that provided motive power for the train and elevation mechanisms, a loud whine started.

When the whine reached a maximum, Big Jackson and the pointer turned their hand wheels in the appropriate directions. Kittredge grabbed the side of the door and the Acey-Deucey players put their hands over the markers on the board. Then the mount began to jitter back and forth and then steadied and swung around to the direction of the sun. The pointer elevated the barrel of the gun until it pointed at the sun. Then the pumps were turned off, the whine subsided to a low growl, and soon stopped all together.

Big Jackson came back to the door and sat down.

Kittredge said, "How come you're a member of a mount crew and all the other stewards are down in the magazines for battle stations?"

Big Jackson laughed. "Chief Williams had a big go-round with Chief Vickers about it. Had to go to de old man. De skipper said to put me here."

"So you like being a hot shell man?"

"Sure." Jackson wiped his brow. "Ahm up in de open, at least when de doors are open."

"Who does your work in the wardroom when you're on watch?"

"Chief Williams. He's always tryin' to improve me. Doan do much good though. I still talk lak a field hand mosta da time."

Kittredge shrugged. "Some times you talk just like the rest of us."

"I can, but I doan wanta get too good. The folks back home would think I was uppity."

"And that means a lot to you?"

"Sure. Home is where it's at."

"But don't you come from the same home town the Exec comes from?"

"Yeah. Near Selma."

"Doesn't he help you?"

"Nah. He's a southerner."

"The Captain helps you, and he's from the south."

"It ain't always where yer from. De Exec's family taught him to be lak he is. He cain't help it."

Big Jackson shifted his position, trying to get comfortable on the hard steel deck, and inadvertently sat on some of Kittredge's books.

"What dese books you readin' all de time?."

"I'm studying to get into the Naval Academy."

"You think you make it?"

"I hope so, but I've got a lot of work to do." A frown passed over Kittredge's boyish face.

"Whatsa matter?" Jackson asked.

''Maybe I won't last that long.''

''Why not?''

''We're bound for the war zone. Neither of us might make it.''

Big Jackson said, ''You right. Sometimes I doan care if ahm gonna make it or not. All I got to look forward to is makin' trainer on dis mount. It ain't much.''

CHAPTER TEN

The next morning they were due to join Task Force 58. Sorenson was up early, pacing the bridge. He hurried his meager breakfast, wanting to be ready in case they were suddenly detached.

About 0900 the *Cabot* ordered a course change, and Sorenson suspected she had made contact with the Task Force on her radar. Because of her higher mast height, she would have a greater radar range capability.

Sorenson was correct. In five minutes CIC reported a radar contact dead ahead. and then many radar contacts. Brophy focused his spotting telescope forward and soon shouted, "Many contacts dead ahead. Looks like a regular forest."

The Task Force ahead approached rapidly and then turned into the wind so the tankers could spread out and fuel them.

In CIC Bronte was plotting the contacts. He reported, "Each Task Group is in circular formation, and the Task Force Commander has closed the Groups in toward him so that they can get to the tankers quicker."

Then the TBS began to spew orders. "Olympia, this is Tyrant. Commence fueling. Banker, direct your ships to join Olympia."

Scorse said, "Banker is the *Cabot,* and Olympia is Task Force 58. Tyrant is the Commander of the Task Force. Now we find out where we go."

The next message came out over the overworked TBS from the *Cabot,* and it was addressed to the *Carson.* "Hustler, join Olympia Two."

Scorse said confidently, "That means we're part of Task Group 58.2."

Jablonski hurriedly opened the over-all Commander in Chief Pacific Fleet Operation Order and thumbed through it. Sorenson watched the light glint off of Jablonski's glasses and the hair in the front of his head fall over his high forehead. He remembered how many times Jablonski's keen mind and skills had helped him before.

Then Jablonski found what he was looking for and said, "Task Group 58.2 is commanded by Admiral Montgomery with his flag in the *Bunker Hill.* The carriers are the *Wasp, Monterey,* and now the *Cabot,* our friend."

"Good," Sorenson broke in. "We'll just follow her to the right Task Group. Go ahead, Jablonski."

Jablonski resumed reading. "The cruisers in the group are all light ones, the *Santa Fe, Mobile,* and *Biloxi.*"

Dubose said, "Some good old southern cities."

Jablonski said, "Commander Destroyer Squadron 52 commands the screen with five of his ships. He also has Destroyer Division 104 with four ships, and part of Destroyer Squadron 1. We're to join him."

"Fast company," Dubose said. "They're all veterans."

Sorenson said, "Not all. This is the second *Wasp.*"

Dubose said, "Well, if you mean long time veterans, only the three in Destroyer Squadron 1, the *MacDonough, Dewey,* and *Hull* are real veterans of Guadalcanal and that era."

Sorenson said, "Except for you, Brophy, and a few others, the rest of us are amateurs out here. I think we'll do all right, though. The Atlantic was a good testing ground."

The *Cabot* speeded up and headed for one of the Task Groups, and Sorenson tailed in behind her. Soon a voice on the TBS said, "Welcome to Olympia two. Banker take station two. Hustler come alongside and pick up guard mail for you and Banker. Deliver same to Banker and then report to Dasher in station one."

Scorse thumbed through the voice call book, obviously enjoying the communications action. "Dasher is the screen commander," He said.

"Brophy, where's the *Bunker Hill*?" Sorenson asked.

Brophy pointed at a carrier. "The big carrier over there bearing two four six."

Sorenson said, "I have the conn. Come to course two four six. Call away the line transfer party. Scorse, go down to the forecastle and get ready to receive the guard mail."

Sorenson headed for the *Bunker Hill* at 25 knots, threading through the screen ships and then the other large ships in the inside of the formation.

Brophy stood near, using body English to try to speed the Carson through its maneuvers as Sorenson repeatedly changed course. "Jesus!," he said. "Never saw so many ships in one place in my life."

Sorenson rounded up astern of the *Bunker Hill,* and when she hoisted a flag indicating she was ready to receive them, he started the ship forward. He turned to the talker. "Tell the forecastle that Mister Auerbach is to leave Chief Bellows in charge and comeup here."

Auerbach came running up to the pilothouse. "Yes, sir?"

Sorenson grinned. "Slow down. I just wanted you up here to tell me about this carrier."

Auerbach said, "But you told me you qualified in flight training by landing on one several times."

"I did, but I never was allowed to get out of the cockpit. I always took off right away. When I landed on a carrier, the flight deck looked like a postage stamp. Now, from down here, the carrier looks like a whole small town."

Auerbach said, "I know. It's almost nine hundred feet long and the flight deck will tower over us when we get alongside."

''How many men does she carry?''

''About four thousand.''

Sorenson whistled. ''How many aircraft?''

Auerbach said, ''I don't know exactly about this one, but the *Enterprise* usually had seventy-two. Sometimes more for special missions. I believe this one is a little bigger and has about ninety. A squadron of thirty-three SB2Cs, a squadron of thirty-seven F6s, a squadron of eighteen torpedo planes, mostly TBFs, and something new to me, a group of four F6Fs specially configured to operate as night fighters.''

''Is this night fighter business something new?''

''Yes, sir. I heard about it at Pearl Harbor. All the big carriers have four F6Fs with pilots who are trained to take off, land, and fight at night. The Japanese are beginning to send out night snoopers and even attack units. Our night fighters will be busy.''

The *Carson* slid alongside the huge carrier. Sorenson could see at least two openings in the side of the carrier about 10 feet above the height of the *Carson's* forecastle. They were fitted with roll-up doors that were now open. Sorenson could see men inside on the hangar deck pushing aircraft around and swarming on top of those aircraft not being moved around.

''Looks like an aircraft factory over there,'' he said.

''It is. They can do any repair that can be done in the States.''

Sorenson stopped the *Carson* with the forecastle abreast of the large opening, and men on the carrier threw over a small messenger line with a monkey fist on the end. Bellows directed his men to retrieve it, and soon a larger line came over. When all was ready, a canvas sack was brought over, and Scorse opened it.

While this was going on, Brophy was communicating with the carrier signal bridge by hand semaphore, his forearms flashing up and down as he formed the letters. He turned to the Captain. ''They want to exchange movies.''

Sorenson grinned. ''They think we brought out some new ones from the States. Tell them we'd be glad to.''

Bentley, the movie officer, was called up to the forecastle and soon a large canvas sack was being pulled back and forth with large metal cans of movies in it.

While this was going on, Sorenson looked up at the soaring carrier superstructure. He tried to sort out which bridge was the flag bridge, which was the ship's navigational bridge, and which was the flight operations bridge, but it was difficult. Auerbach helped him. ''See that officer leaning on the rail up there with the gray hair? That's Admiral Montgomery, our Task Group Commander. Above him is another officer with darker hair. That's the captain of the *Bunker Hill.*''

''So that's the way you tell. What happens if they're wearing hats?''

''No problem now that you know where to look. The third level is the flight operations bridge. The guy in charge always looks over the other side toward the flight deck. Never over this side.''

Sorenson waved at the Captain above and saluted. The officer waved back and nodded.

Sorenson called for Jablonski. ''Where do we go from here?''

Jablonski said, ''Brophy has been getting the dope on the formation and our station from the carrier bridge. They are relaying it from the screen commander on the other side. The formation axis is zero zero zero. The screen axis is also zero zero zero. The screen is on circle eight and has fourteen stations. Our station is seven. The Screen Commander is in station six, and we are to come alongside him after we make the *Boston* with their operation order.''

Sorenson said, ''I guess the Screen Commander wants us in a station close to him so he can keep an eye on us for awhile.''

Auerbach nodded. ''I think it may be a good idea. The rest of these guys are old pros by now.''

The last trip of the canvas bag came back with ten gallons of ice cream. Sorenson waved a thank you to the *Bunker Hill* Captain, and they returned the lines to the carrier.

Brophy said, ''You may not thank him so much when you see the movies we got. The forecastle says we got four John Waynes and three Doris Days. The stuff we gave them was twice as good even if we'd seen it several times.''

Sorenson laughed. ''Too bad. The Executive Officer and I are old horse fans. We don't care who's riding them.''

When the lines were clear, Sorenson took the ship out ahead and looked for the Boston. She was close by, and they made their approach and passed the guard mail they had picked up to her.

Auerbach said, ''She's a heavy cruiser, but she looks like a midget next to a big carrier.''

Sorenson said, ''Did you ever get lost in the Enterprise?''

''Sure. The first day aboard, one of my squadron mates showed me the way from the quarterdeck to my room, to the head and shower, then to the wardroom and ready room. I never went any where else for a month. Then I got curious and went aft and down below. I never felt so lost in my life. You lose all sense of direction. All you can see is a maze of passageways, doors, and ladders. I did learn, though, that when you get lost the thing to do is take the next set of ladders up. Eventually you'll come out on the hangar deck, and then you can go to a ladder you are familiar with and go back down again.''

''That sounds a little like a sea story.''

''No. They used to talk about the new pilot who went to take a shower. He missed the turn and thirty minutes later turned up in the after engine room.''

''I suppose he lost his towel.''

''No, sir, but his bar of soap melted before he could get out of the engine room.''

As they pulled away from the Boston, Jablonski said, "The Screen Commander bears three two one. Distance seven thousand yards."

Sorenson said, "See if CIC agrees with that. We need to check every thing we do carefully from now on."

Jablonski pulled down the handle on the squawk box and asked CIC where the screen commander was. Back came the answer confirming Jablonski's data.

Sorenson said, "Good. Here we go."

In a few minutes they were alongside the *Owens*, the Screen Commander's flagship. The operation order and the set of standing instructions came over rapidly. The Screen Commander gave a wave of welcome, and the Carson was off for her screening station.

When they had settled down in station, Sorenson sighed and eased into his chair. But his feeling of relief was shattered when Scorse brought the two operation orders and sets of standing instructions up to the bridge. Sorenson started thumbing through them. "My God! This is bigger than the San Francisco telephone book."

Dubose, standing behind him, said, "I'd better take those down to the wardroom and hold school for the officers. If something comes up before we figure out what to do on the simplest maneuvers they give you, call me on the telephone."

Sorenson said, "Good idea. The rest of the group will be fueling until dusk, and I don't think there will be any changes of formation until then."

Sorenson sat back in his chair and looked around him. But before he could relax, Scorse came running up to the bridge. "We're supposed to be guarding the screen common frequency. I'll have it on the second bridge speaker in a few minutes."

Scorse trotted off again to make the necessary arrangements. Sorenson watched him go, and noted that he had lost about twenty pounds in the last month. His face was no longer pudgy, but angular. Now he looked more like his Italian forbears, trim and muscular. Sorenson tried to sit down again, but Jablonski interrupted him. "Captain, I've got all of our ships plotted on this plotting board. You ought to take a look at them."

Sorenson walked over to the chart desk and looked at the plot. "Looks like an anthill."

Jablonski laughed. "That's because I have all the destroyers plotted where they are temporarily. There are only seven left in the screen now. The rest are either fueling, standing by astern of the tanker they are about to fuel from, or are on their way back to their screening station."

Sorenson walked out to the bridge wing and looked over the formation. He whistled. "What a mess!" But after a few minutes of sorting things out, he began to see the pattern. Within half an hour he felt right at home, and soon the seeming chaos became quite logical. He went back to his chair and sent for his dinner.

Soon Dubose came up with a brief for him on the data the officers had been able to distill form the orders and instructions. For fifteen minutes Dubose talked, turning the pages to pertinent points. Sorenson felt overwhelmed, but as he absorbed the most important points he soon realized that only a small portion of the order involved the *Carson*, and he began to feel that it wasn't so complicated after all.

When his dinner arrived, he ate it with one hand, leafing through the instructions with the other. He knew he wasn't fully prepared, but he thought they'd do the best they could. He watched the progress of fueling with rising trepidation, and when the last ship broke away, he grabbed a piece of paper and a pencil and stood next to the TBS and screen common speakers.

First, there was a stream of signals over the TBS, all in a simple substitution code. With Jablonski's help and some assistance from Auerbach, who had the deck, he figured out that the Task Group Commander had just set a new course and speed and had declared the formation axis unchanged.

Then the screen common speaker spewed out a set of implementing orders. He soon determined that the screen remained unchanged, but that several other destroyers were to change stations. Jablonski confirmed his decoding of the signals and Sorenson felt better.

When the new course and speed were executed, he watched Auerbach make the changes, and looked apprehensively at the destroyers in the adjacent stations. They seemed to be making the changes easily, and he too relaxed. They had passed their first test.

Darkness came, and Sorenson shifted to the surface search radar repeater. The face of the circular display was black, with a beam of blue light sweeping around it. As the beam passed each ship a blip of light showed to indicate the position of the ships. The blips faded slowly and stayed lit until the next passage of the beam. By using a grease pencil to mark each blip. any relative movement of a blip could easily be detected. If the pencil mark was stationary, then the ship had not moved relative to the Carson. Down in CIC Sorenson knew the CIC watch officer was doing the same thing and would report to the bridge any unusual movement of any ship in the formation. Distant contacts appearing on the radar screen would also be reported.

In CIC, on a radar screen for the air search radar, another operator was plotting air contacts. As Sorenson had seen before, the air search radar did not produce as distinct a contact as the surface search radar, and therefore, air contacts were transferred by telephone and plotted by hand on an air search plotting board.

Sorenson marveled at the advances the American Navy had made in radar since the war had started, and he was amazed that the Japanese were so far behind. Then he remembered their skill in night fighting and torpedo firing and he thought it was all a question of where a navy put its emphasis.

The first night was serene, with a few course changes, and no speed changes, but Sorenson knew the simple business of keeping station would become a nightmare when they began flight operations and would be even worse when they entered combat. He was thankful that they would have a few days to warm up.

CHAPTER ELEVEN

Sorenson was up early, ate his usual meager breakfast of dry toast and coffee, and prowled the bridge, waiting for the day's operations to start. He knew they would begin early and accelerate. He was not disappointed. An hour before dawn the Carrier Task Group Commander promulgated the dawn launch times and assignments. Although Sorenson knew CIC was recording them, he scribbled them down on a spare message form on the chart desk under a red flashlight.

Then the Screen Commander sent out assignments for plane guards, and Sorenson noted that the *Carson* was to act as plane guard for the carrier *Bunker Hill*. He gave CIC a few minutes to plot the assignments and calculate the courses and speeds to their assigned station. CIC sent them up before he had to ask, and he noted the promptness with satisfaction. The ship was making progress.

Steiner had the deck, and Sorenson noted that he was careful, but not particularly speedy. When the screen commander sent out messages, he could not afford to have all ships receipt for the messages. Customarily he asked three ships for a receipt and depended on the rest to receive the messages.

On the message assigning stations, Steiner made the mistake of plotting the stations first before answering the

Screen Commander. Sorenson noticed that he was slow, and started to speak to him.

The Screen Commander said, ''Hustler, did you receive my message?'' There was a patient tone to his voice, but Sorenson ran over to the TBS and transmitted, ''This is Hustler, affirmative. Roger.''

Steiner shook his head. ''Sorry. I'll do it better next time.''

Then the Task Group Commander transmitted, ''Execute,'' and Steiner ordered, ''Right full rudder. Come to course two seven six. All ahead flank.''

The ship swung rapidly and began to accelerate. The dawn was beginning to break, so Sorenson abandoned the PPI and went out to the bridge wing. He lifted his binoculars and scanned the sea ahead to make sure there were not any ships between them and their assigned station. They closed the *Bunker Hill* rapidly. Steiner watched carefully, and brought the *Carson* around to formation course five hundred yards astern of the carrier.

Sorenson nodded appreciatively. ''Well done, Chuck. I hope you've learned a lesson about communications.''

Sorenson spent the morning with Jablonski studying the Operation Order for the forthcoming operation. He discovered that Task Force 58 was headed for the Marshall Islands to attack the main islands of Kwajalein Atoll. The islands of Roi and Namur were at the northern end of the atoll, and were heavily fortified. Roi had a large airfield. At the southern end of the Atoll, the island of Kwajalein also had an airfield. The atoll surrounded a splendid anchorage big enough to hold all the navies of the world at the same time.

After lunch the *Carson* was ordered to take station as plane guard again. Auerbach now had the deck, having relieved Steiner. He was the least experienced of the watch officers, and Sorenson watched him carefully. Auerbach was obviuosly nervous, but he did a good job of taking station.

For this flight operation, four Hellcat fighters took off, and then the four being relieved began landing. The third took a wave off and circled again, obviously in trouble. Half way around light smoke began to come out the Hellcat's exhaust. The pilot cut his downwind leg short and began an abbreviated approach. Just before the aircraft got to the ramp, the engine quit, and the Hellcat plopped down into the carrier's boiling wake.

Sorenson took the conn, and watched the floating aircraft carefully. Its tail was high in the air, and it was evident that it would not float long. The pilot clambered out and jumped over the side. Before the *Carson* arrived, the aircraft slowly sank, and the pilot was alone.

Sorenson headed for a position slightly up wind of the pilot and stopped engines when the khaki-clad figure was just forward of the bow. Then he backed the engines and stopped them again with the pilot a few yards off the forecastle. Bellow's assistant threw a heaving line to the pilot, and he pulled himself to the net. Two men climbed down the net and helped him up.

In seconds Sorenson ordered, "All ahead flank," and the Carson was soon in position astern of the carrier for the last recovery.

Fineman brought the pilot up to the bridge. He had been given a dry set of khakis and a small bottle of brandy.

"How do you feel?" Sorenson asked.

"Fine, but I'll be glad to get back. This thing rolls too much."

After the last recovery, the *Carson* highlined him back to his ship, and the carrier responded with 10 gallons of ice cream.

On the day before the attack, the Task Force Commander broke up the Task Force and sent the four Task Groups off in different directions. Task Group 58.2 went to a point south of Kwajalein and began the approach to its assigned launching area.

Sorenson went over the Operation Order again until he was sure they were ready. He sat back and went over the events of the last few days. He was pleased that they had done so well, and he thought they were ready for the real thing. He left a call for 0400 and turned in in his sea cabin abaft the bridge.

CHAPTER TWELVE

The night during the approach to the launch area south of Kwajalein was tense because they were in range of Japanese night-flying aircraft. The *Carson* stayed in plane guard station astern of the *Bunker Hill* all night. Every hour Sorenson could see and hear the two ready night fighters on the catapults start and turn up their engines. As the powerful engines coughed to a start, smoke and blue flame were visible even in the dark as the engines began to turn over. Then they would catch and accelerate to a roar as they warmed up. After a minute or so, the noise died as the pilots shut down.

Sorenson looked at the Operation Order in the charthouse and noticed that the intellignce annex claimed that there were at least 150 Japanese aircraft based on the airfields in the Marshalls area and that hundreds more could be flown in from distant bases. He hoped that surprise and overwhelming numbers would smother the threat before the Japanese attack and torpedo aircraft could take off and find the American ships.

About 0400 Jablonski came into the charthouse. ''You're up early,'' Sorenson said.

Jablonski yawned. ''Not as early as you are.''

Sorenson said, ''Here's the flight schedule for this morning. Luckily we're already in plane guard station. All we have to do is follow the carrier around to flight course. We'll be going to dawn general quarters in a few minutes, and since you're the officer of the deck for general quarters, you'll be right here. Have you had breakfast?"

Jablonski grinned. "Yes, sir. A half dozen of Chief Williams' good doughnuts."

Sorenson said, "I think I'll send down for some."

"You'd better hurry. They don't last long, and all the officers are up early to eat before general quarters."

Sorenson picked up the telephone and ordered his breakfast. Then he put the telephone down and pointed to the flight schedule. "This is a full day. First the *Bunker Hill* launches a twelve-plane Combat Air Patrol that will stay over the Group. Then the big carriers launch twelve more fighters armed with small bombs and twenty-four SBD dive bombers and six TBMs with bigger bombs. That will be the first strike. Then every two hours another strike of the same size goes off. The Combat Air Patrol will be launched and recovered every two hours."

Jablonkski nodded. "That means the Group will be launching or recovering aircraft every two hours all day long."

"Right. We've got to sandwich in some meal hours. I'm going to stay at general quarters until we see what reaction we get from the Japanese."

The buzzer from the bridge squawkbox rang. Sorenson pushed down the transmitter handle. "Yes?"

"Sir, it's thirty mintes until sunrise. Permission to sound general quarters?"

"Has the crew finished breakfast?"

"Yes, sir."

"Permission granted. I'll be right out."

Sorenson went out to the bridge and sat down in his chair. The strident tone of the general alarm was sounding, and he could hear feet pounding on the decks below as the crew went to their battle stations. Around him the general quarters bridge crew took over their stations. Wencey took over the helm and said, "Good morning, Captain."

Sorenson said, "Good morning, Wencey. After we settle down we may be at general quarters for several hours. Whenever you need rest turn the helm over to Caruso."

Wencey said, "Aye, aye, sir."

Sorenson picked up his binoculars and looked at the flight deck of the *Bunker Hill.* In the slowly growing light he could see that the night fighters on the catapults had been replaced by day fighters, and the flight deck was a teeming ant hill of men scurrying about the deck moving aircraft to their assigned places for the dawn launch. He could distinguish the colored shirts and helmets of the various specialists in the flight deck crew as the men armed the aircraft with bombs, topped them off with fuel, and checked their cockpits.

Fifteen minutes before sunrise, a group of pilots burst out of a door in the side of the superstructure and ran to the various aircraft. They clambered up into the cockpits and were strapped in by their plane captains. Within minutes the blue flames from their exhausts began to wink around the flight deck and then there was a steady pattern of exhausts and a mounting roar of engines.

On the carrier signal bridge the signal flag Fox fluttered half way up to the yard arm. Brophy, watching the carrier signal bridge intently, said, "Fox at the dip."

On the TBS a voice said, "Execute to follow. Turn shackle afirm cast hypo unshackle. Speed shackle george victor unshackle."

Jablonski looked at the decode table on the bulkhead next to the TBS. "Turn two six zero speed twenty five," he said.

Sorenson nodded.

The signal was executed, and Brophy yelled in the pilothouse, "Fox to-blocked!"

The moment the carrier was on the flight course, two jets of water vapor condensing from the burned gun powder behind the speeding catapult piston flew up from the flight deck, and two fighters rocketed off the bow. Then the remaining aircraft began to make running take offs at short intervals from the flight deck. Without the initial thrust of the catapult, they dipped slightly as they cleared the bow ramp and then quickly cranked up their wheels to increase flying speed.

Sorenson watched as the aircraft slowly gained altitude and circled to the left, joining the aircraft that had gone off ahead of them.

The sky was clear, tending toward a typical tropical day with clear sky and light winds. Sorenson stole a look at the other carriers nearby. Off the bow of each was a rising stream of aircraft, each turning into a circle of orbiting aircraft on its carrier's port beam.

Sorenson marvelled at the seeming confusion of all the aircraft buzzing around, but he knew there was a carefully planned allocation of space, both vertically and horizontally, to assure that each segment of the total attack force had its own assembly area, and separate course and altitude to the target.

Soon the various flights had rendezvoused, formed into close vees, and faded in the sky toward Kwajalein.

Sorenson called Scorse and Auerbach to the bridge. "I want you to set a watch on the aircraft strike frequency and keep me informed of the action of our aircraft at Roi and Namur Islands. Auerbach can interpret for you and come up to brief me now and then."

Scorse and Auerbach left, and Sorenson turned his attention to the formation. As soon as the last launch had been made and each carrier had hauled down the fox flag, the Task Group Commander turned back to a course down wind, so that he could maintain roughly the same geographical position. The returning aircraft would need to be able to find them.

Sorenson knew the Task Group Commander could use a moving rendezvous point if he wanted to, but a stationery point would simplify pilot navigation, and this was the first big operation in which many of the pilots had taken part. Getting back home would be kept simple.

Sorenson called Steiner down from the director. Steiner came to the bridge, obviously grateful to be able to stretch his legs. "Yes, sir?"

''Chuck, as you know, there are a lot of Japanese aircraft stationed in the Marshalls. Have your lookouts stay alert and keep your guns trained in the direction of Kwajalein. In a few minutes we'll know how many of the aircraft on Roi and Kwajalein airfields have been destroyed by our first strike. Then maybe your gun crews can relax a little.''

Steiner went back to the director.

Sorenson waited, pacing the bridge. Then Auerbach came racing up the ladder. ''Complete surprise,'' he said with a huge smile. ''The strike commander over Roi Island reports few aircraft got off the ground, and all are being attacked.''

''How about Kwajalein?''

''No report yet. The other Task Group is scheduled to strike it at dawn.''

Auerbach went down below to listen some more. In half an hour he was back. ''The Strike Commander has just given a brief report over the air. He says the first high cover of twelve Hellcats met a whole squadron of Japanese Zeke fighters over the airfeld.''

Sorenson asked, ''Zeke is the new name for the old Zero?''

''Yes, sir. Our fighters shot several down, and the rest fled. Then the escort fighters came in and strafed the field, destroying several aircarft on the ground. The first Zeke group came back and tried to engage the Wildcats strafing, but the Wildcats shot them all down. The strike group of forty-eight SBDs then came in and bombed mainly antiaircraft gun emplacements so that the big TBFs could get in safely and drop fragmentation clusters and heavy bombs on the runway. Six Japanese Bettys were shot down trying to escape. He says he doesn't think any aircraft are coming our way.''

Sorenson sighed. ''I guess that's best, but I was looking forward to seeing a little action out here. So far all we've seen is a lot of garbage going over the *Bunker Hill*'s garbage chute as we followed her around.''

Auerbach laughed. Then he stopped smiling. "We lost five aircraft. Maybe dodging the garbage is better than dodging the Japs."

Sorenson nodded. "Nothing is free," he said.

Throughout the day additional strikes were launched, but most were diverted to Namur Island, the sister island next to Roi. Namur Island contained most of the Japanese defenses, and the Task Group aircraft worked them over for the rest of the daylight hours.

As the last aircraft landed, the sun went down, and Sorenson heaved a sigh. He had secured the gun batteries from general quarters around noon when it was evident that there would be no Japanese aircraft coming after them. A hasty lunch for the crew followed, but now Sorenson was glad they would have a full dinner. It had been a long day, and they would be hungry. Sorenson's stomach began to growl just thinking about it, and he sent for his dinner.

Then he had another thought and sent for the Executive Officer. When Dubose came up, Sorenson said, "Dubose, I want Chief Williams to be allowed to make doughnuts for the signal gang. It will be understood that he will do this on his own time, and I want the cost of the doughnuts added to my mess bill."

Dubose was silent. After a few seconds, he said, "Aye, aye, sir," but Sorenson could tell his heart wasn't in it.

Sorenson took off his cap and rubbed his head with the back of his hand. "Dammit, Forrest, you've seen what these young kids in the signal gang go through on a day like this. Something simple like a doughnut will raise their morale sky high. I don't like to go against you on this, but you've got to learn about morale if you're to take command. Little things like this are important. Am I getting through?"

Dubose's lips had been stretched tight when Sorenson started to talk began, but they began to ease. When Sorenson finished, Dubose managed a grim smile. "To tell you the truth, I snitched one this morning in the ward-room. Brought it up to Brophy. I guess your way is better.''

Sorenson smiled. ''I never felt you were like that. Is this something left over from the previous Captain?''

Dubose said, ''I don't like to make excuses, but he did want everything done exactly by the book. I thought it was the way to do it, because he was a hell of a good skipper. I and a lot of others who served in the ship off Guadalcanal owe our lives to him.''

Sorenson said, ''I don't want to downplay him. Every Captain has his way. Mine is to stretch discipline a little on some occasions. When your turn comes, you'll be different, too. I just want to expose you to some of my ideas.''

That night Task Group 58.2 moved north of the islands of Roi and Namur to make the run in for the morning srikes shorter. Night fighters on the duty carriers remained on alert throughout the night, but nothing marred the beautiful tropical night.

Sorenson watched the moon sail along through small cirrus clouds and thought how little the Marines huddled in the transports and waiting to go ashore could see of it. He shuddered. The Marines could have the mud and dust ashore. At least life was relatively clean and peaceful at sea.

Before dawn the routine of the day before was repeated. All day long strikes left for Namur, and Auerbach reported that they were pounding the fortifications ashore between salvos from the battleships.

That night, just as the last strike aircraft was landed aboard, the TBS erupted. Sorenson listened carefully.

The Task Group Commander detached the three light cruisers, *Santa Fe, Mobile,* and *Biloxi,* to join the *Louisville* for a bombardment of Wotje Atoll. Eight destroyers, including the *Carson* and *Ransome,* were to screen them and join in on the bombardment.

Jablonski hurriedly broke out the chart of Wotje Atoll and tacked it to the chart desk. Dubose, who had just come on the bridge, heard the assignments, broke out in a smile, and started to say something.

Sorenson interrupted him. "Yes, I know, an all southern group of cruisers."

Dubose said. "Sounds good to me."

In a few minutes the *Carson* and the *Ransome* followed the cruisers out of the formation. and joined the other six destroyers.

When they met the *Louisville,* Admiral Oldendorf, in command, headed the group directly for Wotje. During the night he promulgated and transmitted a bombardment plan to his group by flashing light. Sorenson, Steiner, Dubose, and Jablonski took it down to CIC and spread it out on the Dead Reckoning Tracer together with a chart of Wotje and plotted the target assignments.

Sorenson said, "The plan says we're to form a column at 0400, order of ships *Louisville, Santa Fe, Mobile, Biloxi, Carson,* and *Ransome*. The destroyers *Morris, Anderson, Hughes, Fletcher, Mustin,* and *Russell* are to form a column ahead of the *Louisville.*"

Steiner said, "What the hell are we doing back there? There may not be any targets left for us."

Sorenson said, "We've been assigned a gun emplacement at the nearest end of the island. I'm sure it will wait for us."

Steiner muttered, but seemed to be satified. When they had all studied the chart and Jablonksi and Bronte had picked out points on the chart to use for radar navigation, Sorenson proposed that they hit their bunks. "Big day tomorrow," he said.

At dawn the *Carson*'s crew was ready at general quarters. The gun crews had brought up extra projectiles and powder cans. Steiner consoled the 40-millimeter crews who were unhappy because their guns would be out of range at the planned initial range of 8,000 yards.

At 0500 the low-lying fringe of palm trees on Wotje Island could be seen from the bridge, and Dubose reported from CIC that they had an initial navigational fix. The guns trained out to starboard, and the big hydraulic motors began to whine as the 5-inch director pointer and trainer tried to keep them on the target coordinates generated in the computer from information provided by CIC.

Sorenson raised his binoculars and searched the low shore of the sandy atoll. Only tired-looking palm trees and sand appeared in his lenses. It looked safe enough, he thought.

At 0630 Admiral Oldendorf ordered "Commence firing," and all the ship's batteries roared almost simultaneously. Yellow smokeless powder residue flew back across the *Carson*'s bridge and clogged Sorenson's nose. He blew it out and sneezed. Additional salvos roared off, the cruisers ahead seeming to be aflame as they shifted to rapid fire. Under the *Carson*'s gun mounts, brass powder cans clattered on the deck and moved about aimlessly as the ship rolled.

Then the somnolent scene ashore came to life. Orange flashes of fire welled up from emplacements near the bases of the palm trees, and white geysers erupted abreast of the leading destroyers. The first shots were short, but soon one hit a ship at the front of the column. Sorenson raised his binoculars trying to see which ship was hit. He couldn't make it out, but in seconds a destroyer ahead sheered out to port and slowed. Now he could see the bow number as it turned. It was the *Anderson*. The other ships continued on, pounding the source of the Japanese firing, and soon it stopped.

A scratchy voice came up on the TBS. It was the Executive Officer of the *Anderson* reporting that she had been hit on the bridge, the commanding officer and several men were dead, but she was ready to resume her position in the formation.

Sorenson sighed. The luck of the draw, he thought. The *Carson* might have been at the other end of the column and Ferren would have been a widow. He shook his head and tried to keep his mind on the task at hand.

The column ahead was now reversing course inboard, and he cautioned Steiner to be careful with their fire when the ships ahead passed between them and the beach.

The group continued to pound Wotje Island without drawing any more return fire. At noon Admiral Oldendorf called a halt to the bombardment, and the formation steamed off to the west.

Sorenson secured the ship from general quarters, and the crew went below to eat a belated lunch. In half an hour Chief Bellows had some deck hands on the forecastle removing the empty brass cases and sweeping down the powder residue littering the decks.

Jablonski grinned. "Old shaky never misses a trick," he said to the Captain.

Sorenson grinned. "I hope I'm that vigorous when I'm that old."

Jablonski said, "I'm not that vigorous now."

Sorenson had just finished his lunch when Fineman came running to the bridge with a decoded dispatch.

Sorenson said, "Slow down."

Fineman said, "Read this."

Sorenson grabbed it expectantly and read it. Then he grinned. "Exciting, all right, but not as much as you made me think it would be."

Fineman said, "I thought you liked independent command."

"I do. I was just kididng."

Jablonski said, "May I read it?"

"Sure. Read it aloud."

Jablonski read it and said, "It detaches us with the *Ransome* under your command and directs us to proceed and look for a downed aviator outside Kwajalein Atoll."

Sorenson turned and shouted to Brophy. "Hoist a signal asking for permission to proceed on duty assigned."

Brophy looked up the signal and in seconds a hoist whipped up to the yardarm, the blocks screaming in protest as the halyards whipped through them.

Brophy watched the *Louisville* intently, and then he said, ''Acknowledged. He says affirmative.''

Sorenson said to MacIntosh, who had the deck, ''Sheer out and come to 25 knots.''

He turned to Brophy again. ''Make a signal to the *Ransome* to form column.''

Again the blocks screamed, and in seconds Brophy said, ''Acknowledged.''

Sorenson said, ''Execute,'' and Brophy nodded to Caruso. The flags whipped down into Caruso's arms.

Jablonski went over to the chart desk. ''Course two four six,'' he said.

Sorenson turned to MacIntosh. ''Make it so.''

MacIntosh said, ''Aye, aye, sir,'' and gave the necessary orders.

About midnight Jablonski awakened Sorenson, who was sleeping in his chair, and said, ''We're approaching the area we are to search, but I don't think we can see much until daylight.''

Sorenson stretched his arms over his head. ''Maybe so, but the poor bastard in the water may be able to see us, and if he has his survival kit with him, he'll signal.''

Jablonski said, ''We can see the edge of Kwajalein Atoll to the west on radar. It will give us a good fix for our search.''

Steiner now had the watch, and Sorenson said, ''Set up a box search and direct the *Ransome* to take a position on our starboard beam.''

Steiner, aided by Jablonski, plotted the search pattern on the chart and transmitted the necessary orders to the *Ransome*.

Sorenson said, ''We can slow for the search to 15 knots, too.''

At this speed they made two legs of the box before the *Ransome* reported, "Light in the water my port beam."

Sorenson picked up the TBS transmitter. "Investigate," he said.

Soon the *Ransome* reported, "Aviator in a rubber boat. Am picking up."

While the *Ransome* was picking up the aviator, the *Carson* proceeded west toward Kwajalein. They had gone only a mile when CIC reported, "Two contacts coming out a passage in the reef."

Sorenson leaped for the squawkbox transmitter handle, "How big are they?"

"One is about as big as a destroyer. The other is a little smaller. My guess is an escort of some kind and a small tanker or transport."

Sorenson said, "Chuck, sound general quarters. Go on up above to the director. I'll take the deck until Jablonski can relieve me."

Sorenson pulled down the transmitter again. "What's the range?"

"Ten thousand yards."

By now the general alarm was sounding and men were running through the black night to their stations. Sorenson impatiently awaited the reports from the various stations, but relaxed when he realized that the men who had just been rudely awakened were not as alert as he was.

As soon as all stations reported manned and ready, Sorenson summarized the situation over the IMC announcing system and followed it up with specific orders to CIC and Gun control.

"Gun Control, commence firing, using radar control, at eight thousand yards. Target lead ship in the formation. It should be an escort and may fire back at us. Let me know when you're ready."

MacIntosh, standing by his nearby torpedo battery director, said, "Captain, how about letting me take the second target with a salvo of torpedoes?"

Sorenson laughed. "They cost too much. Just watch."

MacIntosh said, ''How about just one?''

''Well, we'll see.''

At 8,000 yards the 5-inch guns forward roared out, and soon Sorenson changed course to port in order to unmask the after guns. Then all four guns began firing. For a few seconds the target did nothing. Then it opened up with at least two guns, obviously aimed at the *Carson*'s flashes. The first shots landed well short, but then they began to creep closer.

The *Carson*'s guns began to hit the target, and it slowed, but kept on firing.

Then Sorenson was aware that MacIntosh was at his side. ''Captain, how about just one.''

Sorenson said, ''All right, just one. Fire it at the ship firing at us.''

Aft the sound of a torpedo being fired followed almost immediately, and Sorenson laughed. ''Damned eager beavers,'' he said.

Steiner kept on firing, but the stubborn Japanese refused to sink or even stop firing. One wild shot hit the edge of the bridge and scattered fragments all over the starboard flag bag, but didn't hit any member of the crew.

Brophy ran over and surveyed the damage in the light of the gun fire. He came back muttering, ''Whole damned bag of flags needs to be replaced.''

MacIntosh, counting the seconds of torpedo run, shouted, ''Now!'' Nothing happened. Then a huge ball of flame erupted, sending smoke and fire hundreds of feet into the air.

CIC reported, ''One target has disappeared.''

Steiner leaned out of the director, and shouted down to the bridge. ''Damn it, MacIntosh, you stole my target!''

Sorenson looked up. ''Never mind, Chuck. There's one left for you, and it isn't firing back.''

Steiner pulled his head back in the director, and soon the 5-inch battery began firing at the larger second target. This time it took only two salvos to set the target on fire.

It was obviously a tanker, and it began to burn fiercely. Large billows of flame lit up its long low hull.

Sorenson ordered, ''Cease firing. Secure from general quarters. Set condition three. Jablonski, give me a course back to the Task Group rendezvous.''

The tanker burned as long as the flying *Carson*, followed by the *Ransome*, could see it astern in the growing light of the tropical dawn.

At noon the next day, CIC reported that they had the Task Group on radar. Sorenson changed course to intercept, and by 1400 they were close enough to report for duty by flashing light. Soon their screen assigment came over the screen common circuit, and they were home again.

Sorenson, pacing the bridge wing, said to Brophy, ''Where's the flagship?''

Brophy pointed out one of the big carriers. ''There she is.''

Sorenson nodded and turned to the officer of the deck, Finlay MacIntosh. ''Take our station.''

MacIntosh said, ''Aye, aye, sir.''

Sorenson watched MacIntosh taking bearings on the guide as he headed for station and gave orders to the wheel. Sorenson thought MacIntosh had lost most of his Scottish burr, and he could only hear it when MacIntosh was excited.

MacIntosh tended to let his shock of brown hair grow too long, and the sharp wind was blowing it in his eyes. Sorenson made a mental note to tell MacIntosh to get a haircut as he headed for his chair.

CHAPTER THIRTEEN

That afternoon the *Carson* resumed her duties in the screen, and Sorenson watched the aircraft taking off to render support to the Marines now ashore on the beaches of Namur Island and advancing against stiff opposition.

Sorenson wrote a quick report describing the rescue of the downed aviator by the *Ransome* and the sinking of the two Japanese ships, and Brophy transmitted it by flashing light to the flagship.

An hour later, while Sorenson was dozing in his chair again, Brophy called out, "The flagship has our call sign at her yardarm. Answer it."

The signalmen on watch scurried to hoist an answering call sign. Then Brophy watched the flagship carefully through his large telescope as a second flag hoist went up. By now Sorenson was wide awake. "What does it mean?" he asked.

Brophy looked at Sorenson and grinned.

Sorenson said, "Why don't you answer it? Don't you know what it means?"

Brophy's grin became even wider. "Sure I know, sir. I'm just enjoying it, and I want all the other ships to see it." Then he said to the watch, "Answer it."

A second hoist streamed up to the *Carson*'s yardarm and was to-blocked.

Brophy said, ''It means 'well done.' Congratulations, Captain.''

Sorenson said. ''We didn't do anything.''

Brophy said, ''I just sent them the message telling them what we did.''

''But that wasn't anything those pilots over there in the carrier haven't done at least twice a day for the last three days.''

Brophy smiled and said, ''In this Navy take it while you can get it. Tomorrow we may catch hell for something we didn't do.''

Through the next day the strikes continued, and then on the 4th of February came the welcome message, ''Cease flight operations.''

Dubose, on the bridge, said, ''What now?''

Sorenson had been listening to Brophy call off words in a semaphore message he was receiving from the flagship. He said, ''I think the answer is coming in now.''

Dubose went over to the signalman who was recording the message Brophy was receiving and looked over his shoulder. In a few minutes he came back. ''The message isn't all in yet, but we're headed for Majuro Atoll. I've never heard of it.''

Sorenson said, ''It was mentioned in one of the operational summaries the other night. We occupied it about a month ago. It's about two days away. It's an atoll about half as big as Kwajalein. Good anchorage, but I doubt if it's been completely surveyed yet. We'll have to wait and see.''

The Task Group steamed southeast toward Majuro for two days. Sorenson looked over at the *Bunker Hill* and noticed the crew of the flagship sunbathing. He promptly passed the word that the crew of the *Carson* could sunbathe, and a loud cheer went up below.

The second night Sorenson started to turn in at 1800. Before he went in to his sea cabin, he looked aft. Men were stretched out on deck under every available patch of shade, under the gun mounts, the boats, and the torpedo tube mounts. Most were using life jackets for pillows, and some who couldn't find shade were stretched out in the sun. Looks like a battle ground, he thought.

Then he went to his sea cabin, flopped down on his bunk, and slept until dawn the next day.

About 0800 of the third day the outline of Majuro appeared over the horizon ahead. Sorenson watched it grow bigger in his binoculars. As they approached, he could see the usual string of small islands surrounding a circular lagoon. The palm trees on the larger islands were relatively undamaged, which meant that it had been occupied without much opposition. Around each island was a shimmering necklace of white sand.

At 1000 the ships of the Task Group began entering the largest passage in the reef, marked by temporary buoys. The *Carson* was amongst the last to enter, and was assigned a berth near the flagship. Sorenson noticed that the large ships of the Task Group were anchored almost in the same relative positions they had occupied at sea. The destroyers were anchored around the larger ships in an approximate circle.

He turned to Dubose. "Look at that. The Task Group Commander must think there's good chance of enemy air attack, and he has arranged us as a screen to protect the big ships from attack."

Dubose nodded. "There are still fields on outlying islands the Japanese could use to reach us."

The *Ransome*'s signal light began to blink. Wencey said, "She wants permission to come alongside us. Her anchor windlass got damaged the other day in the bombardment at Wotje."

"She didn't say anything about it the other day."

Wencey said, "The signalman says they didn't realize it was damaged until they just tried to test it on the way in. They'll have it fixed in a couple of days."

Sorenson said, "Tell them affirmative."

He watched the *Ransome* come alongside, and waved at the commanding officer.

Then he went below to his larger lower cabin below the bridge. It was the first time he had been in it for two weeks. He look a long, luxurious hot shower and got ready for a lunch in the wardroom. He sat down and wrote a letter to Ferren. He had seen several tankers and logistics ships at anchor in the atoll when they had come in, and he knew mail would go off in the next few days when they were scheduled to fuel from one of the tankers. Just as he sealed the letter, Vila knocked on his door and told him lunch was ready.

When he entered the wardroom, the officers were kidding Ensign Bentley, who, as movie officer, had just returned from a trip to the two nearest big ships trying to trade for a good movie or two.

Bentley said, "Nothing but horse operas. Not even a John Wayne."

Sorenson said, "I take it you didn't have any luck on your trip."

"No, sir. I'll try two more this afternoon, but I don't expect to do much better. The carriers say they show as many as six movies a day, and they can't afford to give any good ones up."

Sorenson said, "Well, let's eat. Maybe someone will come up with a brilliant idea before dessert."

The dinner was the best Chief Williams could serve. Just as a baked Alaska dessert arrived, Fineman said, "How about a smoker?"

Dubose groaned. "I don't think anybody wants to box in this heat."

"No," Fineman said. "I guess I mean a musical entertainment."

Sorenson said, "I haven't seen a musical instrument on the ship at any of my inspections."

Reifel said, "There's a small chaplain's portable piano in one of my storerooms. You haven't been down to that part of the ship yet."

Sorenson said, "Where did we get it?"

Reifel said, "Down in the Solomons a chaplain brought it aboard by high line for a Sunday service. By the time the service was over we got him back to the cruiser he came from, but it was too rough to get the piano back. Then the cruiser was sunk the next week. We use it for lay services when I can get to it."

Renard said, "Vila has an accordion."

Scorse nodded. "I've heard Brophy play a harmonica sometimes up on the signal bridge when we were in port. He's not bad."

Fineman said, "That's great. Then we have that great singing group, the Four Hawaiian Haoles."

"Who?" asked Renard.

"Haven't you heard them?"

"I guess not."

Fineman nodded at Reifel, Auerbacch, and Dubose, and raised his hand. When he brought it down they joined him in a long drawn out note.

Renard shook his head. "I don't think that will keep the crew awake."

Fineman said, "Wait until we've practiced a little and put something together."

Renard pursed his lips. "The crew is a pretty tough bunch. They don't like to be conned. He reached in his pocket, pulled out a twenty dollar bill, and slapped it on the table. "Twenty says there'll be at least one man asleep in the front row before the end of the second number by the Four Hawaiian Haoles."

Up the table one person slapped the table. Then another. Then another. Sorenson slapped the table and said, "This is all mine. I'll take the bet."

Renard reached in his pocket, pulled out another twenty, and slapped it on the table. "Twenty more says they'll be booing by the end of the third number."

This time all the officers looked expectantly at Sorenson. He didn't disappoint them. He slapped the table hard. "You have another bet. I think they'll like anything but these damned horse opera movies we've already seen three times."

Dubose declared the wardroom closed for the afternoon over the protests of Renard, and told the officer of the deck to announce that there would be a singing smoker tonight in lieu of a movie. He could hear faint jeers from the crew below, but he resolved to go ahead.

Inside the wardroom, Dubose, Reifel, Auerbach, and Fineman rehearsed more musical numbers. About 1400, Dubose sent for Chief Brophy, who came into the wardroom carrying his harmonica and his Irish Song Book. Vila followed him with his accordion, and Terrill came in with a clarinet.

Then Chief Williams was summoned. He came in carrying a huge soup tureen and two wooden spoons. After a short conference with Fineman, Williams sent for Big Jackson, who entered carrying two large metal spoons. Then a carpenter's mate came in, stayed a while, and left sniggering. In half an hour he was back with two wooden swords with makeshift scabbards and a pointed helmet.

Outside the wardroom Renard paced up and down, wondering if he had been foolish in offering to bet on the outcome of the evening's entertainment. Finally he decided to hedge his bets. He knocked on the wardroom door and pushed it open. A chorus of boos overwhelmed him. He raised his arms in surrender. When the chorus died down, he said, "Gentlemen, I offer to act as master of ceremonies."

"Out!" Dubose said. "Fineman will do it."

After supper, as the short tropical dusk descended, half of the *Carson* crew gathered on the starboard side of the main deck aft, which was below the break of the deck leading up to the forecastle. The area was a natural theater, and it soon filled with canvas stools brought up by the crew. Men could sit on the after part of the various deck levels clear up to the signal bridge, on the torpedo deck, and aft as far as they cared to sit. A few men on the *Ransome* alongside lounged on the rail, idly talking to men on the *Carson*.

A row of wardroom chairs had been placed against the forward bulkhead and aft of them a row of chairs for the chiefs. Most of them were full.

At 1900, as dark fell, Fineman came out of the area behind the chairs and into a lighted area under cargo lights rigged by the electricans. His dark eyes flashed with pleasure as he held up his hand. In his well modulated voice he said, ''Men of the *Caruso* and guests on the *Ransome,* tonight we're trying a change from the same old movies. If you like tonight, we'll do this more. If you don't, it's back to horse operas.''

There was silence amongst the crew, but a few clapped tentatively. Renard's hope of winning his bet increased, and he smiled.

Fineman felt more confident. He looked at the crew and said, ''The first number will be a rendition by the Four Hawaiian Haoles, late the sensation of the Moana Palace Cafe in Honolulu.''

The crew applauded tentatively, and Fineman ducked behind a screen rigged over the entrance to the radio room. Soon the quartet came out wearing palm leaf hats. Fineman and Auerbach carried out the portable piano.

Their first number was 'Aloha Oe,' rendered in the usual combination of English and Hawaiian. Sorenson nodded to Steiner,sitting next to him as the number ended. ''Not bad,'' he said. There was a smattering of polite applause.

Sorenson could see Renard grinning in anticipation of winning the bet, but no one in the front row of the spectators was asleep.

Fineman announced that the crew could sing along with the next number, and they began singing as soon as they found out it was "Home On the Range."

The applause was louder, and Renard squirmed in his chair. Sorenson looked around at the men in the front row. Still no one was asleep, and all of them were smiling.

Fineman announced that the *Carson* band would play the next number, led by Chief Brophy.

Brophy came out with harmonica in hand and his Irish songbook under his arm. Vila followed with his accordion. Terrill with his clarinet was behind Vila, and the surprise of the evening was the rhythm section composed of Chief Williams carrying a huge soup tureen which he upended beteeen his feet and prepared to play with the ends of two wooden spoons. Steward's Mate third class Big Jackson helped Williams with the tureen and then sat down with two large metal spoons poised on his thigh.

The ensemble was complete.

Brophy stepped out in front, and held up his hand. "Gentlemen, the first number is "When Irish Eyes Are Smiling." You may sing if you wish."

After the first bar the words welled up from all over the topside of the ship. Sorenson noticed that about half of the *Ransome*'s crew who had come topside was now sitting in the upper part of the ship and joining in.

The next number was announced by Fineman. "Steward's Mate Vila, the pride of Cebu, will now play the most popular song in the Philippines, 'Planting Rice' Lieutenant Steiner, who, together with Vila and Lieutenant Jablonski is a veteran of the Philippines, will demonstrate how to plant rice. You can join in."

Steiner stood up in front of the musical group. Vila began to play the lively tune, "Planting rice. Planting rice. Planting rice is mighty nice." Steiner leaned over and simulated taking tufts of rice plants from a bag at his side and thrusting them in the mud of the rice paddies. Soon the whole crew was standing, singing the simple words and 'planting rice.' in the steel deck.

When the song was over, a roar rose from both ships. Renard leaned over Sorenson's shoulder and pushed two twenty dollar bills in his hands. ''I know when I'm licked,'' he said.

Chief Williams and Chief Brophy got up and disappeared into the radio room behind the screen.

Fineman announced the next number. ''Gentlemen, you all know the saga of Abdul Abulbul Amir and Ivan Skavinsky Skavar. We are fortunate to have two brilliant thespians here tonight to play the parts of these famous warriors. As we sing the lyrics, Chief Brophy, as Ivan Skavinsky Skvar, the favorite of the Czar, will skirmish with Chief Williams, as Adbul Abulbul Amir, the pride of the Sultan of the Moslem camp. Fanfare, please.'' Fineman stepped off stage and sat in the audience.

All the instruments were blown, banged, or squeezed, and Brophy and Williams strode out, waving wooden swords, the pride of the carpenter's mate. Williams wore a turban made of a wardroom napkin wrapped in medical gauze, and Brophy sported a helmet painted silver and topped with two tired turkey feathers taken from a dust mop. Each had a flowing cloak made of a sheet. As the quartet started to sing the well-known lyrics, the combatants threw off their cloaks, faced each other, and saluted with their swords.

Then, according to the song, ''They parried and thrust, circled in the dust, slashed out and cut.'' As the crew cheered, Brophy got too enthusiastic and almost unseated William's turban. Williams recovered, straightened it, and the crew stood and cheered mightily.

As the saga concluded, the tired combatants sank to the deck. Abdul ''heaved a last sigh,'' and Ivan ''shouted a last huzzah.'' The crew cheered and waved their hats.

Brophy and Williams got up, bowed, and the drama was over.

Fineman announced that the next number was the 'Beer Barrel Polka,' and the noise welled up from between the two ships, even before the number started.

After the end of the first chorus, a messenger leaned over Sorenson's shoulder. "Sir, there's a boat full of armed men approaching our accommodation ladder."

Sorenson started. Steiner said, "Probably just a drill."

Sorenson said, "Maybe, but let's go see what it's all about." He turned to Renard. "Tell Fineman to keep the show going."

Sorenson hurried over to the port side where the petty officer of the watch was standing at the top of the accommodation ladder looking anxiously over the side. Sorenson followed his gaze. A motor whaleboat with about ten men seated in it, wearing helmets and carrying rifles, was approaching the ship.

Sorenson looked aft to see where the *Carson*'s after security watch was located. He was standing just aft of the quarterdeck with his Thompson sub-machine gun trained on the approaching boat. Sorenson grinned and said to the sentry "Good work! But don't take the safety off."

The security watch nodded.

The boat came alongside, and an anxious-faced ensign trotted up the ladder, pistol drawn and held across his chest at the ready. When he got to the top of the ladder and saw Sorenson, he said, "Sir, is everything all right?"

"Certainly," Sorenson said. "And by the way, I'd put that pistol away if I were you. There's a man standing back there with a Thompson sub-machine gun pointed at you."

The ensign looked around at the blue-black muzzle and blanched. He hurriedly jammed the pistol in its holster and stepped down off the grating. "But sir, do you need some help?"

Sorenson said, "No, why do you ask?"

Our officer of the deck heard all the noise over here and thought a riot or a mutiny must be going on. He had our signal bridge call your signal bridge for about five minutes, but couldn't get any answer. Then he called away the boarding party, and here we are."

Sorenson looked up at the signal bridge. Wancey and Caruso were watching the action down on deck and singing at the top of their voices. Sorenson put his fingers in his mouth and produced a piercing whistle. Wencey stopped singing and looked down. Sorenson pointed to the flagship. Wencey blanched and ran to the signal light.

Sorenson said, "Would you like to see the source of all this noise?"

The ensign said, "Well, I need to report to the officer of the deck what was going on."

Sorenson led him over to the starboard side where he could see the musical group. They were giving an encore of "Planting Rice." The ensign watched the bobbing figures. Then he said, "Thank you, sir, I don't understand this, but it's obvious that your crew is having fun. Would you consider sending your group over to perform for us?"

Steiner said. "Their standing rate for a performance is ten good movies."

The ensign shook his head, "That's a little over my head. I'll tell my boss when I get back and let him make the decision."

Steiner led the ensign back to the accommodation ladder, and Sorenson went back to the other side and sat down to see the rest of the show.

When Steiner came back, Sorenson said, "Did you get a better deal?"

Steiner said, "I offered to do it for six movies if they'd supply a guitar player."

Sorenson nodded. "Good deal."

By now the repertoire of the company had been exhausted, but Fineman moved the small piano forward and offered to play anything the crew wanted to sing. For another hour the songs rolled out, and finally Sorenson had to put an end to it.

"The Admiral will be over here himself if we don't quiet down soon," he said.

The next morning Auerbach got permission to take a boat over to his old ship the *Enterprise* to visit his squadron mates. When he came back he was somber. At lunch Sorenson noticed his unhappy mood and asked him to come to the lower cabin after lunch.

Auerbach came in, and Sorenson said, "Please sit down and tell me about your visit to the *Enterprise*. Something's bothering you."

Auerbach sighed. "Yes, sir, many of my old shipmates are gone. A lot of them never made it off Guadalcanal. Some have been sent to the States after a lot of missions. My old roommate was shot down over Kwajalein on a support mission the other day."

"Not recovered?"

Auerbach shook his head. "No chute."

Sorenson said, "I'm sorry to hear that. Was there any other news?"

"Yes. The *Enterprise* and two other carriers are beginning to specialize in night operations."

Sorenson said, "We've already seen the night fighters on the *Bunker Hill* and some of the other carriers."

"It's a dangerous game. Even the best pilot they had, a guy named O'Hare, never came back from a mission."

"Any idea what happened to him?"

"No, sir. He just never came back. He had flown many successful missions. Shot down several aircraft. I also found out that there will be a series of night attacks on Truk in the forthcoming operation. In addition to the night fighters, specially equipped TBMs will be used. The pilots have already been trained at Pearl Harbor in a new school."

Sorenson said, "I'm sorry to hear that your visit was so depressing. Take it easy this afternoon."

Auerbach shook his head. "I'd rather keep busy."

The next evening the *Ransome* volunteered to lead the singing, and the evening event became standard for the few days they were in Majuro. On the last day, the *Ransome* had repaired its anchor windlass, and after getting underway to fuel, the two ships anchored separately.

Fineman decoded a long dispatch just before lunch on the fifth day in port and brought it to Sorenson at the lunch table. Sorenson read it carefully. All conversation stopped as the officers put down their forks and anxiously studied his face.

When he had finished reading it, he looked up and said, "Back to the war. We're going to make the first night attack ever attempted on Truk."

Dubose whistled. "That's the most heavily fortified Japanese base in the Pacific."

Sorenson nodded. "I guess that's why we're going to attack at night."

"Any surface bombardment?" Steiner asked.

"This is just a preliminary message," Sorenson said. "The planners will develop the operation while we steam east, make up a plan, and probably pass it to us at sea in a few days. Scorse, a new tanker just came in. Make a last mail call to her, and all of you get busy and write letters."

An hour later the mail orderly came back in the boat. Brophy was watching the boat approach. "He's smiling. He must have gotten some stateside mail."

When the boat came alongside, willing hands went below to help the mail orderly unload twenty bags of mail. For over an hour the mail orderly worked sorting it. Then he asked the petty officer of the watch to pass the word for the division mail petty officers to draw mail. A cheer went up, and the crew headed for their division areas. They laughed and shouted as the division mail petty officers gave out the mail. Then all was quiet as each man headed for a quiet area to read his letters.

In the wardroom the process was a little quieter, but just as joyful. Sorenson collected six letters from Ferren and took them to his cabin. For over an hour he read and re-read them, savoring each sentence. She was well, missed him very much, and had a bunch of hellions in her class whom she was rapidly whipping into shape. She sounded reasonably happy, but Sorenson detected an air of sadness in her letters. He shook his head. He couldn't expect more from a woman who had already lost one husband on a destroyer.

He reached for a pen and stationery and started a letter to her. If he hurried, it would go back to Pearl Harbor on one of the tankers and then to the States by air.

CHAPTER FOURTEEN

As Task Group 58.2 continued to rest and re-supply, two other Task Groups of Task Force 58 arrived and replenished from the large array of tankers, ammunition ships, and supply ships anchored in the huge lagoon.

By the twelfth of February, all groups were ready, and the sortie began. The destroyers of Task Group 58.2 got under way and formed a screen around the entrance. Then the large ships came out and quickly formed a circular formation. The destroyers broke off from their fixed departure screen and formed a circular screen around the heavy ships. The formation turned north to circle the atoll and then set a course to the east. Looking back, Sorenson saw the other two Task Groups coming out of the atoll entrance. By noon the three formations were close enough to each other to be seen, but far enough apart to give them room to launch aircraft.

Sorenson settled back in his chair to watch. Soon flight operations began, and endless streams of aircraft took off and landed from the carriers as their pilots made refresher landings and takeoffs. Many of the landings were rough, and several pilots had to make second and even third approaches.

Auerbach, who had the deck, said, "They're just like athletes. If they lay off for a week they have to get in shape again."

At dusk the parade of aircraft stopped, and the night fighters took their places on the catapults again, except on the *Enterprise*and the other designated night carriers. CIC reported that aircraft were taking off and landing all night from the carriers designated to make the night attacks at Truk as they trained and rehearsed.

The next day was even busier as the aircraft did more complicated maneuvers, circling to rendezvous next to their carrier, departing, and then returning to bomb and strafe spars towed by their parent carriers.

That afternoon two destroyers were designated to pick up and distribute copies of the Operation Order for the Truk strikes. Scorse brought the *Carson*'s two copies to Sorenson. Sorenson kept one to study and gave one back to Scorse to use in briefing the officers.

By the next day they seemed to be ready, and the Task Groups rendezvoused with five tankers well north of Kwajalein. Fueling took most of the day. At dusk the tankers departed, and the three Task Groups headed east at high speed, keeping well to the north to avoid any possible detection by snooping Japanese search aircraft. Then they headed southeast, cutting through the easy seas at high speed.

By now Sorenson had finished studying the long thick Operation Order and called a conference in CIC of the principal officers who would be involved in the forthcoming action.

When Dubose reported that they were all assembled, Sorenson asked Dubose to stay on the bridge and went below to CIC.

Sorenson said, "Jablonski, start us with a quick review of our target."

Jablonski pointed to the chart he had laid out. "Truk is unique among atolls. It has a protective outer ring of coral reefs. Inside a large circular reef is a series of islands of volcanic origin."

Steiner said, ''We'd have a hell of a time taking those islands with a regular amphibious assault. They'd be dug in hundreds of yards deep, and we'd have to fire at them from outside the reefs.''

Jablonski wiped his high forehead and said, ''The intelligence annex calls Truk the Gibraltar of the east and says it's very heavily fortified. It also has airfields capable of supporting several hundred aircraft, and it says they are strongly protected by many antiaircraft guns.''

Sorenson pointed on the chart to the immense lagoon in the middle of the ring of islands. ''This is a magnificent anchorage, too.''

Jablonksi nodded. ''It's the headquarters for the Japanese Southern Fleet. Limited reconnaissance shows it's always full of ships.''

''Why do we bother?'' Steiner said, ''Why don't we by-pass the damned thing?''

Jablonski said, ''According to the Operation Order, we are. We'll be trying to destroy all the aircraft we can find and sink all the ships possible. Then we'll go away and revisit it periodically.''

Sorenson nodded. ''A good idea. Auerbach, please summarize our attack plan.''

Auerbach stepped forward and opened the Operation Order to the flight schedules. ''We launch generally from a point 90 miles northeast of Truk as early as we can on the seventeenth. The first flight will be mainly fighters to suppress the Japanese aircraft. The Task Group Commander wants to hit Truk as soon after dawn as possible on the seventeenth. Assuming the Japanese fighters are destroyed, there will be thirty strikes that day, each as big as the Japanese strike on Pearl Harbor. They will carry over three hundred thousand-pound bombs, five hundred five-hundred-pound bombs, and about seventy-five torpedoes.''

Steiner whistled. ''We've come a long way. Then what happens? We retire for the night?''

''No. For the first tine in history we stick around and launch night strikes the eighteenth using twelve TBFs.''

Auerbach turned to Sorenson, "They are the ones I told you about the other day."

Sorenson nodded, "This may be the beginning of a new kind of air warfare."

Jablonski said, "That's about all. The rest of the eighteenth will be taken up with surface searches around the atoll for surviving ships and a few air strikes for the same purpose."

Sorenson, eager to get back to the bridge, asked, "Anything more?"

All of the officers present shook their heads, and Sorenson headed back for the bridge. When he came into the darkened pilothouse he sat down. He looked around at the men on watch in the pilothouse. At the gleaming stainless steel wheel was the young gunner's mate, Smith, mount captain of mount 53, his earnest face peering into the subdued glow of the gyro repeater, trying to keep the speeding *Carson* on course. An equally young seaman, Kittredge,stood leaning on the annunciator, ocasionally making changes on the engine turn order as the officer of the deck, Finlay MacIntosh, made sure they were in exact station in the screen. Over in the corner of the pilothouse, young Caruso bent over the quartermaster's notebook, entering the changes as they were ordered, using a masked red flashlight.

MacIntosh prowled the bridge, alternately looking at the formation on the radar PPI and walking out on the wing to survey the rushing seas and the ships next to them. MacIntosh's faint Scottish burr was detectable when he gave terse orders to the man steering. His assistant officer of the watch was Chief Bellows, who was supervising the routine, and occasionally looking at the radar PPI.

Sorenson watched him as he bent stiffly over the luminous face of the PPI. Faint blue light outlined the deep wrinkles in his sixty-year-old face. Sorenson realized that the young men on the bridge could be his sons. Then he thought with a start that Chief Bellows was old enough to be his father.

He looked around the warm, dark bridge again. Somehow the men here felt like the family he had never had. The steady red lights from the instruments lit their faces as they moved about, masking the fatigue in them. Sorenson was content; then he thought about Ferren. Were her school children serving the same purpose, a surrogate family? He hoped so, and he started as MacIntosh said, "Captain, here's your coffee."

Well before dawn the next morning Sorenson was back on the bridge after a short period of sleep. Jablonski came to the pilothouse.

"Good Morning, Captain, we're approaching the launch point."

"Good morning." Sorenson looked at the sky. "It looks like a good day for flying."

Sorenson turned to the quartermaster on watch. "What are the pressure and temperature?"

The quartermaster consulted the last entry in his notebook. "Thirty inches and steady. Eighty-five degrees, sir."

The officer of the deck, Steiner, said, "Captain, request permission to sound general quarters?"

"Permission granted."

"The strident sound of the general alarm split the quiet night. As it rang in his ears, Sorenson thought he would never get used to the offending sound. Three minutes later they were manned and ready, and Sorenson could hear the whir of the hydraulic motors in the director and the 5-inch guns as they tested their control mechanisms. It, too, was a sound he would never forget, and he watched the mounts training right and left and elevating their slim barrels. He thought the ship looked like an insect lying on its back and waving its legs.

Fifteen minutes later the formation turned into the wind, and the plane guards took station. Sorenson could hear the sound of aircraft engines being started and then turned up.

Almost simultaneously the carriers launched the first fighter sweep, and the separately buzzing lights came together in formation, turned off their running lights, and disappeared to the southwest, steadily gaining altitude.

Sorenson had already ordered Auerbach to listen to the strike frequency, and he paced the bridge waiting for word of the strike.

In half an hour, Auerbach came up to the pilothouse. Sorenson could see a wide grin on his face in the increasing daylight.

"Complete surprise," he shouted. "About fifty Zekes, the newer version of the old Zero, managed to take off, but our seventy-two fighters had the advantage of surprise and altitude and shot down most of them. The others fled."

"Where did they go?"

"Out to sea. They'll have to come back and land sometime, and our guys will get them on the next strike. Right now the fighters with ammunition left are strafing aircraft that didn't manage to take off from the three fields."

Auerbach went below, and Sorenson sent for coffee. Before he had finished the cup, Auerbach was back. "The first strike has arrived and made its attack. The flight commander said the first fighters to arrive had counted about three hundred and fifty aircraft on the fields and now only about one hundred were left, some damaged. The other strikes are on the way, and there will be aircraft over Truk all day."

"How about attacking ships?"

"That has started, too. We've sunk at least three light cruisers, several destroyers, and about twenty merchant ships and other miscellaneous ships. The flight commanders say they're having a field day."

Sorenson said, "Well, so much for the Gibraltar of the Pacific."

Sorenson remembered the vast amounts of ordnance the Operation Order had scheduled the aircraft to drop, and he pitied the Japanese. It would be a long day for them, and it was just starting.

It was a long day for the Task Force, too, and it ended about 1800 when the last strike aircraft and the combat patrol overhead came aboard the carriers and were either put below or secured on deck by the weary aircraft handlers.

Sorenson felt that there could not be much life left in the Japanese, but he was apprehensive. They never did what they were supposed to do. He called up to Steiner in the 5-inch director, ''Chuck, I don't trust these bastards. They're always the most dangerous when they're down. Be alert.'' Then over the squawkbox he told Bronte in CIC to have both the surface and air radars keep an alert watch. He delayed securing from general quarters and setting condition III for over an hour. The darkness had closed in, but he was still uneasy.

About 1900, just as he was on the verge of giving the order to secure, CIC reported, ''One of the carriers reported six bogies coming in low. We don't have them yet. They must be very low. Probably torpedo planes.''

The Task Group between them and Truk started to fire. The firing became a black curtain in the faint light of dusk as more ships in the other screen joined in. The fire was so heavy that the aircraft turned away, but they were still on radar.

The Task Group Commander gave the order to hold fire, and one of the night fighters was launched, trailing a blue exhaust as it flew toward the enemy at full speed.

Bronte followed the directions given to it by its controller and reported the night fighter's progress to the bridge. Then he said, ''Damn! Something's wrong. The fighter doesn't answer up, and according to our radar he's passed the bogey.''

In a few minutes his voice became agitated. ''About five bogies are headed this way, right for us.''

Sorenson grabbed the TBS. ''Request permissiion to open fire at approaching bogies.''

''Negative,'' came the answer.

Sorenson watched in agony as the first bogey passed over the screen and headed for the *Intrepid*. That was enough for the Task Group Commander. "Commence firing!" came over the TBS.

Sorenson gave the order to Steiner to fire at the next two aircraft now approaching their sector.

"Solution!" shouted the talker. "We're opening fire."

Sorenson took a deep breath. "Good!" he shouted.

All four 5-inch guns crashed at the same time. The concussion pushed on Sorenson's chest and the smokeless powder residue flew in his eyes as he opened them. He had closed them just before the salvo went off to preserve his night vision. Now the 40-millimeter machine guns opened with a rolling roar, peculiar to their type of loading mechanism. There was enough moonlight to see that the two aircraft split as they approached the *Carson*. One went astern, but the second bored directly in toward the *Carson*.

Sorenson held his breath and gritted his teeth. "Get the bastard!" he yelled.

At about five hundred yards Sorenson could see the moonlight glint off of the metallic surface of a torpedo as it dropped from the bottom of the aircraft, nose over slightly, and splashed nose first into the sea. It appeared to be coming directly at the *Carson*.

Sorenson shouted, "Left full rudder!"

The ship began to swing, and he knew the torpedo would miss, but the aircraft kept on coming right at the middle of the ship. It was so low Sorenson didn't think it would clear the ship. His hands grabbed the wooden rail on the ship's bridge, and he tried to will the pilot to pull up.

"Up! Up!' he yelled. "Pull up, dammit!"

As the *Carson* swung, the aircraft slowly drew aft until it was headed directly for the 40-millimeter mounts. The frantic mount crews were pouring rounds into the aircraft, and Sorenson didn't see how it could survive. A hundred yards from the ship a 5-inch projectile burst directly in it, and pieces of it flew in all directions. Only the heavy engine section came on at them, and from the bridge it appeared to hit the 40-millimeter mounts. Sorenson groaned and turned to the talker. "Tell the after 5-inch mounts to render assistance to the 40s."

The talker delivered the message, and Sorenson waited anxiously for an answer.

Then he realized that there might be other aircraft making attacks, and he asked CIC for a report. "Screen is clear," came the answer.

On the port side of the bridge, Jablonski was watching the *Intrepid*. "Captain, the *Intrepid* is hit pretty badly. She has sheered out of formation and seems to have lost steering control."

Sorenson waited impatiently for a report from aft, and also a report on the TBS from the *Intrepid*. The report from the *Intrepid* came first. A strong, but slightly shaky voice said, "Torpedo hit on starboard quarter. Lost steering control. Can steer using engines. Some flooding. Several dead. Ready to depart if you can spare me."

The Task Group Commander promptly detached the *Intrepid* with an escort of the *Cabot*, two cruisers, and four destroyers.

"Jesus," Sorenson said, "That's half of the Task Group, and we've got tomorrow to get through."

He called down to CIC. "Dubose, go aft and see what happened."

Five minutes later the Executive Officer puffed up the ladder. When he had his breath back, he said, "All communications to the 40s are out. Nobody was killed, but there are several wounded. Fineman has them below."

Sorenson said, "How could we get off that easily? The heaviest part of that aircraft appeared to crash right into the 40s mounts."

"No, it went right over them. scraping the top of the gun sights and some other equipment off. The guns are a mess, and some men were wounded by flying parts of the gun sight."

Sorenson shook his head. "We were very lucky." He sat down in his chair to write a report to be transmitted the next morning, but gave up the attempt. He could not hold the red flashlight or the pencil steady enough to write, and he jammed both into the space behind his chair.

Dubose, watching him, said, "Captain, I think we should secure from general quarters now. I'll write a rough of the report in CIC and have it for you in the morning."

Sorenson sighed. "Thanks. I didn't realize how tired I was. I haven't been this bushed since my days in the Atlantic."

The respite was short, and the Task Group was scheduled to launch its night strikes shortly after midnight. Sorenson stayed at condition III during the launch. Most of the 12 TBFs were launched from the other Task Groups, and CIC followed them on radar. When they were over the radar horizon, Auerbach went below to listen on the strike circuit. When he came up to the bridge later, he said, "Captain, I can't tell you much. The strikes seemed to surprise the Japanese, but after that the strike leader didn't say much. Maybe he was too busy."

Sorenson said, "That's probably it. I wouldn't like to try to fly one of those clumsy TBFs, find a target, and report what all my aircraft were doing. We'll find out more later when they come back."

Two hours later they were all back, but still there was no word.

Sorenson dozed in his chair until morning general quarters. The day dawned clear and warm, and Sorenson wondered how many Japanese wouldn't see another morning. Some of the Americans wouldn't either, but so far he could count only four aircraft down from the preliminary reports. Some of the pilots would be recovered by the large surface force now sweeping around Truk to catch and sink any Japanese surface forces trying to escape. Already there had been a report of several sinkings, and the surface force was still reporting contacts fleeing from them.

At dawn Brophy sent the report of the shooting down of the Betty torpedo bomber the night before and the damage to the *Carson*. A few minutes later Renard brought up a decoded dispatch from the Task Force Commander to the Commander of the Pacific Fleet giving the results of the strikes. According to the report, the night attack had resulted in a number of sinkings of several kinds of surface ships.

Sorenson said, "Show this to Auerbach. He thinks night attacks are the future of naval aviation, and he may be right."

The next day they withdrew at high speed to a fueling rendezvous. When the *Carson* completed fueling, the Task Group Commander sent them a dispatch. "DETACHED WITH REGRET. YOU HAVE BEEN A VALUED MEMBER OF MY TEAM. PROCEED AND REPORT WITH RANSOME AND WINONA TO GUADALCANAL. DETACH WINONA AT GUADALCANAL AND PROCEED MILNE BAY NEW GUINEA AND REPORT ON ARRIVAL TO THE COMMANDER SEVENTH FLEET. STAY WELL CLEAR OF JAPANESE SHORE AND AIR FORCES ENROUTE."

CHAPTER FIFTEEN

The Task Group pulled away rapidly, leaving the *Carson, Ransome,* and the fleet tanker *Winona* steaming along slowly. As soon as the last ship of the Task Group was clear, Sorenson ordered Brophy to hoist a signal meaning, ''Take course one eight zero. Speed one two.'' The tanker turned south and Sorenson then formed a two-ship screen in front of it. When the small formation was settled down, he ordered it to zigzag, and then he went down to CIC. Dubose and Steiner were already there, and he sent for Jablonksi. Jablonski brought down the chart for the route they were to take to Guadalcanal and to New Guinea.

Sorenson said, ''First, spread the charts from here to Guadalcanal out on the DRT and let's see what route we'll take.''

Jablonski unfolded the chart, smoothed it out, and taped it to the top of the DRT.

''Where are we?' Sorenson asked.

Jablonski pointed to a spot about 100 miles northeast of Truk. ''Right here.''

Sorenson ran a pencil line down from their position to a point half way between Truk and Ponape. ''We should be able to pass Truk during the night and end up out here in the open ocean early tomorrow. Then we'll set a course directly for Guadalcanal. Do you all agree?''

All except Steiner nodded.

"Well, Chuck?"

Steiner put his finger on Rabaul, a Japanese stronghold about 600 miles northwest of Guadalcanl. "I'm not sure about passing this close to Rabaul."

Sorenson measured the distance from the closest point of their track. "Four hundred miles," he said. "That seems pretty safe."

"I know," Steiner said, "but the Japanese have been running searches out to five hundred miles and following those up with attacks by Bettys at least that far."

Sorenson said, "Forrest, what's your opinion?"

Dubose shook his head. "We're giving the Japs too much credit. They'll never bother us this far out."

Steiner's face reddened. "What about Truk? The fly-boys said they'd destroyed all the aircraft there. Then that night the Japanese attacked us and put the *Intrepid* out of action. Those bastards never quit."

Dubose sniffed. "I still think they won't bother us. Rabaul's been pounded by air for months. They're dead on the vine."

Steiner gritted his teeth. "Some vine! I think they've got plenty left, and we'll hear from them."

Sorenson rubbed his chin. "I think that's a risk we'll have to take. If they come out, I think we can defend ourselves."

Jablonski calculated the course they had agreed to take, and Sorenson called it up to the bridge with instructions to make the change. Soon the DRT bug indicated they were on the new course, and Sorenson leaned back against the DRT, relaxing.

He looked at Dubose, "Forrest, I thought the show Fineman put on in Majuro was excellent. Your quartet showed a lot of talent. We'll have to do it again."

Dubose grinned. "It was a lot of fun."

Sorenson took off his cap and rubbed his facial scar. "I thought Chief Williams was particularly good."

"Yes, they all have rhythm."

Sorenson stopped rubbing his scar, and his face darkened. ''That wasn't what I was talking about. I meant his peformance as Abdul.''

Dubose turned a little pale even under the subdued lighting of the CIC. He opened his mouth, but then closed it and said nothing.

Sorenson, waiting for an answer, glared at him. When Dubose remained silent, Sorenson said, ''Dammit, Forrest, you've got to realize that Chief Williams is the equal of any man on this ship, including you and me.''

Dubose looked at the overhead.

Sorenson stalked off to the bridge. Steiner and Jablonski quietly left the CIC, leaving Dubose alone with his thoughts.

That night they passed through the area between Truk and Ponape without any contacts, and for the next two days steamed over increasingly warm water as they approached the equator.

The days got very hot. The temperature of the crews' living compartments soared. Many men brought mattresses or pieces of canvas topside at night. During the day, they sought shade where they could find it, under mount overhangs, under boats, and on the shady side of the ship. Fineman had the pharmicist's mates pass out salt pills in the mess line.

Sorenson considered having an initiation as they crossed the equator, but decided against it, and the ship merely announced the fact over the IMC announcing system.

The next day they were abreast of Rabaul. The weather was beginning to cool slightly. Steiner still seemed to be anxious about enemy threats. He repeatedly admonished the lookouts to stay alert and visited the crews of the guns being manned at condition III. By this time the gunner's mates had been able to make temporary repairs to the 40-millimeter machine gun sights so that they could fire in local control.

Late that afternoon, with the sun about to set in the west in the direction of Rabaul, the three ships steamed southeast over a leaden sea. Low-hanging clouds were moving in from the west, but Sorenson thought the situation was safe enough for the ship to remain at condition III instead of going to general quarters.

He checked their position on the chart with Jablonski. Jablonski pointed to his latest navigational fix and the dead reckoning he had used since the fix. "Right here."

Sorenson said, "How far to Rabaul?"

"Three hundred and eighty miles."

Sorenson looked at the weather moving in. "I hope they're closed in over there."

Jablonski said, "Possible, but not probable. The weather report doesn't indicate any widespread storm. This is probably local. Besides intelligence says the Japanese now have search radar in some of their aircraft."

Sorenson said, "I don't feel right."

Jablonski shook his head. "The last time I heard you say that the *O'Leary* ran into a huge new submarine in the Atlantic."

Sorenson shuddered. "I'll always remember that, and I feel the same, now. I'm going to sit here in my chair just in case."

Jablonski shrugged. "If you don't need me, I'm going below for evening meal."

Sorenson looked over at the *Ransome,* on the other side of the screen, and at the tanker, plodding along in the rear. He called the talker over, "Tell gun control to keep the lookouts alert."

Sorenson looked aft. Mount 53 was manned for condition III and was trained out to starboard. The starboard 40-millimeter machine gun was manned, but its director was still out of commission. Two 20-millimeter machine guns were ready, the crews leaning on their shields.

He sat back and put his head against the bulkhead behind his chair. He began to think about Ferren, wondering if she was doing well with her school class. Then he thought about his brother Ed, back on the ranch, making money in spite of himself. He smiled. Someday he'd be able to enjoy the money that was piling up in his bank account.

Then his instincts took over. He sat up abruptly and looked to starboard. He blinked his eyes. There were two specks on the horizon. He knew they were enemy aircraft. Neither radar nor lookouts had reported anything, but he realized that they were too low for the air search radar to pick up and too high for the surface search radar to find. He blinked his eyes again. They were still there and they were bigger. They were approaching at high speed. Now he was sure. He leaped to his feet. ''Aircraft starboard beam!'' he shouted. ''Commence firing!''

The talker started to fumble with his transmitter.

''Dammit, tell them!'' Sorenson yelled. He ran out on the bridge wing and shouted up to the director, ''Air action starboard beam!''

Steiner poked his head out of the top of the director, and Sorenson realized he was up there for the same reason he was on the bridge. Steiner had suspected something. The director slewed around to starboard, and Sorenson could see the 5-inch mount aft pointing at the targets. The 40-millimeter mount trained around on the targets.

Two aircraft were now closing fast, and they were close enough so that Sorenson could see that they were Bettys, each with a large torpedo slung under its belly.

The guns aft started to fire. The officer of the deck had sounded general quarters as soon as Sorenson had yelled the first time, and below the crew was racing to its stations.

Then mount 52 forward of the bridge started to fire. Sorenson guessed that Steiner had put the crew of the gun in standby near the mount and they had been able to man their mount and start firing quickly.

Black bursts began to blossom in front of the two aircraft. The lead aircraft suddenly pulled upwards and began a turn away. The second Betty kept coming straight for the *Carson*. Five-inch bursts completely surrounded it, and then tracers from the 40s began to streak past it.

Then one 5-inch projectile burst against its cockpit, and it began to disintegrate. In an apparent last gesture of defiance, the pilot dropped his torpedo, but he was too high, and the fish began to nose over as it dropped. When it hit the water it plunged straight down.

The Betty nosed up and then stalled as it lost motive power. It fell back on its tail in a huge splash, and disappeared.

The first Betty cruised around out of range for a few minutes and then turned back into the clouds, gaining altitude. CIC reported that they had it on the air search and that it was headed toward Rabaul.

Sorenson turned to Jablonski, who had taken the deck. "What do you make of that?"

"I think they were out here on a search mission. They found us, and the leader tried to pull away to report us to his base. The other pilot got too eager, and bought the farm, Japanese style."

"What do you think the pilot will do now?"

"I think he's reporting our location to his base and to any of several submarines out here."

Sorenson shrugged. "Just in case you're right, we'll change course to the left twenty degrees."

Jablonski went over to the TBS and transmitted the order.

Sorenson said, "Set condition III. Gun control, well done all the way."

Steiner came down from the director grinning. Sorenson said, "You were right all along. Congratulations."

Steiner said, "I remembered the time in the Atlantic, too. When you say you're uneasy, I listen."

Then Sorenson noticed that someone was standing behind him. He turned and looked at Dubose.

"Well, Captain," Dubose said. "I was wrong. Steiner was right, and I apologize."

Sorenson grinned. "No need to apologize. I asked you for your opinion, and you gave it to me clearly and forthrightly. You might have been right. I took all of the views given to me and added my own. Then I made a decision. I was as wrong as you were. But in the end it came out all right."

Dubose looked puzzled. "How so?"

"We reduced the Japanese Navy by one aircraft."

Dubose laughed. "Thank you, Captain, you make me feel better."

Sorenson thought his change of course had eluded any submarine that might be around, but he was wrong. About 1600 Terrill, the senior sonarman, reported over the squawkbox, "Sonar contact! Bearing one eight three! Range two five double oh! Probable submarine!"

Sorenson waited for several more pings, listening intently on the bridge speaker to the signals coming back. Steele arrived on the bridge, puffing heavily, and listened, too. Then he said, "I think Terrill has a live one. I'm going to sonar."

Sorenson gave the order to sound general quarters, and ordered Wencey, who had the watch, to hoist a signal ordering an emergency turn to port of ninety degrees.

Over the TBS he told the *Ransome* to take charge of the tanker and that the *Carson* was attacking.

Steele called out from sonar. "Up doppler! Submarine is headed directly for us!"

Then Sorenson could hear a babble of voices in the background. Steele came on again. "The submarine has fired a torpedo at us. So far it seems to be headed slightly to port."

Sorenson shouted, "Jablonski, come right!"

Jablonski gave the order, and all on the bridge waited tensely.

Above, a lookout shouted, "Torpedo wake. One point on the port bow. Sorenson heaved a sigh of relief, and took the conn again. "I'm resuming the attack," he told sonar.

By now the contact had closed to just over one thousand yards, and the *Carson* was making 17 knots, its best attack speed.

From sonar came, "Contact changing course to the left. Speed 5 knots."

Sorenson changed course slightly to compensate for the submarine maneuver, and told the talker to tell the depth charge battery to stand by for a medium pattern. The depth charge battery acknowledged.

The range wound down rapidly, the outgoing signals coming more rapidly as Terrill shortened the scale.

Steele said in his deep voice, "Lost contact due to short range! Recommend drop on time!"

Sorenson swallowed, looked at the drop table posted on the bridge, and started the stopwatch. At the indicated time, he shouted, "Drop depth charges."

After a few seconds of silence, the K-guns aft went off with a characteristic pop, and Sorenson knew the men aft were rolling a series of charges off the stern rack.

Then he remembered that the *Carson* only had one depth charge rack, unlike the two he had been used to on the *O'Leary*, and he resolved to make sure of his contact before he dropped any more.

The men on the signal bridge reported that there was no debris in sight, and Sorenson swung in a wide arc for another attack.

This time the sonar team had settled down, and the reports from sonar were more consistent. Steele's voice was confident as they bored in toward the target, and after they had dropped, Sorenson felt that they had excuted a good attack. His feeling of tension began to evaporate, and he felt more confident.

He started to open the range after the last charge had rolled. This time a single heavy explosion followed the normal multiple explosions of the depth charges. Steele said, "I think we hurt him." Then he added, "I hear sounds of blowing ballast. I think he's coming up."

Sorenson turned to bring the contact on his beam and passed the word to gun control to be ready. The director and all four gun mounts trained out on the expected bearing of the submarine.

Sorenson and the personnel on the bridge waited tensely. Dubose, down in CIC, reported, "The DRT plot shows him stopped."

Suddenly a black bow burst through the surface, and thrust upwards, trailing water and foam.

Up in the director, Sorenson could hear Steiner ordering, "Commence firing."

Before Sorenson could open his mouth, four projectiles rocketed toward the helpless hulk. At that range it was impossible to miss, and Sorenson could see at least three dull red flashes at the base of the conning tower as the projectiles hit the thick steel of the hull beneath. Salvo after salvo poured out, enveloping the submarine in cascading water, smoke, and fire. The submarine had now fallen back to level and was slowly sinking back into the sea.

One projectile of the last salvo hit its conning tower and then there was a spurt of foam and mist high above the top of the conning tower. Bubbles boiled up as it disappeared.

Sorenson said, almost wistfully, "Cease firing!"

The guns stopped, and Steiner poked his head out of the director hatch. Sorenson looked up at him. "Nice shooting!"

Steele came out of sonar and watched as Sorenson conned the ship through the area where the submarine had disappeared. Oil was spreading rapidly as they passed through the slick at slow speed. One lifejacket and a few papers floated on the surface. Sorenson stopped the *Carson*, and Chief Bellows fished the debris up with a bucket and grapnel.

Sorenson realized he had a responsibility to the other two ships, and he ended the search for debris with the command, "All ahead full. Come to course zero nine six,'' the bearing of the rapidly disappearing tanker and the *Ransome.*

Then he returned the deck and conn to the officer of the deck and ordered him to secure from general quarters and to join the other two ships.

Steele, still standing by him, said, ''I think we can claim to have sunk this one. Some of the papers we recovered are written in Japanese.''

Sorenson nodded. ''I'm sure we can, but right now I'm concerned that there may be another sub around.

After the *Carson* rejoined, Sorenson resumed command of the formation and put an even more radical zigzag plan into effect.

Dubose came up to the bridge. He grinned. ''Well, Captain, as you would say, we've reduced the Japanes Navy by one submarine. Congratulations.''

''Thanks, but the credit goes to Steele and Terrill.''

''I understand that,'' Dubose said, ''but I also understand that as commanding officer, you also deserve credit.''

''And if we had failed, then the discredit.''

Dubose said, ''I understand that, too.''

''Then you've learned something more about command.''

The rest of the day and the next were quiet, and the temperature and weather moderated. They passed around the eastern tip of Malaita Island the next morning and headed for the anchorage off Guadalcanal.

Later, as the formation approached the anchorage, Auerbach, Steele, and Steiner stood on the deck aft of mount 52 and watched the Guadalcanal shoreline grow bigger. Steele said, ''Dick, tell us how Guadalcanal has changed since you saw it last.''

Auerbach laughed. ''I only saw it one day. The second day I had bandages across my eyes. But I'll try.''

As they drew nearer to the anchorage, he looked closely at the shore line and the flat land behind it. ''Well, for one thing, when I was here, the airfield control tower was a ramshackle building. Now they have a much better one. We had to live in tents. That's all there were except fox holes. Now I see many metal Quonset huts and even some prefabricated wooden buildings. There are storage buildings and dumps way back in what used to be boondocks.''

''Boondocks?''

''Yeah. Out where there's just tall kunai grass and even patches of jungle.''

Steiner said, ''I see some piers ahead made out of several connected pontoon sections. Looks almost like a regular port.''

Auerbach shook his head as the ship drew closer. ''Hard to believe it's the same place. I keep expecting to hear the air-raid siren.''

On the bridge, Sorenson ordered the tanker to leave formation and proceed to the open anchorage off the beach. After the tanker had dropped her anchor, the *Carson* and *Ransome* went alongside her and fueled.

While they were fueling, the commanding officer of the *Ransome* came over to call on Sorenson. The two Captains exchanged information and went over the events of the past two months.

Then Sorenson said, ''I'd like to get out of here as soon as we've fueled. The water is shallow enough to discourage submarines from coming in close, but after the other day, I feel that the Japanese may be turning to submarines to take up the slack from their other failed offensives using surface ships and carriers.''

''Suits me,'' said the Commanding Officer of the *Ransome*. ''I don't want to contribute to their success.''

By noon they were underway and headed for Milne Bay, a port on the extreme southern end of New Guinea, a two-day trip.

Sorenson watched the shore of Guadalcanal and nearby Savo Island fade into the distance. He realized they were passing over the watery grave of thousands of American sailors, six Allied cruisers, and over a dozen destroyers and smaller ships. For a moment he was very depressed, but he realized that the survivors had to keep going to seek revenge for those who could no longer fight, and he left his chair and began to pace up and down the bridge wing, thinking about the future in order to try to forget the past.

CHAPTER SIXTEEN

Sorenson stood on the bridge watching the lush green coast of Guadalcanal disappear behind him. He ordered the *Ransome* to take station two thousand yards on the *Carson*'s port beam and commenced zigzagging.

The trip to Milne Bay would take two days, and he looked forward to a rest during that period. The weather, although still tropical, was more pleasant.

But before he began his rest period, he decided to give himself and the officers something to think about. He sent word to Dubose to have Jablonski bring all the information he had on New Guinea and the Seventh Fleet to the wardroom.

He left MacIntosh with the deck and went below. Jablonski had spread a chart of New Guinea on the wardroom table and had several reference books with him.

Sorenson sat down and said, "John, tell us all you know about New Guinea, and Doc, don't tell us you've already been there."

Fineman shook his head and shuddered. "I understand it's a regular hell hole. I never went there."

Jablonski stood up so he could see the chart better. "I don't know about its being a hell hole. I think it's too wet to burn. Some parts of it get one hundred inches of rain a year, and others have some rain over half the days of the year.''

Renard looked at the chart. ''It's just slightly south of the equator. Why wouldn't it be hot?'' Renard wiped the perspiration off his brow.

Jablonski said, ''Oh, it's hot all right, but not as hot as equatorial Africa, for instance. It's about a steady ninety degrees, and always very humid. Just slightly hotter than the area we're in now.''

Renard was still looking at the chart. ''Funny looking island. Looks like a bird.''

Jablonski said, ''That's where it got it's name. It looks like an African Guinea hen, a bird about as large as a chicken.''

Bentley said, ''I don't see any feet.''

Jablonski smiled thinly. ''Don't be so literal. It's flying.''

Bentley laughed. ''I guess you weren't a farm boy like I was. Guinea fowl don't really fly. They just skitter along on the ground with their wings out.''

Jablonksi said, ''Then how do they get up in trees to roost at night?''

Bentley said, ''They make it somehow, but it isn't a pretty sight.''

Renard said, ''Well, it looks like a bird to me. I see Vogelkop up to the north, which means bird's head. It even has a mouth.''

Jablonski said, ''And on the other end a tail. That's where we're going. Milne Bay is right at the end of the tail feathers.''

Sorenson said, ''I take it we'll be sticking to the coast for operations. Tell us what you found out about the interior.''

''Not much. There are about one thousand tribes on the island, which incidentally is the second largest island in the world. Each tribe speaks its own language. The mountains are so high and the valleys so deep there isn't much travel or communication, except by boat.''

Renard asked, ''What's this vertical line in the middle?''

''That marks the boundary betwen Papua on the south, which is controlled by the Australians, and Dutch New Guinea on the north, controlled by the Dutch.''

Sorenson traced a finger along the south coast. ''I take it the Australians and Americans control the coast up to about the Huon Peninsula.''

''Yes, the Japanese in 1942 began a push south, but the Australians stopped them short of Port Moresby and Milne Bay and then drove them back to the north to the present positions in very bitter fighting.''

Sorenson pointed to the groups of islands off to the east of the coast. ''What about these?''

Jablonski followed his finger. ''Those are the New Britain Islands and up north the Admiralty Islands. We control them except for Rabaul in New Britain and Kavieng on the Island of New Ireland.''

''I take it we say we've neutralized the positions at Rabaul and Kavieng.''

''Yes, that's what the Operation Plan says.''

Steiner shook his head and muttered, ''That's what it says, but the guy who wrote it didn't see those Bettys coming out of Rabaul the other day.''

Sorenson nodded. ''Neither did our lookouts.''

Bentley asked, ''I keep hearing about Operation Plans and Operation Orders all the time. What's the difference?''

Scorse sat forward. Sorenson noted that he seemed to have lost at least twenty pounds and his face was lean and almost gaunt. His black eyes were intent. By contrast, Reifel, across the table, had added twenty pounds and looked human again. Scorse said, ''An Operation Plan is a general document setting forth the objective, giving the forces available, listing the enemy forces to be expected, and then giving a general plan of operation for an indefinite time. An Operation Order is more specific, and gives the exact forces and factors to be used in carrying out a short operation in support of the Operation Plan.''

Bentley asked, ''While I've got the floor, what happens to our mail?''

Scorse said, ''Good question. The mail system is very good. The day we were tranferred to the Seventh Fleet, some postal clerk back in the Fleet Post Office in San Francisco changed our name from one hole to another, and the sacks of mail began to pile up in a new hole. When a tanker was ready to come out here, our sacks were put aboard with the sacks for all the other ships out here, and they'll be in Milne bay thirty days later. We should have mail the second week we're there.''

Jablonski nodded and said, ''Well, that's about all I have. Shall I go into the command structure?''

''No that's Scorse's territory. Go ahead, Scorse.''

Scorse stood up. ''We will work for the Commander Seventh Fleet, Vice Admiral Kinkaid, who in turn works for General MacArthur.''

Sorenson said, ''This is quite a shake up. We've worked for the Commander of the Pacific Fleet so long we'll have to make a lot of changes in a hurry.''

''Yes, I have a set of the Seventh Fleet's regulations. The good part of them is that they're very brief. The bad part is that they don't give us much help.''

Sorenson said, ''Well, we'll just go along as we were until someone tells us differently.''

Scorse said, ''Our tactical boss will be Rear Admiral Barbey, who is in command of what's called the Attack Force, or Task Force 77. Admiral Barbey is usually with General MacArthur and Vice Admiral Kinkaid, at their headquarters, but for operations he embarks in a destroyer.''

Steiner asked, ''How big is the Seventh Fleet?''

''Not many big ships, but a lot of small ships and landing craft. Only two American cruisers and two Australian cruisers. However, there are about fifty American destroyers and ten Australian destroyers. Also a division of amphibious shipping of APAs, AKAs, and an LSD. In addition it has several destroyer escorts and many fast destroyer transports.''

''What about aircraft?''

''There is Task Force 73, land-based and tender-based patrol aircraft, and Task Force 78, the escort carrier groups, with eight escort carriers.''

''And submarines?''

''A good many, but they operate by themselves up north, and we won't see much of them.''

Sorenson said, ''Fineman, please ring for some iced tea. This is making me thirsty.'' He turned back to Scorse. ''What's this about a lot of smaller craft?''

''When this campaign was being planned in Australia, apparently General MacArthur thought he would need a lot of small amphibious craft to move up the coast of New Guinea from place to place. He didn't think there would be much need for embarking in big amphibious ships as there has been in the Pacific with longer distances and more heavily defended beaches.''

Dubose interrupted, ''They say MacArthur's a military genius.''

Steiner looked at the overhead and muttered, ''Guess you haven't heard about Clark Field and the bastards who starved on Bataan.'' Jablonski ignored him and went on, ''The Navy said it was too busy and didn't have enough personnel to man such a force, so General MacArthur gave the job to the Army Engineers. Now they have a small navy of their own manned by yachtsmen and Army Reserves.''

Dubose nodded. ''The Navy made a mistake.''

Sorenson said, ''What kind of small craft?''

''LCVPs, LCMs, LCTs, and a special adaptation of the LCI called a LCIG. It's a standard LCI fitted with rockets and extra machine guns.''

Dubose said, ''The Navy designed that version for them. The Pacific Fleet has some. They really chew up a beach just at the time the landing waves need support.''

Sorenson said, ''So much for the hardware. Now how do we operate?''

''I don't know much about that. Apparently you'll get detailed information when we arrive at Milne Bay and you call on Admiral Barbey in his flagship.''

Dubose stirred. ''How about calling on General MacArthur?''

Steiner sneered. ''He won't be that near to the front lines. He's taking it easy back in Brisbane.''

Dubose cleared his throat. ''I don't think you should say that about one of our most famous generals.''

Steiner sat upright. ''I happen to know a lot about General MacArthur. I was out in the Philippines when he botched the job there.''

Sorenson said, ''I never thought those stories about Dugout Doug were warranted. After all, he was exposed to enemy fire repeatedly in World War I, and his personal bravery was never questioned.''

Steiner said, ''I'm not talking about that. He was personally brave enough, but he wasn't morally courageous. He made many mistakes in command and never admitted any of them.''

Dubose's face was reddening. ''You're talking about a general who is almost as famous as Robert E. Lee.''

''Lee is a man I can respect.''

Sorenson asked Dubose, ''Why are you so taken with General MacArthur?''

Now Dubose was falling back into his Alabama accent. ''I remember he was born in Arkansas. He's a good rebel, and a great general.''

Sorenson turned to Steiner, ''And why are you so against him?''

''He damned near wiped the Asiatic Fleet out and he did wipe out the Army Air Force in the Philippines. He was also responsible for the debacle at Lingayen gulf and Bataan and Corregidor.''

''How do you know that?''

''I was there. The old *O'Leary* was lying off the Cavite Navy yard, ready to go in for overhaul, when all this happened. We knew that Pearl Harbor had been bombed at three o'clock in the morning our time. General Brereton, in command of the Army Air Forces at Clark Field, tried to get General MacArthur to let him attack Formosa at dawn, but General MacArthur wouldn't even talk to him. Told his chief of staff to tell him not to attack until we were attacked first. At noon the whole Army Air Force was caught on the ground at Clark Air Field and destroyed. Soon the Asiatic Fleet had no air cover at all. The Japs just cruised over and bombed us at will."

Sorenson said, "Couldn't the submarines still operate?"

"Not very well. MacArther declared Manila an open city without consulting Admiral Hart. As a result of that decision, Admiral Hart couldn't legally move the submarine torpedoes and spare parts out of Manila, and the submarines had to move to Australia."

Dubose was getting angry and red-faced. "I don't believe all that."

Steiner was also getting upset. "I know it was true. I was there. What was worse, General MacArthur had earlier ordered his Army staff to position all their food supplies out in the plain to the east of Lingayen Gulf, where he said he was prepared to fight the Japanese in the open area. The only trouble was the Filipinos didn't know anything about maneuver warfare, weren't equipped for it, or for much of anything else, and retreated rapidly after the Japanese landed, leaving all the rice and ammunition they had out on Lingayen Plain. Consequently, they had nothing to eat or shoot at Bataan and on Coregidor, and you know the rest. It was tragic."

Dubose said, "Well, I never heard anything done about it. I never heard of any investigation like there was after Pearl Harbor."

Steiner said, "That was the final straw. Admiral Kimmel and General Short were investigated and fired, but no one ever said a word to General MacArthur."

Dubose stood up. "Well, he's a national hero to the Filipinos, and to me. In the future, please don't talk like that about him when I'm present."

Dubose stalked out of the wardroom.

Sorenson sighed. "Chuck, I'm afraid you've hit a nerve. You'll have to cool down and apologize to him.

The rest of us will have to hope General MacArthur has learned something since those tragic days."

Sorenson spent a restless night, mulling over the conversations in the wardroom. By the second day Steiner had reluctantly apologized to Dubose, and calm prevailed in the wardroom as the officers talked about the hoped-for pleasures of Milne Bay.

Early the morning of the second day, they steamed into Milne Bay, followed by the *Ransome*. The bay was filled with American and Australian ships of every category, but it was so big that the berths assigned to the two arriving ships were not crowded. Sorenson turned his binoculars on the shoreline surrounding the bay. There was an almost complete ring of green surrounding the bay, broken only in a few places by small buildings. If there was civilization there, he thought, it was well back in the thickly growing trees. They were assigned anchorages, and soon the *Carson*'s anchor plunged down to the muddy bottom.

Sorenson sent a message to the commanding officer of the *Ransome*, proposing that they call on Admiral Barbey that morning, and then he sent a second message to the flagship requesting permission to call.

An hour later Wencey came down to the cabin with an answer, and at 1300 Sorenson picked up the commanding officer of the *Ransome* in the *Carson* boat and they were on their way to call.

Two hours later Sorenson was back and Dubose met him at the top of the Ladder.

Sorenson said, "Let's have a conference."

Dubose grinned, "The officers are all in the wardroom waiting."

Sorenson went below and threw his cap on a chair. All the officers were standing, smiling expectantly.

Renard said, "Any liberty, Captain?"

"Yes and no. I'm glad we brought all that beer. That's all we'll get."

The officers sat down after Sorenson was seated. Sorenson said, "There isn't any general liberty ashore here. The place is too small. But there is a small beach a mile up the river where we can send swimming parties."

Renard asked, "And beer parties?"

Sorenson laughed. "That, too. I was figuring out in my head on the way back how to do it best. Do we have enough beer to provide two bottles per man?"

Renard said, "Yes, sir, and then some."

"We can send twenty men at a time to the beach for four hours. In the two weeks we will be here that will get each man ashore once with two beers. We will have to say that any man who doesn't drink his beer will have to bring it back and can't give it to another man."

Dubose said, "I've already figured out that each party will have to have an officer or chief petty officer in charge. He'll have to dole out the beer."

Sorenson said, "Well, so much for this important stuff. Now for the trivial. We'll be here at least two weeks. We have to fuel, top off our spare parts, provisions, and ammunition, and get some repair work done."

Steiner said, "We can do some ourselves, but we'll need some parts and help for the 40-millimeter machine gun sight repair. The Australian repair ship will do it. The Australians use the same kind of machine guns."

MacIntosh asked, "What about a replacement torpedo?"

"The ammunition ship has some."

Sorenson asked Reifel, "Chief, what about the engineering department. Do you need help?"

"No, sir. Just time to clean boilers. Two weeks should do fine."

Dubose asked, "What about operations?"

Sorenson said, "There's a big operation coming up. General MacArthur is about to move along the coast of New Guinea to thenorthwest. We'll be a part of that. In the meantime we'll go out on some other smaller operations. Now how about lunch? I'm starved."

The next morning the first of the swimming parties left. Chief Bellows was in charge, and Doctor Fineman went along to make an inspection as to whether ot not the area was medically safe.

When they arrived they found the beach was isolated and apparently not much used. The sand was whitish-brown and undisturbed. About twenty yards behind the beach a thick stand of trees and bushes enclosed the beach like a green wall. The water was calm, transparent, and inviting.

Chief Bellows shepherded the beer in a large galley pan out of the boat and back into the shade of the trees. Fineman looked carefully at the area and took a sample of the water. "Looks okay to me," he said. "I'll go back in the boat and put this under a microscope. If the boat doesn't come back in half an hour, start swimming."

Bellows grinned, "Ve drink de beer first."

Two hours later most of the beer was gone, and the men were neck deep in the green water. Bellows had made them keep their underwear shorts on. "In case de ladies show up." There was a loud protest over this, but the water looked so good the noise didn't last long.

Suddenly Wencey looked toward the beach. "Jesus!" he shouted. "Look at that!"

Everyone stopped splashing and looked toward the fringe of trees back of the beach. A group of about twenty Melanesian men was standing there watching them. All were dressed only in loin cloths. Most were short and slightly beer bellied, but one man standing in front was different. He was six inches taller than the rest and a lighter shade of black.

Wencey said, "We'd better get up there before they steal our clothes."

Bellows and Wencey led the way out of the water, followed by the rest of the party.

As the group approached the black men, they could see some of them picking up the *Carson* group's clothes and hanging them on tree branches.

Bellows noted that three of the men in the front row carried long knives.

Wencey said, "Look, they're going through our clothes, and I don't like those toad-stabbers."

As they approached nearer the group of black men, the tall man stepped forward. Bellows and Wencey stopped in front of him.

Bellows said, "Ha-whaddaya dunha-wit hour ha-clothes?"

The black man's eyebrows went up, but he didn't say anything.

Wencey said, "Let me try." He stepped forward and raised his hand, palm outward, "How," he said.

The black man looked at him. "How what?"

Wencey said, "You speak English?"

The black man said, "Certainly, mate, what does your friend speak?"

Wencey said, "He speaks English, too, but he put his dental plates in his pocket when he went swimming. Where did you learn your English?"

"Long story, mate. My tribe comes from the interior. Some missionaries discovered our tribe several years ago. And a white trader discovered my mother, too. That's why I'm a lighter shade. Anyway, when I was twelve, I had learned all the missionaries could teach me and they sent me away to school in Australia. After a few years I came back. Couldn't stand all the clothes. My name is David, after the guy in the Bible."

Wencey said, "I hope you aren't going to use those knives on us."

David laughed, "Not on you, mate. We used them to cut a path down here from our village."

"And your men won't steal our clothes?"

"Certainly not, we aren't savages. You should never leave your clothes on the sand. A little devil known as a sand mite will get in them. They bite badly."

Wencey said, "Why did your men come all the way down here?"

"We wanted to trade, mate. You got anything?"

Wencey scratched his head. "Nothing but these bottles of beer and some loose change."

"All good stuff, mate, paricularly the empty beer bottles. Also the metal tops. That bottle opener you have there will sell, too. We'll make an ornament out of it. And the coins will be big sellers, too."

Wencey was getting in to the swing of things. "What have you got to trade with us?"

"A lot of good stuff, mate, but first we have to prove to our women that you're safe."

"Where are your women?"

David pointed back over his shoulder in the bush. We can't let them come out until we've seen the color of your penises."

"What!"

"I know it seems rude, mate, but for decades our older men have taught the women that men with white penises are second rate and that black penises are great. I know that's open to question, but it works, and it keeps the women happy and handicaps the white men."

"What happened with your mother?"

"She doesn't rightly know, mate. She says it was a dark night, and she wasn't too careful."

Wencey conferred with Chief Bellows. Bellows shook his head, but Wencey argued with him. Then Bellows nodded and Wencey said, "Okay, men let them have a look."

All the men standing behind him laughed and pulled down their shorts.

David said, "All right, that's enough." He sent a man back in the bush, and in a few minutes he returned leading a half dozen giggling black women out to the beach.

The men stared in amazement. All the women were bare to the waist, but most of their breasts hung pendulously half way down to their navels. Each carried a woven bag over her shoulder.

With the novelty over, trading began, and after half an hour all the empty beer bottles were gone together with all the loose coins. Each *Carson* man had a souvenir of some sort ranging from carved wooden heads to short knives and spears. Fierce masks made out of grass were very popular. When they had finished trading, Wencey asked, ''Do you have any shrunken heads?''

David laughed. ''Curious you should ask. We have a model made expressly for tourists.'' He beckoned to one of the women, and she pulled a grass wrapped package out of her sack. She unwrapped it and put it on the sand. The *Carson* men gathered around it.

Wencey said, ''It looks like it must have been a Japanese.''

''Sure,'' David said. ''Who else? We haven't killed any friends for years.''

Wencey shuddered and moved upwind to get away from the odor. ''How do you shrink it?''

''We don't actually shrink the skull. We strip the skin and hair off the skull, remove part of it, break the dental arches, and then stuff the inside with grass. Don't look too closely. I wouldn't let them sell you that one.'' He motioned to the woman, and she put it back in her sack.

Wencey said, ''More of our men will be coming over here for the next two weeks. Will your people be here?''

''Most assuredly, mate, they know a good market when they see one.''

The *Carson* group said good bye and started to wade out to the incoming boat. David called out, ''You'd better swim for a few minutes with your clothes on to drown the sand mites.''

Bellows led them back into the water and in a few minutes they were back in the boat, dripping and wet, but happy.

Over the next several days the tales told by the swimming parties got bigger and wilder as each party embellished the last account. The ship became a curio shop, with masks and spears hanging all over the living compartments.

On the last day of the swimming parties, at breakfast in the wardroom, Dubose called Chief Williams and Big Jackson into the Wardroom.

''Chief, I haven't seen your name or Big Jackson's on the swimming party list. Don't you want to go?''

Williams looked up at the overhead and then back at Dubose. ''No sir.''

''Why not?''

''Sir, I didn't come half way around the world and fight a lot of battles just to be discriminated against by other blacks. It's bad enough in the States with the whites.''

''I don't understand.''

''I hear they won't let any one swim over there who has a black penis.''

Sorenson turned to Dubose. ''Is that right?''

Dubose said, ''I hear that's what's going on, but they have a good reason for it.''

Sorenson looked down the table to the other officers. ''Is that right?''

Steiner said. ''That's right, sir, but it hasn't really come up yet since neither Williams nor Big Jackson has been ashore. Little Jackson is scheduled for the last swimming party.''

Sorenson said, ''How can they do that?''

Steiner said, ''There are a couple of men standing there with large knives that look pretty dangerous, and they don't want any competition for their women from other black men.''

Sorenson bristled. ''I'll send over some armed men of our own.''

Chief Williams interrupted. ''Please, Captain, don't make an issue of it. I feel bad enough as it is.''

Fineman said, ''I've got an idea. We could paint your offending member with white zinc oxide. You'd be sensational.''

Williams laughed. ''No, thank you, it's the principle of the thing.''

Dubose turned to Big Jackson. ''How about you, Big Jackson?''

Big Jackson giggled. ''That cold beer sounds mighty good. Can I drop down to sick bay and get some of that white stuff?''

Fineman said, ''Sure. Right after I have some more hot cakes.''

Chief Williams and Big Jackson withdrew to the security of the pantry.

Dubose sat over his coffee for several minutes, with Sorenson careful not to disturb him. Finally Dubose said. ''That was funny, but sad. I'm beginning to see Chief Williams's side of the picture.''

CHAPTER SEVENTEEN

At the end of the second week in Milne Bay the *Carson* crew completed her repairs and the loading of spare parts, provisions, and ammunition. MacIntosh drew a torpedo from the ammunition ship, and the torpedomen lovingly prepared it for a war shot and loaded it in the long-vacant tube. Reifel's engineers completed cleaning the sooty firesides of their boilers, and all of the firemen involved were given a special swimming party to soak off the soot and grime.

Reifel went with them, and when they came back, he reported that in place of David and his group of tribesmen there was an Australian soldier with a rifle. Reifel said, "When I asked him what had happened to David, the soldier said, 'Had to send the black blighters back to the bush. They was littering the beach.' "

Dubose came to Sorenson and reported the ship ready in all respects for getting underway. Mail had arrived the day before, and morale had risen as the men caught up on news from home.

Bentley found a dozen movies in the Seventh Fleet movie exchange they had not seen before.

Sorenson went to Admiral Barbey's flagship, the *Blue Ridge,* to report their readiness. He was back soon and called the usual officers' conference.

Calling for iced tea to replace the usual coffee, he started right out. "We're to join the destroyers *Ammen, Daly, Hutchins, Beale,* and *Mullany* in conducting a bombardment of Wewak. Jablonski, show us where it is on the chart."

Jablonski stood up and leaned over the chart spread on the wardroom table. "You all will remember that New Guinea looks like a bird with its beak pointing west. Wewak is right in the middle of its back. Right here." He stabbed at the chart with his finger.

Steiner said, "Are we going to land there later?"

Sorenson shook his head. "No. That's the point. General MacArthur has decided to land farther north at a later date. This will be part of the continuing operation that will make the Japanese think we're going to land at Wewak. Actually we'll land farther north at Hollandia at a later date."

MacIntosh asked, "Will there be other actions taken to mislead the enemy?"

"Yes. General Kenney's air force will bomb Wewak also. Then there will be some deceptions carried out. PT boats will patrol off Wewak several nights, making a lot of noise. Dummy parachutists will be dropped behind Wewak to simulate scouts, and a submarine will float in some vacant life rafts to make the Japanese think we've landed reconnaissance teams. Altogether a strong effort."

Dubose took a deep breath and grinned. "Damned smart generalship by MacArthur."

Sorenson looked at Steiner, expecting some reaction and preparing to step in, but Steiner kept on looking at the chart and said nothing.

Sorenson turned to the chart again. "We hope the Japanese will begin to move their troops south from Hollandia toward Wewakin anticipation of our landing there. Their movement south will take about three weeks. Once they get there, they can't get back in time for the Hollandia landings. The roads are almost non-existent. The air force will conduct daily reconnaissance along the trails to try to pick up any movement."

Steiner asked, "Will there be any naval action on the part of the enemy?"

Sorenson pondered for a minute, rubbing his facial scar. "The Japanese have something they call the Ninth Fleet in the area. It has just a token force of minelayers, subchasers, barges, and about three hundred ground troops for its own defense. It actually has a Vice Admiral in command of it."

Dubose snorted. "Not much of a force for a Vice Admiral."

Sorenson nodded. "And not much is expected from it, either. Maybe we can shoot some of it up during our bombardment. But at least we have to be alert for any action they might try to take."

Reifel asked, "What about air opposition?"

"The Japanese still have aircraft on inland fields and farther up the coast. They may stage some in to the Hollandia airfields from Borneo. Our air force will have aircraft over us all the time."

Now Steiner came to life. "I hope General MacArthur does a better job than he did for us in the Philippines."

Sorenson jumped in quickly before Dubose could say anything. "I think defeat was inevitable no matter what MacArthur did. As it was, you got out with out being sunk. If you'd have stayed around you might not be here now."

Dubose was still silent, but Sorenson could see a slight smirk on his face.

The conference broke up soon after, and all the officers went off to brief their men and to make last minute preparations.

On March 17th, the *Carson* got underway and took station in column behind the other five destroyers. They steamed northwest at a steady 18 knots, zigzagging and on the lookout for stray Japanese aircraft.

Just before 2200 the next night, the Division Commander turned to approach the coast just north of

Wewak. Bronte, in CIC, sweated nervously as they plotted radar bearings of prominent points on the coast as they closed it. Then he relaxed as he realized that the lead destroyer would go aground long before the *Carson*, at the end of the column, would reach shallow water.

In a few minutes, the Division Commander turned south east to parallel the coast, and the column approached its initial firing position.

Sorenson had sent the *Carson* crew to battle stations an hour before, and all was ready. Fire hoses were laid out. The gun control mechanisms had been tested, and Sorenson was sure they were ready. He listened as the hydraulic motors of the gun mounts brought the individual mounts to starboard to match the director orders. He knew that down in CIC Dubose and Bronte were working to put accurate navigational fixes on the chart using radar so that they could send range and bearing to the targets ashore assigned to the *Carson* by the Division Commander.

Then Dubose called up on the squawkbox, "On target and tracking. Ready to fire."

Sorenson leaned out of his chair and acknowledged the information on the squawkbox. "Stand by," he said.

The guns began to train aft slowly as the ships barrelled down the coast. Just when Sorenson was afraid they had gone too far, the order came over the TBS, "Commence firing!"

Sorenson repeated the order to his talker, and in seconds the first four-gun salvo boomed out to starboard.

Sorenson had closed his eyes just before the salvo was fired to preserve his night vision, and when he opened them, he could see about twenty tracers arcing toward shore. Then other salvos followed at five-second intervals, and he lost his night vision. It made little difference now because the projectiles landing ashore ignited large fires.

Sorenson, looking through his glasses, shouted. "There goes some ammunition! A helluva show!"

Jablonski said, "That's some that won't be fired at us."

But the Japanese were not caught entirely by surprise. Guns ashore began to wink, and a few splashes rose short of the speeding column.

The Division Commander reversed course, and the ships repeated their firing run, helped now by the light provided by flaring fires ashore. More and more enemy shells landed around them, but as far as Sorenson could see, none of them hit any of the ships.

Almost at the end of the second leg, the lookouts reported a small sub-chaser along the shore. Sorenson grabbed the TBS transmitter and requested permission to fire at it. Even before the Division Commander said, "Permission granted," Steiner had swung his guns toward it. Then the *Carson's* guns roared, and the first salvo erupted around the fleeing ship. Two more salvos started a large fire on it, and three more sent it to the bottom, leaving sparks and smoke on the surface.

Sorenson reported its sinking, and Steiner resumed fire on the shore targets.

One last time the Division Commander reversed course and a third set of salvos went out. When the forward guns could no longer bear, the Division Commander gave the order to cease firing and set a course toward Hansa Bay about 50 miles down the coast of New Guinea where they were scheduled to make a dawn shore bombardment under the cover of Army Air Force aircraft.

Sorenson set condition III, and the gun crews stayed around long enough to gather up and stow the brass powder cases rolling around on the deck in their aluminum containers.

Dubose had planned an early breakfast an hour before dawn, and the crew not on watch headed to their bunks for a short rest.

At 0400 the word was passed to, "Turn out and show a leg," an ancient and meaningful expression to get the reluctant sailors out of their bunks.

Caruso groaned and turned over to try to go back to sleep. A sailor getting out of an adjacent bunk noticed his still form and slapped him on the back. "Rise and shine, Caruso, The Japs won't wait."

Caruso turned back over and sighed. "Some day I'm going to sleep all day."

"Not until the war's over."

On the bridge, Sorenson slipped back to his sea cabin, brushed his teeth, and managed a face wash and a quick shave. Then he went back to the bridge and ordered breakfast sent up. By the time qeneral quarters was sounded, he was finished with his usual sparse breakfast and was pacing the bridge, trying to see through the darkness.

In the tropics, the darkness grew to light in about twenty minutes, and he searched the coast trying to see prominent landmarks Jablonski was looking for. But neither had much luck, and it was left to CIC to find their position and targets by radar.

Just after dawn, nine Army Air Force fighters thundered overhead and took up a patrol position just over the beach.

Sorenson looked up at ther circling aircraft. "Very comforting," he said to Jablonski.

Steiner, with his head poked out of the director, looked down at Sorenson, pointed at the fighters, and raised his fist. Sorenson grinned. He knew what Steiner was thinking about and on an impulse said to the talker, "Tell Mister Dubose in CIC we have nine aircraft overhead."

The talker hesitated, "Sir, I think he knows it."

Sorenson said, "I'm sure he does, but tell him anyway."

By 0800 the destroyer column eased around the entrance to Hansa Bay until they were in a position to fire on the

Japanese installations intelligence had told them were on the shore and slightly inland.

This time the prominent landmarks and the daylight made navigation easier, and Sorenson was sure they could do a good job firing on their assigned target.

Within minutes after they could see into the bay, CIC reported having located the correct target, and Sorenson in turn reported to the Division Commander that the *Carson* was ready.

As soon as all ships reported ready, the Division Commander ordered ''Commence firing!'' over the TBS and, as at Wewak, the opening salvos from all ships went out at almost the same time.

Sorenson watched the projectiles land ashore. Huge pieces of roof and buildings rose in the air and fell back. Fires started almost immediately, and black smoke welled up over the harbor.

Then the euphoria was interrupted. CIC reported, ''Bogies coming in from the west.''

Sorenson looked up. The fighters overhead were orbiting as if nothing was happening. He grabbed the squawk-box transmitter. ''What about the fighters? They're still overhead.''

Bronte answered. ''The Division Commander can't seem to communicate with them.''

''Use our radio and break in. The Japs will be here any minute.''

Sorenson went out on the open bridge and looked up again. ''Damn!'' he said, ''They're here now.''

The space overhead became a swirling, milling mass of aircraft as the Air Force fighters mixed with the oncoming Japanese fighters. They were too high for Sorenson to hear their machine guns, but he could see puffs of smoke as the aircraft turned and twisted. Then one of the fighters burst into flame, and a parachute blossomed.

The Division Commander designated one of the other destroyers to recover the pilot, and the remaining ships completed the last few salvos of the bombardment.

Sorenson kept an anxious eye on the aircraft overhead, and toward the west, hoping the fighters were not a diversion for incoming bombers. CIC said the west was clear of bogies, and he turned his attention to the fighter battle overhead which was coming lower and lower as the aircraft lost altitude. By now they were so low he could identify the types of aircraft.

Then one pair came so low that they were about to pass over the *Carson*. Sorenson watched in fascination as the American fighter closed on the speeding Zeke. A final burst took off one wing, and the remaining wing and fuselage began to corkscrew down. Sorenson realized the remains of the aircraft were heading directly for the *Carson*. "Right full rudder," he shouted.

But it was too late, and the rapid descent of the wreckage was too unpredictable to avoid completely.

Sorenson watched helplessly as a piece of the burning engine crashed into the ship aft. A towering flame shot up, and Sorenson banged the rail in frustration. He turned to the talker. "Tell the repair party to get aft in a hurry. We've been hit and there's a big fire back there somewhere!"

The talker delivered the message, and almost immediately said, "Mount 53 says the wreckage lit in the whaleboat, and it's on fire. The mount crew, the after repair party, and the 40-millimeter crew are manning fire hoses."

Sorenson said, "Good! Tell CIC to have the Executive Officer go back there and take charge."

In CIC DuBose heard the explosion aft and the reports and headed for the door even before he heard the order from the Captain. He ran aft and noticed the towering flames as he approached.

He got within a few yards of the boat, but the flames were so hot he had to retreat. He saw the men aft of the fire playing mist on the boat, and huge clouds of steam were rising from it.

Then behind him he heard the forward repair party pounding down the deck. Chief Bellows stopped by his side. ''Not so bad,'' he said. ''Ve stop it.''

He turned to the forward repair party and gave a rapid set of orders. One man in an asbestos suit picked up a hose and started for the boat. As he advanced, he turned it on the boat, and the cooling water enabled him to get almost underneath it. By now flaming diesel fuel from the boat's engine and tank was spilling out through a burned-through hole in the boat's bottom and running all over the K-guns and their depth charges in adjacent racks on that side of the deck. Dubose yelled. ''We've got to cool all those depth charges! Get a hose on them!''

Bellows sent another man with a second hose to wet them down. By now a third member of the forward repair party had climbed to the torpedo deck and was dragging a hose back so that he could play it down into the boat from above.

''That did the trick!'' Dubose shouted.

The remaining diesel fuel was flushed out of the boat bottom and over the side. The fire began to die, and a last convulsion of white smoke went skyward.

Dubose knew it was over, and he heaved a sigh of relief. Losing a boat wasn't so bad, but if the depth charges had gone off, he would have been dead, or at best, swimming a long way from the ship. He turned to the chief. ''Nice work, Bellows.''

Bellows nodded. ''De men did it. De gun crew helped.''

Dubose trudged back to the bridge to report to the Captain. He suddenly realized he was so weary he felt like he was walking through sand.

On the bridge, Sorenson watched the dying phases of the air conflict above.

Then the TBS crackled. ''Hustler, this is Mangrove. Do you need any help?

Sorenson picked up the TBS transmitter. ''Mangrove this is Hustler. Negative. Thank you. Ready in all respects except for one boat and my K-gun battery.''

The Division Commander acknowledged the transmission and Sorenson put the TBS transmitter back in its holder.

He walked out on the bridge wing and watched Dubose climb slowly up the ladder to the bridge. ''Is the fire all out?''

''Yes, but Chief Bellows is keeping a hose on the depth charges until they cool down.''

''Were we in danger of losing our after section?''

''About fifty-fifty. The depth charges were all set on safe, but we couldn't get to them to jettison them. Still, it would have taken a lot of heat to set them off.''

''Burning diesel oil can get pretty hot.''

''Sure, but our gun crews started cooling them fairly quickly. If they hadn't reacted so fast, we might have been in trouble. Maybe we should take the fuel out of our boats before combat next time. We used to off Guadalcanal.''

''Yes, but your boats used gasoline then. Diesel oil is much safer. We have to have our boats ready for rescuing pilots, survivors, or for abandoning ship. I think it's a risk we have to take.''

Dubose nodded. ''I agree.''

''How did the repair parties do?''

''They were great. Between the crew of mount 53, the 40-millimeter crew, and the after repair party, they started the hoses going right away. Chief Bellows and his forward repair finished up. There wasn't much for me to do but watch.''

''Sometimes that's the hardest thing for an officer to do. Well done.''

''Thanks, but the credit goes to Chief Bellows. I'll never think of him as an old man again.''

''I hope he had his dental plates in.''

''Oh, yes. The men had no trouble understanding him, even if I did.''

Sorenson laughed. ''They're used to him. The officers and crew seem to be getting used to your accent, too. Maybe I was a little too heavy on the subject.''

Dubose laughed. ''I've tried to change, and I think I've partially succeeded. The other day a couple of southern boys asked me if I was turning Yankee. I had to tell them I was trying to get in the middle. But you were right,-- and I'm making progress.''

Two days later the *Carson* was detached, steamed into Milne Bay, and went alongside a tanker to fuel. While they were fueling, a representative of an Australian repair ship came aboard. Sorenson, Dubose, Steiner, and Auerbach went aft with him to plan repairs.

The Australian looked at the burned out hulk of the whaleboat at the davits and shook his head. ''Junk! We'll give you one of ours. They're about the same. We make them in the Sydney shipyard from your designs.''

''Can you repair our K-guns?''

''Easy, mate. The racks are just angle iron. The projectors themselves are relatively undamaged. You ought to replace all the depth charges that were close to the fire. Your ammo ship has lots of them.''

Sorenson said, ''I think the rest of the damage is small stuff our crew can handle if we have time in port.''

The Australian said, ''They told me you'd have seven days. Let me know if you need help. You'll need lots of paint for the deck and sides.''

Auerbach shook his head. ''We'll have to paint the whole ship aft of the torpedo mount.''

Dubose nodded. ''Just be glad we still have that part of the ship. We might have lost it.''

For the next seven days the crew worked hard to restore the after part of the ship. A new boat was delivered and painted Navy gray.

Toward the end of the period the *Carson* went alongside an ammunition ship to replace the ammunition expended at Wewak during the bombardment and replaced most of her depth charges.

She was as ready as her officers and men could make her.

Sorenson made two trips to the *Blue Ridge,* Admiral Barbey's flagship, and on the last trip came back with the news that a big operation was coming up soon and that the *Carson* would be part of it.

He dropped hints in the wardroom, but refused to give any details. On the sixth day he said at dinner, "I'll tell you all about it at a conference at 0800 tomorrow."

CHAPTER EIGHTEEN

Sorenson came to breakfast early the next morning in a somber mood. Only Doctor Fineman was there, stirring his black coffee and nibbling his dry toast.

Fineman looked up the table at Sorenson. ''I see somebody with a problem. Want to talk about it?''

''Not really, and it's not actually a problem. Sometimes I get pissed off over the slow progress of this war. I'd like to get it over with so we can all go home.''

''So would we all, although I don't have the same pleasures and comforts waiting for me at home that you have. Is that your problem?''

''I think about Ferren a lot. Of course I'd like to see her for my own selfish reasons, but I feel for her, all alone in Coronado for months and months.''

''Last time I heard she had twenty-eight close friends on her hands all day long.''

''Yes, all day long, but the nights and weekends must be very lonely for her.''

''Then she can use that time writing to you.''

''She has, but that isn't the way she planned her life.''

''I take it you've heard from her recently.''

''Yesterday. Maybe that's what made me mad when I heard the big operation I've been hearing about has been postponed for a month.''

"What's the trouble? Don't we have enough forces?"

"There's nothing wrong with our forces. They're ready to go. It's the damned Japs. They're having trouble moving south away from our next objective at Hollandia and down to Wewak. It seems they're having to hack trails through the deep jungle."

"Can't they travel by coastal shipping?"

"They could, but we destroyed all of their coastal transport when we bombarded Wewak."

Fineman laughed. "Hoisted on our own petard."

"Something like that."

"Surely the bigwigs will think up something for us to do in the meantime."

"Oh, yes. We got the Operation Order last night for an interim operation. We're going to be part of a group taking Los Negros Island, near Manus Island in the Admiralty Islands."

"What do we want with it?"

"It has a fine anchorage named Seeadler Harbor and an airfield named Momote."

"Seeadler? Sounds like a sea monster."

"I don't know the origin of the name, but it sounds ominous."

"We'll see whether anybody else knows where the name came from. We'll have a conference right after breakfast."

When the breakfast dishes were cleared, Sorenson began the conference by turning to Jablonski. "John, for once we don't need the chart of New Guinea. The big operation I've been hinting at has been postponed for a month."

There was a murmur of disappointment around the table.

Sorenson raised his hand. "I know how you feel, but, we'll be kept busy. We're to be part of a Task Group taking potential bases in the Admiralty Islands."

Jablonski produced charts of the Admiralty Islands and spread them on the table.

Sorenson said, "Los Negros is a small island just east of the bigger island of Manus. It has a sort of hour glass shape. One indentation on the west is called Seeadler Harbor. The indentation on the east is called Hyane Harbor. Momote Airfield is to the south of Hyane Harbor."

Fineman asked, "Does anyone know the origin of the name Seeadler?"

Steiner said, "Sure. Seeadler means sea eagle in German. That was the name of the German commerce raider Count Von Luckner brought to the Pacific during World War I. The western harbor was named after the raider because it was rumored that he visited there. There's a lot of argument about how far west he sailed."

Fineman said, "Thanks. I should have known that."

Steiner asked, "Is it well fortified?"

Sorenson nodded. "There are several large guns situated so they face to the west into Seeadler Harbor."

"So we're going to land in Hyane Harbor behind the gun emplacements," Steiner said.

Dubose broke in. "Right. A typical MacArthur ploy."

Steiner nodded, and Sorenson looked at Dubose out of the corner of his eye. Dubose was studying the chart.

Sorenson said, "We'll need the harbors for basing sea plane tenders and the airfield for basing long-range search aircraft."

Auerbach asked, "What kind of search aircraft will be used?'

"Three seaplane tenders will move into Seeadler Harbor as soon as possible, and each will operate thirteen PBY Catalinas. Another squadron of Navy Liberators will be based at Momote Airfield. They'll be able to cover the sea approaches clear up to the Southern Philippines."

Dubose put his finger on the chart and measured the distance from Wewak to the Admiralties. "I see the Admiralties are at least a hundred miles northeast of Wewak, but they should be safe from Japanese sea forces."

Sorenson said, "I agree. Now let's turn to the forces involved."

Dubose asked, "Will it be a big force?"

"No. Surprisingly small. The landing operations in the Cental Pacific run to twenty or even thirty APAs and AKAs carrying two divisions of troops and having six battleships prepare the landing area by days and days of bombardment. Our operation is a mere flea bite compared to those operations."

Steiner said, "There's a reason for it. The Japanese land forces in those areas run to thousands of well dug in troops, and it takes a lot to root them out. For some reason, in New Guinea, the Japanese fight differently. They don't dig in, and they often surrender in large numbers."

Sorenson said, "I think the reason we'll use such a small force is that the intelligence types don't think the Japanese are there in any strength. On the 23rd, a reconnaissance aircraft reported that they couldn't see any Japanese or even any signs of them, although the original intelligence estimate was about four thousand.

"This scouting report is what set up our operation. Three APDS embarking about a thousand soldiers of the First Cavalry Division will land at dawn at Hyane Bay in what is called an armed reconnaissance. This is an Army euphemism for, 'If the bastards kick us off, we'll say we were just looking to see if anybody was there.' "

Dubose sat forward. "I think it's a wise move, and typical of General MacArthur's flexibility."

Sorenson smiled. "I apologize for my remark. You're right."

Steiner said, "You were about to tell us which of our forces will be used."

"Ah, yes. The three APDs, of course, and the thousand troops. Then nine destroyers will escort the APDs and provide a short pre-landing bombardment. If any opposition is encountered, we'll be there to fire at it. There will be a covering force of two cruisers and six destroyers off shore to take care of any Japanese surface force that might show up."

Sorenson turned to Dubose, ''Forrest, you'll be interested to know that General MacArthur will be embarked in the *Nashville*, the lead cruiser.''

Steiner grinned. ''How many Japs did you say were present a minute ago?''

Sorenson realized he had put himself in a corner by pointing out that the early intelligence estimate was that there were no Japanese there. He could see Dubose clasping his hands to retain control. Sorenson said, ''General MacArthur will go ashore only if there are Japanese there.''

Dubose nodded in agreement, and Sorenson went on, ''We'll get under way tomorrow, and arrive off Hyane Harbor at dawn on the 29th. Are there any questions?''

There were none, and Sorenson went back to his cabin to re-read Ferren's last letters.

The trip to Los Negros was uneventful, and the ships steamed in formation, zizagging except at night. The trip up took two daylight periods, and even the rushing breeze from the 20 knots they were making failed to compensate for the equatorial sun beating down on the steel decks as they pushed north toward the equator. Sorenson looked over at the crowded APDs. The fast destroyer transports had been converted from four-stackers like the *O'Leary* in which he had served as executive officer in the Atlantic. Their forward boilers had been removed and troop berthing installed in the vacated space. Sorenson knew that even with this added space, the berthing compartment would only take about one hundred and thirty men. There were about three hundred and thirty soldiers on each APD. That meant that at least two hundred would have to spend at least one night sleeping on the hot decks.

Sorenson raised his binoculars and studied the topside of the APD nearest them. He saw Army soldiers wandering around on the topside. There was a long line forward waiting to get down to the messhall, and another long line aft waiting for a turn at the head. In between, soldiers had rigged pieces of canvas and blankets between the four landing craft the APDs carried aft to form tents. Many men were sprawled under this crude cover. Others sat on the upper parts of the ship with their shirts off. Many wore bush hats or pieces of cloth over their heads.

Sorenson sighed. In another day the men would either be enjoying swimming in the surf at Los Negros or fighting for their lives inland. War was a very iffy thing, he thought. Who knew what might happen to any man on any given day. Swim or die. Take your pick.

The second evening, just before the landing, Scorse brought up a decoded dispatch and handed it to Sorenson. Sorenson read it and shook his head. "It says General Krueger didn't trust the aircraft reconnaissance reports that said there were no Japanese on Los Negros and sent some scouts in from a Catalina flying boat. They landed in a rubber boat but didn't stay long. Their report was that the island was 'lousy with Japs.' But the message says we'll go ahead with the landing anyway."

Sorenson said to Scorse, "Route this around."

Sorenson sat back in his chair, thinking about the troops on the nearby APDs. Just like that the decision had been made for them. No swimming on an undefended beach; fighting instead. Sorenson was glad he was in the Navy. The fighting was just as tough, but in the Navy it seemed a little easier to control your destiny, and a lot more comfortable, he thought, as he ate a huge dinner from a tray Chief Williams had sent up.

After dinner Dubose came to report that the ship was ready for battle and that breakfast would be served to the crew at 0400.

Just after dark, Sorenson went to his sea cabin and laid down on his bunk fully clothed. He tried to sleep, but there was too much racing through his mind. About 0300 he got up, shaved, and went out to the bridge.

By now the air had cooled, and the 20 knot breeze racing by was very pleasant. Sorenson hoped the troops on the APDs were enjoying it. For some it would be their last earthly pleasure.

An hour before dawn the general alarm was sounded, and the crew raced to their stations. Sorenson sent his breakfast tray below and put on his rubber life preserver. He liked the new rubber belted-type designed for the tropics. It was lighter and less cumbersome and certainly cooler, but he remembered the old kapok type with fondness. The heavy kapok had caught many a sharp shard of glass or piece of steel shrapnel.

Scorse came to the bridge wearing a radio head set and plugged it into a receptacle on the bridge.

Sorenson said, "I take it that's going to be on the landing force frequency you were talking about."

"Yes. sir. I'll also have the circuit on the speaker up here, but I'm afraid at times it will be so loud and so busy you'll decide you want to turn the speaker down and have me summarize what's going on ashore."

"Good idea. Let's start out with the speaker."

Just at dawn the speeding destroyers slowed while the navigators picked their way into the unfamiliar harbor. The APDs went in to about five hundred yards off shore and lowered their LCVPs. The *Carson* and one other destroyer were ordered to take station on the flanks of the APDs and conduct preliminary fire against the beach.

Steiner swept the beach area with the director optics. "Don't see a damned thing except sand and palm trees and not many of them." Then he said, "I can see the backs of some heavy guns, but they're all sited to fire out into Seeadler Harbor."

Jablonski looked at the chart. "The neck of land between the two harbors is only about a half mile wide in the narrow part. The Japs outsmarted themselves. They thought anyone would naturally land on the beaches of Seeadler Harbor."

Sorenson said, ''Anyone but General MacArthur. Maybe Dubose has a point.''

Sorenson said to Steiner, now leaning out the hatch of the director. ''Put a few salvos into the back of the gun positions in case the Japanese crews are there somewhere out of sight.''

Steiner nodded, pulled his head back inside the director, and in a few seconds four-gun salvos were kicking up dirt and dust around the guns.

Between salvos Sorenson could hear the landing force circuit coming alive.

Then the firing ceased from the destroyers, and Steiner began to search the beach for possible return fire, but there was none.

Sorenson bent over the speaker listening to the crackle of radio transmissions and scratchy background noise. ''Get that damned rifle butt out of my ribs,'' came an irate voice.

Scorse laughed. ''That transmission must have come from someone in the company commander's boat. He had his transmitter button down.''

Sorenson asked, ''Where is it?''

Jablonski, who had been watching the progress of the first wave of boats toward the beach, said, ''About fifty yards from thebeach.''

Then another voice said, ''Any fire yet?''

Scorse said, ''That's the landing force commander. He's scheduled to go ashore in the third wave.''

Then over the landing force circuit there was the roar of a boat exhaust and a heavy splash. ''The first ramp is down,'' Scorse said.

Jablonski lowered his binoculars. ''That's right. There are eight boats on the beach and another four just behind in the second wave. I don't see any firing.''

Then the voice in the first boat said, ''No fire from ashore. Disembarking.''

Then there was a heavy splash and a curse. Scorse laughed, ''Sounds like he made it the hard way.''

There were sounds of heavy breathing and then another report, ''No opposition. I'm in the tree line.''

Sorenson looked at the chart. ''Then he's practically on the edge of Momote Airfield.''

Almost as if the voice had heard him, it reported. ''On the edge of the airfield.''

The landing craft were now back at the APDs loading troops, and soon they had landed them and were back for a third and final load.

By 0800 the APDs were empty and headed out the harbor.

At 0950 the voice reported, ''Occupied Momote Air Field. Have set up a perimeter four thousand yards from beach. Safe for resurrection.''

Sorenson said, ''What the hell does that mean?'

Scorse shrugged. ''Code word, I guess.''

Jablonski turned and looked toward the harbor entrance behind them. The Cruiser *Nashville* was nosing into the harbor. He said, ''There's your answer.''

Sorenson said, ''Resurrection is General MacArthur?''

''Who else?''

The *Nashville* closed the beach and lowered a boat. Sorenson watched as it came alongside the cruiser's side and loaded. ''Jesus! There's more brass in that boat than at a West Point parade.''

The boat left the side and went to the beach. Sorenson could see a large group of officers and men gathered to meet the boat. He shook his head. I hope the Japs don't counter-attack right now. Threre's nobody left in the front lines.''

But there was no daylight counter-attack, and Colonel Chase, in command ashore now, wisely pulled his perimeter back to fifteen hundred yards after General MacArthur had departed.

After General MacArthur left, the situation returned to normal, and the *Carson* remained in Hyane harbor on call to provide gun fire support in the event of a night attack on the First Cavalry forces dug in ashore.

That night, about 2300, the landing Force circuit came alive. ''Enemy on our front,'' came a voice. Gunfire flashed ashore, apparently small arms.

Sorenson had gone to general quarters at the first shots. Five minutes later the request came for gunfire support, and down in CIC Dubose and Bronte plotted the coordinates of the target and calculated the range and bearing from the travelling point of light on the DRT. In seconds all four guns roared, and the darkness was split by the four bright tracers winging their way ashore. The explosions of the projectiles ashore could be seen as bright flashes and then heard clearly.

''Down one hundred,'' came the voice of the controller ashore.

Another salvo went out. Sorenson waited impatiently.

Then the voice said. ''No change! Rapid fire!''

The guns began to crank out salvos every five seconds, and a huge pall of smoke rose in the expanding illumination of the explosions.

The speaker crackled urgently. ''Cease firing! They're infiltrating us. Shift to illuminating fire!''

Main battery plot calculated new gun orders designed to put star shells a thousand feet above the area.

The guns, with the new orders, rose in elevation and when the fuses of the starshells had been set and the starshell projectiles loaded, the *Carson* resumed fire. Twenty seconds later greenish blue lights blossomed above the area of combat ashore. Parachutes deployed above each flare, and the brilliant stars of illumination slowly descended to the ground.

''Great!'' came the voice over the speaker. ''Keep it up.''

For half an hour the *Carson* lobbed starshells over the area so that a new salvo burst just before the last one went out.

Then a triumphant voice said over the radio, ''We got'em all. Cease firing and thanks. There must be three hundred Jap dead around us, and the rest are bugging out.''

Sorenson secured from general quarters and set condition III, with one mount ready to fire if called for.

Daylight was almost full as the men left their guns and made their way down to the living compartments for breakfast.

As he watched his men move below, Sorenson thought again about the soldiers of both armies on the beach. This morning many who were alive last night would never see another tropical night, and many more would die. It was a tough war, and it would get worse as they moved nearer and nearer to the Japanese homeland.

Sorenson sent for his breakfast and sat down in his chair to wait for it. He was bone weary, but not nearly as exhausted as he had been in the punishing Atlantic where the weather had been as much of a foe as the big German submarines.

Vila brought his breakfast up, and he was just getting through the first order of scrambled eggs he had eaten for a week when the TBS squawked. ''Hustler, take position in Seeadler harbor and prepare to bombard gun emplacements.''

''What!'' Sorenson said, ''We did that yesterday from this side of the isthmus.''

Dubose came running up with a piece of toast in his hand. ''CIC sent word down that we're to move.''

Sorenson said, ''Yes, and I don't understand exactly what we're to do. I'm going to move to Seeadler harbor and see what the situation is like there. While we move around, you might see if you can pin the Army down as to where their frontline positions are. We don't want to hit any of them by mistake.''

Dubose crammed the last bit of toast in his mouth. ''On the way.''

Sorenson reluctantly called Jablonski back to the bridge. Jablonski came up the ladder buttoning his shirt and rubbing his eyes.

Sorenson laughed. ''How did you get to sleep so soon?''

''I skipped breakfast. I guess that was a mistake.''

''No, but you may be up here for some time. I'll send down for some for you. Plot a course out of here and around to the other side of the island to Seeadler Harbor. Let me know how long it will take us to get there as soon as you can. We'll leave right away and steam at 20 knots.''

Jablonski busied himself with the chart, with Sorenson looking over his shoulder.

They both agreed on a course out of Hyane Harbor and Sorenson gave it to MacIntosh, who had the deck.

Jablonski drew a track on the chart and measured the distance. ''Thirty minutes,'' he said.

Sorenson turned to MacIntosh. ''I hate to do this, but pass the word that we'll go to general quarters in thirty minutes.''

The boatswain's mate of the watch blew his pipe and passed the word. When he had finished there was a collective moan from those on watch on the bridge.

Sorenson grinned. ''Boats, get men up here after they've eaten to relieve the watch so they can all have breakfast. We'll delay entrance to Seeadler harbor a few minutes if we have to so that all hands can eat.''

The boatswain's mate grinned. ''Thank you, Captain, my stomach was about to rebel.''

On the trip around the island, Scorse turned the radio speaker on the bridge tuned to the landing force circuit back on.

At first there were a meaningless series of reports. Then Sorenson realized they were numerical coordinates and that he would have to see the chart to recognize them. He left the bridge when they were clear of Hyane Harbor and went down to CIC. Dubose and Bronte were bent over an Army Map of the island of the kind used to make shore bombardments. Terrain lines in light blue showed the altitude above sea level at ten foot intervals. Terrain features were clearly labelled, and most important of all, the map was gridded with a series of numbered lines. Each grid had a number and the lines were at one hundred meter intervals. The first number located a line. The second number located a point on it to ten meters. The third number located the point even closer to one meter. Thus, a six figure number could locate a square meter section of the island. Unless the enemy had a copy of the chart, the location was secure. Using it, an observer ashore could quickly and easily designate a target to a ship, which would then plot the target on the Army map and measure off the range and bearing from its own position on the chart to the designated target. In seconds the information could be applied to the computer in the five-inch fire control system, and the projectiles could be on their way to the litle square meter of sand. Of course, errors were introduced, and the subsequent salvos had to be corrected, but the system was accurate and rapid.

As Sorenson came into CIC, Dubose and Bronte were examining the Army map for the location of possible targets. Indentations in the terrain lines and other geographical features indicated where the Japanese might have emplaced guns.

Finally, Dubose raised his head. "I don't see any logical locations. We'll have to wait until the Army tells us what they want us to shoot at."

Bronte was copying a series of six number designations. Dubose said, "He's copying the location of the front lines."

When the transmission ceased, Bronte began plotting the locations. Sorenson and Dubose crowded over his shoulder. Sorenson said, "Looks like there is a strip of beach front about a mile wide fronting Seeadler Harbor that the Japs still control. There must be other guns we didn't see from the rear the other day."

In half an hour Dubose reported the crew had all eaten, and Sorenson ordered MacIntosh to sound General Quarters. Within minutes, the *Carson* rounded the northern extreme of Seeadler Harbor and slowed.

Sorenson said to the talker, ''Tell the gunnery officer to search the beach and the land behind it. Be prepared to open fire if we're fired on.''

Then he said, ''Tell CIC to ask the Army what targets they want destroyed.''

Sorenson heard the message going out on the bridge speaker. There was an interval before a reply came back. Sorenson listened to it open-mouthed. ''Hustler, there are enemy guns just behind the beach, but we don't know where they are. We'd like you to draw their fire so you can locate them and then destroy them.''

When the last part of the message had come in, Sorenson banged his fist on the wooden bulwark. ''What do they think we are, a target in a shooting gallery?''

Dubose's voice came over the squawkbox. ''Captain, I know you're angry, but we can do it. I have faith in Steiner.''

Sorenson was still boiling but said, ''Acknowledge the message.''

Sorenson called Steiner down to the bridge and explained the situation to him. ''You will have to be able to switch targets in a hurry. At the first sign of enemy activity, I'll maneuver radically. That will bother them more than it will you. By the way, the Executive Officer expressed great confidence in you.''

Steiner grinned, but said nothing.

''Go on back up to the director. CIC will give you the initial coordinates of the most suspicious areas. Let me know when you're ready.''

Steiner left, and in a few minutes the talker said, ''The gunnery officer says he's ready.''

Sorenson went to the IMC internal communication transmitter and pulled down the transmitter lever. ''This is the Captain speaking. We're about to conduct a dangerous mission. We'll fire at suspected targets ashore in order to try to make them shoot at us. Then we'll take them under fire. All men topside not part of the 5-inch battery take cover below decks.''

Sorenson turned to the talker. ''Commence firing.''

A salvo crashed out, and Sorenson raised his binoculars. Dirt rose in huge mounds. Above the bridge the director slewed quickly to the next bearing and another salvo followed the first, extending the line of rising dust. Several more salvos went out before any reaction came. Then Sorenson saw a winking flash at the base of the last explosions ashore.

Jablonski shouted, ''That did it. They're firing at us.''

Sorenson waited anxiously while the projectile was on its way. Above he could hear Steiner calmly giving orders to shift their fire to the location of the flash. Then the single projectile hit a hundred yards short. Sorenson was tempted to turn toward the splash, but resisted the impulse and turned away instead. Two more guns opened up ashore. The *Carson*'s 5-inchers roared in rapid fire, and Sorenson did not see how anything ashore at that close range could stand up to the hail of steel and explosives.

Several Japanese projectiles landed even shorter than the first, and Sorenson was glad he had turned away. Steiner was raking the area with four projectiles arriving at five-second intervals. One enemy gun stopped firing, and then there was a huge explosion in the vicinity of the other two. The enemy fire stopped. Even before Sorenson could give the order to cease firing, the Army commander said, ''That did it. Your first salvo blew the camouflage off the guns and your last salvo did the trick. You got all three. We can see a lot of Japs lying around the guns, and we're about to attack. Please cease fire.''

Sorenson gave the order to stop firing and sent the word down to CIC to acknowledge the Army request.

He sat down wearily and said to MacIntosh. ''Tell all stations 'well done.' Secure from general quarters and set condition III.''

Twenty-four hours later another destroyer was ordered into Seeadler Harbor to relieve the *Carson*. When they were relieved, the *Carson* joined the patrol group off the harbor.

On the Army communication net Sorenson could hear the Army reporting their casualties so far as eighty-five dead and the count of Japanese bodies as over a thousand.

Fineman came up to the bridge. Sorenson could see him looking closely at his face. "What's the matter? Didn't I shave closely enough?"

Fineman shook his head. I'm not interested in your face. I want to know how your mind is."

Sorenson pointed at the peaceful sea around them and the gentle bow wave coming back under the forecastle. "Not as peaceful as this scene. Just a few miles over there men are killing each other."

"And we've just finished our part of it."

"Yes, I suppose it was our duty, but it was all pretty impersonal."

"Are you beginning to feel a little battle fatigue?"

"My God, no! This is a piece of cake compared to what you and I went through in the Atlantic. Another beautiful day like this and I'll be raring to go."

Fineman pulled a piece of paper out of his pocket. "I just decoded this. Maybe it will help."

Sorenson read it. "We're detached with two other destroyers tomorrow and we're to proceed to Milne Bay."

Fineman said, "A great place to recuperate."

Sorenson smiled. "That's where the mail is."

"I thought you'd think about that," Fineman said.

"Yes. But we're off again in a very big operation in about a month."

"Good," Fineman said, "But let's enjoy the moment now. It's a beautiful scene out there."

CHAPTER NINETEEN

Two days later the *Carson* and her accompanying destroyers entered Milne Bay, and the *Carson* went alongside a tanker to fuel. An hour later the mail orderly brought aboard four sacks of mail. While it was being sorted, Sorenson let Bentley get the ship underway and take her to an anchorage. Bentley made it with out damage to the ship, but not without sweating his shirt through.

Then all hands answered mail call, and there was silence broken by occasional whoops of joy as individual men received good news.

Sorenson read Ferren's letters with relief. Other than an outbreak of chicken pox among the children, Ferren was having little trouble with her young charges. Sorenson heaved a sigh of relief.

Early the next morning Sorenson went over to Admiral Barbey's flagship. On the *Carson*, breakfast was over quickly as all the officers awaited the news from Sorenson. After he returned, he deliberately prolonged his breakfast, asking for extra cups of coffee.

Finally Renard put down his own third cup and said, "Come on, Captain, stop stalling. We want to know all the dirt."

Sorenson laughed. "You were very patient." He turned to Jablonski. "John, bring down our New Guinea chart."

Jablonski reached down behind the sterilizer and pulled it up. "Had it right here all the time, Captain, but I thought it might grow mold on it while you were getting ready."

Jablonski spread it on the wardroom table, and the officers gathered around.

Sorenson cleared his throat ostentatiously. "Here we go. You will all remember what we said last conference about drawing the Japanese southeast toward Wewak with our bombardment and deception plans. Well, we finally did it, after a month's delay. Fifth Air Force reconnaissance shows Japanese forces now moving down the trails from Hollandia toward Wewak. By the time of the next operation, they'll be there in force and the areas we are going to attack will be severely weakened. The bush up there is so heavy and the trails so primitive that the Japanese will take at least a month to get back to Hollandia."

Steiner said, "I'll be the first to admit that General MacArthur's plan shows some military genius. All I can say beyond that is that I wish he'd demonstrated it in the Philippines."

Dubose nodded his head, but didn't say anything.

Sorenson stood up and leaned over the middle of the chart. "You know where Wewak is, about the middle of the back of the bird. We are going to make three separate landings in the Hollandia region north of Wewak. The three sites are Aitape, Tanahmerah Bay, and Humboldt Bay. "Aitape is on the coast about 50 miles northwest of Wewak. But the 50 miles are almost impassable, as the Japanese have just found out."

Bentley chuckled. "We should have offered to take them down there in our landing craft."

The older officers groaned, and Sorenson continued, ''A force called the Eastern Attack Group, will land at Aitape. This force will be composed mostly of APDs but will also include an LSD and an AK. There will be an ample number of destroyers for screening and fire support.''

Dubose said, ''A pretty small operation.''

Sorenson nodded. ''There won't be many Japanese there, and the Army thinks the force is adequate for the task.''

''Who gets Tanahmerah Bay?'' Steiner asked. ''That seems like a small operation, too.''

Sorenson said. ''The Western Attack Force under Admiral Barbey. There are two schools of thought here. One says there aren't any Japanese there. The other says there probably is a good-sized force there. The planners have designated a strong force to take it. The fact that Admiral Barbey himself is in command means that he thinks it will be difficult.''

Reifel asked, ''What forces will he have?''

Sorenson said, ''Two Australian transports, One American transport, one LSD, seven LSTs, and sixteen LCIGs. Of course an adequate number of destroyers.''

Steiner said, ''You haven't mentioned us yet. I suppose you're saving the best for last.''

Sorenson said, ''At least I'm saving the biggest part of the operation for last. Humboldt Bay is about 50 miles farther north than Aitape and has the most potential for future use. It can be developed into a major base. The Central Attack Force will take it, led by Admiral Fechteler. His force won't be any bigger than the others, but we'll be part of it, and that ought to count for something.''

The officers down the table grinned. Renard said, ''If necessary we could sing the Japs to sleep.''

There was a groan, and Renard shrugged his shoulders.

Sorenson said, ''There will also be a sizeable group of PT boats covered by two Australian cruisers, two Australian destroyers, and two American destroyers, working over the coast between Aitape and Wewak. They'll bombard as far inland as they can reach, and the PT boats will go in next to the beach looking for small craft trying to ferry troops back up to Aitape. As soon as the Japanese figure out we are going to bypass them, they'll head north by every means possible."

"After the bombardment we made, there shouldn't be much left in the way of coastal shipping," Steiner said.

Dubose said, "Probably not, but the Japanese are very tenacious. They'll repair every vessel they can, and they'll even use native canoes."

Sorenson went on, "Well, so much for the forces and their objectives. We need to study the forthcoming Operation Order for our part in it."

"When will we get it?" Dubose asked.

"Tomorrow, I hope. We need every day we can get. We get underway the sixteenth."

Two mornings later Scorse came back from the flagship with two copies of the Operation Order for the Hollandia landings. All the officers gathered in the wardroom, and Sorenson divided one copy of the Operation Order into sections and passed them out to the responsible officers. The other copy he took the binding off of and started to read through it. As he finished each page, he handed it to Dubose. In an hour they had all digested their portions, and Sorenson called for a general discussion.

"First," he said, "I'll summarize the movement order. We get underway on the sixteenth with almost the whole Seventh Fleet. This will be the largest operation yet in this part of the world. We will go by a circuitous route to a point about a hundred miles north of Seeadler Harbor. The LCIs will have left early and will let the troops aboard go ashore at Seeadler to rehearse. Then they'll leave to rendezvous with us. The next day we'll meet and start south toward the landing areas. This route should confuse any submarine or aircraft reconnaissance the Japanese may be able to mount. The eight escort carriers and their screening destroyers will rendezvous with us and will then provide continuous combat air patrol and antisubmarine patrol. When the three groups arrive off the landing beaches, the escort carriers will also furnish prelanding air strikes and air support after the landings.

"As we head southwest, the Southern and Northern Attack Forces will peel off and head for their areas. We will continue on and head for Humboldt Bay. The day for the landings has been set for April 22."

Dubose nodded. "Sounds good. I don't see anything I would change."

Steiner said, "A bold plan. The General is learning all the time."

Dubose looked at the overhead and visibly gritted his teeth. Sorenson, watching him, hurried on. "Our job will be as part of the antisubmarine screen for the transit to the area. After arrival at Humboldt Bay, we take positon as a member of the bombardment group. Chuck, this is your business. Tell us what we'll do."

Steiner stood up and pointed to the portion of the chart containing Humboldt Bay. "First, Humboldt Bay has great potential as a base for future operations. The bay itself is about four miles wide at the mouth and three miles deep. It will be difficult to provide protection for large ships against submarines for larger ships, but I suppose the bay will be used mainly by small amphibious craft. There is a small inner bay named Jautefa Bay at the center of the big bay. Small landing craft can get into it with difficulty. Beach White One is planned for the middle of the base of Humboldt Bay and Beach White Two is just inside Jautefa Bay. LSTs will beach at Beach White One, but only LVTs, DUKWs, and LCVPs can get into Beach White Two. The exit areas from both beaches are difficult, but what's new about that?"

Dubose said, "That probably has been taken into consideration."

Steiner said, "I hope so."

Bentley asked, "Just what do these LVTs and DUKWs look like?"

Steiner said, "The LVT is a tank-like craft developed by the Marines for transit across reefs and shallow water. A lot of them were used at Tarawa to cross the reef. The Army developed and prefers the DUKW. It's a combination vehicle and boat, operating like a truck on land. In the water, its body will float like a boat and it even has a propeller sticking out the back. Both of them will make about four knots afloat, and the DUKW's wheels will outrun the LVT's treads ashore. Neither has much armor."

"Thanks," Bentley said. "I'm glad I'm not riding in either one of them."

Steiner said, "Now comes our part. We take position on the north side of the transport area and boat lanes together with one light cruiser and two other destroyers." He pointed to the chart. "Here's our operating area."

Sorenson said, "What about the other side of the transport area?"

"Two cruisers and two destroyers will take care of it."

Sorenson said, "Well, so much for the plan. Now we get ready for the actual battle. Let's study this order some more and make sure we have our communications set up for it. Scorse, this will be the most complicated communication plan we've had so far. Are you set up for it?"

Sorenson noticed how lean Scorse had gotten. The eyes that had looked like buttons in a fat bun a few months ago now peered out of a very lean and angular face. His hair was black and curly, and Sorenson thought how much he now looked like the pictures of old Roman warriors in his history books. Now he was almost too thin, and Sorenson thought he would ask Fineman to take a look at him.

Scorse spoke up confidently. "There will be times when we'll have to make some fast shifts of equipment, but we can cover all of our assigned frequencies and still put an extra landing force frequency up on the bridge like we've done before."

Sorenson nodded. "Good. Chief, is the plant ready?"

Reifel, unlike Scorse, had put on weight, and Sorenson noted a new confidence in his deep voice as he said, "Ready now, Captain."

Sorenson turned to Steiner. ''Chuck, we're scheulded to load ammunition tomorrow. Then I assume you'll be ready.''

Steiner nodded.

Sorenson said, ''Then I guess we're all ready.''

Auerbach spoke up, ''You didn't ask me.''

Sorenson laughed. ''You're always ready.''

CHAPTER TWENTY

On the sixteenth most of the ships in Milne Bay got underway. Many of the APAs, LSTs, and LCIs had already loaded their troops from staging areas farther south, and joined the formation off Milne Bay.

The *Carson* was assigned a screening station and began to patrol. In the pilothouse, Sorenson looked at a chart on which Jablonski had laid out the proposed track to a point well north of Seeadler Harbor. He said to Jablonski, "If I didn't know where we were going, I'd think we were lost."

Jablonski nodded. "That's what the Japs are supposed to think."

Sorenson took off his cap and ruffled his blond hair. "I wonder what's going on in the minds of the Japanese defenders on Los Negros Island?"

Jablonski said, "I made a trip to the flagship for some new charts. They said we've captured the whole island and have landed on Manus Island, the big one next door. We lost about three hundred men overall, but the Japanese lost over three thousand. The Navy is going to move a seagoing drydock and moor many large repair and logistics ships in Manus Harbor. That will make up a large naval base there."

Sorenson said, ''Maybe we'll go there next for some overhaul.''

Jablonski grinned, ''More like Sydney. I asked about it, and they said we had a good chance in a month or so. The repair facilities are very good in Sidney. Almost like the States.''

''And I suppose there are other interesting things there?''

''Oh, yes, they told me that that kind of thing in Sydney is better than it is in the States.''

The formation, held to a low speed by the slower amphibious craft, steamed slowly along. Sorenson wiped his brow frequently. In the southern hemisphere, April was like fall in the States, but they were so close to the equator that there wasn't much seasonal difference. Every day was hot. Some more than others. Now, at midday, Sorenson's shirt was soaked through. He tried to stand where the slight breeze made by the ship's motion could cool him, but even this didn't help much. While the sun was near the vertical at noon, everyone just suffered. He looked over at the LSTs, LCIs, and transports. All the men who could crowd up on the upper decks were either walking slowly about the decks or sitting on the deck. The ships looked like they were covered with green ants.

Sorenson sent for some iced tea, feeling guilty that he should have such a privilege while many men on ships nearby were undoubtedly drinking tepid, chlorine-flavored water. He drank it quickly. He knew the men on the transports couldn't see him that far away, but he felt less guilty.

By nightfall the weather had cooled, and the next day was cloudy and rainy. The heat was replaced by humidity, and Sorenson was grateful the next day when the sun came back and dried out the canvas gun covers and other equipment topside before mold could start.

Two days later, they passed Seeadler Harbor, and the LCIs there came out and joined them.

That afternoon they saw the first of the aircraft flying from the eight escort carriers, and from then on there was a combat air patrol of fighters overhead in daylight hours and an antisubmarine patrol of SBDs around the screen.

Sorenson felt safer, and he was sure the convoyed ships did. Standing next to Auerbach, he watched the aircraft flying overhead, and he asked Auerbach if he still missed flying.

Auerbach thought for a minute. Then he said, ''If I can leave aviation as you did and get command of a ship, then I'll be reasonably happy. I'd still like to fly, but I can't.''

Sorenson said, ''It's all up to you. You've made a good start. I suggest you start studying to be Steiner's replacement. That's the next step up the ladder to command of a destroyer.''

Auerbach said, ''I already have. I've completed the course on how to be a gunnery officer, and Steiner has told me to come up to the director for the next firings if you approve.''

''Certainly. That's where you'll learn the most. You've made a good start.''

The Center Attack Group steamed south during the night, and about 0300 Jablonski called Sorenson on the telephone and told him they had Cape Soeadja on the radar. Sorenson yawned and slapped his jaw, trying to wake up. Jablonski said, ''It's the cape at the north side of the entrance to Humboldt bay and is a prime radar mark. We'll be off the bay by 0500, right on schedule.''

Sorenson got up, washed, shaved, and dressed and sent for his breakfast. He went out to the pilothouse just as the officer of the deck sounded general quarters. He looked at his radium-dialed watch. "Just on time. Did all the crew get to eat?"

Steele, who had the deck, said, "Yes, sir. Renard says in one meal they went through his whole week's ration allowance."

"Good. They might not get anything but sandwiches on station the next few days."

At 0530 Admiral Fechteler broke up the formation, and the tranports and landing ships headed for their areas off the middle of the Bay. Two destroyers and two cruisers headed for the south side of the transport area. Sorenson looked at the area Jablonski had marked on the chart. "I see the positions the other ships are going to. Is this northern one still ours?"

"Yes. The Cruiser *Nashville* is outboard of us, and we two destroyers take station just inside the harbor's northern edge. We're supposed to remain underway, but lie to in the same location."

"I suppose General MacArthur is embarked in the *Nashville*?"

"Yes, sir. He'll be looking right down our back."

"I hope Dubose knows about this. He'll be wanting to catch a glimpse of his hero."

Jablonski laughed. "I'm sure he will. I'd just as soon Steiner didn't know. He might be tempted to get off a salvo backwards."

The sea was calm, with hardly a ripple. There was some overcast, but usually it burned off just after dawn, and today seemed to be no exception. Sorenson looked at the bridge clock. It was just 0550, and he knew sunrise would be about 0634. In a few minutes the short tropical period before daylight would begin.

He paced back and forth, watching the clock. Just as the hands reached 0600 the guns on the *Nashville* to seaward of them boomed out. The sound was overwhelming. The 6-inch projectiles rushed overhead, seemingly just missing the mast head of the *Carson*. Sorenson thought he could feel the hot wind as the first salvo went over. There was a short period while the gun crews in the mounts on the *Nashville* worked to load the 6-inch guns. Sorenson was glad they weren't the 16-inch guns of battleships. Then another salvo went out, and others followed quickly.

Sorenson lifted his binoculars, looking for the explosions ashore.

''There!'' Jablonski said. ''Their target is three 3-inch antiaircraft guns in the tall Kunai grass on Pancake Hill, the slight elevation just back of the harbor and just beyond the right edge of Beach White One.''

Sorenson searched the area, but waving Kunai grass was all he could see. The projectiles exploded in the grass, huge clouds of dust rose high in the air, and then the flattened Kunai grass straightened up again. ''The damned stuff is like wire!'' he said.

He glanced at the transports and landing craft unloading on their port beam. Small LCVPs, DUKWs and LVTs scurried around the larger ships, loading troops. Beyond them, on the other end of the bay, the other two cruisers pounded the area around Cape Dejar on the other extreme of the Bay.

He looked at the clock again. It was 0615. There were still 15 minutes before the *Carson* and the other destroyers were scheduled to begin the bombardment. Now Steiner was training the 5-inch battery on the elevations above the beach watching for fire that might come out from the beach.

No response came from the Japanese, and at 0630 the *Carson*'s 5-inch guns thundered. The cruisers stopped firing, their mission completed. Steiner raked the beach first and then lifted his fire to the elevated highlands beyond the beach. For half an hour the *Carson* poured a steady stream of steel and explosives into the most probable areas of gun emplacements ashore. Some small fires flared. Just bfore 0700, the scheduled time of the landings, a group of carrier aircraft roared in from the northwest and zoomed over the beach, strafing and dropping bombs. Sorenson knew from the operation order that Avengers were laying antipersonnel bombs back of the beach and other bombs designed to detonate Japanese antipersonnel mines in the beach area.

Sorenson estimated that by now the cruisers had fired almost two thousand rounds of 6-inch ammunition and that the destroyers had fired about four thousand rounds of 5-inch.

The *Carson* was still firing at the area back of the beach and was supposed to keep firing even after H-hour at 0700.

About 0715 it became evident that there would be no return fire, and Sorenson ordered, "Cease firing."

The bridge crew took the cotton out of their ears and rubbed them. Sorenson noticed that his were still ringing, and he rubbed his head vigorously. The rubbing didn't help his ears, but it eased the muscle tension in his scalp. That felt so good he took off his steel helmet and rubbed the rest of his head.

In the lull, he went to the port wing and watched the landing craft go by. Each was full of helmeted and heavily equipped men. Some of the LCVPs in the later waves carried artillery pieces.

Scorse had been listening to the landing force circuit during the firing, and now that there was a lull in the firing, he turned the bridge speaker up. Sorenson said, "What's been happening on that circuit?"

Scorse said, "It's been very quiet. The first wave landed on time with no opposition. They say in the center of Beach White One there is a huge pile of Japanese equipment including ammunition. The beach and the area behind it are very small, and they are having a hard time getting through all the Japanese junk. Many of the men are stopping to take souvenirs."

Then a voice came up on the landing force circuit. "We've just entered what must be the Japanese headquarters here. The rice on the table is still warm. They left in a hurry."

Then there was a noise in the background, and the radio operator forgot to, or couldn't, release his transmitter button. On the *Carson* bridge they could plainly hear a man curse loudly. "Jesus!" he shouted. "This fish tasted like some body has already eaten it!"

Another voice said, "Shut up, Fatso, I can't get this transmitter button to release and the colonel can hear everything you say."

Fatso said, "Well, tell him not to eat the fish when he gets here."

Sorenson shook his head. "Why is it the Japanese in the Central Pacific are dug in so well and fight so hard, and these bastards down here run away?"

At 0800 troops reported occupying Pancake Hill, the site of the three antiaircraft guns at which the *Carson* had fired. On the landing force circuit came the report, "Two guns are destroyed, but one undamaged."

Sorenson shook his head. "I can't believe we laid all that ammunition up there and one gun lived through it without a scratch."

On the circuit came the word that they had captured many prisoners and that there had been only a few enemy rifle shots.

At 0900 the landing force commander, General Fuller, landed and assumed command ashore. Sorenson said, "Keep an eye on the *Nashville* and ask the Executive Officer to come up to the bridge."

Dubose came up the ladder on the run, puffing slightly. Sorenson said, "You and I need a workout. Remind me when we get back to port."

Dubose grinned and said, "You sent for me?"

"Yes. I wanted you to have a chance to salute your hero at close range in a few minutes."

Sorenson and Dubose went out on the port bridge wing and leaned against the bulwark, watching the bustle on the *Nashville* close astern. A boat was lowered and rapidly filled with the usual cargo of brass-hatted officers.

Promptly at 1000 General MacArthur embarked, and the boat headed for shore. Sorenson thought it would pass close aboard the *Carson*, and it did, barely 30 yards away. General MacArthur stood in the stern, wearing sunglasses and a crushed hat with a gold-braided visor, and smoking his corncob pipe.

Dubose watched, his mouth partially open, and when the boat passed, he snapped a smart salute.

Sorenson wasn't sure, but he thought he could hear a rude noise from the gun director above.

The telephone talker smiled. "Mister Steiner says that only an idiot would smoke in a boat. He deserves to be blown up."

Sorenson glanced apprehensively at Dubose, but he was still absorbed in watching the departing boat.

Sorenson said, "Tell Mister Steiner to keep a close watch on the hills above the beaches. This may not be over yet."

The Japanese offered no opposition, and the troops occupied all their objectives by nightfall.

The *Carson* withdrew and took her place in an antisubmarine screen off the entrance to the harbor. Sorenson secured the crew from general quarters, and the men had their first meal since before dawn. During the day the cooks had distributed hundreds of sandwiches, but Sorenson knew they didn't fill the stomachs of the hardworking men serving the guns and feeding the boilers below.

Sorenson kept the landing force circuit on the bridge turned up and sat in his chair listening to the reports from shore. Now that the landing force commander was ashore, they were sparse and laconic. At one point the landing force commander reported that he had lost only six men. Then he said the congestion on the beach at White One was getting worse instead of better and that the engineers would be working all night to bulldoze a road from the beach to the heights above.

Sorenson picked up his binoculars and scanned the Beach White One area. Darkness had fallen, but there was a steady glow from a fire that illuminated the whole area. The huge piles of American equipment and supplies had been added to the Japanese stores, and the whole beach was unbelievably crowded. He could see men and vehicles moving around the piles. Sorenson was concerned. The fire was growing in size, and no one seemed to be trying very hard to put it out. About midnight weariness overwhelmed him, and he slept in his chair until dawn general quarters.

The next day the landing force continued to press west toward Lake Sentani, about four miles to the west. The Japanese had begun the construction of three airfields there, and the Fifth Air Force wanted to take them and use them as soon as possible.

At noon Doctor Fineman brought up a decoded dispatch giving a summary of the landings at Aitape and Tanahmerah Bay. Sorenson scanned the dispatch and noted that the landings were progressing on schedule. The dispatch said that the landings here at Humboldt Bay were also progressing on schedule, but Sorenson's instincts told him there was trouble ahead. He raised his binoculars and scanned the area behind Beach White One. The pile of equipment and supplies was just as big as it had been the day before, and the fire was still smouldering. Occasional sparks flew up and landed in the adjacent piles.

During the day, several LSTs from a follow-on echelon entered the Bay and added their cargo to the mess on the beach.

Shortly after 2045 that night, an aircraft droned over head. Sorenson went to general quarters, but the aircraft dropped a single bomb near the fires on Beach White One and beat a low level retreat across the mountains.

Sorenson started to secure from general quarters, but something told him to wait. Within minutes there was a volcanic explosion ashore. Pieces of vehicles and equipment flew high in the air. The shock wave threw the men on the bridge against the bulkhead.

The talker got up and said, ''Mister Reifel down in the engine room wants to know if there's been an earthquake.''

Sorenson said, ''Tell him it's worse. An ammunition dump ashore has blown up.''

Then additional explosions split the night. These were obviously more Japanese ammunition from the captured stock, and projectiles and flares rose into the air and exploded like a fourth of July display. Pieces of projectiles landed three miles away from the beach, and Sorenson kept the crew at general quarters and the machine-gunners under cover for protection from the falling debris. He stayed inside the pilothouse watching the explosions. Again and again the ship shook as the explosions ashore continued.

By 0400 the explosions and fires had subsided enough for Sorenson to secure from general quarters, but throughout the next morning fires raged through the dump.

At midmorning several more LSTs arrived and milled around until the landing force commander ordered them to unload at Beach White Two.

A message that Renard decoded said that sixty percent of the equipment and supplies unloaded on Beach White One had been destroyed.

The next morning the destroyers were detached and ordered to return to Milne Bay. As they steamed south the column of smoke was visible for 50 miles. The Hollandia operation had been a success, but the one lone Japanese airman who had dropped a single bomb on the ammunition dump had done more than he would ever know to slow the American advance.

The day before the *Carson* and her accompanying destroyers were due to arrive at Milne Bay, the officer of the deck reported, ''White smoke from the stack.''

Sorenson got up from his chair and looked aft. A large volume of white smoke was spewing from the stack. Sorenson knew white smoke meant water was mixing with the fuel oil. Then the ship slowed.

Sorenson waited patiently for a report from Main Engine Control. In a few seconds the report came. "Water in the fuel oil. We're shifting suction to a new tank."

Sorenson watched the white smoke clear to a light black haze. Down below the turbines speeded up again. He headed for his chair, but before he reached it, more white smoke poured out of the stack, and the ship slowed again.

This time Sorenson was less patient. "Ask the Chief Engineer to come up to the bridge as soon as he's solved the problem," he ordered.

In a few minutes Reifel came up to the bridge, wiping his hands on a rag.

Sorenson looked at him. It wasn't necessary to ask him any questions. Reifel said, "We've got at least two tanks with water in them. We were close to the bottom of each of them. I've shifted to a full one, and we should have no more trouble until we get in."

"What then?"

"We ask for the Australian slush barge and pump off the bottom oil from the contaminated tanks. We'll also test the remaining tanks as soon as they've had time to settle."

"What do the Aussies do with the contaminated fuel?"

"The repair officer told me they give it to the natives who use it to burn off Kunai grass so they can plant new areas."

Sorenson said, "I can see why they need to use it. That Kunai grass behind Humboldt Bay was plenty tough."

Reifel said, "There's more to it. In New Guinea, with the rain every other day, the grass never gets dry enough to burn between rains. Using the fuel oil is the only way they can get a fire started and keep it going."

When they entered Milne Bay the flagship directed them

to fuel from a tanker, but Sorenson had to request anchorage instead so they could process their fuel oil.

Bronte brought the ship to the anchorage and managed to hit their assigned berth within a few yards. ''Not as easy as I thought,'' he said, after the anchor was let go.

CHAPTER TWENTY-ONE

After the Carson anchored, Sorenson sent an urgent message requesting the slush barge, and it rumbled alongside about noon, bashing a groove in Chief Bellow's paint job in the process.

Bellows leaned over the side, tufts of gray hair bobbing at the back of his cap. ''Ha-dammit! Ha-look at ha-paint job!''

The Australian coxswain looked back up at him and grinned, showing a few missing teeth. ''Pop, you got more teeth missing than I have. You ought to see a paint job when I really mess the bloody thing up.''

Chief Bellows took a deep breath and started to open his mouth. Auerbach stepped forward. ''Now, Chief, take it easy. You might dislocate your dentures. He's doing the best he can.''

Bellows subsided, obviously still angry. He muttered, ''Ha-damned Ha-Aussies.''

The Chief Engineer soon had men connecting hoses and pumping fuel out of the offending tanks. In an hour Reifel reported to Sorenson, ''The rest of the tanks are okay. We can fuel now.''

Sorenson requested a fueling assignment, and the *Carson* fueled in the early afternoon.

That night a message came in ordering the *Carson* and *Ransome* to proceed to Seeadler Harbor. The short trip barely gave the crews of the *Carson* and the two accompanying destroyers time to catch up on their sleep.

As they neared the beautiful broad bay, Sorenson noticed three destroyers patrolling off the entrance. The mouth of the bay was so wide some protection against possible incursion by Japanese submarines was needed and the width of the mouth of this bay made it impracticable to install nets.

As they approached the bay, the signal light on the *Nashville* began blinking, and it was promptly answered by Brophy. In a few minutes Brophy brought a rough copy of the incoming message over to Sorenson.

Sorenson read the message carefully and then handed it to Dubose. While Dubose was reading it, Sorenson said to Jablonski, ''The message gives us our anchorage and says we will stay there three days. We are to expect to get underway for the next operation in three days.''

Jablonski said, ''Sounds fair to me. I'm ready for a few days off.''

Dubose finished reading the message and handed it to Jablonski so he could plot the anchorage.

Sorenson said, ''It gives us the privilege of sending a twenty-man liberty party over to the beach for two hours a day. That doesn't sound very encouraging.''

Dubose shrugged, ''Maybe the prohibition against swimming because of sharks has something to do with it.''

Sorenson nodded. ''Maybe, but I'd like you and Steiner to be in the first party so you can look around ashore in the vicinity of the gun targets we fired at. You were responsible for plotting their positions and the range and bearing we used to open fire, and Chuck was responsible for shooting at them when he could see them.''

Dubose said, ''I'd like that. We might learn something.''

Sorenson said, ''I've noticed Scorse has been a little down lately. Would you mind taking him with you?''

Dubose said, "Not at all. A little liberty would do him good. He didn't even go ashore in Mare Island."

As they eased toward their anchorage, Brophy brought a list of ships present in the harbor to Sorenson. He read it carefully. "Look at that. He ran his finger down the list to the group of Australian ships. "Wonderful names their destroyers have. *Warramunga, Arunta*. They even sound fierce."

Jablonski said, "We'll be surrounded by them. Both destroyers are in adjacent anchorages."

Exactly at 1200 the *Carson* dropped her anchor in her assigned berth. Brophy looking at the adjacent ships, said, "Captain, it looks like a small riot over on the Australian destroyer's forward gun decks."

Fineman, standing next to Sorenson, laughed. "Just a daily occurrence. Promptly at 1200 each day in port the liquor mess on all British and Australian ships opens for a short period. It opens for a much longer period before dinner."

Brophy said, "I heard that, but they're dragging wicker chairs and tables out under the awnings they've rigged over mount two."

"Why not," Sorenson said. "They know how to live. By the way, Forrest, if we have any beer left aboard, take some with you this afternoon when you go ashore."

Dubose grinned. "Thank you."

The bridge crew watched the Australian officers stretched out in their chairs, and as the word was passed to "Splice the mainbrace," they could see a long line of men form on the main deck and line up in front of a large wood tub.

Brophy groaned. "I can't watch."

The next morning Dubose watched the beer being loaded into the boat and then followed the recreation party down the ladder. At the small landing ashore, the boat coxswain came alongside carefully, and Dubose directed several members of the recreation party to carry the beer inland and put it under a group of palm trees. He left Chief Brophy in charge of the beer, and led the officers on a tour of the island.

Their first stop was the cemetery. "My God!" Reifel said, "There are thousands of Japanese here."

Scorse nodded, "And three hundred of ours."

Steiner pointed to a single grave marker of an old piece of coral. He bent over it. "I can't read the inscription too well. On top it has a crude carving of a sea eagle. Then the name Ruge and the date 1916. Under the date is the word Seeadler."

Dubose nodded. "It must be the grave of one of the crewmen of the Seeadler commanded by Count Von Luckner."

Scorse came to life. "I'd like to be buried here someday."

Dubose frowned. "Why wouldn't you want to be buried in the States near your home?"

Scorse shook his head. "I'm an orphan, and I don't have any home. I enlisted in the Navy from an orphanage, and the Navy is my home."

Dubose led the group away from the cemetery. They found an Army colonel lounging in a beach chair in front of the biggest shack on the island. The colonel stirred heavily and got up slowly. "What can I do for you?"

Dubose said, "We'd just like to look around. First, can you tell me a little about these shacks I see over there." Dubose waved a hand toward a group of about twenty grass shacks in a grove of beaten-up palm trees.

"Sure. what do you want to know?"

"How do they survive a typhoon?"

The Colonel laughed. "They do it the easy way. The natives seem to know when one is coming. They bury all their valuables in the sand, tie themselves to a palm tree, and then just wait. Along comes the typhoon and the grass shacks are promptly flattened. When the typhoon is past, the natives untie themselves, dig up their valuables, and prop the shack walls back up again. It seems to work well. The Army could learn a lot from these guys. At least I've learned to take it easy.'' The colonel sighed, stretched, and sat down heavily in his chair.

''May we look around?'' Dubose asked.

''Be my guest,'' the colonel said. ''You'll find a beer party from the *Warramunga* back in the bushes.''

Dubose led the officers toward the sound of singing and soon found the party. In a few minutes the two parties had joined and the *Carson* quartet broke the ice by singing a few selections. The Aussies responded with ''Waltzing Matilda,'' and the beer flowed freely.

''Blimey,'' an Australian officer said. ''How about coming to the *Warramunga* for dinner?''

Dubose laughed, ''We'll be there.''

When the beer ran out, Dubose gathered the Carson group and brought them back to the ship.

At 1700 the quartet, resplendent in clean khakis, and led by Dubose, got in the boat and left for the *Warramunga* in the next berth.

Sorenson saw them off and then went up to the forecastle to pace up and down in the coolness of the early part of the evening. He could see the quartet debarking on the *Warramunga*'s quarterdeck and being escorted up to the area under the awning.

A mutter of polite conversation carried over the water, and Sorenson regretted that he had not invited himself. Then, as the cocktail hour progressed, the muttering became laughter, and soon the strains of ''Aloha Oe'' floated across the water. Loud applause followed, and then came the words of ''Waltzing Matilda.'' The quartet answered with ''Roll Out the Barrel,'' and the laughter and applause crescendoed.

Sorenson shook his head and smiled. Then, when he could take the merriment no longer, he went down to dinner.

After a quiet dinner in the wardroom, he went back up on deck. The singing was even louder, and he was happy for those who were forgetting their troubles. He thought about Ferren, and wondered if she was happy with her large school family. For the first time since he had been married, he thought about having children, and he thought it might be just what they needed. If only the war would end and they could lead a normal life. But would life in the Navy ever return to the leisurely pace of the days in Long Beach and Norfolk before Pearl Harbor? He kicked at a minute piece of paper on the deck, but it wouldn't move, and he leaned over and picked it up, crumpled it, and threw it over the side.

A gale of laughter erupted on the *Warramunga*. Sorenson had had enough. He went below to the loneliness of his bunk.

At breakfast the next morning the quartet was present, but subdued.

Sorenson laughed.

Dubose squeezed his eyes together. "Please, Captain, not so loud."

Sorenson said, "You all didn't seem to mind the noise last night."

Reifel, holding his eyes open with some difficulty, said, "It was a wonderful evening, but I don't want to do it again soon."

Auerbach put down his coffee cup, trying not to spill it with his shaky hand. "But, you will. I heard the Exec invite the Captain, four officers, and ten men over for dinner and a sing along tonight."

Dubose groaned, "What have I done?"

Sorenson turned to Fineman, who seemed not to have suffered as much as the other members of the quartet.

''How about it, Doc? You must have been relatively sober.''

''Yes, I learned early on a previous trip to Australia that the Aussies seem to have bottomless stomachs. I think it's bred in them.''

''What's the secret of your success?''

''Early on I find a position next to the rail. Then, frequently, while nobody is looking, I put my glass behind me and water the fish.''

Reifel said, ''I'll remember that, but what do you remember about the Exec's invitation?''

''I heard him give it. They were very enthusaiastic, even when I reminded them we couldn't serve any booze. They said they liked our coffee and were looking forward to it. Seems their Captain makes them stick to tea, and they hate the stuff.''

Promptly at 1700, a boat load of Aussies from the *Warramunga* approached the accommodation ladder. Sorenson, with Dubose at his side, was on the quarterdeck to meet them. Brophy and Wencey were also on hand to meet and escort the four chief petty officers invited and the ten enlisted men to the appropriate messes.

Sorenson met the commanding officer at the top of the brow. After he had saluted the colors and asked permision to come aboard, he turned to Sorenson, extended his hand and said, ''Cunningham.''

Sorenson grinned, ''Sorenson here. Welcome aboard. This is my Executive Officer, Forrest Dubose.''

Cunningham shook hands with Dubose and said, ''Yes, I know him well.'' Cunningham was about Dubose's height, but twenty pounds lighter.

Sorenson said, ''Dubose will take the officers to the wardroom and Chief Brophy here will take charge of the Chief Petty officers. Behind him is Petty Officer Wencey who will take your enlisted men.''

''Sounds top hole,'' Cunninham said.

"If you'll follow me, I'd like to talk a little over a cup of coffee in my cabin before dinner. I'm sure you know we can't carry liquor aboard except for use ashore."

Cunningham sighed and rubbed his lean belly. "I can do with your coffee. I need a little change."

When they were seated with coffee, Sorenson said, "You seem to be British. Is it common for Australian ships not to be commanded by Australians?"

"Sometimes, but not common, old chap. Admiral Crutchley, over there on the HMAS *Australia,* is a Brit. Actually I'm English. Some of us from the Royal Navy fill in where the Aussies are short. I enjoyed your quartet last night, and I'm looking forward to tonight's do, also."

Sorenson knew he would like Cunningham. He said, "I hope so. We can be pretty noisy."

Cunningham laughed, and his bright eyes sparkled. "Don't worry. Our chaps will keep up."

Dinner was pleasant. Captain Cunningam in his clipped British accent, moderated by long exposure to the Australians, entertained with many stories from his early days in destroyers in the Atlantic, and Sorenson responded with a few of his own from his time with the convoys in the Atlantic.

One of the *Warramunga* officers said, when the steak was served, "Haven't seen anything but mutton for months. Well done."

Fineman said, "Not all of it. There are a lot of rare pieces, too."

There was a groan up the table.

Before coffee, the quartet excused themselves to prepare for the entertainment. After coffee, Sorenson led Cunningham and his officers out to the quarterdeck and to some waiting chairs.

After a few minutes, Doctor Fineman got up and introduced Chief Brophy. The entertainmnet started as a duplicate of the sing along in Majuro, but the Aussies quickly joined in with their version of ''Waltzing Matilda.''

They learned how to ''Plant rice,'' and roared with the crew through the verses of ''The Beer Barrel Polka.''

Then came the rendition by Chief Brophy and Chief Williams. The Australians cheered the competitors, and became so enthusiastic two of them tried to join Abdul Abulbul to put Ivan away. They were restrained by two laughing Aussie chief petty officers and taken back to their seats.

As the evening went on, the noise reached almost epic proportions and Sorenson told Cunningham about the incident in Majuro Atoll when they had been boarded by a rescue party. Cunningham laughed. ''No chance of that here, old boy. More likely the boat would have been full of chaps wanting to join the party.''

By 2300, both commanding officers agreed that Admiral Crutchley's sleep was important, and the sing along was stopped to a chorus of boos.

Sorenson saw Cunningham and his officers and men off at the quarterdeck and headed for his bunk. He took a deep breath. He was bushed, and his throat and lungs hurt from the singing.

The next day the ships stood out and formed up. The *Carson* and the other ships of the screen formed an anti-submarine screen around the large ships.

Just after they had settled down in station, the flag-ship's signal light began to blink.

Brophy received the message and brought it to Sorenson. Sorenson read it and said to MacIntosh, who had the deck, ''Pass the word that we're going to go alongside the *Nashville*, pick up guard mail and deliver it to the other cruisers. We'll be followed by another destroyer that will make deliveries to the other destroyers. I think it's the Operation Order for the next event.''

When MacIntosh had passed the word, Sorenson said, ''Take her alongside the *Nashville*. Then we'll get Scorse and Chief Vickers up here and let them try their hand at conning the ship alongside.''

MacIntosh did fine, and they headed for HMAS *Shropshire,* with Scorse at the conn.

Dubose was standing beside Sorenson watching the proceedings. Scorse was standing behind the pelorus, the best position from which to conn a destroyer alongside another ship. His feet were widely placed although there wasn't much roll. His hands gripped the bulwark in front of him. He took off his cap and jammed it behind the pelorus.

Sorenson, watching him, seemed to be mildly amused. He raised his hand and behind it said to Dubose, ''Look at him. His short, curly hair and that patrician nose make him look like a Roman charioteer.''

Dubose nodded. ''I see what you mean.''

Scorse did a good job coming alongside, and Sorenson took his eye off of him and glanced up at the Australian captain standing on the *Shropshire*'s bridge. He waved and saluted.

The Australian captain waved back and picked up a megaphone.

''Captain, congratulations.''

Sorenson was puzzled and he took the megaphone handed to him by Caruso and raised it. ''Thank you, Captain, but what for?''

The Australian said, ''I was talking about your feat of making more noise than the *Warramunga* the other night. You are now the fleet champs.'' He shook his head. ''Those cobbers are the loudest group this side of Sydney, or were until you came along.''

Sorenson grinned and said, ''Thank you, sir. We'll treasure the honor.''

Sorenson turned to Chief Gunner's Mate Vickers. Vickers was a slightly fat, florid man of average height. He was obviously nervous, and he was standing aft in the pilothouse, clasping and unclasping his hands, obviously hoping Sorenson would forget to call on him.

Sorenson said, ''Your turn, Vickers. Are you sure you want to do this?''

Vickers cleared his throat, ''Ain't my cup of tea, Captain, but I'll try her.''

Vickers took the conn and headed for the last cruiser.

He gave too many orders, and the *Carson* jockeyed back and forth. Sorenson let him alone and eventually the task was done.

Vickers sighed deeply as he headed the ship away and turned the conn over to MacIntosh.

Sorenson said, ''Good try, Vickers. Come up to the bridge more often and watch the others.''

Vickers shook his head. ''Captain, if it's all the same to you, I'll stay down in my battery.'' Then, as he headed down the ladder, he turned. ''Captain, if you'd like come down to my battery next time it fires, you can train a mount.''

Sorenson laughed. ''Thanks, Chief, I might just do that.''

Sorenson ordered MacIntosh to take their station in the screen and he headed for his cabin to see what the operation order they had just picked up would hold for them at Biak.

CHAPTER TWENTY-TWO

Sorenson went to his sea cabin and settled down to read and study the operation order for the Biak landings. He read and re-read it right through the dinner Vila brought up for him.

After dinner, he went out to the bridge and paced up and down, thinking about the difficulties of taking Biak. There was no doubt why General MacArthur wanted it. The three Japanese bomber strips would be very useful as the push north to the Philippines developed. But the price of taking them could be high.

In the first place, intelligence had no firm idea how many troops were on the islands. Estimates ranged from two thousand to ten thousand. The intelligence experts finally compromised by estimating that half of any numbers present were probably engineers.

Then the terrain would cause difficulties. The island was quite large, 45 miles by 20 miles, and it was covered with thick jungle, both trees and bushes. The vegetation had already made the task of aerial reconnaissance difficult, and it would be difficult to fight through. In addition, there were many natural caves.

Steele had the deck, and Sorenson trusted him above all of his watchstanders. He decided to break his custom of never leaving the bridge at sea, and he sent word down to Dubose to assemble the officers after dinner in the wardroom to go over the operation order.

Half an hour later Sorenson hurried down to the wardroom, not wanting to leave the bridge any longer than necessary.

When they were ready, he said, "I assume you've all had a chance to study your part of the next amphibious operation at Biak."

The officers all nodded.

Sorenson went on. "This operation worries me. The intelligence is mushy. Furthermore, I suspect the Japanese Navy is about to respond."

Dubose said, "I agree. Also, the landing force may have a tough job just getting ashore and moving off the beach. I understand the battleships off Tarawa fired at the fortifications for hours and didn't do much to them. We expect to do the job with 6-inch gun light cruisers and destroyers firing for a relatively brief period of forty-five minutes."

Sorenson said, "We meet the landing force on the 28th after it leaves Humboldt Bay. Then we approach Biak at low speed. We'll be held back by the slow landing craft.

"Before we talk about the landing, Auerbach, tell us about the air preparations that are going on."

Auerbach said. "The airfields we've captured lately are already in heavy use by both fighters and bombers. The Fifth Air Force has been bombing Biak Island for three weeks. They have also bombed the Japanese airfields on Borneo and farther north. Even with this effort, they expect the Japanese to bring in air reinforcements from as far away as the Philippines. Starting on Z-day, an alternate expression for D-day, the first day of the landing, the Fifth Air Force will have fighter cover over the landing area all day long."

The atmosphere in the wardroom was glum, and the conference broke up soon so the officers could get to their bunks early.

About 0615 on the morning of the 28th the attack force approached the coast of Biak through a muggy atmosphere. A low overcast delayed the coming of dawn. The American cruisers *Boise, Nashville,* and *Phoenix* were in position along the southern coast of Biak Island so they could bombard the three airfields just inland from the coast.

The destroyers, including the *Carson,* closed the landing area to the east of the location in which the cruisers were operating, and when the cruisers opened fire, the destroyers joined them in delivering a forty-five minute preparatory bombardment of the areas back of the beach.

The overcast, the heavy air, and the lack of any winds made the heavy dust and smoke hang over the landing area. Soon the jetties and the actual landing beach were obscured.

When the preparatory fire was completed, Sorenson watched the LVTs and DUKWs approaching the beach. Something was wrong with the picture, but he didn't know exactly what it was. ''Jablonski, how are your fixes?''

Jablonski said, ''Because of the dust we have to use radar. We're getting a current of two to three knots along the beach.''

Sorenson said, ''That's the trouble! Those landing craft are headed for the wrong beach area. They can't see the jetties and they don't know the current is pushing them west.'' Sorenson grabbed the TBS transmitter and called the control ship. ''There's a heavy current along the coast, and the landing craft are going to the wrong beach.''

There was silence for a few minutes. Then the control ship came up on the circuit. ''Thank you, Hustler. I'm sending a destroyer off the jetties to locate them by radar. The LSTs following the landing craft now should be able to get to the right beach.''

Scorse, listening to the landing force circuit, said, ''The boats are squared away now, and the next wave will land at the jetties. The LSTs will also land there. The first troops ashore report no resistance.''

Sorenson shook his head. ''Wait until they get to the caves and airfields.''

By afternoon there were 10,000 troops ashore and enough tanks, artillery, and supplies to support them.

The troops moved inland and west toward the airfields, and soon reported heavy fighting.

The cruisers withdrew and left half of the destroyers including the *Carson* and *Ransome* to render fire support.

The night was quiet, except for an occasional call to furnish harassing fire to the troops around the first airfield.

Shortly after dawn, Sorenson was congratulating himself that there had been no air attacks on them when one of the lookouts shouted. ''Aircraft coming over the land.''

Four fighters, followed by four twin-engined bombers, roared over the crest of the hill and spread out to attack the ships off the beach. Antiaircraft fire burst from all ships, forming a black curtain in front of the attackers.

''Look out!'' Jablonski yelled as one dissolved in a ball of fire, and the remnants rained down on a nearby destroyer.

''There goes a second one!'' Sorenson yelled, as a twin-engined Betty caught a wing in the water and cartwheeled.

Another Betty headed directly for the destroyer *Sampson,* Admiral Fechteler's flagship, obviously trying to crash into it. Heavy fire from all ships tore off one wing, but the rest of the aircraft kept going long enough to pass over the *Sampson*'s bridge.

Sorenson let out his breath. ''We damned near lost the big cheese!''

The remains crashed just beyond the *Sampson* and careened into the SC-699. Huge fires broke out, and Sorenson headed for the burning craft to assist. A fleet tug, the *Sonoma,* got there first and succeeded in putting out the fire.

A nervous calm descended over the area, and the LSTs went back to work unloading.

Sorenson set condition III and sat down in his chair. For a few minutes he was numb, and then he began to review in his mind the recent attack. He could see again the Betty flying low over the *Sampson*, and he knew how close Admiral Fechteler had been to death. He wondered if a Betty would find the *Carson*'s bridge and he would die in the flames of the burning aircraft. He shuddered. At least that kind of death would be quick and his body would be buried at sea so Ferren would be spared his burial. He sighed. What the hell, he thought, live now and forget the worrying.

''Messenger,'' he said, ''Please send down to the wardroom for coffee. Black and bitter.''

That afternoon Fineman brought a decoded dispatch up to Sorenson. Sorenson said, ''It orders us to leave with the *Ransome* and join the covering force of cruisers now in Humboldt Bay. The covering force is fueling and getting ready to defend against a Japanese naval force they think is coming south.''

Sorenson turned to Scorse, the officer of the deck, and said, ''Pass the word that we're departing for Humboldt Bay. Take a course southwest to clear Biak and increase speed to 20 knots.''

Just as they had speeded up and the *Ransome* had come out to join them, the newly formed antiaircraft warning system broadcast, ''Air warning red.''

Sorenson said, ''Go to general quarters.''

As soon as they were manned, Sorenson asked CIC, ''Where's the bogey?''

Dubose said, ''We don't have it on radar. Must be north of the island and low.''

In a few minutes two fighters burst over the island flying just a few feet above the ground and headed for the ships there.

The ships nearby put up heavy fire at the rapidly moving targets. One Zeke began to smoke, and then exploded and fell near an LST.

The second Zeke kept coming, its propeller glinting in the sun. It turned slightly and headed for the *Carson*. Steiner opened up with all batteries, and the fighter wobbled. The pilot seemed to be fighting for control of the aircraft, but just before he passed over the bridge of the *Carson*, the pilot opened up with machine-gun fire. The line of bullets walked over the water toward the *Carson* and then up across the signal bridge. Since the ship was at general quarters, all the signalmen except Caruso, who was the quartermaster in the pilothouse, were standing on the signal bridge watching the approaching aircraft. The line of projectiles plowed through them.

The Japanese aircraft plunged into the green water just over the *Carson* and cartwheeled into oblivion.

The guns stopped firing, and in the silence Sorenson could hear shouting from the signal bridge. He ran aft. All four signalmen were lying on the deck. Blood had spattered the deck and bulkheads.

Sorenson yelled, "Get Doctor Fineman and stretcher bearers up here on the double!"

Dubose came pounding up the ladder from CIC. When he saw the carnage, he said, "Jesus! What happened?"

Sorenson said, "A Zeke machine-gunned us. Help me with the wounded until Fineman gets here."

But Fineman was right behind Dubose, and he bent over the prone figures.

The first man was Wencey. Fineman examined him quickly and then pulled a rubber tube out of his pocket and applied it as a tourniquet around Wencey's leg to stop arterial bleeding.

Fineman turned to the stretcher bearers and said, "Take him first. Right to the wardroom. Show the wound to the chief pharmacist's mate."

Dubose, leaning over Brophy, said, "Brophy's unconscious, but I don't see any arterial bleeding. He took one in the back."

Fineman said, ''Leave him there. I'll get to him in a few seconds.''

Fineman bent over the other two men. ''Penetration wounds. No arterial bleeding. Take them down next.'' Then he went over to Brophy. Caruso and Dubose were leaning over him. Fineman said to Caruso, ''How come you didn't get hit?''

Caruso said, ''I had the quartermaster watch in the pilothouse.''

Dubose said, ''My God! That means you're the only signalman left.''

Sorenson rubbed his chin. ''And tomorrow we join up with the covering force. We'll be in a hell of a shape for visual communications.''

Fineman cut Brophy's shirt off, turned him sideways, and looked at his wound. ''Lucky,'' he said. ''It struck him in the back and bounced off his shoulder blade.''

Fineman took an ammonia ampule out of his pocket, broke it, and held it under Brophy's nose.

Brophy gasped, and his eyes opened. ''What happened?'' He struggled to get up, and Fineman pushed him back to the deck.

Fineman said, ''The whole signal gang except for Caruso here got wiped out.''

''Damn!'' Brophy said. ''Caruso is a good kid, but he can't run the whole thing. Get Chief Williams up here. He can do it.''

Dubose said, ''What are you talking about? He's a steward's mate.''

Brophy said softly, ''Sure he is, but he's also the second best signalman on the ship. Well, maybe after Wencey. But he can run the signal bridge. He's been up here for hours in port. Also there's a kid named Kittredge down in the deck force, who's a trainer on mount 53. He wants to be a signal striker. He can help.''

Dubose stood up. ''I don't care. Williams is still a steward, and he can't do it.''

Sorenson's lips thinned, and his voice was cold and controlled. ''He's our best bet. Get him up here.''

Dubose started to say something, but he glanced at Sorenson's closed fists and hard eyes. He walked away stiffly and went below.

Sorenson went into his sea cabin and sat down. His emotions were boiling. Dubose's conduct had been upsetting, but even worse for the second time in recent days he had come close to death. He thought how vulnerable a destroyer was--to air attack--to submarine torpedoes--to guns from surface ships. The only defense a destroyer really had was speed and manueverability, and these had to be used by a bold, fearless, and capable captain. He wondered if he really met those requirements. Then he shrugged. He must have met them. He had escaped death several times when in command, and he had only lost one ship, the *O'Leary*.

He got up and called the bridge. When the boatswain's mate of the watch answered, he said, "Please have the messenger find Doctor Fineman and ask him to come up and see me."

Sorenson sat down again. He thought about Ferren, and he wondered what she would do if she lost him. The loss of her first husband on a destroyer in the Atlantic had devastated her for a long period. If she lost him, too, she would suffer badly.

There was a knock on the door. Sorenson said, "Come in."

Fineman opened the door and came in. "Got a headache?"

Sorenson laughed in spite of his somber mood. "More like a mindache. Please sit down."

Fineman sat down and said, "Tell me about it."

Sorenson sighed. "I just don't know where to begin, but I'll start by giving you this."

Sorenson moved over to his desk and wrote rapidly on a piece of stationery. Then he sealed the paper in an envelope and held it out to Fineman.

"What's this?" Fineman asked.

Sorenson said, "I should have let you read it. It says if I'm killed in action I want to be buried at sea. I hope you will see that my wishes are carried out."

Fineman said, "Certainly, but why do you want to do this? I would have thought you would want to join our shipmates at Seeadler."

"I can see why you'd think that way, but my problems are different from Scorse's."

"How?"

"I would want Ferren to be spared the emotional trauma of even dealing with my body or my grave. I want my burial to be clean, quick, and final. She will need to have all the possible help in carrying on her life. A double tragedy would be hard for anyone."

Fineman said, "I see your point. But what brought this on?"

"I guess seeing the *Sampson* almost get hit the other day followed by the action on the bridge a while ago. That was the last straw. I've always known the risks we were taking, and I don't see how our luck can hold out much longer. I was lucky today. I missed death by inches."

Finman said, "An inch is as good as a mile."

"Sure, but what about the next time, and the one after that?"

"You feel you're not going to make it?"

"I don't have any real feelings about that. I just know we're pushing our luck."

Fineman sighed. "I hadn't thought about it that way. We'll be in the same ship. We both may buy the farm. Then who will take care of both of our bodies?"

"I thought about that. Your battle station is in the wardroom. That's quite a distance from mine. Any serious explosion would probably spare one of us. If the whole ship goes up, it won't make any differnce."

Fineman nodded. "I guess that's the best we can do."

Sorenson said, "Thank you, David, I feel better. I'm not really pessimistic, just being careful."

The next day the *Carson* and the *Ransome* steamed into Humboldt Bay. Chief Williams hovered over Caruso and Kittredge as they exchanged calls with the flagship, and personally received the message assigning them a berth.

Sorenson, watching, sent for Chief Yeoman Carmody.

When Carmody arrived, Sorenson said, ''Carmody, you know what happened to the signal force?''

''Yes, sir, I hear they almost got wiped out.''

''Chief Williams is doing a good job, but he'll need more help when we get to sea with all these big ships. I'd like you to report to him for duty until Brophy is up and around. You can record messages the others are receiving and write them up.''

Carmody scratched his head. ''I can do more than that. I was a Boy Scout and pretty good with the Morse code. Also, I remember some semaphore from boot camp.''

''Good. Maybe Chief Williams can teach you something.''

Carmody grinned. ''Maybe I can teach him something, too. About how to make Texas chili.''

Sorenson laughed. ''I'd like that. I thought I'd never eat any again after I left Texas, but now I think I'd like some.'' His face sobered. ''Carmody, thank you for volunteering. I'll remember it.''

Carmody said, ''Captain, I don't remember exactly volunteering, but I'm glad to do it. Williams is a heck of a nice guy.''

The *Carson* was told to fuel from a tanker before anchoring, and Sorenson watched young Bentley chew his nails to the quick as he brought the *Carson* alongside with only a slight bump.

While the *Carson* was fueling, Kittredge received a message calling the commanding officer of the *Carson* and two other destroyer commanding officers over to the flagship. Sorenson called for the gig and left immediately. He climbed up the cruiser's accommodation ladder, saluted the quarterdeck, then the officer of the deck, and asked for permission to come aboard.

"Permission granted," the officer of the deck answered. "The ceremony is on the forecastle. The Flag Lieutenant will escort you."

Sorenson turned to a young lieutenant wearing the blue and gold aigulettes of an aide indicating he was the aide to a rear admiral. He was standing near the officer of the deck. "What ceremony?" Sorenson asked.

"Three commanding officers are being awarded Silver Stars," the Flag Lieutenant said.

"But I haven't done anything to deserve that."

The Flag Lieutenant grinned. "That's not what the citation says. Sinking a submarine and shooting down five aircraft deserves at least a Silver Star, sir."

Sorenson protested again. "But my crew did that. I don't deserve any particular credit."

"The Admiral thinks you do, sir, and I suggest you shouldn't argue with him. If you think members of your crew deserve awards, I'll be the one to process them. I suggest you forward them as soon as we're in company again. Now, if you'll follow me, the others are all assembled."

Sorenson followed the Flag Lieutenant to the forecastle and headed for a position next to the other commanding officers. One of them was Commander Cunningham, captain of the *Warramunga*. Sorenson fell in beside him.

Cunningham winked at him and said out of the corner of his mouth, "Nice to see you, old chap."

Sorenson nodded and smiled.

The Flag Lieutenant disappeared through the door into flag quarters and reappeared almost immediately, followed by Admiral Barbey. The Admiral was obviously in a hurry to get the ceremony over so his force could get underway, but he made sure the proceedings were dignified and meaningful to those receiving awards.

Each officer was called forward in succession and stood at attention in front of the Admiral while the citation was being read. When it was Sorenson's turn, he listened carefully to the citation, thinking that he would use some of the words in the citations he would write for the awards for Dubose, Steele, Steiner, Williams, and Terrill.

Then the Admiral stepped forward and pinned the five pointed Silver Star hanging from a red, white, and blue ribbon on his khaki shirt. The Admiral shook hands with Sorenson, returned his salute, and stepped back. The ceremony was over.

The Admiral turned on his heel and headed for the flag bridge. The Flag Lieutenant looked expectantly at the commanding officers.

Cunningham said out of the corner of his mouth without moving his firm jaw, "He's trying to tell us to 'get going,' as you Yanks would say. I think the force is about to 'haul ass,' also as you would say."

Sorenson said, "You speak our language very well. He doesn't have to tell us twice. Let's go."

After fueling, Reifel took them to their anchorage, his deep voice reverberating as he gave orders to the helm and annunciator.

Sorenson grinned. He turned to Dubose who was standing near his chair. "Sounds just like a Baptist preacher," he said.

Dubose nodded. "That's what he used to be before the war."

CHAPTER TWENTY-THREE

On the Afternoon of the third, a signal went up on Admiral Crutchley's flagship, the *Australia,* for all commanding officers to report on board.

Sorenson hurriedly shifted into a clean uniform and called away the gig. He hustled up on deck and down the accommodation ladder and ordered the coxswain to make the *Australia*.

An hour later he was back and asked Dubose to call the usual conference of all officers.

When all the officers were assembled in the wardroom, he went down below to join them and threw a small sheaf of papers on the table. "There it is," he said. "The Australians are like the British. They don't think much of paper work."

Dubose picked the papers up and shuffled through them. "Is this all? Just a few lists of communications call signs and a formation or two?"

Sorenson laughed. "I'm over-simplifying. They did give us some intelligence and said they'd send out a daily set of changes. Right now they think the Japanese are loading troops in the Philippines for a reinforcement run to Biak. Admiral Crutchley has been ordered to leave tonight and take a position northeast of Biak to be ready to intercept it. Of course he doesn't know yet just exactly when the Japanese will sail or what part of Biak they intend landing on.''

Dubose said, ''I take it we have a lot of reconnaissance forces out in the forward area.''

''Yes. The Fifth Air Force and our Navy long range Liberator aircraft are going to make day and night searches as far north as Davao and Zamboanga in the Philippines, and we have submarines off both ports. We'll know when the Japanese leave.''

Steiner put down his coffee cup and asked, ''What forces will Admiral Crutchley have?''

''The Australian cruiser *Shropshire* is in Sydney under repair and the *Nashville* is somewhere with General MacArthur. That leaves the light cruisers *Australia, Phoenix,* and *Boise,* our old friends and song mates the Australian destroyers *Warramunga* and *Arunta,* and American Destroyer Divisions Forty-two, Forty-seven, and Forty-eight. We'll be there with the *Ransome* as Destroyer Division Fifty-nine. We won't know much more until after we sail. My guess is that there will be a real ruckus.''

Steiner said, ''My boys are ready for one.''

Sorenson turned to Scorse. ''Can Chief Williams and his patched up signal gang do the job?''

Dubose was silent, looking down into his cup of black coffee.

Scorse said, ''So far he's doing all right. Chief Brophy is up and about with his arm in a sling. He wants to come up to the signal bridge.''

Sorenson looked at Fineman and said, ''How about it?''

Fineman shook his head. ''Too soon. He can do a little light duty up there in about five more days when I take the stitches out.''

Sorenson said, ''Is Chief Carmody doing any good?''

Scorse said, ''Sure, sir. He's even beginning to send and receive a little.''

Just before dark the signal was made to get underway, and the ships stood out with the cruisers in a column and the destroyers in a circular screen. Just outside the harbor the *Nashville* steamed up and joined the formation.

Renard and Fineman stayed close to the communication decoding machine and brought a stream of traffic up to Sorenson. The first message was from Admiral Kinkaid telling Admiral Crutchley to arrive at a point 25 miles north of the eastern end of Biak Island at 1715 June fourth. Thereafter Admiral Crutchley was to engage Japanese forces if they appeared. If the Japanese did not arrive the night of 4-5 June, Admiral Crutchley was to retire toward Hollandia and repeat the performance each night thereafter.

''Jesus!'' Sorenson said, ''We'll feel like we've been in a runaway elevator.''

Jablonski, plotting the position off Biak Island on the chart, said, ''It won't be so bad. We're only going to make sixteen knots.''

The next decoded message brought the information that intercepted communications had indicated that a Japanese search plane had sighted the Crutchley force and that an air attack on the force should be anticipated in the next twelve hours.

Sorenson sent word to Steiner. ''Tell him to be careful,'' he told the messenger.

Crutchley turned the formation toward Biak.

Down in CIC Bronte reported that thirty-five bogies were headed their way and were about 50 miles away. Then Sorenson could hear him swear over the squawk-box. ''The damned Fifth Air Force fighters are leaving the area and heading back to Wakde Island. They say they have to get back before dark.''

Sorenson swore. ''Maybe we should tell the Japanese to go back to their airfields because it's dark.''

Admiral Crutchley, apparently also hearing the reports, put the cruisers in a circular formation and ordered the destroyers to close in to a close circular anti-air formation outboard of them.

Sorenson took the conn and ordered Auerbach to sound general quarters. The strident sound of the general alarm echoed through the bridge structure. Sorenson thought he would hear it in his sleep the rest of his life.

In two minutes all stations were manned and ready and Steiner had the 5-inch battery trained out in the direction of the approaching bogies.

At 1830 the sun was low over the horizon in the west where the bogies were reported, and Sorenson ordered Steiner to train the guns toward the sun area. It was a wise decision. In minutes Bronte reported many bogies at low altitude. Sorenson shaded his eyes and looked at the sun. Minute specks grew into larger ones and then into winged spots. Steiner had seen them too, and all the *Carson*'s guns were ready to open fire. As the first Japanese aircraft reached the range of the 5-inch battery, the guns began to boom. Black bursts blossomed in the middle of the oncoming aircraft formation, and in seconds the other ships in the formation began to fire.

Sorenson held his breath. "Damn!" he shouted. "Get the nearest one!"

Steiner did. Sorenson could see a projectile burst cut away a wing. The Betty dipped to that side briefly and then cartwheeled, the water putting out the beginnings of a fire.

Sorenson shifted his eyes to the next Betty. It was dangerously close to its drop point, but the 40s cut it to pieces.

Then another aircraft began to smoke, and the smoke grew and turned into flames. In seconds it was a ball of flame.

The pilots of the trailing aircraft in the second wave seemed to lose their nerve as they saw the first wave going down. They began to turn away by twos and threes, and then the whole wave broke away short of their drop points.

"We did it!" Jablonski shouted.

Bronte was exultant. "Who needs the Air Force!" he shouted over the squawkbox.

Sorenson started to laugh, but then he felt his stomach turning. He realized it was the reaction to the tension of the recent attack, and he felt sympathy for all the officers and men who undoubtedly felt the same. He began to think about Ferren, and how she would feel if he had been killed. Their luck had been good, but it could not hold out forever. He breathed deeply, and the sick feeling went away.

Brophy yelled, "Signals on the way! Stand by your bags!"

Crutchley formed the cruisers into a column and headed for the south coast of Biak. The destroyer divisions were ordered to form individual columns on the bow of the cruisers.

Sorenson secured the ship from general quarters and asked Dubose to supervise the feeding of the crew so thay could be ready to go back to general quarters as soon as they had eaten. Then he called down to the wardroom for his dinner and asked if Renard and Fineman had any recent messages to explain why they were headed for Biak.

Fineman answered the telephone. "Renard is typing a message up. It says Admiral Crutchley intends passing close to the south coast of Biak Island and sweeping west to the western tip of the island. He doesn't know if the Japanese forces will be there, but he's going to make sure they don't surprise us."

Sorenson had kept the crew at general quarters during the coastal sweep, but now he considered securing them. Something told him not to, and at about 0100 his caution was rewarded. Four torpedo planes came in low ahead and dropped torpedoes. Bronte picked them up on the air search radar and transferred the contact to Steiner's firecontrol radar. Steiner reported acquiring them on fire control radar and soon began to fire on the streaking enemy aircraft. All four dropped their torpedoes from ahead. For some reason Admiral Crutchley did not maneuver the formation, and Sorenson searched ahead for oncoming torpedoes. All the lookouts were alerted and scanned the black but moon-illuminated water ahead. The bright full moon should have made the task of seeing the faint rising pattern of bubbles easy, but nobody reported any wakes.

Then Chief Williams, his eye glued to a signalman's telescope, shouted, "Torpedo wake one point on the port bow. Come left! Come left!"

Sorenson could not see the wake, and he was doubtful about the wisdom of turning the ship toward the torpedo, but he trusted Williams. He ordered the helmsman to put the rudder over full left. The ship's stern quickly began to swing out to starboard, and Sorenson anxiously searched the black water ahead.

"There it is!" Jablonski yelled. "It's headed for our port quarter, but it's going to miss our stern by twenty feet."

The stern was still swinging to starboard away from the torpedo from the action of the left rudder. Sorenson let his breath out. "Williams, you saved us. That sucker would have blown off our stern if you hadn't told me what to do."

Williams laughed. "Any good signalman would have done the same. I had the biggest glass."

"Is Chief Carmody helping?" Sorenson asked.

Williams smiled. "Sure. He handed me the long glass I used."

An hour later the formation had cleared Biak Island and turned south in the direction of Hollandia. Sorenson said, "Back to safety."

Fineman, who had just come to the bridge with a decoded diapatch, heard him. "Don't speak too soon. Read this."

Sorenson pulled out his small red flashlight and read the message. "How far are we from Wakde Island?" he asked Jablonski.

"We'll be passing it on the way south to Hollandia in two hours."

Sorenson said, "When we pass by we ought to have some sort of service for the Fifth Air Force. The fighters that couldn't stay with us earlier because of the approaching darkness went back to Wakde and parked on the airfield wing to wing. I guess they thought the Japanese couldn't fly at night either."

"What happened?" Jablonski asked.

"Two Japanese bombers came in low and bombed and strafed over a hundred fighters sitting on the airstrip. They destroyed most of them. Wakde won't be operational until the Fifth Air Foce can fly in some replacements."

Jablonski said, "I hope they find some pilots who aren't afraid to fly at night."

Sorenson saluted toward the air field as they passed Wakde, and at dawn they turned around and headed north again. It had been a short night.

CHAPTER TWENTY-FOUR

On the sixth of June the Covering Force worked its way north to the familiar position 25 miles northeast of Biak Island. As they steamed along in calm seas, Sorenson sat in his chair in the pilothouse reading a group of messages just decoded by Fineman.

Sorenson laughed. ''These are summaries of intelligence about the recent attempt of the Japanese to land troops on Biak Island. Sounds like a Keystone Cops comedy. First they loaded troops at Davao and Zamboanga in the southern Philippines. Then they started south and were discovered by one of our submarines. Then they turned around and went back to port. Then they started out again and were discovered again by our aerial reconnaissance. They were apprehensive about this, so they unloaded their troops at Sorong, a port at the bird's beak of Northern New Guinea.''

Fineman said, ''Where are the ships now?''

''They went back to Davao, but one of the destroyers was sunk as it tried to enter the harbor by our submarine stationed off the port.''

Fineman said, ''Well, that'll be one less for them to use for the next effort.''

''Good thought, because intelligence says they're going to load up for another try soon.''

"Maybe the eighth of June."

"That means we have to keep doing this yoyo bit for a few more days."

On the seventh, while the Covering Force was fueling at Humboldt Bay, Sorenson noticed that the flagship suddenly left the tanker. He called down to the decoding shack. "Is something coming in?"

Renard, who was decoding, said, "Yes, sir. A long intelligence dispatch was just interrupted by a priority message to Admiral Crutchley. I'll read it to you off the tape. "GET UNDERWAY IMMEDIATELY AND PROCEED TO POSITION OFF KORIM BAY NORTHERN NEW GUINEA BY 2200 JUNE 8."

Sorenson said, "Thanks. Bring the intelligence message up when you have it typed." He turned to Jablonski, "Where is Korim Bay?"

Jablonski pointed to the chart desk in the pilothouse. "In the middle of the north coast of Biak Island."

Renard brought the long intelligence dispatch up, and Sorenson read it carefully. He said, "It says the Japanese are sending several destroyers to Sorong to re-load the troops they left there the other night. Some troops will be loaded on barges that will be towed by the destroyers."

Jablonski shuddered. "What a hell of a way to go to war. North of Guadalcanal the Japs tried using barges to ferry troops. When our destroyers caught them, the Japanese destroyers just abandoned the troop-filled barges and took off. Our ships pounded the hell out of the helpless barges and killed hundreds of troops."

Sorenson pursed his lips thoughtfully. "The Japanese never developed the kinds of amphibious ships and craft we have. I guess they have to improvise for operations like this."

"Yes, sir, but abandoning the helpless troops isn't my kind of warfare. It doesn't jibe with the conduct of the Japanese when they have to defend a place like Biak or Tarawa. They fight to the last man."

Sorenson shrugged. ''Their Army and Navy don't get along too well. Maybe this is a case of that failing.''

''If it is, I hope they do the same thing tomorrow night.''

Kittredge, the young seaman who had been drafted to augment the signal force, came into the pilothouse. ''Captain, there's a signal flying from the *Australia* to get underway immediately.''

''Thank you, Kittredge. How do you like the signal bridge?''

Kittredge smiled broadly. ''Fine, sir, I hope I can stay up here.''

Chief Vickers says he needs you, too, in Mount 53. If we can find a relief for you somewhere, I'll bring you up here permanently.''

Kittredge beamed. ''I'd like that, sir.''

Sorenson turned to MacIntosh, who had the officer of the deck watch. Sorenson had kept the steaming watch on even though they had anchored after fueling. ''MacIntosh, pass the word that we will get underway immediately.''

Sorenson noticed a bustle on the top decks of the *Australia* as men ran about bringing in the mooring lines from the tanker. The other cruisers, already fueled, were hoisting their anchors.

The *Carson* joined the rapidly forming screen off the Bay, and in minutes the Covering Group was formed and heading north at 20 knots.

In the early afternoon, a message came in saying that the few reconnaissance aircraft left at Wakde Airfield and some from the Lake Sentani airfields had located several Japanese destroyers steaming south toward Sorong.

''That's the group we'll be looking for,'' Sorenson said to Dubose who had come up to the bridge to plan meal times for the crew. ''We'd better plan on an early dinner for the crew and then sandwiches and coffee on station from then on until we see an end to this.''

Dubose agreed, and just as he was leaving, another message came up.

"Wait a minute," Sorenson said. "Let's see what this says." He read it quickly and smiled. He said, "Our Fifth Air Force friends have located the force and made several attacks. They claim sinking one destroyer and damaging two others."

"Great!" Dubose said.

"Just the same, the other destroyers picked up survivors and continued heading south. I think the game is still on for tonight."

When the Covering Force was still about 120 miles from Korim Bay, radar reported a bogey circling out of gun range. "Damn!" Sorenson said. "We need our own combat air patrol, either from carriers or from the Air Force. This bastard will report our position, and we can't do anything about him."

About 2100, with Korim Bay nearby, bogies began to appear on the air search radar screen. Bronte reported, "They don't seem to want to attack."

Sorenson answered, "Maybe they have trouble seeing us. There's an overcast with many rain showers. Keep a close watch on them."

Half an hour later a bogey approached within 3 miles of the formation on the other side of the screen and a destroyer opened fire. The bogey quickly scooted out of range.

As the task group approached Korim Bay, Admiral Crutchley formed the cruisers in column and placed a division of destroyers on each bow. A third destroyer division made up of the *Warramunga* and *Arunta* formed astern, and Sorenson's two-ship division was sent out ahead three miles.

No surface forces appeared as they passed Korim Bay. Admiral Crutchley detached the destroyer *Mullany* to search Korim Bay, and the remainder of the covering force continued northwest along the coast of Biak Island.

Soon after they had passed Korim Bay, a report came in from a searching Navy Liberator on the aircraft resonnaissance circuit, "Five unidentified ships course southeast speed 12 knots."

The *Mullany* came back at high speed and re-joined her division.

From CIC, Dubose sent a recommended course to intercept, and Admiral Crutchley soon changed to approximately that course. Destroyer division 42 was ordered to change station from the head of the formation to back on the quarter, but seemed not to get the message. Sorenson laughed. "He's stalling. He doesn't want to miss the action."

Bronte sent word up that Destroyer Division 42 was increasing speed to thirty knots. Sorenson laughed again. "Doesn't sound like he's going back to the quarter."

Dubose reported, "The enemy ships have slowed and turned north. From the way the radar contacts look, they're casting off their barges and leaving the area. What we think are barges are dead in the water, and the destroyers are forming up and increasing speed.

Then Dubose reported. "They've turned toward us."

Sorenson said, "Watch them closely. They may be turning to unmask their torpedo batteries."

Two minutes later, Dubose reported that the contacts had turned north and were increasing speed.

Sorenson said, "They've fired torpedoes! Gun control, keep a sharp lookout for wakes! Talker, alert the lookouts!"

The night was so dark and the overcast so low Sorenson knew they would probably not see the faint torpedo wakes, but on the other hand the Japanese could not have seen the ships clearly either, and probably had fired a spread on an approximate bearing. In any event, they had to press on.

Sorenson swallowed. This was another time when they had no choice. He had to take the risk. If they failed to avoid the torpedoes, many of his officers and men would die, and the ship would surely sink. He thought briefly of Ferren, but a message coming in brought him back to the present.

Over the TBS came the order from Admiral Crutchley, "All destroyers pursue and attack!"

Sorenson grinned. "I understand that order. Admiral Nelson would be proud of his descendant."

Now the destroyer divisions were well on their way toward the enemy, and no torpedoes had been sighted. Sorenson breathed easier. Desdiv 47 was about a mile to the east of them, and Desdiv 48 was coming up astern. The two Australian destroyers were trying desperately to close the gap. Sorenson's division, with a head start, was to the east and abreast of the leading division.

Sorenson called down to Main Engine Control. Reifel answered. Sorenson said, "Give us all you've got."

The RPM indicator crept up as the engineers below opened the burner nozzles wide in the four straining boilers and the throttlemen coaxed a few more turns out of the screaming turbines.

CIC reported that the enemy had split into two columns, one with three destroyers and the other with two. Well astern of their own formation they could see the helpless barges disappearing off the radar screen.

From CIC came the report. "They're making 32 knots."

Sorenson looked at the annunciator. It showed turns for 35 knots. The *Ransome* astern had fallen back a few hundred yards, but otherwise was keeping up with the flying *Carson*.

Back in the cruiser formation there were reports of passing torpedoes and the cruisers individually changed course to avoid them. They had missed the American destroyers, but Sorenson remembered that Japanese destroyers carried re-loads. In about fifteen minutes the American destroyers would be in mortal danger again.

The range closed tantalizingly. It was now about 16,000 yards, just out of 5-inch gun range.

Just after 0100, Commodore Jarrell, in Desdiv 47, turned his division to port to unmask his after guns and opened fire.

Sorenson said, ''Clever maneuver. Now let's see what the Japanese do.''

The Japanese reacted by turning to starboard.

Sorenson said, ''This may let us close the range, but it also gives the Japanese time to fire a salvo of torpedoes.''

Jablonski said, ''That's right. They've had time to reload the spare torpedoes they carry.''

But the change of course let Desdiv 47 and Sorenson's division close the range to 15,000 yards, just inside the range of the 5-inch guns.

Sorenson ordered, ''Commence firing!''

Steiner's response was immediate. Four projectiles were on their way, their tracers arcing high in the air because the guns were elevated to almost 45 degrees. After the tension of the long chase, the blast was almost welcome, and more salvos poured out in a long-awaited catharsis.

Suddenly Sorenson thought about the depth charges. They had been kept ready when the destroyers were in an antisubmarine screen, but when the ships had been shifted to an attack formation, Sorenson had forgotten to order the depth charges put on safe in case the ship was sunk. Depth charges not set on safe could kill survivors in the water when the charges on a sinking ship reached the depth set on them.

Scorse had just brought a message up to the pilot house, and Sorenson said to him, ''Please check to see that the depth charges are set on safe.''

Scorse said, ''Aye, aye, sir,'' and left the bridge.

Five minutes and several salvos later a dull red flash blossomed on one of the fleeing enemy ships about five miles ahead, and CIC reported a blip dropping behind. Steiner shifted fire to another ship in the fleeing formation, but the ship that had been hit soon speeded up and rejoined.

Then Admiral Crutchley ordered the destroyers to break off the attack and rejoin.

''What!'' shouted Jablonski. ''He can't quit now.''

Sorenson shook his head. ''He has to. He was ordered to break off by 0230.''

Sorenson, who had the conn, reluctantly gave the order, ''Left full rudder. All ahead full.''

Just as they were half way through the turn, a salvo of Japanese projectiles landed near the fantail. The ship shook, and huge geysers of water rose from the near misses.

''Jesus!'' Sorenson shouted, ''Where did those things come from?''

Jablonski said, ''The right hand column is shootng at us.''

Sorenson knew there was nothing further that needed to be done to avoid succeeding salvos. They were already in a tight turn. He waited anxiously, hoping the next salvo would be shorter. But it wasn't, and there was a loud explosion aft. The flash was yellower than the near misses had been.

''Damn!'' Jablonski said, ''We've been hit.''

Sorenson continued the turn to the left until they were headed for the cruisers and then steadied on the bearing of the cruisers. He called down to CIC. ''Tell the Executive Officer to go aft and see what the damage is.''

Below on the main deck Sorenson could hear feet pounding on the deck as Chief Bellows and his forward repair party made their way aft to join the after repair party.

Sorenson headed for the cruisers at 25 knots, hoping the hits aft had not impaired the engineering department.

He called the forward engine room and asked to speak to Reifel. Chief Machinist's Mate Hodges came on the line and said, ''Captain, Mister Reifel has gone to the after engine room to see what the damage is there.''

Sorenson asked, ''Do you have any idea what happened there?''

''No, sir. We can't communicate with them, but they're answering all bells.''

''Ask Mister Reifel to call me when he comes back to the forward engine room.''

''Aye, aye, sir.''

Dubose ran aft as fast as he could in the dark. When he got to the main deck near the K-gun, he could dimly make out two men leaning over someone on deck. The figure was inert, one leg bent at an odd angle, and it was dressed in officer's khaki. He went over to the group and leaned down, trying to identify the man on deck. Chief Bellows straightend up and said, ''Ha-Mister Scorse. Ha-he dead.''

Dubose swore, ''What happened?''

''Ha-look over dere.''

Dubose looked at the deck edge outboard of where they were gathered. There was a four foot square hole in the deck where the K-gun and its rack of depth charges had been located.

Dubose leaned over the side. He could see that the hole began about two feet above the waterline and extended upwards to join the hole in the deck. The area looked like a huge shark had taken a bite out of the *Carson*'s side.

He turned back to Bellows. ''Any more men dead or injured?''

''Ha-can't find none, sir.''

Dubose said, ''Get the stretcher bearers to take Mister Scorse's body down to the wardroom and then see what you can do about patching up that damned hole. We need to keep water out of the engine room. If we hit bad weather we might flood it.''

Dubose went back to mount 53 and knocked on the side door. The mount captain opened it. Dubose said, ''Did you see Mister Scorse back here just before we got hit?''

Smith said, ''Yes, sir. He was looking at the depth charges. I guess to see if they were set on safe. Then he started back up forward and the explosion went off over there. Did he get hit?''

''Yes. He's dead.''

The mount captain shook his head. ''Too bad. I liked him.''

Dubose headed back for the bridge.

Sorenson watched Dubose and Reifel slowly come up the ladder to the bridge. As they stepped up on the signal bridge, he said, ''Bad news?''

Dubose said, ''Yes. We took a Japanese projectile hit in the side just below the starboard K-gun.''

Reifel nodded. ''It came through the skin of the ship and detonated on a pump just inside the after engine room. The force went upwards and out and blew a good-sized hole in the side. The bottom of it is only two feet above the water line. Chief Bellows and my gang are putting a temporary patch over it with mattresses and shores. We'll have to get it fixed soon before we hit any weather.''

''Lots of damage in the engine room?''

''No, sir. Not much. The pump it hit was demolished, but we can bypass it. The explosion cut some wiring, including the telephone circuit to the forward engine room. That's why we couldn't communicate with them. Several men caught some flying shrapnel.''

Dubose cleared his throat. ''I'm afraid we weren't so lucky topside. Scorse is dead.''

''No! What was he doing back there?''

''You remember you asked him when he was on the bridge to make sure the depth charges were set on safe?''

''Sure, but I didn't expect him to do it himself. He should have called down to the chief torpedoman.''

''Apparently he didn't. The mount captain of mount 53 saw him going forward from the depth charge rack just before the explosion.''

Sorenson turned white in the red gleam of the pilothouse lights. He clenched his hands. ''Damn! I sent him to his death.''

Dubose said, ''No, you didn't. He shouldn't have gone back there himself.''

"He went because he was so damned conscientious."

"Yes, and you can't blame yourself for that."

Sorenson shook his head and clenched his hands. "I'll always blame myself. That's one of the terrible things about being incommand."

Sorenson secured the ship from general quarters and sent for some coffee. He eased back into his chair and sent for Carmody. When Carmody arrived, he said, "Take this dispatch down. 'Suffered projectile hit vicinity starboard K-gun. K-gun and its depth charges missing. Four foot hole in side and also on deck at former location of K-gun. Temporary patches being put on holes. Recommend availability for permanent repairs soonest. One officer killed. Eight men lightly wounded."

Carmody said, "Got it. I'll tell Chief Williams to get it off right away by flashing light."

Shortly after dawn, Wencey, who was now back on duty and had the signal watch, said, "Flagship calling. Stand by to write."

Sorenson got up out of his chair and went over where he could see the clip board over Carmody's shoulder.

Carmody wrote on a message blank on the clip board, "Detached immediately. Proceed with *Ransome* to Manus for temporary repairs. Then proceed to Sydney for permanent repairs and well-earned recreation. Sorry to hear about your loss. Well done. We will miss you. Crutchley."

Sorenson thought the message in normal times would have been welcome, but all he could think of was Scorse, lying alone in his bunk.

He turned to Wencey, "Tell the *Ransome* to fall in astern."

Then he turned back to the officer of the deck, "Ask Jablonski for a course for Manus and head for it. I'll be in the sea cabin."

He turned in in the sea cabin bunk in his clothes, but couldn't sleep. He got up, put on his shoes, and went below to Scorse's room. He pushed back the curtain and went in. Scorse's body was lying in his bunk covered with a sheet.

Sorenson reached down and pulled the sheet back from Scorse's face. Scorse looked very peaceful. His curly black hair was neatly brushed, and his patrician nose rose at a slight angle. Fineman had placed bandaids over several cuts on his face.

He looked at Scorse for several minutes. Tears began to form and then coursed down his cheeks. When he could stand it no longer, he pulled the sheet back over Scorse's face and left quietly.

Back in the sea cabin he took off his shoes and got in his bunk again, but he couldn't sleep. It was one of the longest nights of his life.

CHAPTER TWENTY-FIVE

The next day the *Carson* and *Ransome* steamed over glassy seas, zigzagging and searching methodically with their sonars. Sorenson had little interest in the short trip to Manus, and spent most of it pacing the bridge wing. Vila brought a grilled cheese sandwich to the sea cabin, but Sorenson sent it back untouched.

Vila tried again at dinner with one of Sorenson's favorite dishes, pork chops and mashed potatoes, with the same results.

Sorenson slept little that night, got up before dawn, and took a shower. This time Vila brought up some toast and coffee, and Sorenson finished it. At 0800 the lookouts reported the high green hills behind Manus Harbor in sight and soon the lower outlines of nearby Los Negros Island and the beaten palms behind Seeadler Harbor came in sight over the horizon.

Neither Sorenson nor Jablonski had ever been in Manus Harbor, but the piloting instructions, describing its pre-war condition, painted it as a sleepy tropical port. Sorenson was surprised when the sides of the harbor opened up to see a large group of logistic type ships anchored around the spacious harbor. Repair ships, a floating drydock, ammunition ships, supply ships, and tankers almost filled the harbor.

Ashore dust rose from dozens of bulldozers, clanking in the coral dust and red volcanic soil, building roads and leveling foundations for the many buildings being erected by bustling Army Engineers and Navy Seabees.

As the two ships rounded the edge of the harbor, Brophy, now back on the bridge with his arm in a sling, shouted, "Senior Officer Present Afloat is calling us."

Wencey said, "I got it," and flashed the appropriate signal to the signal light operator on a tender to commence sending.

Brophy, balancing a clipboard on the signal bridge desk with his bad hand, wrote down the incoming message. In a few minutes he took it to Sorenson. Sorenson was looking straight ahead. "Read it to me," he said.

Brophy looked at Sorenson. "Dammit, Captain, stop blaming yourself. The whole crew knows you aren't responsible for Mister Scorse's death. The Goddam Japs killed him. Not you. Now stop moping and listen to this dispatch. Life has to go on."

Sorenson turned his head slowly toward Brophy and grinned bleakly. "Brophy, you are a helluv an Irishman. You guys know how to meet death, and I thank you for the advice. Now read the damned dispatch."

Brophy cleared his throat and grinned tentatively. "It says to moor to the port side of the repair ship in berth sixty-one for temporary repairs."

Sorenson said to Jablonski, "When you can, identify Berth sixty-one."

Jablonski came over to the captain's chair and pointed ahead. "Just behind the tanker with the two destroyers alongside to port."

"Thanks," Sorenson said. "Auerbach, take her in. Call away the linehandling and anchor details."

Auerbach relayed the order to the boatswain's mate of the watch, and Sorenson listened as the boatswain sounded his pipe and passed the word.

When all stations had reported manned and ready, Auerbach said to the talker, "Tell Chief Bellows I'll be up on the bridge while we come alongside."

The talker relayed the word. Then he laughed. ''Chief Bellows says he'll rig an additional fender alongside and please don't scratch his paintwork too much.''

Sorenson, listening, managed a faint smile, and he realized he was coming back to normal. After all, he thought, he was still responsible for over three hundred other officers and men of the *Carson,* and they deserved his best efforts.

Auerbach managed the landing without a scratch, and Sorenson set the port watch and went below to take a shower.

An hour later, he left to call on the Commanding Officer of the repair ship. The Repair Officer, in company with the Executive Officer, Reifel, and Auerbach, had already completed a preliminary inspection of the damage to the *Carson.*

When Sorenson arrived at the Commanding Officer's cabin, he had just finished a conference with his Repair Officer over the *Carson's* condition.

After Sorenson had introduced himself and accepted a cup of coffee, the Commanding Officer said, ''We can fix you up in three days. The Repair Officer, here, will give you the details.''

The Repair Officer consulted his notes and said, ''We'll have to put in a strength member along the edge of the deck. Then we'll trim the edges of the hole and weld a plate over the side hole and another over the deck hole. It won't be pretty, but it will be strong and watertight. You'll get a new K-gun in Sydney. We'll have to run temporary wiring around the wires cut in the explosion. Again, Sydney will run more permanent wiring. You'll be able to do anything you could do before except use the K-gun. You just won't look very pretty back there.''

Sorenson thanked the Repair Officer and asked to talk over something else of importance with the Commanding Officer.

"Certainly." the Commanding Officer turned to the repair officer and said, "Harry, thank you. Go ahead with the work as you outlined it."

After the Repair Officer had left, the Commanding Officer said, "How can I help you?"

"Just some advice. I have an officer who was killed in the action off Biak two nights ago. He wanted to be buried in the cemetery at Seeadler Harbor, and we have to do it within a day or too because the body won't keep too long in the tropics. I need to find a means of transporting it and a funeral party to Seeadler Harbor. Our whale boat would take all day."

The Commanding Officer thought for a few seconds. Then his face brightened. "I have the solution. There are four PT boats on my other side completing a short overhaul. One has to get under way and run his engines in this afternoon. I'm sure he'll be glad to do it. You go back to your ship and make the arrangements and I'll have his PT boat alongside you at 1400."

Sorenson said, "That takes a load off my mind, and I thank you very much. If I can ever do anything in return, let me know."

The Commanding Officer screwed up his face. "Say, isn't the *Carson* that can that's famous for sing alongs? Maybe we could borrow your group some night."

Sorenson nodded. "We're the culprits, all right, but I'm afraid we're not in the mood right now. Maybe we can do it later."

Back on the *Carson*, Sorenson sent for Dubose and explained the arrangements he had made.

"Fine," Dubose said. "Chief Vickers wants to send an eight-man firing squad, and Terrill volunteered to play taps on his clarinet."

Sorenon raised his eyebrows.

Dubose said, "Don't worry. We've had a practice run, and it sounds okay. Maybe better than a bugle."

''What about a service?''

''Reifel will do it. He's all set.''

''But Scorse was a Catholic, and I think Reifel's a Baptist.''

''I don't think it makes any difference in the Navy. Reifel will use the standard Navy service designed to be used for all religions just like all chaplains use. After the service and his prayers, the quartet will sing Eternal Father, the Navy hymn.''

''I think that sounds like just what he would have wanted.'' Sorenson said, ''Let's get started, We leave at 1400.''

At 1400 the petty officer of the watch reported a PT boat coming alongside, and Sorenson got up to the after part of the deck in time to see it make its approach. The PT's powerful engines were throttled down to idle, but still the burbling roar drowned conversation on the deck nearby.

When the PT was moored to the *Carson*, it shut down its engines, and the Captain came aboard. Sorenson met him and shook hands after the routine ceremonies of boarding. ''Thank you for your help. it means a great deal to us. We never could have made it to Seeadler in our whale boat.''

The PT boat captain grinned. ''I have to make full speed to test our engines. We should make it in about twenty minutes.''

Sorenson said, ''I didn't think about where we would land. We were here when the island was taken, and there weren't any piers.''

''That's changed in a hurry. The Seabees put in a pontoon causeway, and we'll have no trouble. We're ready to go when you are.''

Sorenson nodded to Dubose and Dubose turned to Chief Bellows. Bellows went forward and soon six men appeared carrying a stout wooden coffin that had been made hurriedly by the repair ship.

Other men on the deck of the PT boat grabbed the outer edge of the coffin and it was handed over and placed in the center of the deck. Men on the PT boat lashed it securely in place, and Wencey boarded the PT and placed an American flag over the crude box. He lashed it securely to the edges of fittings on deck. Some of the PT men, watching him, shook their heads and added to the lashings.

One said, "Forty-five knots will carry away just about anything. You may have to sit on it."

Wencey nodded. "I will if I have to."

Then Chief Gunner's Mate Vickers and eight men wearing leggings and carrying rifles boarded and took their places next to the coffin.

Wencey, now worried, said, "Sit on the flag, but only if you have to.

Dubose, Reifel, Auerbach, and Fineman then boarded and went up to the tiny wardroom. When Sorenson boarded, the Captain invited him to use his miniscule cabin, but Sorenson said, "May I join you on the bridge?"

"Of course," the PT Captain said. "Follow me, sir."

The PT Captain nodded to his Chief of the Crew and started the engines. They coughed, spewed a stream of smoke out their exhausts, and quit.

The PT Captain said, "Don't worry. That's why we're running them in."

On the next start, they coughed again but caught and began to work up to a roar. When the Captain was satisfied, he raised a hand to his crew chief and the crew chief in turn gave hand signals to the men standing by the mooring lines.

The mooring lines were taken in quickly, and the PT boat began to back away.

Sorenson looked back at the *Carson*. Although he had not given any orders to do so, the officers and men of the *Carson* were standing on the topside and saluting. Sorenson returned the salute for Scorse, and again he felt the tears forming in his eyes. There was nothing like the crew of a ship that had been welded together by action, and he felt very proud of the *Carson* and her crew.

The PT boat stopped clear of the *Carson's* stern and the Captain shoved the throttles partially ahead. Sorenson felt the hull surge under him and grabbed the bridge rail. Still, he was unprepared when they cleared the harbor and the PT Captain shoved the throttles all the way forward. The roar of the engines increased to the point where they hurt Sorenson's ears, and he almost missed the rail when he grabbed for it.

The PT Captain grinned and shoved a piece of cotton toward him. Sorenson put pieces of it in his ears and felt better.

Sorenson looked aft to make sure the coffin was secure. It was fine, but Chief Vickers and his firing squad were trying frantically to control the flapping flag. Finally Vickers sat on one corner of the coffin and the others joined him. The flag still flapped, but now it stayed in place.

Just as the PT Captain had predicted, they slowed and burbled in to the steel pier at Seeadler Harbor in about 20 minutes.

Dubose supervised the lifting of the coffin off the PT boat, and willing hands carried it up the pier and back to the small cemetery a hundred yards behind the beach.

Sorenson went to a small shack next to the cemetery and knocked. There was a small sign next to the door saying "Army Graves Registration Service."

An Army soldier dressed in khaki shorts, no shirt, a forage hat, and sandals came out and said, "What can I do for you, sir?"

"We'd like to bury an officer from our ship in your cemetery. Is there a section consecrated for Catholics?"

"Yes, sir. Follow me."

The soldier led Sorenson to an area where there were three open graves and a group of natives nearby digging several othergraves.

Sorenson said, "Why are there so many unused graves here?"

The soldier said, ''The Army is still digging Japs out of the caves over on Manus. Some of our troops get killed in the process. We get several customers every day. You can take your pick of the grave sites, courtesy of the Army Graves Registration Service.''

Sorenson chose an open grave with one end pointing to Seeadler Harbor and beckoned the rest of the funeral party over. They picked up the coffin and carried it over to the grave Sorenson had chosen. Sorenson looked around the cemetery. Except in the new section they were in, he could see neat rows of graves marked with small headstones.

He said to the Army sergeant, ''Where did these head markers come from?

The sergeant grinned and hitched up his shorts. ''They always arrive just after the Army lands. We strive to please.''

Sorenson sent Chief Vickers and his firing squad to form up a hundred yards away in the shade, and Terrill with his clarinet in the other direction.

Reifel placed his cap on a nearby bush and opened his Navy Hymn Book. When Sorenson indicated he was ready, Reifel began to read the standard Navy service from the Navy Hymn Book in his deep rolling voice. Then he opened a Bible and read in Latin some of the passages used in Catholic Masses.

When he had finished, he read a prayer and nodded at Sorenson. Sorenson stepped forward and gave a brief eulogy, stumbling at times when tears welled up in his reddened eyes.

He finished his brief remarks and turned to Chief Vickers and waved. He could hear Chief Vickers giving orders to the firing squad, and then three volleys rang out.

Sorenson turned to Terrill and nodded. Terrill began to play taps softly on the clarinet. The notes were true and lingering.

When the last note died, the firing squad stacked their arms and came forward to lower the coffin into the open grave.

While they were getting ready, Fineman led the quartet in singing the Navy Hymn. The words moved Sorenson. "Eternal father, strong to save," and he remembered that Scorse had known no other Father but the Navy. The Hymn went on, "Whose arm hath bound the restless wave."

When it was over, Sorenson turned to Vickers. Vickers found two pieces of line and passed them under the large box. Before the men started lowering the flag-draped box, Vickers said, "Captain, should we take the colors off to forward them to his family?"

Sorenson shook his head. "He had no family except his shipmates. Let's leave the colors with him."

Vickers nodded and gave the orders to his men. They slowly lowered the coffin into the open grave. When they finished, Dubose looked inquiringly at Sorenson.

Sorenson said, "Go ahead back to the PT boat. I'll be with you in a minute."

The funeral party trudged across the sand toward the pier, and the natives nearby, who had been leaning on their shovels watching, started toward the grave to fill it. Sorenson held up his hand, and they stopped and leaned on their shovels again.

For several minutes Sorenson stared down at the coffin and its covering colors. Then he pulled out of his pocket the Silver Star Medal he had recently been awarded, leaned over, and tossed it on top of the starred portion of the flag covering the coffin. It bounced once and turned over so that it was upright.

Through welling tears, he said, "Lieutenant Sydney Scorse, I hereby award you the Siver Star Medal for Gallantry in action. You did more to earn it than I did."

Sorenson wiped the tears from his eyes and beckoned the party of natives to come forward. They shuffled to the side of the grave and began to shovel sand into the gaping hole.

Sorenson watched until the shining medal and the flag were covered with sand, and then he turned and walked slowly toward the PT boat. All the way there he could hear the plop of shovelsfull of sand landing on the coffin.

The trip back was just as quick as the trip to the island had been, and Sorenson boarded the *Carson* after thanking the PT Captain for his help. He went to his lower cabin, sat down, and put his head in his hands.

Doctor Fineman followed him and knocked on his door. Sorenson said, ''Come in.''

When he saw who it was, he said, ''David, I don't want to talk now.''

Fineman said, ''This is the time to talk, while you still remember clearly. First, I know you are blaming yourself for Scorse's death. You shouldn't, and nobody thinks you should.''

Sorenson grinned. ''Yes, Brophy set me straight, but that doesn't take the pain away.''

''Are you beginning to realize that you gave an order under extreme stress and it was a good order that you'd probably give again under the same circumstances?''

''Yes. Dubose told me that.''

Fineman said, ''You take chances all the time when you let the officers and chief petty officers handle the ship.''

Sorenson sighed. ''I may have worn out Chief Vickers.''

''No, you haven't. He may not want to do it again, but I've heard he's been bragging in the CPO mess. This is a good thing you do, and it makes the officers and chief petty officers feel they're a part of the ship.''

Sorenson nodded. ''That's why I do it. You should have seen Scorse when he was coming alongside a cruiser a few days ago. Dubose and I remarked about how he looked like a Roman charioteer.''

''Yes. Scorse talked about it in the wardroom for days.''

''He had no relatives. No family. The *Carson* was his family and home.''

''Then shut the other thoughts out of your mind and think about how you brought his family to life. You made him very happy.''

''If only he hadn't been so conscientious.''

''That, too, was a good quality, and you wouldn't have wanted him to change.''

Sorenson looked at Fineman. ''By the way, you haven't handled the ship yet.''

Fineman paled. ''Er, no, that's not my field.''

Sorenson grinned. ''Why not? You said you'd sailed a lot.''

''Ah, yes, but just small stuff. This damned thing is huge compared to a cat boat.''

''It works roughly the same. It just puts out a lot of smoke and soot. Come up to the bridge tomorrow when we get underway.''

''You're not thinking of---?''

''I'm your patient. You ought to see if I'm all right.''

Fineman tried to change the subject. He said, ''You're getting a lot of good advice from all of us. Now take it.''

Sorenson sighed and yawned. ''I'll try.''

''When did you last sleep?''

Sorenson shook his head. ''I honestly can't remember.''

Fineman took a bottle of pills out of his pocket and handed two to Sorenson. ''Take these with a full glass of water as soon as I leave and get into your bunk quickly. Otherwise you may go to sleep on the deck.''

Sorenson grinned. ''Are they that fast?''

''Trust me.''

After Fineman left, Sorenson went into the head and took the pills. They were not quite as fast as Fineman had said they were, but Sorenson slept through the evening and well into the next morning.

CHAPTER TWENTY-SIX

Late the next morning Sorenson was awakened by the sound of chipping hammers clack-clacking on the forecastle deck. For a moment he couldn't remember where he was. Then the memories of the day before and the sad occasion of the funeral flooded back. He thought about them, but he was now more nearly able to accept what had happened.

He looked at his watch. Breakfast in the wardroom had long since ended. He rolled out of his bunk, rang the telephone bell to the wardoom pantry, and ordered breakfast brought up to his cabin.

Meanwhile he shaved, showered, and dressed, and as he was tying his shoe laces, Vila knocked and brought his breakfast in.

"Good morning, Captain," Vila said. "I see you're ready to eat again. I've added some doughnuts that Chief Williams made to your order."

Sorenson stood up and headed for his desk where Vila had placed his breakfast tray. "Thank you. This looks good. My compliments to Chief Williams."

Vila said, "Big Jackson fixed this. He's a good grits man. Would you like to try some?"

Sorenson said, "Sure, but this will hold me for now. I'll try some tomorrow. How's the weather outside?"

''For Filipinos and Texans, almost coolish. For others, hot as hell.''

Sorenson went topside and back to the area where the projectile had hit. Repair ship personnel in leather welding suits and darkened glass face masks were working on the plates, welding them to the fore and aft strength member they had already welded in place.

Sorenson shielded his eyes from the flashing electric welding arcs of the welders' equipment.

Auerbach was also watching, and came to his side.

Sorenson said, ''How's it going?''

''Fine, sir. They're on time. Other men are below working on the replacement wiring. We can plan to leave day after tomorrow.''

''Good,'' Sorenson said. ''We'll get underway at 0800 and stop at Milne Bay to fuel. Let me know if there's any change in our progress.''

Sorenson left the scene of the repairs and sent a message to the *Ransome* anchored nearby to be ready to get underway at 0800 two days later.

At 0730, on the day they were to get underway, Sorenson sat in his bridge chair watching Steele, who had taken Scorse's place as officer of the deck for special sea detail.

Steele was supervising the testing of the steering system, the engine order telegraph, and the gyro-compass repeater.

Bronte came by, turned on and tested the surface search radar PPI, and said good morning.

Sorenson got up and went back to the signal bridge to see if there were any doughnuts left. He was too late. All that remained were a few crumbs of sugar. He went back into the pilothouse and said to Steele, ''Please send for Doctor Fineman. Tell him I want to see him on the bridge as soon as possible.''

Three minutes Fineman came up the ladder, puffing, and said, ''Where's the patient?''

''Over here,'' Sorenson said, ''I'm the one you're supposed to see.''

Fineman looked at him closely, and put his fingers on his wrist. ''Your eyes are clear and your pulse is normal. Do you have a temperature or any other symptoms?''

''No. I seem to be fine.''

''Then what's wrong?''

''Nothing really, but two days ago you said to call you if I needed anything. I just wanted you up here to take the ship away from alongside the repair ship and out of the harbor.''

Fineman blanched. ''Ah, er, I don't think---.''

Sorenson stopped him. ''Let's think positively. You can do it. I'll back you up and make sure you don't get into trouble. You said you've sailed.''

''But just a cat boat. This hunk of steel is a lot different.''

''No, it isn't. Steele will keep the deck and run the administration. All you have to do is get the ship away from the repair ship and out of the harbor.''

Fineman looked up at the high, bluff side of the repair ship and then at the ships anchored in the crowded harbor. ''Would you try to take an appendix out?''

''Sure, if you stood behind me.''

Fineman shook his head. ''I give up. It's on your head. What do I do first?''

''You tell the helmsman and the man on the engine order telegraph that you have the conn.''

Fineman repeated the information, and the men on the wheel and the engine order telegraph grinned broadly and said, ''Aye, aye, sir.''

Fineman said, ''Now what?''

''You remember from all the times you've been up here when we've left another ship or a pier, that we have to back out because the stern moves when we use the rudder and engines. The bow doesn't move much. It's not like an automobile, which is just the opposite.''

''Oh, yes. I remember. You take in most of the lines and put the rudder over toward the repair ship. Then you go ahead on the outside engine and back on the inside engine until the stern swings out.''

''So far so good. They're called the outboard engine and the inboard engine, not the outside and inside engines. When you have the stern where you want it, you take in the last line and back away.''

Fineman said, ''I think I have it.'' He began to pace back and forth in the pilothouse, muttering practice orders to himself.

When Steele reported that the ship was ready for getting underway with all lines singled up, Sorenson said to Steele, ''Tell Main Engine Control to stand by to answer all bells.''

Sorenson turmed to Fineman. ''Okay, Doctor. The patient is ready. Time to operate. Let's go out on the starboard wing so we can see better.''

Fineman followed Sorenson out to the starboard wing, looked aft, and said in a shaky voice, ''Take in all lines except two.''

Sorenson laughed. ''Don't just tell me. The men inside the pilothouse have to hear you. Steele is standing in the door to make sure they get the word right.''

Fineman turned toward Steele and repeated the order in a louder voice.

Down on the forecastle and aft men scurried around the deck taking in the lines. On the forecastle, a single line leading aft to the repair ship held the *Carson*.

Fineman looked astern of the ship. Sorenson said, ''Good. You looked aft, and all is clear astern. Go on.''

Fineman looked uncertain, but he gave the order, ''Port engine ahead one-third, starboard engine back one-third, right full rudder.''

The ship surged ahead slowly against the remaining mooring line, and the stern swung out. Fineman watched it and when it was about ten degrees out, he looked at Sorenson. Sorenson nodded.

Fineman said in an increasingly confident tone of voice, ''Take in two. All engines back two-thirds. Rudder amidships.''

Inside the pilothouse Steele pulled down the whistle cord and sounded a long blast. Fineman started when the blast began, but soon regained his composure.

As the *Carson* backed clear of the repair ship, Sorenson searched the area astern. Fineman noticed what he was doing, and followed his movements. When Sorenson was sure there was clear space astern he nodded at Fineman. Fineman seemed uncertain as to his next move, and Sorenson said, "Now twist her and head for the harbor entrance."

Fineman gave the order, "Starboard ahead two-thirds."

When the ship lost sternway, he added, "Left full rudder."

"Good," Sorenson said. "Now look through the sight on the pelorus over there and pick out a course to the entrance."

Fineman bent over the sight vanes on the pelorus at the edge of the bridge, shut one eye, and looked through the other. "Two four six," he said.

"Fine. Now tell the helmsman."

Fineman shouted in a firm voice, "Steer two four six." The helmsman acknowledged by repeating the order and spun the wheel.

Sorenson said, "Your port engine is still backing."

Fineman looked surprised and glanced over the port side. The propeller was churning up foam and pushing it forward. "Port ahead two-thirds," he shouted.

Back came the acknowledgement, the churning stopped, and the ship slid slowly ahead. The delay in changing the port engine had offset the course of the *Carson*. Sorenson squinted ahead and noticed that the heading now pointed them directly at the stern of a moored tanker. He pointed at the tanker and said, "Unless you come left a little, you're going to end up in one of that guy's fuel tanks."

Fineman looked at the tanker and said, "Right ten degrees rudder." Sorenson said nothing, and the helmsman looked confused. He began to turn the wheel slowly.

Sorenson said, ''Ah, Doctor, your right hand knoweth not what your left hand doeth.''

Fineman noticed the slow swing of the ship and said, ''Damn! I'm used to putting the tiller of a sail boat to the right in order to come left.''

''Well, then, you'd better tell the helmsman.''

Fineman said, ''Forget the last order. Left ten degrees rudder.''

The helmsman looked relieved and spun the wheel rapidly to the left. The ship began to swing clear of the tanker.

Sorenson said, ''Every profession has its own language. It's customary to say 'belay the last order' rather than to say 'forget it.' ''

Fineman said, ''One thing at a time. I saved us, didn't I?''

''Yes, you did, and a fine job it was, too. Now you can turn the conn over to Steele.''

Steele grinned and said, ''I have the conn. Good job, Doc.''

Fineman let out a huge sigh. ''I feel like a large weight has been lifted from my shoulders.''

Sorenson grinned. ''You're not supposed to feel that way. You should feel fulfilled.''

Fineman grinned weakly. ''I guess I do a litle. Sort of like the satisfacion of giving birth.''

Sorenson laughed, ''And for you, almost as painful.''

They steamed south for two days, and entered Milne Bay to fuel. That morning after breakfast, Fineman came up to the bridge and said good morning to Sorenson. Sorenson said, ''Up here to bring the ship in, or just to say you're not mad at me any more?''

Fineman said, ''No. Just up here to laugh at the next sucker.''

Sorenson said, ''You're looking at him. I'm taking the ship alongside. I need the practice.''

When they were alongside a tanker, the mail orderly came back with the news that all of their mail had been forwarded to Sydney.

The bad news speeded up the fueling, and soon they were out of Milne Bay and headed south.

Sorenson followed their progrees south toward Sydney on the navigational chart Jablonski kept. For the first time in months they were out of radar range of land, and Sorenson was in charge of the two-ship formation. That meant that Jablonski had to navigate by the stars, sun, and moon, taking sights with a sextant and working out their position.

Sorenson watched him taking sextant sights at dawn and for practice took some sights himself and worked out the sights with him. When they had both finished and made their plots, Sorenson's fix was within two miles of Jablonski's and he was satisfied that he could still read a sextant and work out the results.

As they got farther south he relaxed the requirement for morning general quarters and let the crew sleep in.

"Gotta get them in shape for Sydney," he told Fineman. "They haven't been ashore in a civilized town for a good many months."

Fineman raised his eyebrows. "You're not talking about Sydney?"

"Sure. But I've never been there. Have you?"

"Yes. It's civilized, all right, but maybe too much. The Aussies are tough customers and won't take anything from our sailors. I predict a lot of fights and a good many stitches."

Each day they made about four hundred miles to the south, passing through the waters of the Coral Sea on the first and second day.

Auerbach, on watch, said, "There are some of my friends at the bottom of this sea. The Battle of the Coral Sea was a bloody one."

On the third day the weather had changed noticeably. Biak had been just south of the equator, and now, a thousand miles south, the weather was like that of San Diego in February. The seasons were reversed in the southern hemisphere, and winter was coming on.

On the fourth day they rounded the easternmost part of Australia off Brisbane and changed course slightly to the west to head directly for Sydney.

That night Sorenson broke out a blanket, and the next morning put on a sweater for the bridge.

On the morning of the fifth day, Sorenson kept the uniform khakis, but issued foul weather jackets.

About 0600 the lookouts sighted the twin headlands flanking Sydney Harbor. Jablonski recommended a course for the entrance, and they stopped just short of it to allow the net vessel to pull the antisubmarine nets back.

Just inside the net vessel, a pilot boat was waiting. Jablonski said, "In Sydney a pilot is mandatory. We'll have to pick one up."

The pilot boat came alongside, and Dubose went aft to meet and escort the pilot to the bridge.

Soon Dubose's head appeared at the head of the ladder, and he stepped aside to introduce the pilot following him.

Sorenson looked at the pilot. He was about five feet five, and skinny as a stick. His nobby knees connected equally thin tops and bottoms of his legs. A pair of baggy shorts stayed up only by using a long thick belt with a flapping end. On his head was an Australian desert campaign hat and at the other end was a pair of desert sandals. Sorenson estimated his age at sixty.

He raised his hand in an imitation of a salute and said, "Morning Captain. Sutter here. I'm your pilot. I know your conning commands and I won't break up your nice boat. If you're ready I'll take her in."

Sorenson remembered to return his salute and said, "She's all yours. This way to the pilothouse."

Dubose spoke up. ''Would you like some tea?''

The pilot snorted. ''Hell no, Mate. How about some of your American coffee?''

Dubose nodded. ''Sugar and cream?''

''None of that slop, Mate, just plain.''

Sorenson looked at the pilot's feet. ''Don't you get cold in that rig?''

The pilot grinned, showing several missing teeth. ''Sometimes. Then I put on a long-sleeved shirt.''

Jablonski asked, ''Can you tell us what berth we're going to?''

''Sure, Mate. Two berths astern of the *Warramunga* in berth thirty-two. When I brought the *Warramunga* in a coupla days ago, Captain Cunningham said he knew you were due in today and not to put you next to his ship. Something about there'd be too much racket, and the yard boffins wouldn't like all the noise.''

Sorenson laughed. ''Both ships sing a lot.''

The *Carson* steamed at a steady 10 knots under the Sydney Harbor Bridge and toward the distant Cockatoo Navy Yard. As they came out from under the bridge, local boat traffic increased. Several small ferries scooted under their bows, but the pilot paid little attention to them, disregarding their right of way. Once Sorenson almost stepped in and took the conn, but the pilot, noticing his concern, said, ''Captain, you never let the little blighters get the best of you. If one sees you giving in, the rest will want to do the same thing, and we'll never get there.''

Soon they rounded the end of the Navy Yard piers and Sutter took them to a berth, easing into a crowded space without a scratch.

''There you go, then, Captain. I'm off to bring another one in. Captain Cunningham is looking forward to seeing you.''

That morning was filled with conferences with Navy Yard repair planners, but by noon repairs and overhauls had been arranged.

After lunch Sorenson sent for Bentley. "Bentley, please go to the *Warramunga* and ask Captain Cunningham when it will be convenient for me to call."

In a few munutes Bentley was back. "Captain Cunningham presents his compliments. He will be away all afternoon, but he invites you to join him and Mrs. Cunningham at dinner at their home. If you can make it, he will drive by and pick you up at 1730 today, and unless you send back word otherwise, he will assume you accept."

Sorenson grinned. "Wouldn't miss it for the world."

At 1730 Sorenson was standing on the quarterdeck. A few minutes later a small red Austin two-seater drove up to the brow.

Cunningham, driving it, waved, and Sorenson walked down the brow to meet him.

Cunningham said in his clipped British accent, "Glad you can make it, old boy. My wife is dying to meet you. Watch your legs getting into this contraption. It isn't made for American legs."

Sorenson folded his legs and eased them into the leather seat.

Cunningham gunned the engine and zipped down the pier with a medium amount of abandon. He said, "I drive a little fast. Just like all good destroyer sailors. We're about 15 minutes from my home. Be there in a jiffy. By the bye, my first name is Colin. I'd like it if you'd call me that. What is your, er, moniker? Did I get that right?"Sorenson laughed. "No. That's for New Yorkers. In Texas we use the word 'handle.' "

"I understand. Then what's your first handle?"

"My name is Alden, but I'm called 'Tex.' "

"If you don't mind I prefer Alden. More British, I suspect."

Cunningham drew up to a small house in the eastern suburbs of Sydney. "Here's our spread, as I think you

Texans call it.''Cunningham leaped lightly out of the Austin, but Sorenson struggled to make it without falling. Cunningham said, ''That's all right, old chap, you'll soon get the hang of it.''

Sorenson followed Cunningham up the walk, and the door opened.Cunningham smiled at his wife, and said, ''Molly, dear, this is Captain Alden Sorenson, the Yank I wrote to you about.''Molly was petite, blonde, and very pretty. She smiled and said, ''Welcome to Cunningham manor. It's small, but we like it. I hope you will.''

Sorenson shook her proffered hand and found it unusually strong.

Cunningham noticed his reaction and said, ''Molly is an accomplished violinist. That's why her hands are so strong. I met her at a concert of the London Philharmonic Orchestra and stole her from them.''

Molly ushered Sorenson into the small living room and took his cap.

Cunningham headed for the bar. ''I know you've been a long time at sea. What can I mix for you?''

Sorenson said, ''Just a double Scotch with water and no ice, please.''

Cunningham said, ''There, Molly, I told you he was a pearl of great price.''

Molly laughed. If you'll pour me a sherry, I'll head for the kitchen. Alden, if I may call you that, I hope you like curried lamb. Mutton and lamb are all we have in Australia these days.'' Cunningham said, ''I've seen lots of your western movies, and I know how you Texans hate sheep. If you don't like mutton, you can take comfort from knowing you've helped destroy one of your enemies.''

Sorenson laughed. ''I'm sure the curry will disguise anything.'' He took a deep swallow of the dark brown glass of strong Scotch. ''After this nectar, I'll like anything.''

Dinner was very good. The Cunninghams had two small children, but in accordance with British custom, they were brought in to be introduced and then disappeared somewhere with a nanny.

As the pleasant evening progressed, Sorenson found himself thinking about Ferren and how much he wished he could be sharing this occasion with her.

Molly sensed his mood and began to ask him questions about her.

Just talking about her cheered him up, and soon the dinner was over and Molly brought in coffee.

Sorenson said, "I hear you're a classical violinist. I love classical music. Could you play something for us?"

Molly said, "I'm pretty rusty, but I'll try."

She brought out a violin and began to tune it.

Sorenson recognized its excellent tone as she frowned and turned the pegs. In a few minutes she was satisfied, and began to play.

As Sorenson had suspected, she was superb, and the classical airs she played stimulated him.

Then she stopped after the end of an aria, and said, "Our orchestra made a tour of America, and I learned this piece there. It's called 'Laredo Rag.' "

She hitched up her skirts a little, revealing graceful knees, and began to play. Sorenson was startled. He knew it was indeed the "Laredo Rag," and she beat her foot to the time and sawed at the strings like a true Texan.

Sorenson began to tap his foot, and then began to stomp. Even Cunningham was moved to follow the intense beat.

She finished with a flourish, stood up, smiled, and bowed.

Sorenson yelled, "Ya-hoo!"

Cunningham said, "Molly, you surprised me. You never played that for me before."

Molly laughed, "If I had, you'd have thought my violin was out of tune."

Later, Cunningham drove Sorenson back to the *Carson*. When they arrived, Sorenson was able to imitate Cunningham's exit by jumping out with out falling.

He turned to Cunningham. "Colin, a fascinating evening. I hope you and Molly can visit me at my ranch some day. We'll try our best to equal your hospitality."

"As long as I don't have to ride a horse," Cunningham said. "I hate the beasts. By the way, it's rumored your ranch takes up half of Texas."

Sorenson laughed. "it is pretty big, but I try to keep the facts quiet. There will be plenty of room for all of us."

The next morning the mail they had been expecting arrived. When Sorenson had finished reading his mail from Ferren and the financial reports from his brother about the ranch, he rang for Carmody. Carmody appeared at his door carrying a large box of official mail. He was frowning. "Sir, you're not going to like this."

Carmody put the box of mail down on Sorenson's desk, picked up the top piece, and handed it to Sorenson. Sorenson read it and frowned. "It detaches Lieutenant Commander Reifel and sends him to a new construction destroyer as executive officer. Who the hell is supposed to relieve him as chief engineer?"

Carmody picked up another piece of paper. "This is probably the answer." Sorenson read it. "It promotes Chief Machinist's Mate Lloyd to Ensign. Get Mister Reifel for me."

Carmody said, "He's right outside." Carmody opened the door and gestured to Reifel. Reifel came into the cabin. "I see you've read my orders. I don't want to leave the ship." Sorenson frowned. "You have to. I can't violate the orders, and you've earned it."

"But this has turned into the best ship I've ever served in."Sorenson shook his head. "Then you've learned enough to make the next ship just as good."

"But what if my next skipper isn't like you?"Sorenson grinned, "Then use your influence and make him good. An executive officer can really turn a ship around if he uses a little diplomacy. Now what do we do about a relief?

I suppose you've heard that Chief Lloyd is to be promoted to ensign. I think the Bureau of Naval Personnel is planning that he be the chief engineer."

"He's qualified, all right. I highly recommend him, and he deserves it."

"All right. Turn over to him, and when you're satisfied, I'll detach you. You should be back in the States in two weeks. I'd appreciate it if you'd call on Ferren." He smiled. "You can tell her how well I'm resisting these Australian sheilas."

Carmody said, "There's other bad news."

Sorenson sighed. "Out with it."

"We also lose six petty officers to new construction. There are six brand new seaman on the quarterdeck reporting as their replacements."

"Well, that's something. Let's wait on the rest of this paper work. I want to go up to the quarterdeck to welcome them."

Sorenson went to the quarterdeck. When he stepped out on deck, the Petty Officer of the Watch called out, "Attention on deck!"

Six men, standing by their seabags, snapped to their best recruit training braces. The Chief Master at Arms was standing beside them.

Sorenson walked over and stood in front of them. He looked each one of them in the eye, slowly turning from one to the other. Then he said, "I'm Commander Sorenson, your Commanding Officer. Welcome aboard. We'll soon be returning to the war zone, and we'll need you all."

There were some barely repressed grins on the fresh young faces. Sorenson noticed them. "War is a very serious business, and it demands that all of our ship teams be highly trained. You will soon be assigned battle stations in those teams, and I expect you to do your utmost to learn your new duties. You will have battle experienced teachers who will make sure you know your stuff. The better you do, the more chance this ship and you will have of surviving the war. The Chief Master at Arms, here, will give you your berthing assignments and turn you over to the petty officers of your divisions. Good luck to you all.''

Sorenson turned and walked forward. Carmody was waiting at his door with the rest of the paperwork. ''Any more bad news, Carmody?'' Sorenson asked.

Carmody shook his head. ''That's enough for one day.''

Two days later the wardroom officers had a rousing send off party for Reifel, and he left the next day, looking a little beaten up, but resigned.

The next day Chief Lloyd was given a wetting down party by the chief petty officers, sworn in by Sorenson in a ceremony, and moved into the wardroom, wearing his new insignia. His seat was next to Fineman, who soon put him at his ease.

The time in Sydney was growing short, and Sorenson and Dubose inspected the permanent repairs daily to make sure they would be ready when the ship sailed.

Auerbach went with them on the last inspection, and when they had finished, Sorenson turned to Auerbach. ''I take it you had a good time in Sydney?''

Auerbach's eyes lit up. ''Wow! We met a couple of sheilas who wouldn't quit.''

''We?''

''Yes, I took young Bentley over the second night and got him shaved, shampooed, and schmoozled.''

''Schmoozled?''

''That's Australian for —.''

''I can guess. I hope you didn't get Bentley in trouble.''

''No way! Doc Fineman gave him a half hour lecture before we left the ship and a pocket full of equipment when we left.''

CHAPTER TWENTY-SEVEN

The last few days in the Cockatoo Navy Yard passed quickly, and Sorenson enjoyed walking about downtown Sydney. The crew managed to keep out of major scrapes with the Sydney constabulary.

Sorenson turned in early the last night hoping that they would get by without major problems ashore.

But in the middle of the night there was a loud knock on his door. Sorenson turned over and looked at the radium-dialed clock on the bulkhead. It said 0300.

''Yes?'' he said.

''Sir, it's the messenger on watch. There's an Aussie constable on the quarterdeck. He brought an important message for you.''

Sorenson turned on the light over his bunk and said, ''Come in.''

The messenger opened the door and thrust a folded note into his hand. Sorenson opened and read it. ''Jesus!,'' he said. ''Is the constable still there?''

''Yes, sir.''

''Please ask him to wait, and tell him I'll be there as soon as I can get dressed. Then call Doctor Fineman and ask him to get dressed and meet me as soon as possible on the quarterdeck.''

Sorenson dressed quickly, put his wallet and checkbook in his pocket, and went to the quarterdeck. He walked over to the Australian constable and said, ''Can you tell me anything at all about this note?''

''Sorry, mate, I was just told to deliver it and bring you to the station if you wanted to come down with me tonight.''

''I do. Please wait just another minute until my doctor gets here.''

The constable said, ''I don't think you'll need a doctor, mate. More likely a lawyer.''

''Thank you,'' Sorenson said. ''If you'll wait in the car, we'll be over to the pier in a minute.''

The constable left the ship and went to his car. In a minute Fineman came to the quarterdeck buttoning his shirt. ''What's the trouble? Do you want me to get the ship underway? Is someone hurt?''

''Neither. Read this. It's from the Executive Officer, and he's in jail. He wants us to come down to the jail and get him out.''

Fineman whistled. ''Do we break in?''

Sorenson said, ''Don't be funny at this hour of the night. Read the note.''

Fineman went over to the quarterdeck and held the note under the desk lamp. As he read it, his eyebrows got higher and higher. When he finished it, he looked at Sorenson and said, ''He says he's been accused of rape.''

''Yes.'' Sorenson said.

''I don't believe it. There's been some mistake.''

''I hope so, Let's go.''

The constable was a fast driver and there wasn't any traffic that early. After a bumpy ride and some sprightly attempts at conversation by the constable, the car pulled up in front of the police station in downtown Sydney.

The constable said, ''In the front door and turn to the right. The sergeant will take care of you.''

Sorenson said, ''Thanks for the ride.''

They followed the constable's directions and ended up in front of a very sleepy sergeant. ''Yes, mate,'' he said. ''What can I do for you?''

Sorenson said, ''You are holding a Bedford Forrest Dubose for raping a girl?''

The sergeant searched his papers. ''Ah, yes, here it is. He's in cell two.''

''Can we see him?''

''Sure, mate, follow me.''

Sorenson and Fineman followed the sergeant to cell two. He unlocked the door, let the two in, and locked the door again. ''Let me know when you want to be let out.''

Dubose was sitting on a lower bunk with his head in his hands.

Sorenson said, ''What happened?''

Dubose looked up and blinked his eyes. ''Thank God you're here. These bastards won't listen to me.''

Sorenson sat down next to him. ''Now calm down and tell us what happened.''

Dubose took a deep breath and shuddered. ''Well, I went ashore yesterday and spent several hours walking around Sydney. About 1800 I got thirsty and went into what I thought was a small cafe. I sat down at a table and ordered a beer. Before I finished it, a young lady came over to my table and asked if she could join me. I got up, bowed, and said, 'Certainly, Ma'am.' ''

Dubose paused, obviously thinking back to the scene.

Sorenson said, ''Go on.''

''She was a nice enough looking girl, a little dark complected, but a lot of these Aussies have good tans. I asked if I could buy her a beer, but she said I wasn't allowed to. We talked for almost an hour. Between my accent and hers we had a little trouble communicating, but she managed to tell me a lot about something called the outback where she said she was from.''

Fineman said, ''I think we'll find out that your girl friend was a part aborigine bar girl.''

Dubose sighed. "After a little over an hour, I decided it was time to go back to the ship. I put an Aussie pound note on the table for the drinks and stood up. She looked at the money on the table and then at me, and said in a loud voice, 'You raped me!' I was shocked. I said, 'I never laid a hand on you!' She pointed at the money on the table and said again, 'You raped me.' "

"The bartender noticed and said to the girl, 'What's wrong, Duba?' "

"She said, 'He raped me.' "

"The bartender looked at me and said, 'Yank, that's not nice.' "

"I said, 'I never touched her.' "

"He said, 'Are you going to make it right?' "

"I thought they were going to try to extort me. I said, 'I don't think I should.' "

"The bartender sighed and motioned to a couple of big men who were sitting at a table. They came over to me and gripped my arms. The more I struggled, the tighter they squeezed. The bartender picked up the telephone and called the police."

" 'Mate,' he said over the phone. 'I got a live one here. He needs some treatment.' "

Fineman said, "I suppose they showed up in a hurry."

"Yes. In a few minutes the two big policemen arrived, handcuffed me, and brought me and the girl here. I tried to talk to them, but they told me to tell my story to the sergeant."

Fineman asked, "Is the girl still here?"

"I suppose so. The sergeant said I would have to wait until 0800 when the judge got here. She's supposed to be a witness."

Fineman called the sergeant and was let out of the cell. "I'll be back in a few minutes," he said. In five minutes he was back. "Let's go," he said. "You owe me two pounds."

Dubose looked up, his mouth open. "What?"

Sorenson said, "What happened?"

Fineman said, "Just a misunderstanding. The Executive Officer didn't understand their language, and they wouldn't listen to his."

"I don't understand," Dubose said.

"You didn't understand the girl either. I talked to her, and she has dropped the charges after I paid her fee and gave her a generous tip."

"Fee?"

"Sure. She is part aborigine and is a bar girl. She charges a pound an hour for talking to customers. You owed her another pound for the second hour, as well as the bar charges."

Sorenson said to Dubose, "You should have asked if she was a bar girl."

Dubose bristled. "That would have been an insult to her womanhood!"

Sorenson smiled. "Maybe in Alabama, but not in Australia."

Dubose said, "But they kept saying I had raped her. My God! We were right out in the open all the time."

Fineman said, "No. She said you had reaped her. When the Ausralians say reap, it sounds just like they say rape. It's an Aussie expression for cheating. She thought you hadn't paid her what you owed her for her services. So did the bartender."

Dubose got up unsteadily. "I'd like to get out of here as soon as possible."

Sorenson thanked the sergeant on the way out, and the constable took them back to the *Carson*. As they drove up to the brow, Dubose said, "I didn't get any dinner. I sure am hungry."

Sorenson looked at his watch. "I'm afraid we're too late for breakfast, but we might find some left-over doughnuts up on the signal bridge."

Dobose sighed. "You're a tough schoolmaster, Captain, but I'm learning. Thanks for getting me out. I thought I'd be sent to a penal colony."

Sorenson said, "Don't thank me. Thank Fineman. I thought I might be going with you."

Just prior to getting underway, Sorenson went ashore and sent a huge bouquet of flowers to Molly Cunningham and an equally big box of cigars to Colin Cunningham.

The *Carson* left at noon. Sutter, the Australian pilot, took them out. ''I requested to take you out specially, Captain, you have the best coffee of all the Yanks I've piloted.''

''Thanks,'' Sorenson said. ''I hope you'll accept a couple of pounds to take with you.''

''Sure, mate. You won't have to twist my arm, as you Yanks say. By the way, the weather blokes say there have been reports of a Willy-willy forming north of here along the path you're going to take. The weather reports will give you more exact dope.''

Jablonski said, ''Yes, we know. I've been plotting the data in the weather reports.''

At the entrance to the net the pilot took his departure, a brown package under his arm. ''Good luck, mates,'' he yelled up at the bridge.

Sorenson waved. ''Nice old geezer,'' he said.

When they were outside the net and steadied on a course north with the *Ransome* on their beam, Sorenson said, ''Let's look at the Willy-willy plot, as the Aussies call it.''

Jablonski led him over to the navigational chart. ''Here's the last location. It's just south of Espiritu Santo, headed about two two five, and has fifty knot winds. It will get worse and also re-curve to the south. I'll keep you informed. In twenty-four hours we'll pass abeam of Brisbane and then we'll have to decide what to do to avoid it.''

Sorenson said, ''I understand a Willy-willy is the Australian name for a typhoon. In this hemisphere, they rotate clockwiseinstead of counter-clockwise and move to the south instead of to the north. Other than that, they're the same as typhoons.''

''That's right. I saw a lot of them in the Philippines. Chuck Steiner was on the China Station a lot longer than I was, and he's an expert on the subject. I'll ask him to brief us tomorrow after we've received the latest weather report.''

''Good idea. We'll meet in the pilothouse right after dinner.''

CHAPTER TWENTY-EIGHT

The next morning after breakfast, Sorenson hurried to the pilothouse to meet with the other officers about the typhoon. Jablonski, Dubose, and Steiner were already there, looking at an area chart of the stretch of ocean from Sydney clear up to Milne Bay.

"Let's get at it," Sorenson said. "John, show us where we are, where we'd like to go, and the plot of the typhoon movement."

Jablonski leaned over the chart with the others looking over his shoulder. He pointed to his 0800 navigational fix. "Here we are, about three hundred miles northeast of Sydney, making sixteen knots. I've laid out a course almost due north for the next few days. Here are the 0800 positions for each day, assuming we do not have to change course or speed to avoid the storm."

Sorenson pointed to the small island of Espiritu Santo, over a thousand miles to the northeast. I assume this is where the last sure fix of the typhoon was when it passed near land."

"Yes," Jablonski replied. "It was forming then, and the island escaped serious damage. Now it's up to sixty knots near the center and is moving southwest at about 10 knots. Fixes on it are approximate now."

"Why?"

"Up ahead of us is a thousand-mile stretch of open water. There aren't any weather stations in it. The only information General MacArthur's weather service has to go on is from ships passing through the area and the aircraft flying north and south from Australia to New Guinea. There aren't many ships out there. The main route to the States is over here, well south of the typhoon, and aircraft naturally tend to give a storm a wide berth."

"That means we'll be the best weather station they've got."

"I'm afraid so. Soon we'll know more about it than the weather guys."

Dubose said, "I don't believe that. Surely they must know more than that about it if they can put out such exact weather reports on it."

Steiner laughed. "Believe him. They don't know their butt from first base. Out here we can see, hear, and even smell the storm better than they can back there in a cosy weather center where they dream up these reports."

"All right, let's not argue." Sorenson said, "John, where does the latest weather report say the storm is located?"

Jablonski pointed to a plotted point on the chart. "Here, eight hundred miles due north of us."

Sorenson looked out at the sea. It was a little oily in appearance, but calm. The wind was light, and the clouds were cirrus, high overhead. He said, "Around here it's good weather. Let's use today to secure the ship for heavy weather and meet up here again at 0800 tomorrow."

Chief Bellows, followed by Lieutenant Auerbach, cruised the topside the rest of the day, ordering the securing of all top side equipment that couldn't be stored below. They doubled the lashings on the life rafts and boats, and double-checked the depth charges to make sure they were on safe and lashed so that heavy seas couldn't carry them away.

Auerbach, watching Chief Bellows lash them, said, "What will we do if we have to use them on a submarine?"

Chief Bellows patted a large knife in a leather holder on his belt. "You gotta get one. You in de deck force."

Auerbach grinned. "I will."

Below, Chief Williams rigged the wardroom table for heavy weather, lashing the chairs to stanchions, and instructing both Jacksons about how to serve in heavy weather without spilling soup down the officer's necks.

Big Jackson grinned and said aside to Little Jackson, "I ain't gonna try too hard not to do dat."

By late afternoon the ship was as secure as they could make it, and Sorenson passed the word to turn in early so as to be rested for the probable ordeal ahead.

Just after breakfast the next morning, Sorenson bounded out to the bridge. As they had been yesterday, the three officers were waiting for him. Dubose and Steiner were glowering at each other, but when Sorenson approached, they smiled and said, "Good morning, Captain."

Sorenson said, "I detect a little disagreemant here."

"Yes," Dubose said, "But first let Jablonski brief you."

Jablonski pointed to the next 0800 position on the chart and said, "We're here, three hundred and eighty miles farther north. The storm, according to the latest weather report is here." He pointed to a position about a hundred miles west of their northerly projected track. It has winds of 60 knots and is moving just a little west of south."

"Bull shit!" Steiner said loudly. "The damned thing is directly ahead of us and has alredy started to re-curve to the east. It's moving almost due south and will change course slightly to the east soon."

Dubose said, "But the weather report puts it a hundred miles to the west of our track. How can you say otherwise?"

Steiner shook his head in exasperation. "That's the trouble with all these weather jockeys and even with us.

You can't deal with a typhoon inside an office or even inside a pilothouse. Let's go outside on the wing.''

All the officers followed Steiner out to the port wing. He pointed to the sky. ''Look at those clouds. You can see the long streamers of moisture. Sure sign of trouble. Look at the water. There are the beginnings of long swells coming from due north.''

Sorenson said, ''I can feel them. The ship isn't pitching, but going up and down like an elevator. They are very long.''

Steiner went on. ''The center of an approaching typhoon is always within ten degrees of the direction of the swells. As the day goes on, the swells will grow hourly. Then there's the barometer. Yesterday at this time it read 30.00, about normal. Now it reads 29.50, a half inch low. It will continue to fall as we approach the center of the storm. The closer we get the lower it will go.''

Sorenson said, ''That's exactly what we want to avoid, the center of the storm.''

''Ha!'' Steiner said. ''We want to do more than that. The center is bad enough, but the dangerous semicircle is almost as bad. Come back into the pilothouse, and I'll show you on paper.''

When they were bent over the chart again, Steiner drew a series of roughly concentric circles. He put arrows on the circles with numbers representing the velocity of the winds at the circles. At the center was a small circle with no velocity.

Steiner paused and looked around at the assembled officers. ''These circles represent the speeds of winds as you see them at the various locations relative to the center of the storm. This small circle at the center is almost a dead calm. Then the circles nearest it are the maximum velocities. This one, as you see, has winds near the center of about 60 knots. The velocities diminish as you get farther from the center, but they can do a lot of damage, when combined with the long heavy seas, at as much as a hundred miles from the center. The whole complex is moving ahead along this line.''

Steiner drew a slight curve with an arrow on it labelled 10 knots. ''You all remember your vector analysis from mathematics. That means in this semicircle, the dangerous one, over here to the east, the 10 knots of forward advance is added to the 60 knots of circular motion to make surface winds of 70 knots. Whereas, over here in the safe semicircle, the speed of advance is subtracted from the 60 knots of circular speed to make only 50 knots at the surface.''

''A helluva lot of difference,'' Jablonski said.

Steiner went on, ''Not only that, this baby will speed up to about 20 knots or more. They all do. That makes at last 80 knots in the dangerous side, but only 40 knots on the safe side.''

''That's for me,'' Sorenson said. ''The difference would be 40 knots.''

The quartermaster of the watch interrupted them, ''Sir, the barometer has fallen to 29.40 and the wind is up to 15 knots from the southeast.''

Steiner said, ''That's another indicator. There's an old Asiatic Fleet rule. Face the wind and the center of the typhoon is one hundred and twenty degrees to the right when you are in the northern hemisphere. Down here, of course, the typhoon is one hundred and twenty degrees to the left. It's east of north all right.''

Sorenson said. ''I think we ought to go to the northwest to avoid the storm and to get into the safe semicircle as Chuck recommends.''

Dubose said, ''I still think we should wait to see if the weather predictors at headquarters change their minds.''

Sorenson scratched his head. ''All right, Forrest, but not beyond this afternoon. We'll meet up here after dinner.''

The evening meal was a sober affair. Dubose and Steiner hardly spoke, and Sorenson tried to keep the atmosphere light by describing his dinner in Sydney with the Cunninghams and the violin concert given by Molly Cunningham.

Steiner looked up from his plate with interest as Sorenson described the "Laredo Hoedown" as played by Molly. Sorenson took advantage of the opening. "Chuck, I didn't see much of you in the wardroom in Sydney. Did you find something interesting ashore?"

"Yes, sir, I met some old friends I had made in Surabaya in the early part of the war when I was there in the *O'Leary*. We went through Java on our way to Australia. These friends were Dutch, and they escaped from Java on an old tramp steamer before the Japanese arrived."

"What are they doing in Sydney?"

"There's quite a large Dutch colony there now. Many of those who escaped from Java came there to await word from those they left behind. Not many have heard anything."

Sorenson nodded. "I heard it was a hell of a mess."

Steiner lapsed into a thoughtful study, and as soon as Sorenson had finished his coffee, he headed for the bridge. This time he paused out on the wing and observed the weather. Large, long swells had built up since 0800, and he noted they were almost dead ahead, or even a little on the starboard bow. The *Carson's* bow rose majestically as each swell lifted the forecastle and then passed back along the side. Now an occasional wave splashed over the amidships section of the main deck. Sorenson made a mental note to tell the officer of the deck to pass the word for all hands to keep off the main deck. The high clouds had now turned to a solid overcast and had lowered. A slight rain had begun to fall. The wind was up to 30 knots and still from the southeast. When he went inside the pilothouse, the officer of the deck said, "Sir, the barometer is down to 29.00, a full inch below normal."

Sorenson nodded and walked over to the chartdesk, carefully timing his progress to coincide with slack times when the ship was not pitching.

''What's the dope?'' he said.

Steiner said, ''No change as far as I'm concerned. The typhoon is now about five hundred miles ahead and slightly on our starboard bow. At this rate, if we don't change course, we'll be in at the center or in the dangerous semicircle in twenty-four hours.''

Sorenson turned to Dubose. ''Forrest, what's your recommendation?''

Dubose was pale and obviously upset. ''Captain, I can't ignore this latest weather report which says the typhoon is over here.'' He put his finger on a pencilled notation a hundred miles to the west of their track. I think we should avoid by changing course to the east.''

Steiner rolled his eyes and looked at the overhead, but said nothing.

Sorenson said, ''I can't wait any longer. Officer of the Deck, change course to the northwest, three one zero will do it. Notify the *Ransome*.''

Dubose said, ''But Captain---.''

Sorenson interrupted him, his mouth a straight line. ''Dubose, if you don't agree, put your recommendation in the quartermaster's log and sign it.''

Dubose sighed. ''Captain, I don't agree, and I couldn't say otherwise. I'm not about to disagree with you any further. This is your decision. I gave you my best advice, and now your decision is my decision.''

Sorenson smiled. ''I hoped you'd say that.''

Steiner said to Dubose, ''I suppose if I'm wrong I'll never hear the last of it.''

Dubose shook his head, ''No, I respect your professional opinions just like I hope you'll respect mine. I'll never say a word about it.''

Steiner thought for a second. Then he said, ''I really appreciate what you just said. It makes our profession a lot easier. It's a tough one at best.''

Dubose nodded. ''Tough as hell, just as the next forty-eight hours will be tough, regardless of which one of us is right.''

Auerbach, who had the deck, gave the order to the helmsman, and the ship began to swing across the swells, Immediately the ship began to roll instead of pitch, but the motion with the swells on the bow and the wind on the quarter was bearable, but uncomfortable.

Sorenson watched the ship labor for a few minutes and then said, "This won't be too bad."

Then Wencey said, "The *Ransome* is signalling." He came into the pilothouse in a few minutes with a brief message. Sorenson read it and frowned. Then he read it aloud. "You are standing into danger."

He turned to Dubose. "The *Ransome* agrees with you."

Dubose shrugged. "No he doesn't. I agree with you."

Sorenson laughed. "I'll send him a message." He went over to the chart dask and wrote a message. When he had finished, he said to Dubose, "How does this sound? 'I FEEL THE WEATHER REPORT IS WRONG AND ACCORDING TO LOCAL SIGNS NOT AVAILABLE TO THE WEATHER CENTER THE TYPHOON IS DEAD AHEAD. I AM CHANGING COURSE TO PASS IT IN THE SAFE SEMICIRCLE. IF YOU DISAGREE, PROCEED INDEPENDENTLY. INFORM COMMANDER SEVENTHFLEET OF YOUR ACTIONS.' "

Dubose said, "You told it like it is. We should send a report of our actions and our estimate of the location of the typhoon to General MacArthur's headquarters and to Commander Seventh Fleet."

"Right. Please take care of it."

Dubose went below to write up the message and have it encoded.

The seas slowly increased to just short of mountainous, and Renard had to feed the crew sandwiches and coffee. The wardroom did the same.

At dusk Sorenson felt the tension grow on the bridge. Sorenson couldn't see the swells as clearly in the complete darkness, and the wind increased to 40 knots. The rain thickened, bouncing off the steel decks like continuous hail.

Sorenson sat in his bridge chair all night, wedged in against the corkscrew rolls that occasionally caught the laboring hull. The swells were so big and so long the *Carson* rode up over the tops of most of them with a sickening elevator-like rise and fall. Some of them caught her stern and pushed it over so that the helmsman had to turn the wheel furiously to regain course. Some of the rolls were to 45 degrees, and Sorenson noticed that the members of the bridge crew were watching the roll indicator anxiously. The *Carson* still had most of her fuel tanks full, and Sorenson felt ballasting would not be necessary.

Late that night Sorenson thought the weather was improving slightly, but he couldn't see anything out the bridge ports. At dawn he looked out the bridge ports at a seething sea. The rain was slackening, and the wind was down to 30 knots. "How's the barometer now?" he asked.

The quartermaster of the watch said, "Sir, It's 29.00 and steadying."

Sorenson looked along the direction of the approaching swells. They were now almost from the south. He smiled and said to Steiner, who had the watch, "We've done it! We're passing the center of the typhoon abeam. Then he frowned. "I hope the *Ransome* is all right. Have we heard anything from her?"

"Only her departure report from our formation."

The communication messenger brought up the latest weather report, staggering along the pilothouse deck.

Sorenson said, "How's it below decks?"

The messenger shook his head. "You don't want to know, Captain."

"Yes I do."

"Well, every one except the old hands is seasick, and they're lying all over the compartments. The deck is covered with sandwiches, some not eaten and a lot that were eaten. It's a mess, sir."

Steiner had been plotting the weather report. He banged his fist on the chartdesk. ''Hot damn, those Kangaroo kiddies have finally seen the light. The latest position of the typhoon is right where I said it would be!''

Sorenson said, ''I never doubted it.''

Steiner grimaced. ''But the Executive Officer did.''

''Chuck, that's his job. It will be your job when you get to be an executive officer. He's supposed to give his honest opinion. You know how much he admires General MacArthur. He thinks the General's organization must be good, too.''

Steiner sobered. ''I can't agree about his weather jockeys, but I've gained a new respect for MacArthur's generalship. We could have been still slogging around in the mountains of Southern New Guinea if he hadn't been so bold and decided to take the risks of bypassing large groups of Japanese.''

By midafternoon the rain had slackend to a drizzle, and the seas were around to the quarter. The wind was still at 25 knots. The roll had diminished as the seas began to lift under the counter. Sorenson changed course to north, and the seas began to roll them again. He wedged himself into his chair and drifted off into a shallow sleep.

He thought he was dreaming when the telephone talker said in a loud voice, ''The man on watch in mount 53 reports man overboard to starboard!'' Sorenson jerked upright in his chair.

Steele, who now had the watch, ordered, ''Starboard engine stop! Right full rudder.'' This was standard procedure to assure that a man overboard would not be cut up by the churning propellers.

The Boatswain's Mate of the Watch promptly passed the word over the loud speaker system, ''Man overboard!''

Sorenson rushed to the starboard wing of the signal bridge. Brophy was bent over the signal bags, telescope to his eye.

"Do you see him?" Sorenson asked.

"Both of them," Brophy said. "Looks like Vila and Williams."

Then Sorenson watched in horror as a third figure jumped overboard just aft of the break of the deck and started swimming toward the other two.

Brophy said, "The whole place has gone mad. Who's going over next?"

Then Sorenson realized that he had neglected to worry about the ship, and a large sea caught the *Carson,* now broadside to the swells, and rolled her over 50 degrees. Sorenson pulled himself back into the pilothouse and looked at the inclinometer. At the same time he said to Steele, "Bring her back to port!"

Steele gave the order, "Left full rudder." It did little good, and he gave the order, "Starboard engine ahead full."

The ship hung and then went even farther over to port. Back aft there was a crack like a rifle. The ship's inclinometer steadied, and the ship slowly began to right itself.

Sorenson let out his breath with relief. "Brophy!" he called out the pilothouse door. "What the hell happened down below?"

Brophy had given the resposibility for following the men overboard to Wencey and was leaning over the starboard flag bags looking down. He straightened up. "The turnbuckle on the starboard guy to the mast gave way in that roll. I thought the mast and all the radar antennas were going over the side. The mast bowed like a green stick."

"What's going on down there now?"

"Chief Bellows has a party that is trying to fix the problem. A man just came out of the compartment with a chain fall and a wire loop."

"Do they have safety lines on?"

"Sure. Old shaky wouldn't forget that. One man would have been washed over already if his line hadn't stopped him."

Brophy was watching the scene below intently, now and then nodding in agreement. In no more than two minutes he pulled his head up and said, ''It's fixed temporarily. You can maneuver any way you want.''

Steele had slowed to steerageway so as not to leave the men in the water too far behind.

Sorenson said to Steele. ''Now bring her around slowly to starboard. Don't let us get caught in irons again. Use all the engine power you need. When you're around, head to bring the men under the starboard bow. Not too close. The wind is still strong. I'm going out on the signal bridge to help spot the men in the water.''

When Sorenson got out on the signal bridge, he came up behind Brophy, who had the telescope again. ''Can you make out who the third man is?''

Brophy laughed. ''I can't because he's turned away from us, but Wencey says it's the Exec.''

''My God! What's he doing there?''

''I don't know, Captain, but the Exec gets around. I hear he was chasing a little girl on the beach in Sydney.''

Sorenson said, ''That's a lot of bull. It was a misunderstanding, and I'd appreciate it if you'd get the word out correctly.''

Brophy said, ''Wencey says he'd know the back of the Exec's head anywhere. He says you're usually better off staying astern of him.''

''Any guess as to why the Exec went overboard?''

''None at all, but they're real cosy out there. They're all hanging on to the life ring the man on watch aft threw over.''

Steele had swung the ship slowly so that it was heading south with the seas and wind on the bow. As the ship approached the men, Sorenson noticed that the bow of the *Carson* went up and down as the seas passed under her counter. He knew that they could not afford to get too close to the men in the water, but they would have to pick them up from the high and rearing forecastle. He looked aft at the seas breaking over the amidships area, and realized that men could not work aft.

He went into the pilothouse and said to Steele. "Stop her with the men abeam of mount 51. Stay at least fifty feet to windward of them. We'll bring them up one at a time by hauling them in on a line and lifting them over the lifelines when the bow heaves up."

Steele said, "I don't think a heaving line will carry that far in this wind, and if it does it won't be strong enough to lift them with."

Sorenson said, "I'll take care of that. I'm going down to the forecastle."

Sorenson found Chief Bellows making up a heaving line to throw to the men in the water.

Sorenson said, "Chief, that heaving line won't do it. Give me that one-inch messenger you have back there."

Bellows brought the line forward and put it at Sorenson's feet. Sorenson bent over, brought one end back with an eight foot bight, fashioned a small bowline in the end, and passed it over the standing part of the line. When he stood up, he had a heavy lariat in his hand. He took two bights of line in his right hand with the loop and three others in his left hand. "Chief, I'm going to throw this line. It's heavy enough to carry in this wind. Stand behind me and pay out as many bights as are necessary."

Chief Bellows looked skeptical, but took his position behind Sorenson and picked up the rest of the line.

The *Carson* slowed and backed with the bow in perfect position. Sorenson stepped to the rail, swung the loop and bights twice around his head, and let them go. The loop soared out and landed just a few feet short of the trio. Dubose swam quickly to the loop and swam back to the other two. Williams was lolling in the water, with Vila trying to keep his head up. Dubose slipped the noose over Williams's head and under his arms. He looked toward the forecastle and raised his hand.

Back on the forecastle, six men hauled in the line, the loop tautened under Williams's arms and Williams seemed to fly over the water. Just short of the side, the men on the forecastle stopped heaving, and waited until Chief Bellows, gauging the rise and fall of the deck edge of the forecastle, said, "Ha-heave ha-round!"

Williams shot up over the lifelines, and other strong hands lifted him over the top line and put him on deck.

Sorenson took the line off and coiled it again for another throw. This time he hit Vila squarely. Dubose put the loop over Vila's head and he was soon added to Chief Williams on deck where Fineman was rendering first aid.

Dubose started swimming for the side, but Chief Bellows motioned him back, and he stopped. This time the throw was shorter, and Sorenson hit him easily. In seconds he was on deck, and men were taking the line off his shoulders.

Sorenson said, "I'm glad to see you back, but I want an explanation as soon as we can get some medicinal brandy in you. Can you walk?"

Dubose laughed. "Sure."

They followed stretcher bearers taking Williams and Vila down to the wardroom. Fineman put Williams on the wardroom table face down. He was breathing but unconscious. Big Jackson came out from the pantry and put a bucket under his face. Fineman pressed on his back, and a stream of water plopped into the bucket. "Good," Fineman said. "He'll come around in a minute. Let's look at Vila."

Vila was lying on the wardroom floor, pale but conscious. Fineman looked at him closely. "He needs some brandy, too, but he'll be all right." Vila smiled and reached for the small bottle of brandy the pharmacist's mate handed him. He upended it and said, "Mabuhay!"

Sorenson went to the chair where Dubose was sitting. Big Jackson had put towels under the chair, but they were completely soaked. Sorenson sat down next to Dubose. "Now tell me all."

Dubose said, "I don't know all. I'd like to wait until Chief Williams comes to. I need to know why he did what he did before I can tell you the full story."

Just then Williams tried to turn over. Fineman helped him. Chief Williams sat up on the wardroom table and said, "Where am I?"

Big Jackson, standing next to him, grinned and said, "You in de belly of de whale."

Williams focused his eyes on big Jackson and said, "Don't talk like a field hand! How many times do I have to tell you that?"

Big Jackson straightened up. "You're in the wardroom of the United States Ship *Carson*."

Chief Williams said, "That's better, but how did I get here?"

Dubose stood up and walked over to Williams. "Chief Williams, that's what I want to know, too."

Williams rubbed his wet head, and Fineman gave him a dry towel. Williams said, "I remember now. I was in the pantry. I told Vila to take the garbage out and empty it over the side. Then I looked up and noticed he'd left his life jacket in the pantry. I always told the men to take their life jackets when they went topside in bad weather. I grabbed mine, put it on, and took Vila's life jacket with me. I went out on the main deck, and there was Vila emptying the garbage over the starboard side. Then a big wave came over the port side, lifted him up, garbage and all, and pushed him over the starboard side. I knew he couldn't make it without his life jacket, so I jumped over the side with it."

Dubose looked at Sorenson. "He did that, and he can't swim!"

"Can't swim? How do you know that?"

"In Milne Bay, when we asked him why he hadn't gone swimming, he gave us a good answer. He said it was a matter of principle. And I'm sure it was. But I got suspicious. I went over his service record and there wasn't any record of his swimming qualifications."

Sorenson looked at Williams. "Can you swim?"

Williams said, "No, sir. I managed to be in sick bay the day we took our tests in boot camp."

Dubose said, "I took him out to Bondi Beach in Sydney to try to teach him how to swim, but it was too cold to do much."

Williams shivered. "I've never been so cold."

Sorenson said to Dubose. "Now part of this is cleared up. Why did you go over the side?"

I was sitting in the wardroom when I heard Williams yelling at Vila. I went out there to see what was happening. I saw Williams disappearing up the ladder and I followed him. I got to the main deck just in time to see him going over the side clutching Vila's life jacket. I knew he couldn't swim so I knew I had to go after him."

"So you just jumped over the side."

"Well, not exactly. I dove over and then pulled the toggles on my rubber life belt."

Sorenson said, "Weren't you afraid you might not make it?"

"No, why should I have been? I looked up at the signal bridge, and I saw Wencey looking aft. I used to swim the mile in college. This was a breeze. Hardly even got warmed up."

Sorenson shook his head. "Please come up to the sea cabin and see me when you get dried off and in clean clothes."

Sorenson left the wardroom and went up to the bridge. Steele had steadied the ship down and was back on course north at 16 knots. Steele said, "She rides well now. The seas are going down, and the wind is diminishing."

Sorenson said, "Thanks for the good job. I'll be in my sea cabin."

Half an hour later Dubose knocked on Sorenson's door and came in when Sorenson called.

"Sit down, Forrest," Sorenson said.

Dubose sat down and looked up expectantly. He said, "Before you say anything, Captain, I'm sorry to leave the ship like that, but I'd do it again under the same circumstances.''

''The circumstances are what intrigue me. Here you are, a prime example of southern bigotry, and you risk your life for a black man and a Filipino. I don't understand it.''

''I think you do. They were members of my crew. I'd do anything for them. Color doesn't matter.''

''Ah, that's what I've been waiting to hear you say. It doesn't, and I'm glad you've discovered it. I no longer think of you as bigoted, and as far as I'm concerned, I now consider you completely qualified for command. When we get to Milne Bay, I'm going to send a letter to the Chief of Naval Personnel recommending that you be assigned to command as soon as possible.''

Dubose was silent. Then he said, ''I appreciate your confidence in me, but I don't want to leave the ship as long as you are in command.''

Sorenson said, ''That makes me very proud, but with all the new ships being built, the Navy can't spare you. I'll recommend, however, that you stay in command of the *Carson* and that I go to new construction. I think that's the custom now, anyway.''

Dubose said, ''I guess that's a compromise. But I don't particularly like it. Tell me, how can you recommend me when I've disagreed with you so many times?''

Sorenson laughed. ''That's part of being a good executive officer. You're supposed to express your opinions. I didn't always accept them, but I don't always accept my wife's recommendations either. You were also very good with Steiner. I know he irritated you, but you never took off after him. You let him have his say. And you've learned to accept Chief Bellows, Ensign Bronte, Doctor Fineman, and the others I brought with me from my old ship.''

Dubose laughed. ''They've been the mainstays of this ship.''

Sorenson said, ''You didn't always think that, but you kept an open mind. I wish you the best of luck when the time comes for us to separate, and I know you'll do well."

The next day the skies began to clear and the swells died to normal waves. On the day before they were to arrive at Milne Bay the water had returned to a clear tropical blue, and the weather was once again hot and humid.

The day after the green shores of the southern end of New Guinea came over the horizon, and by 1000 they were anchored in Milne Bay.

That afternoon Renard brought a dispatch to Sorenson. Sorenson read it and shook his head. "The *Ransome* says they are returning to Sydney for repairs. They experienced winds of 80 knots, lost both their boats, lost their mast and both radar antennas, and have several flooded compartments."

He looked up at Renard. Renard shrugged. "Some commanding officers are dumber than others," he said.

CHAPTER TWENTY-NINE

The *Carson* slid neatly into Milne Bay, Ensign Bentley at the conn, and dropped anchor. Even before the anchor chain was secured, Chief Bellows had men working to fix the minor damage to equipment about the decks. Two shipfitters put in place a new shackle for the main guy wire to the foremast. Here and there paint had been stripped off the upperworks by the high winds and furious rain, and soon blotches of red lead covered the bare spots, waiting for the final coat of gray.

Sorenson came down from the bridge and walked around the topside with Chief Bellows and Lieutenant Auerbach, commenting on the minor damage they saw.

Auerbach shook his head and said, "It could have been worse if we'd gone the other way. I heard the *Ransome* almost bought the farm."

"Not that bad," Sorenson said, "but they had to go back to Sydney."

Auerbach laughed. "What a terrible punishment," he said.

Sorenson looked at him out of the corner of his eye. "I take it you found Sydney interesting."

Auerbach sighed. "Very, and I'd like to go back there again."

Bellows said, "Ha-lousy warm beer, and ha-closed up too ha-soon."

Sorenson looked at Bellows. "Chief, do you need another fitting on your dentures?"

"Ha-yes. Ha-ain't ha-wearing em. Ha-got banged up inna ha-storm."

Sorenson said. "If you have any trouble getting dental care, let me know. I'm going to the flagship this afternoon, so you can come with me."

Bellows said, "Ha-thanks, sir."

At 1300 Sorenson, with Bellows in tow, came to the quarterdeck to leave for Admiral Fechteler's flagship. As he stepped into his gig, he noticed a motor launch from the station ship getting ready to come alongside. He could count ten men with the clean uniforms and squared caps that marked them as recruits, and he made a mental note to speak to them as soon as he returned to the ship.

He had arranged by message for a call on the Admiral at 1315, and the Flag Lieutenant met him at the top of the accommodatiion ladder. "I'm glad you arranged to call. The Admiral wants to see you."

Sorenson asked, "Do you know what about?"

"No, but I don't think it's bad. Something about the storm, I think."

Sorenson followed the Flag Lieutenant to Admiral Fechteler's cabin, and the Flag Lieutenant knocked at the door. There was a gruff, "Come in," from behind the door. The Flag Lieutenant opened it. "Commander Sorenson," he said.

Sorenson followed him in, and Admiral Fechteler rose to meet him. The Admiral smiled, stepped forward, and extended his hand. "I'm glad to see you. I've been wanting to hear about that typhoon. Please sit down."

While coffee was served, The Admiral said, "Tell me what happened and why the *Ransome* had so much more damage. We can't spare her for the next operation."

Sorenson said, "I understand that she had extensive damage, but nothing that can't be fixed in a couple of weeks. When is the next operation, sir?"

''D-day is tentatively 2 July, and we assault Noemfoor Island.''

Sorenson said, ''She won't be able to make that date, but she'll be ready for the next one.''

Fechteler wasn't pleased. ''This next operation is going to be preceded by the biggest shore bombardment the Seventh Fleet has ever attempted, and every ship will be needed.''

Sorenson asked, ''Any intelligence on the landing beaches?''

Fechteler frowned. ''They may be expecting us and they now know the beach we'll be landing on.''

''Some breakdown in security?''

''You might call it that. I call it stupidity. General Kreuger sent a reconnaissance force up last week to land on the beach we'll be using. The Japs detected them, and are now reinforcing the defenses around the beach.''

''Couldn't we shift to another?''

''No. It's the only useable one. That's why we must make the bombardment so heavy. General MacArthur is in a hurry to take the island. It has two excellent airfields on it ready for use. Now tell me about the typhoon.''

''In the first place, we confirmed that ships in the area east of Australia can't place too much reliance on weather reports.''

''Why not? Our aerologists are supposed to know their business.''

''They undoubtedly do, but they don't have much data to go on. Not many ships transit the vital area where the storms form, and when they do form, aircraft give them a wide berth. The predictions of location of the center of the storm we encountered were off by over a hundred miles.''

''Enough for the *Ransome* to go the wrong way?''

''Yes, sir.''

''Why did you ignore the prediction and go the other way?''

''I was lucky. I had an old China Hand aboard, and he gave us all a lesson in typhoon prediction. He was exactly right.''

"What can we do to make sure his knowledge is distributed to the Seventh Fleet?"

"I've asked him to write up a report on this incident and his recommendations of how to maneuver in the vicinity of a typhoon and when he's finished I'll forward it to Admiral Kinkaid."

"Forward it via me, and I'll strongly recommend that he promulgate it to the Seventh Fleet. We can't afford to have ships damaged or lost needlessly."

Sorenson said, "Sorry about the *Ransome*. I had to let him do whatever he decided was best for his ship."

Fechteler nodded. "You have already missed a chance to practice on the shore bombardmant range on that small island at the entrance to Milne Bay. I'll make arrangements for you to use it tomorrow. Then you'll come back into the bay, fuel, replace the ammunition you use, and depart right away to join Admiral Berkey's forces. Well, if you don't have any more questions, I'll wish you good luck on the next operation and I'll probably see you in two weeks. We have another operation at Sansapor coming up then."

He called in the Flag Lieutenant who ushered Sorenson to the quarterdeck of the flagship. Chief Bellows was waiting there.

Sorenson said, "How did the dental appointment go?"

Bellows grinned widely, showing his dentures, "Good as ever," he said.

Back on the *Carson* Sorenson asked Dubose to send for the new draft of recruits so he could talk to them.

Dubose nodded toward the forecastle. "They're already on the forecastle waiting for you."

Sorenson went forward and gave the new men the same speech he had given the group in Sydney. As he was walking down to his cabin with Dubose, he said, "We get underway at 0600 tomorrow. If you'll assemble all the officers in the wardroom, I'll tell them all about it."

Sorenson began, "We get underway at 0600 tomorrow and go to the shore bombardment range at the mouth of the bay. We'll do as much practicing as we think we need."

Steiner said, "We don't need any practice. We've been doing this for months."

Sorenson said, "That's what I thought at first, but then I remembered all the new men we have and all the ones we've lost. Also we haven't done much to provide for the training of replacements in case of casualties. For tomorrow, The Executive Officer will get the ship under way and conduct the exercise. Chuck, You'll go down to CIC and act as Executive Officer. Bronte will take over the shore bombardment plotting. Auerbach will act as Gunnery Officer and will man the director."

Fineman grinned. "What will you do? Take a nap?"

Sorenson said, "No. Chief Vickers invited me to come down to a mount for a firing. I'm going to help man Mount 53."

The next morning Dubose got the ship underway with Sorenson sitting in his chair. When the ship was headed for the bombardment range, Sorenson sent for Chief Vickers. Vickers came up to the pilothouse and said, "Yes, sir, you sent for me?"

Sorenson got out of his chair. "Yes, chief, a few weeks ago when you were up here conning the ship, you invited me to come down to a mount with you and watch a firing."

Vickers blanched. "But Captain, I didn't really mean it."

Sorenson laughed. "You can't back out now. Let's go down to mount 53."

While they were going back to mount 53, general quarters sounded, and as they arrived the crew of the mount was just manning it.

Big Jackson was looking out at the Captain walking down the deck. Sorenson could hear him say, "Jesus, what the old man doin' here?"

Sorenson heard Kittredge, undoing his phone set, said, ''The Captain can go anywhere he damned well pleases, and today this pleases him. Don't get in his way.''

Sorenson climbed up the rungs of the ladder in the side of the mount and stepped inside the enclosure. Vickers climbed up behind him.

Sorenson saw Kittredge standing there and said, ''Kittredge, what station do you have?''

Kittredge said, ''Trainer, sir.''

''Good. I'm going to take your place for the first firing. Show me what you do.''

Kittredge pointed to the side of the gun where the trainer's seat and station were located. ''Up there, sir. You sit in the seat and I'll show you how the controls work.''

When Sorenson was seated, Kittredge leaned over and turned on the switch to the hydraulic motor. It started to whine, and Sorenson shouted over the din, ''It makes a helluva racket.''

Kittredge shouted back, ''You get used to it.''

Sorenson tried out the hand wheel in front of him, and the mount jerked right and left. Kittredge put his hand on the wheel. ''Not so much motion. The hydraulic motor does it all. You'll knock the crew in the mount on their cans if you train that fast.''

Sorenson said, ''What's this switch?''

Kittredge said, ''It puts the mount in automatic control. Then the director controls the train.''

''And then I just sit here on my butt?''

Kittredge said, ''You've got it, sir.''

Thirty minutes later Sorenson heard over the phome, ''Coming on the range. Mount 53 will fire first. Mount 53, go to automatic.''

Sorenson reached down and turned the automatic switch. Kittredge nodded approval.

Then the voice on the phone said, ''Coming on the range. Target has been designated. Stand by to commence firing.''

Seconds later the word came, ''Mount 53, commence firing, one round.''

The loading crew began to load, and Sorenson could hear loud metallic sounds behind him culminating in a rumble in his ear as the spademan drove the shell and powder cases home into the gun barrel with the rammer. Then there was another clank as the heavy breech closed.

The salvo buzzer sounded, and the gun boomed. Sorenson was pleased to note that the sound of the explosion wasn't as loud as he had expected.

Three shots later the word came to cease fire.

Sorenson turned the trainer's controls over to Kittredge and went aft in the mount.

Vickers said anxiously, ''How did it go, sir?''

Sorenson said, ''Not enough action. I'm going to try one of the loading positions for the next run.''

Vickers paled. ''But Captain---''

Sorenson interrupted him. ''Big Jackson. what job do you have?''

''Hot shellman, sir, but you don't want to try it.''

''Why not?''

''You'll get your uniform all dirty.''

Sorenson grinned and looked at Jackson. ''Then Vila will have to clean it up.''

Big Jackson grinned. ''Well, that's all right. Here's what you do. See this little hole in the deck?''

Sorenson noticed a small scuttle he had almost tripped over when he had entered the mount. ''I see it.''

''Well, you take these gloves, stand behind the breech, and grab the hot brass powder case when it comes out. Then you shove it down the hole, and it falls on deck.''

Sorenson said, ''I think I can do that.''

Vickers said, ''But Captain, It takes practice to do it right. You might get hurt.''

''Those empty brass shell cases don't weigh much. I should be able to handle them.''

''But, Captain---''

Sorenson interrupted him. ''How soon before we fire again?'

Kittredge, now manning the phones again, said, ''The forward mounts have finished their runs and mount 54 is about to fire.''

The first round from mount 54, just aft of them, took Sorenson by surprise, but he was ready for the next few. Then Smith, the mount captain, yelled down from his perch above, ''The next run is ours. Stand by!''

Sorenson took his stance behind the breech of the gun. Big Jackson nodded approval, but Vickers wrung his hands.

Then the mount captain shouted, ''Stand by! Coming on the range.''

Sorenson wondered if he had been wise, but he didn't have much time to think about it. ''Commence firing!'' Smith shouted.

In front of him Sorenson could see a blur of movement. The man with the brass powder case dropped his case in the big breech chamber. The projectile loader lifted the projectile out of the fusesetter and slammed it into the breech ahead of the powder case. Then the ram carried both into the gun barrel and the breech slammed shut after them. Just as Sorenson was taking a deep breath, the gun went off. Back behind the gun the noise and movement of the breech were louder than they had been at the trainer's station. Sorenson was unprepared for what happened next. He heard the sound of the spade, which could be lifted vertically to allow the expended brass case to be ejected backwards. Then under the bottom of the spade a brass casing rushed at him. It's speed threw his timing off. He grabbed at it with his heavy gloves. He could feel the heat of the casing through the gloves. His right hand slipped, and the base of the casing fell against his foot. He could feel moderate pain, but he reached down and got a firmer grip on the casing. He missed the first time he poked it at the hole in the deck, but made it on the second try.

Then he crouched again behind the moving breech block, determined to do a better job on the next round.

The gun crashed again, and this time he thought he would be ready. He managed to grab the back of the slippery brass casing with his right hand, but his left hand slipped off the front, and the open end of the casing flew up and banged against his face. He could feel the sharp edge of the opening cutting into his face. He grabbed again at the front of the casing, felt it secure in both hands, and this time hit the opening in the deck on the first try.

As he moved back to his station behind the breech, he could feel the warm blood begin to flow down his face, but he could see all right and he managed a perfect catch on the next round. Then came the welcome word from the mount captain, ''Cease firing!''

Sorenson stood up and grinned. For the first time Chief Vickers realized what had happened, and his mouth flew open but he couldn't say anything. Finally he grabbed the first aid box and hauled out a compression bandage.

Vickers pressed the bandage to Sorenson's cheek and held it there. Finally he found his voice. ''Captain, I told you not---''

Sorenson grinned through the bandage and said, ''Best workout I've had in months.''

Vickers looked down at the deck. ''Blood all over the place,'' he grumbled.

Sorenson put his hand on the bandage and looked down at the blood on the deck. He said to Big Jackson, ''Please tell the mount captain I'm sorry to louse up his deck.''

Smith, the mount captain, watching from above, heard him and said, ''No problem, Captain, best show we've seen since the last sing along.''

After the completion of the firing, a quiet and solicitous Vickers accompanied Sorenson up to his cabin.

Just before they got to the door, Sorenson said, ''Chief, I thank you very much. I'd like to do it again. But I have some requests to make of you. I want to put young Kittredge up on the bridge as a signal striker. He was very good when he went up there temporarily. You have just the man to replace him.''

''Ah, who's that, Captain?''

''Big Jackson.''

''But, Captain---''

Sorenson went on, ''I'll appreciate it if you can make those changes as soon as possible and let them get in a little practice on the way up to the next operation. I'll even let you take your pick of the strongest of the draft of new men to replace Big Jackson as hot shellman.''

Vickers sighed.

Sorenson said, ''You have some problem?''

Vickers shook his head, ''Captain, I can do it under two conditions.''

''What are they?''

''First, you promise never to come down to my mounts again.''

''And the second?''

''You promise never to haul me up to the bridge again to conn the ship.''

Sorenson laughed. ''A deal.''

Sorenson sent for Fineman as soon as he got to his cabin. Fineman came in grinning. ''I hear you tried to eat a brass casing.''

''Not quite. It missed my mouth, but I think you'll have a few stitches to take.''

Fineman took the compression bandage off and looked at the wound. ''About six, I'd guess. You'll have a nice match with the scar on the other side of your face. Looks like a couple of parentheses.''

CHAPTER THIRTY

After the shore bombardment exercise, The *Carson* returned briefly to Milne Bay for fueling and ammunition replacement. While they were fueling, Renard came up to the bridge, obviously nervous.

"What's the trouble?" Sorenson asked.

Renard said, "Yesterday I ordered an emergency delivery of sides of beef, but the supply ship couldn't get them to us that fast. Some excuse like having to supply the flagship that day. They promised them today, but I don't see them yet."

"Why such a hurry? Didn't we get plenty of meat in Sydney?"

"Sure. All mutton."

Sorenson shuddered. "No wonder you're worried. How did the crew take it?"

"Not very well. They threatened to throw the Chief Commissary Steward over the side unless we got some beef. I can't spare him."

Sorenson laughed. "I didn't taste any mutton in the wardroom chow."

"That's because Chief Williams knows you're from Texas, and he's been serving chicken and canned meats. Even Vienna sausage. Then last night we had meat loaf."

"There was mutton in it?"

''Yes, but a little pork and even some beef brisket we had left over. Now we're even out of that. Tonight it's curried lamb.''

Sorenson said, ''I agree, you do have an emergency. Take the gig and go over to the supply ship. If they don't deliver by the time we're through at the ammunition ship, I'll lie to next to the supply ship. Tell the skipper that. I don't think he'll want Admiral Fechteler to know he can't deliver on time.''

Just before the *Carson* was due to pull away from the ammunition ship, a motor launch from the supply ship, closely shepherded by Renard in the *Carson's* gig, pulled alongside. When the working party, which had hastily been assembled to unload the boat, saw the sides of beef, a loud cheer went up.

Renard climbed aboard over the side to the cheers of the crew and the relief of the Chief Commissary Steward.

As the ship cleared the harbor, Sorenson tried not to look astern where he knew several carcasses of mutton were going over the side.

At lunch, Big Jackson, serving steak to Sorenson, leaned over and said, ''Captain, I'm grateful to you for fixing it with Chief Vickers.''

Sorenson selected a juicy steak and said, ''Big Jackson, you have the job now strictly on merit. At first Chief Vickers needed a little, er, encouragement, but now that he's seen you in action, he says he's glad to have you.''

Big Jackson beamed, ''Thank you, sir.''

As the officers chewed happily, Sorenson said to them, ''Stay on after lunch and we'll talk about the next operation.''

MacIntosh turned to Doctor Fineman, ''Doc, what happened to the leg of lamb I thought we were going to have for lunch?''

Sorenson heard him and grinned. He said, loud enough for MacIntosh to hear, ''Damned sheepherders almost won again, but the cow hands came through. I think the mutton jumped over the side."

Fineman laughed. "There's your answer. You'll have to wait until you get home again."

After coffee, the table was cleared, and Jablonski automatically brought out the battered chart of New Guinea from behind the sterilizer.

Sorenson started talking after he had fixed his coffee. He patted the bandage on his cheek. "First, the rumor that I tried to eat a brass powder casing is wrong. It tried to eat me, and I've decided to turn the job of hot shellman over to a recruit of Chief Vicker's choice."

Dubose grinned, "He's already picked out a husky farm boy with good hands. A shortstop, I believe."

Sorenson said, "Now to the important news. We're on our way to join the Covering Force for the invasion of Noemfoor. John, show us where it is."

Jablonski put his finger on a small island. "Here it is, a small island beteeen Biak Island and the neck of the bird. It's about ten miles in diameter and is completely surrounded by coral reefs."

"How do we get ashore?" Auerbach asked.

"LVTs and DUKWs. Medium-sized landing craft, LCIs, and LSTs have already loaded all the landing force and their landing craft at Finschafen. They've been at sea several days already on the eight-hundred-mile trip. Fortunately, the weather is good, and they're almost there."

"Don't we get any operation order?"

"No. The operation is so straight-forward and the time is so short there doesn't seem to be a need for any overall order. We'll get target asignments for shore bombardment and Army charts, but that's all."

"Who's in the Covering Force?" Dubose asked.

"Commodore Collins of the Royal Australian Navy is now in overall command in place of the British Admiral Crutchley. Admiral Berkey will command the American contingent, and we'll work directly for him. Since the *Ransome* won't be there, I suspect we'll get a lot of independent assignments. There will be five cruisers and fourteen destroyers altogether."

''A lot of fire power,'' Steiner said.

''Yes,'' Sorenson said, ''Admiral Fechteler said he intends to make this the most powerful shore bombardment of the New Guinea campaign.''

Steiner said, ''Unfortunately it doesn't approach the shore bombardment levels in the Central Pacific. I hear Admiral Nimitz uses six battleships for a week, and still that's not enough.''

Sorenson said. ''Admiral Fechteler told me there were two airfields on Noemfoor, but I see three on the chart. I think three is probably correct. When he talked to me, he was pretty mad at General Kreuger for sending some PT boats up to scout the landing beaches. The Japs detected them, and are now, according to aerial reconnaissance, re-inforcing their defenses. You'll all be glad to know that the Fifth Air Force will have a CAP over us day and night.''

Down at the end of the table there was a loud cheer.

Steiner asked, ''Are there caves and such?''

Sorenson shook his head. ''Not many. Just a high seven hundred foot hill behind the beaches. By the way, D-day is 2 July.''

Dubose said, ''We don't have much time.''

''No. We join the Covering Force on the first. Let's get ready and give these new men a few drills. We can fire a few rounds on the way. I know the new hot shell man on mount 53 can use a little breaking in.''

On schedule the Covering Force showed up on the *Carson's* surface search radar early the morning of the first, and then loomed out of the morning mist as the *Carson* closed the formation and reported for duty.

Soon they were alongside the screen flagship to be passed a copy of the shore bombardment assignments, and then they took their place in the screen. Sorenson sat back in his chair. ''Sydney was great, but it's good to be back to work,'' he said to Jablonski.

Jablonski said, "The sooner we end this war, the sooner we get home."

Sorenson shook his head. "I'm afraid the Philippines is home to General MacArthur. I hope somebody else speeds up the rest of the war toward Japan. That's the way we'll get home early."

Jablonski said, "There is another way, but I don't like to think about it."

"You mean getting badly damaged or sunk?"

Jablonski sighed. "Yes, sir."

Sorenson pursed his lips. "I don't want it that way either."

That night the formation approached the island of Noemfoor from the north to bring the ships that were scheduled to bombard it to the northwest section of the coast where the landing was to take place.

Sorenson had the crew called early for breakfast, and at 0500 he sent the crew to general quarters.

From CIC, Bronte reported, "The Combat Air Patrol says there are no aircraft on any of the fields. We don't have any air contacts on air search radar."

"Thank you," Sorenson said. "Keep it that way."

Sorenson looked over the side, remembering the seas and wind on the way north. Now there was hardly a ripple, and the slight overcast would probably burn off soon after daylight.

Bentley, who had taken Scorse's job as communications officer, came up to the bridge with a portable Army radio tuned to the Landing Force Commander's circuit.

Sorenson asked, "Anything yet?"

Bentley said, "Just testing. The only word is that the surf is minimal."

At 0530 the ships with individual bombardment assignments were detached to proceed to their positions. The *Carson*, assigned to hit a battery of antiaircraft guns, left formation and steamed slowly to her area. When Jablonski determined that they were there, Sorenson stopped the engines. The ship glided forward a few hundred yards, and Sorenson adjusted her heading so that the target was on the beam.

Sorenson watched the cruisers taking their positions like so many ugly and menacing bumps on the otherwise smooth surface of the sea. He tried to remember how many times they had seen the same scene, but as he was counting, the first salvo from a cruiser went off. ''Commence firing,'' he shouted.

All four mounts spewed noise, smoke, and flame. The dimness of dawn was dissipated by a continuous curtain of flame from the guns of the cruisers and destroyers.

There was no return fire, and the LVTS and DUKWs started for the reef and the beach behind it, called Beach Yellow. Behind the beach and up on the bluff was the small settlement of Kamiri and an adjacent airfield. There were some known antiaircraft emplacements around Kamiri airfield, and the *Carson* was assigned one particular gun. Spotting aircraft had been launched from the cruisers and circled around the target area.

CIC reported to the bridge that, according to the spotting aircraft, their salvos were hitting the assigned target.

Sorenson, his binoculars glued to his eyes, said, ''It's too far over the edge of the cliff to see. We'll just have to take their word for it.''

At the end of the scheduled bombardment the beach was obscured by dust and gun smoke.

Bentley, listening to the landing force circuit, said, ''The control vessels report that the visibiity is so bad they've had to rig searchlights pointing to seaward so the LVTs can see where to go.''

Then, in a few minutes, Bentley said, ''The first wave got ashore without trouble and reports that the LCIs can beach in goodwater.''

''Good,'' Sorenson said. ''That means all those troops don't have to tranfer to LVTs to get across the reef.''

Bentley began to laugh. ''Here's a good one,'' he said. ''The landing forces report that the Japanese put a lot of land mines on the beaches recently but also put signs on them so their own troops wouldn't run into them. Our troops have at least one Japanese interpreter with them, and he spotted the signs. Now they've put signs in English on them. The troops swiped all the Japanese ones for souvenirs."

A shore bombardment firing mission came in for the *Carson,* and Jablonski carefully plotted their position. With their position known, Dubose in CIC could plot it on the Army chart and determine the range, direction, and altitude of the target. Soon the first salvo went out and then corrections came in. After four more salvos went out, the spotting aircraft reported, "Target destroyed. Cease Firing. Good shooting."

Bentley reported, "The Landing Force Commander says there are hundreds of Japanese wandering around the area in a daze and more are coming out of caves. He says this is the most Japanese he's ever heard of giving up."

About 1100, Bentley reported, "There will be a big parachute drop on the island soon. Watch put for the incoming aircraft."

Soon several troop transports began to fly over Kamiri Airfield, and parachutes blossomed as troops jumped from the aircraft.

Sorenson watched the men dangling and swaying in the air as they descended. He shuddered. "Not for me," he said.

Bentley said, "Not for me, either. There were 56 casualties reported on that last run."

Sorenson shook his head. "I thought some of those aircraft were too low. Some of the parachutes barely opened before the men hit the ground."

In spite of the mishap with the parachutists, the landing force continued to press inland, and by nightfall the Covering Force withdrew, leaving the *Carson* and two other destroyers behind to render fire support called for by the troops ashore.

Sorenson secured the ship from general quarters and set the condition III watch, augmented in order to be able to render fire support with one gun.

The *Carson* was assigned several routine missions the first night, but then the Japanese retreated so far back in the hills no further missions were necessary.

On the 5th of July the Japanese made a final counterattack which was quickly taken care of, and the Landing Force Commander released the destroyers.

By nightfall the three destroyers were in column headed for Humboldt bay. Sorenson felt the situation was so calm he could eat in the wardroom, and went below for dinner.

After the soup course, Big Jackson and Little Jackson began removing the soup plates. Sorenson said, ''Big Jackson, how did the new hot shellman do?''

Big Jackson chuckled. ''Well, Captain, he's a big strong guy. When he pushes the hot shell down the hole in the deck, he really does it. But the first one wasn't too good. He aimed it at the hole and let it go. He missed, and it bounced back into the air. The projectile man was leaning over to pick up a projectile from the fuze pot, and the hot shell hit him right in the butt.''

The long recital was too much for Big Jackson, and he lapsed into his childhood language. ''Hee hee,'' he said, ''he gotta cut onna cheek just lahk you did. Only lower down.''

Sorenson looked inquiringly at Fineman.

Fineman said, ''Only four stitches. His pocket took most of the damage.''

After dinner, Sorenson went back to the bridge and sat in his chair. The soft air of the tropical night coming on and the setting of the sun lured him out to the bridge wing, and he leaned on the rail, watching the sun in the west as its lower limb touched the horizon.

Fineman came up to the bridge and leaned on the rail next to Sorenson. He watched the setting sun for a few minutes. Then he said, "The sunsets are more beautiful in the tropics, but they don't last long."

Sorenson said, "I'd trade them all for just one sunset in Coronado."

Renard came up to the bridge and went into the pilothouse. "Where's the Captain?" he asked.

"Out here," Sorenson called out. "What's up?"

"A message for us, sir. I think you'll want to go down to the CIC to read it. You'll need the chart." Sorenson turned to Fineman. "Take charge of the sunset."

CHAPTER THIRTY-ONE

Sorenson took a look at the other two destroyers in the column ahead and decided the situation was safe enough so that he could leave the bridge. He went down to CIC and walked inside. Dubose was there with Auerbach.

Dubose said, "I asked Dick Auerbach to join us as soon as I saw the message you have there. It concerns air sea rescue, and he's an expert by default. He's been rescued twice."

Auerbach laughed thinly. "I don't think that makes me an expert, but I'd like to hear what's going on."

Sorenson spread the message on the DRT table and read, "*Carson* proceed Wakde Island at best speed and pick up rescue team. Then proceed as directed by officer in charge of rescue team to Point Markis and effect rescue of downed pilot. Officer in charge has details. After rescue proceed Humboldt Bay for upkeep." He turned to Dubose, "Let's go."

At 0600 the *Carson* eased into the area south of Wakde Island where the ship had bombarded several weeks before and the Army had landed. Now the area was a bustling port complex, full of unloading merchant ships and landing craft. As they closed the landing beach, an LCVP headed out toward them. It came alongside and three men in Army uniforms climbed up the ladder rigged over the side by Chief Bellows. Dubose went aft and met the party.

In a few minutes he was back and introduced the party to Sorenson. "Captain Sorenson, this is Major Barrett of the Fifth Air Force. He's in charge of the rescue team. With him are First Lieutenant Dillon and Sergeant Fellows. Their equipment is back on the after deck."

Sorenson shook hands. "We're at your disposal. What can we do?"

Major Barrett said, "First, I'd like to start for the area as fast as possible. Our pilot may be injured. He was on a bombing mission from Wakde Island airfield and was hit over the target. On the way back his engine kept acting up and finally he had to bail out over Markis Point."

"Then you think he's alive?"

"Yes, sir. I'd like to show you the area he landed in and describe the problem of getting him out. We'll need a chart."

Sorenson said to Dubose, "Forrest, go up to the bridge and get us started for Markis Point at twenty-five knots. I'll take the party to CIC."

Sorenson led the group to CIC and introduced them to Bronte and Bentley. "Here's the chart which includes Markis Point," he said.

Barrett bent over it. With a pencil he indicated an area about a hundred yards behind the beach. "There was a large rock just off the beach. Our pilots saw our lost man parachute along the coast and land here. The rock will make a good landmark for navigation. The pilots who saw him go down circled as long as they could but never saw him come out to the beach."

"Did he have a radio to make contact with them?"

"Yes, they heard the radio functioning, but they never heard him transmit on it and they never saw him. They think he mayhave been injured when he went down. The trees come down close to the beach and are very thick, so thick that they couldn't even see his parachute."

"How do you want us to go about rescuing him?"

"We don't think there are any organized Japanese units in the area, but there are many individuals and small groups of them wandering around in the bush after their organized units were wiped out. I'd like to go in with a boat and about eight of your armed men. Lieutenant Dillon will go with us and advise your men. He's an infantryman. Sergeant Fellows will stay with you. He will have an Army portable radio to communicate with me."

Sorenson took some measurements on the chart. "We'll get there about 1200. Will that be all right?"

"Fine. Maybe we can have something to eat first. We should also take some rations and water with us in case we get pinned down by enemy forces. Also one of your medics. Pharmacist's mates, I think you call them."

Sorenson looked at Dubose, who had come back to CIC. "Does that sound okay to you?"

Dubose nodded. "I'll get Chief Vickers with a Browning automatic rifle and seven other men with rifles ready. Major, if your party will come with me, we'll all have some chow."

Shortly before 1200, the Carson eased slowly towards the beach off Markis Point. There was no surf, and the water was a uniform green, but Sorenson could see the beginnings of coral heads underneath the sea. Chief Bellows kept a man in the chains with a sounding lead. The water was deep enough to approach the beach to within five hundred yards. Sorenson had the ship at general quarters in case there was rifle fire from the beach.

Aft, the whale boat was at the rail, and Chief Vickers and seven men were standing by to board it. A pharmacist's mate with a large first aid kit slung over his shoulder was also ready. All wore leggings and helmets.

On the bridge, Sorenson and Major Barrett searched the foliage back of the beach for signs of the enemy or the downed pilot. Sorenson said, "Looks like nobody has been there for a hundred years."

Barrett nodded. "The foliage is dense, too."

Sorenson said, "Chief Vickers has machetes for cutting through the brush if necessary. I'll be sending in an officer with you and another to stay in the boat. Lieutenant Auerbach is a former carrier pilot who was shot down and rescued twice. He'll go into the bush with you. Lieutenant MacIntosh will stay in the boat as boat officer. He is senior and will be in charge of the boat. He'll take orders from you unless he thinks they will endanger the boat and its crew. Then he's in charge."

"I understand," Barrett said. "I hope we won't have any trouble."

After a thorough search of the area behind the beach with binoculars and the director optics, Sorenson gave the word to load the boat and proceed to the beach. Barrett and his men went aft and climbed into the boat with the *Carson's* officers and men. The boat was quickly lowered and chugged off toward the beach. The bow hook was keeping a careful watch over the bow for coral heads and carrying a sounding lead for possible use.

Sorenson watched the boat ease through a passage in the reef and nose gently up on the sandy beach. Vickers and his men got out first and quickly spread out along the beach and took firing positions. "Ha!" Sorenson said, "Just like a bunch of Marines!"

Dubose said, "I think we'll find the infantry lieutenant helped."

Then the rest of the party got out, and the men disappeared in the bush.

Ashore, as the men under Vickers clambered out of the boat, Chief Vickers shouted, "Let's go, men!"

Lieutenet Dillon said in a quiet tone, "Ah, just a minute, Chief. We should give our orders quietly---the Japs may hear us--and we should spread out until we're sure they aren't waiting for us."

Vickers nodded appreciatively. ''I see, sir, why don't you take charge. I don't know much about this stuff.''

Dillon said, ''I'd be glad to.'' He turned to the other armed men wno were all looking at him and motioned for them to join him.

Vickers said, ''But you said to spread out.''

Dillon nodded. ''Yes, Chief, we've done that, and now we have to enter the undergrowth. We'll have to go single file behind a point man with a machete. He'll have to hack his way into the growth.''

Dillon picked out a husky man and quietly ordered him to start cutting. As the flashing machete moved forward, Dillon led the way in with the others behind him. He drew his pistol and placed Chief Vickers with the Browning Automatic rifle just behind him.

Dillon said, ''Chief, if I shoot at something, put a good burst at my target, even if you don't see anything.''

In a few minutes, Dillon began to call out the pilot's name. At first there was no answer, but then a faint voice said, ''Over here.''

Dillon changed the direction of the column's advance, and the point man soon said, ''There he is.''

They hacked a small clearing around the aviator, who was hanging in a parachute harness from a low limb. Auerbach said, ''Here's his radio and provisions. He couldn't get to them.''

The pharmacist's mate directed the lowering of the aviator. ''Gotta broken leg,'' he said. ''No wonder he couldn't get down.''

Fifteen minutes later the group was back on the beach. As they emerged, Chief Vickers said, ''Damn! We didn't even get to fire our rifles!''

Dillon laughed. ''You were lucky. Those Japs are mean when they're cornered.''

Sorenson waited anxiously for a half hour. Then the group emerged from the bush carrying a man in a makeshift stretcher made from a parachute. They carefully put him in the boat, and it backed off the beach and started back through the channels in the reef.

Sorenson heaved a sigh of relief. In a few minutes the boat was alongside and was being hoisted aboard. When the boat was clear of the water, Sorenson backed away from their position and then turned the ship and headed back for Wakde Island at 25 knots.

When he was sure the ship was squared away on course and speed, he headed for the wardroom.

When he got below, he found the pilot stretched out on the wardroom table with Doctor Fineman cutting his flight suit away from his right leg.

Sorenson knew before Fineman said anything that the pilot had a badly broken leg. He said to Fineman, ''We'll be at Wakde Island in five hours. I can cut it to four if necessary, but we don't have much fuel.''

Fineman looked up. ''I'll need some time to work on his leg and to make sure I've got shock under control. Five hours will be about right. He's very dehydrated, too. I'll need the time to get some fluids in him.''

The pilot looked up weakly and smiled. ''Boy, was I glad to see these guys. At first they made so much noise I thought they were Japs.''

Sorenson laughed. ''They aren't professional soldiers. Marines would have done better.''

''They did just fine. Thanks.''

Fineman said, ''I'm giving you a pretty large dose of morphine. You shouldn't talk any more.''

Sorenson motioned to Major Barrett, who was standing nearby, and Barrett folowed him out of the wardroom and up to CIC.

Sorenson said, ''We were pretty tense back here when you were away. Can you tell us how it went ashore?''

''Yes, sir.''

Sorenson said, ''Let's go to the wardroom for early dinner. The rest of the officers will want to hear about your expedition, too.''

Just before dark the *Carson* entered Wakde Island Harbor again, and an LCVP came out to the ship to take the wounded pilot and the rescue party ashore.

Ensign Lloyd came up to the bridge. "Captain, if we don't get some fuel soon, we'll have to burn salad oil."

They requested and received a fuel assignment from a tanker and in two hours were headed for Humboldt Bay and a much needed rest.

CHAPTER THIRTY-TWO

The *Carson* glided into Humboldt Bay and anchored near a repair ship. Several destroyers were already alongside, so the *Carson* had to make do with an overhaul at anchor.

Sorenson called Ensign Lloyd, the new chief engineer, up to his cabin. When Lloyd knocked, Sorenson asked him in and ordered coffee. "Well, chief, how's it going?"

Lloyd said, "The title chief for chief engineer is the same as I used to have as a chief petty officer, but it's a new ball game. I find the responsibilities of an officer more than I'd ever figured they would be when I was a chief petty officer."

"You seem to be handling them all right."

"Oh, yes, but where I used to go up to the chief's quarters at the end of a busy day and play acey-deucey, now I go to my room and wrestle with logs, paperwork, and other stuff. I appreciate the fact that I don't have to stand watch. I don't know how the guys who do stand watch manage to make ends meet. Every twenty-four hours they stand eight hours watch, try to spend several hours taking care of their men and their equipment and records, and then find a few hours for three meals, a shower, and shave. What's left is for sleep, and it's usually about three hours."

Sorenson laughed. ''A lot of lost sleep for sure. Now you'll have to plan our engineering upkeep without being alongside a tender.''

Lloyd nodded. ''Yes, sir, I've already done that. We have to clean two boilers and fix a few pumps. We'll finish in time.''

Sorenson nodded approvingly. ''I know you're busy, but when you have time, come up to the bridge and watch operations. When you're ready I'll let you handle the ship. You are a line officer, and you need to learn something beside engineering.''

Two days later Sorenson was called to a conference on the flagship. When he came back, the officers had not bothered to assemble in the wardroom as they usually did when Sorenson was away at a conference, and Dubose had to send for them.

While they were waiting for the officers to assemble, Sorenson said, ''These operations are getting to be too routine. Nobody even takes any interest in them.''

Dubose nodded. ''Is this one any different?''

''No, except that we don't even do any shore bombardment.''

The last officer came in, and Sorenson began. ''We leave in a few days for the invasion of Sansapor. As usual General MacArthur wants it for more airfields for the forthcoming action against Morotai.''

Bentley said, ''That must be a lot bigger operation.''

Sorenson nodded. ''Much bigger, and we'll be in on it along with a lot of other ships.''

Dubose said, ''You told me this operation that Sansapor was so routine there wouldn't even be any shore bombardment.''

''Yes. There has been a lot of reconnaissance around the landing area, and they haven't discovered any recent signs of the Japanese. There are two half-completed airfields, but the construction on them stopped some time ago.''

Steiner said, ''If we don't do any firing, what do we do?''

''We go to Wakde Island on the 26th and escort the amphibious landing ships and craft carrying the landing force. It leaves Wakde Island on the 27th.''

Jablonski groaned. ''All at 9 knots.''

Sorenson shook his head, ''More like seven.''

Dubose said, ''Either way, a long slow trip of about three days.''

On the 25th of July, the Carson buttoned up her boilers and got underway. Sorenson noted that Ensign Lloyd was on the bridge, and he took time to explain what Steiner was doing as Steiner got the ship underway. ''Glad to see you up here,'' Sorenson said.

Lloyd grinned. ''Thank you, sir, for the invitation. I've always wanted to see what it was like up here.''

Sorenson nodded approvingly. ''I'll give you a chance to handle the ship soon.''

He also noted Kittredge, sending a message by flashing light to the flagship, and when Kittredge had finished sending, Sorenson walked over to him and said, ''How do you like the signal bridge?''

Kittredge smiled broadly, his young face beaming. ''Best thing that ever happened to me. I couldn't stand the smell of all that machine oil back in the mount. Here there's fresh air everywhere.''

Sorenson looked at the perspiration beginning to stain Kittredge's clean shirt. ''Doesn't all this heat and sun get to you?''

''Oh, yes, sir, but it's clean heat, and I can take a lot of sun.''

Sorenson turned to leave. ''Well, let me know if you want to go back to the mount. I'm sure Chief Vickers will welcome you.''

Kittredge shook his head. ''I don't think so. He thinks Big Jackson is the best trainer he ever had.''

The next morning the *Carson* and nine destroyers patrolled off Wakde Island Harbor. At the last minute the *Ransome* boiled over the horizon and took her place in the screen. Sorenson sent her a welcoming message. Back came a sheepish reply.

Then a stream of amphibious vessels came out of Wakde Harbor. Sorenson counted 5 APDs, 19 LCIs, 8 LSTs, a fleet tug, and 4 PC patrol craft that would act as control ships. He watched expectantly, waiting for them to assume some sort of formation, but after an hour they were still straggling in a nondescript bunch.

Jablonski shook his head. "Looks like they're all hanging back to make sure they're the last to reach the beach."

By nightfall, the amphibious ships were in an approximation of a square formation, and the destroyers assumed a circular screen. The *Carson* was at the rear of the screen. "Damn!" Sorenson said, "These bastards ahead of us will be dropping back on us all night long."

Sorenson slept in his chair all night. Periodically the officer of the deck awakened him with a report of a ship dropping back. Each time Sorenson sighed and said, "Go up alongside him and ask if he needs help."

Each time the offending ship said no and put on a burst of speed.

The second day one of the LCIs broke down, and the fleet tug had to take it in tow. The tug could only make 5 knots with the LCI streaming behind it, and she gradually dropped behind, shepherded by one destroyer.

The second night was a little better, but just at dawn a second LCI broke down, frantically signaling for a tow.

Sorenson kept his fingers crossed, but soon the order came for the *Carson* to take the LCI in tow.

Sorenson disgustedly had the officer of the deck pass the word to standby to tow, and in a few minutes he could see Auerbach and Chief Bellows supervisng the break out of their towline aft.

Sorenson left formation and circled to come around behind the LCI. As he approached the gently rolling ship, the word came up over the telephone, "Ready to tow."

Sorenson increased speed and came up to the beam of the LCI about 50 feet away. He stopped abeam and sent word back to the fantail, "Pass the tow line."

Chief Bellows sent over a heaving line and then a larger diameter messenger. Sorenson leaned on the rail and watched the activity on the deck of the LCI. Although there was only a slight swell, the heavily loaded and topheavy LCI rolled almost 10 degrees. Many soldiers lined the rail, obviously seasick, and others waited to take tbeir turns for a clear space to heave their breakfasts into the calm blue waters.

Jablonski said, "I wonder what they'd do if it were rough."

Sorenson said, "They wouldn't wait in line."

In less than five minutes the tow wire was over to the LCI, and Sorenson went ahead slowly to pay it out. Then he stopped again and the LCI made its end fast to the anchor chain.

When the LCI signalled that they were ready to go ahead, Sorenson increased speed gradually. Then he tried 5 knots, went up to 7 knots, and then to 9 knots. The LCI seemed to be riding nicely, and he put on turns for 11 knots.

Jablonski said, "The formation is only about 10 miles ahead, and at this speed we'll catch them in four hours."

"Good," Sorenson said. "We'll have time to do a little sunbathing."

Fineman, coming up to the bridge, said, "I heard that. You can't stay out in the sun at this latitude in mid-day. Jablonski tells me we're about to cross the equator again."

"Again! We cross it frequently these days."

Sorenson motioned toward Kittredge, standing by the port flag bag watching the formation ahead for signals. "What about him?"

Fineman walked over to Kittredge and looked at his face. "How long have you been up here in the sun?"

"About six days, sir."

"I'm going to send my pharmacist's mate up with some skin lotion. Keep your hat on all the time and find a shady spot whenever you can."

By mid afternoon the LCI sent a message saying they had completed repairs, and the *Carson* directed them to cast off their tow line. When it was safely in, the *Carson* went back to her place in the screen. The last night was uneventful. The amphibious ships settled down in formation and by dawn were ready to approach their assigned positons for unloading.

Sorenson felt uneasy as he watched the LVTs alongside the APAs being loaded with troops. There had not been any preparatory bombardment, but nothing happened. There was no fire from the shore. The LVTs left their area on time and the first waves hit the beach right on time without any opposition.

Bentley, listening to the landing force circuit, said, "The Landing Force Commander tested the circuit and then there haven't been any other transmissions, not even the usual unneccessary junk."

By evening the LSTs were completely unloaded and the Landing Force Commander reported all objectives achieved without any contact with the enemy.

Brophy said, "I feel like I've paid my fee at the cat house and found that the ladies have all gone home."

The next morning the destroyers were released and the *Carson* and the *Ransome* were directed to proceed to Humboldt Bay.

As they steamed south, Sorenson said, "We're not going to get off that easy at Morotai Island. I don't even like the name."

Jablonski, standing next to him, said, "It could turn out to be a helluva melee."

CHAPTER THIRTY-THREE

The *Carson's* stay in Humboldt Harbor was brief but productive. The mail orderly came back to the cheers of the crew with a huge load of mail bags, and several men went down into the boat to help him bring them on deck.

Sorenson waited patiently for the mail to be sorted and was rewarded when Vila's smiling face peered in the door of his lower cabin. "Captain, you made a big strike. Ten letters."

"Thank you, Vila, I hope you did as well."

Vila's face fell. "No, sir, I get maybe a letter a year through the Red Cross."

"Maybe you'll get one next time," Sorenson said.

Sorenson settled down to read his letters. He carefully arranged Ferren's letters by date and then opened them and read them slowly. Another letter was from Brother Ed reporting on their cattle business and enclosing a generous check that Sorenson looked at briefly, endorsed to Ferren, and put in a letter he was writing to her. Jokingly he added a postscript. "Buy a house if you want one." The check was big enough to buy any one of the houses he had seen in Coronado.

Sorenson spent the rest of the day making sure the *Carson* was being readied for the next operation. He found Renard busy ordering fresh provisions and trying to make sure he was not stuck with more then the mandatory quota of Australian mutton.

On the second day the *Carson* was ordered to get underway and fuel. Sorenson called for Ensign Lloyd to come to the bridge andconn the ship alongside the tanker. Lloyd arrived and frowned slightly when Sorenson suggested that he take the ship alongside. Sorenson saw his expression and said, ''There's nothing to worry about. It you begin to get in trouble, I'll take over and bail you out.''

Lloyd gamely stepped behind the helmsman and said firmly, ''I have the conn.''

Lloyd did very well, approaching a little too wide, but Sorenson let him go ahead, and he made a tentative but satisfactory landing. Lloyd's shirt was soaked, but he was smiling. Fineman, who had been watching, said, ''Good job, Lloyd. I'll be glad to help you anytime.''

Sorenson said, ''I hate to tell you, but his landing was better than your last conning job. Maybe you ought to stay up here and take us away from the tanker.''

Fineman grinned. ''Ah, I have several patients waiting. Maybe next time.''

The next morning the Covering Force Commander, Rear Admiral Berkey, called a conference of all commanding officers of the force. When Sorenson entered the mess room, he saw Captain Cunningham and went to sit beside him. Cunningham greeted him cordially and pulled out a huge cigar of the brand Sorenson had given him.

''Alden,'' he said, ''these damned things cost a dollar apiece, and that bunch of flowers you sent Molly goes at least a hundred American dollars in Sydney. It must be true, then, that what I hear about your Texas ranch and what is on it?''

Sorenson laughed. ''I don't know what you hear, but it has a lot of mesquite on it.''

Cunningham shook his head. ''That's not what I meant. I meant a lot of cows.''

"Not many cows. Enough to give milk for the house. Also quite a few out on the range for breeding."

"What do you call the kind that you've, er, fixed?"

"Steers."

"And you've got a lot of them?"

"Well, yes, we keep well stocked, but the government is buying a lot of them."

"And paying you a lot of money?"

"Some."

Cunningham shook his head, "You Texans understate worse than the British, and all the time your American movies have been trying to convince me that you Texans are big talkers."

Sorenson pointed at the cigar Cunningham was rolling in his mouth and said, "I hope you enjoy them, but I recomend that you don't light up until you see if Admiral Berkey smokes. Some of our crusty old admirals are real bears about smoking indoors."

Admiral Berkey came in and started right off without lighting a cigarette, so Cunningham eased his cigar back into his shirt pocket.

When Sorenson returned to the *Carson*, Dubose was waiting for him on the quarterdeck. Sorenson said, "We'll have a conference as soon as you can assemble the officers."

Dubose said, "They're waiting in the wardrom."

Sorenson's eyebrows lifted. "They must think we're back with the first team."

Dubose nodded. "They do. Are they right?"

"Yes. This one will be an all-out affair and the last operation before we start landing in thne Philippines. General MacArthur really needs these landing fields that we'll capture to use for bombers."

"On Morotai?"

"How did you know?"

"It's the most logical place."

"I hope the Japs don't reach the same conclusion."

When Sorenson sat down in the wardroom, he said, ''I see all of you want to know what we'll be doing.''

Steiner said, ''Yes, sir, we've loafed long enough. We want to get on with the big show up north so we can all go home.''

Sorenson said, ''Jablonski, you can junk that chart of New Guinea. Let's see one that includes Morotai and Halmahera.''

Jablonski was ready and took the new chart out from behind the sterilizer. He spread it on the wardroom table, and the officers near the corners put their coffee cups on them to hold them down.

Jablonski said, ''Be careful with that coffee. The last chart was so full of coffee rings I'll have to get rid of it.''

Sorenson said, ''As you can see, Morotai, the island chosen by General MacArthur's planners, is about half way between New Guinea and the southernmost island of the Philippines. It's also just above Halmahera, a Japanese stronghold. Strangely, the Japanese don't have too many men on Morotai, but they should be able to reinforce easily from Halmahera and the other islands. The fixed defenses on Morotai are better than those we have encountered so far in our earlier landings, and there will be a need for a lot of shore bombardment.''

Steiner asked, ''Who'll do it?''

''Admiral Berkey will command the Bombardment Force, and when it has finished its task, it will become the covering force again. He will have the same five light cruisers, Destroyer Division 24, and the *Carson* and *Ransome*. There will also be eight CVEs nearby rendering air support for the troops when they go ashore and air cover for us.''

Dubose said, ''We're back in the big leagues. How about air opposition.''

Sorenson said, ''The CVEs and the Fifth Air Force will do all they can to destroy Japanese aircraft as far east as they can reach, but that dosn't mean the Japanese can't bring in extra aircraft from their Borneo airfields. Maybe the air situation in a day or two after the landings will be more dangerous than at D-day. By the way, D-day will be 15 September.''

MacIntosh asked, ''Where will the landing force assemble, and who will be in it?''

Sorenson said, ''They'll assemble and load at Aitape, and this time we won't have to drag along behind them and play nursemaid.''

A murmur of approval went around the table.

''As for the Army, the 31st Division, plus a regiment of the 32nd Division, will be the landing force. About eighteen thousand men including the artillery and a good many Army Engineers and their heavy earth-moving equipment going along to finish the airfields. The Army Engineers expect to have the fields operational by D-1.

Sorenson looked around the room, and there seemed to be no more questions or comments. He said, ''We leave tomorrow morning. This is going to be the biggest and most probably the most dangerous operation we've been part of. As usual I'm optimistic about our chances, but the odds are getting worse every day against us. I suggest you all write letters home to catch the mail that will go off this afternoon.''

Sorenson left and went back to his cabin. Fineman followed him in a few minutes and knocked on his door. Sorenson said, ''Come in.''

Fineman came in and sat down. ''You look like you needed a shoulder to lean on. I've never seen you so down since we fought the *Sea Wolf* in the Atlantic in the *O'Leary.*''

Sorenson sighed. ''You're a good doctor. I was trying to hide my feelings from the officers, particularly the young ones.''

''Why do you feel so down? The operation seems straight-forward, even if it is bigger than the last ones we've been in.''

Sorenson got up and looked out the port at the small boats hurrying around the harbor. ''Some of it I can explain, and I want to have Dubose and Steiner listen to that part of it.''

Fineman pursed his lips. ''You're losing me.''

Sorenson waked over to the telephone and told the quarterdeck watch to send up Dubose and Steiner. He came back to his chair and sat down. ''While they're being rounded up, I'll tell you some things I won't go into with them. In a few minutes I'll tell you all why I think this operation may be the most dangerous we've ever been a part of. Other than that, I have a foreboding that I haven't had since in the Atlantic with the *Sea Wolf*. I know there's something evil about this operation, but I can't quantify it. Even the name of the island gives me the jitters. The name Morotai seems unusual and even morbid, if I can use the word. Maybe mordant is better. I know that's not enough to account for this feeling. It's just part of it.''

Fineman nodded. ''Well, you were right a year ago. The *Sea Wolf* really creamed us.''

There was a knock on the door. Sorenson opened it. ''Come in and sit down.'' Dubose and Steiner took seats around a small table.

Sorenson said, ''I want to talk to you about a few things I didn't want to go into with all the officers in the wardroom.''

Dubose nodded. ''I could sense that you were holding back, but I didn't want to ask any more questions at the meeting.''

Sorenson smiled. ''Now we're in a better relationship. A good executive officer should always be able to read his skipper's mind.''

Steiner said, ''What's the trouble? The operation seems okay to me.''

''Wel, in the first place, if you'll look at this chart, you'll see that Morotai Island is five hundred miles from Biak Island and a thousand miles from Wakde Island. That means there won't be any Fifth Air Force fighter cover for us until the Morotai airfields are ready to receive the fighters.''

Steiner said, ''But you said they'd be ready by D-1''

Sorenson turned to Steiner. ''No. I said the Army Engineers said that. Frankly, they're just guessing. They don't know what kind of soils they're built on. Also our fighters are much heavier than the Japanese Zekes. The Fifth Air Force bombers have enough range to bomb, but they won't do it without their own fighter cover.''

Steiner said, ''But we have something better. The fighters from eight CVEs.''

Sorenson shook his head doubtfully. ''Yes, but for how long?''

Steiner said, ''I don't know. I suppose for as long as we need them.''

Sorenson said, ''That's the rub. I couldn't say anything about it to al1 the other officers because it's really top secret and tightly held. The Pacific Fleet will invade Peleliu Island in the Palaus group on the same day. A division of Marines will land there.''

Steiner said, ''So? Only a little more than a division of Army troops will try to take Morotai.''

''Peleliu is a different kind of problem. It's hilly, full of limestone cliffs and caves, and is strongly defended by deeply dug in Japanese troops in great strength. Mark my words, after the first day, even though the Pacific Fleet planners won't admit it now, the Marines will be screaming for more air support.''

Dubose nodded. ''And the CVEs will leave in a cloud of smoke.''

''Good God!'' Steiner said, Those high ranking planners in Washington really screwed up.''

''Right. By that time all of the Covering Force except the *Carson* and *Ransome* will have gone north to see that no Japanese surface forces can come south to bother us or the landing force.''

Steiner said, ''Well, isn't that what we want?''

Sorenson pointed to the chart. ''Look at this. There are a dozen Japanese airfields on Halmahera in fighter range of Morotai.''

Steiner said, ''But the operation order provides for neutralizing all of them by D day.''

''I see why you're worried,'' Dubose said. ''You can destroy aircraft, but the airfields are a different matter. The Japanese can fill up craters in twenty-four hours.''

''They've done so before, and they can do it this time. Probably on about the second day, they'll fly aircraft in from Borneo to Halmahera, and after that, well, look out.''

Steiner said, ''You mean, we'll be on the bull's eye?''

Sorenson sighed. ''Exactly. They can't do much to the Landing Force ashore because of the heavy jungle cover, but ships off the beach will be obvious targets. They'll come right at us. If all this happens the way I think it will, we may be in for a lot of trouble.''

Steiner got up and paced up and down, running his hands through his crew cut hair. ''What can we do about it?''

Sorenson, watching him, said, ''Nothing but pray and keep a sharp lookout.''

Sorenson excused Dubose and Steiner, but Fineman remained behind. When the two had left, he turned to Sorenson. ''I see now why you were talking like that earlier. You not only feel a foreboding, there is one. I'm going down to get my sickbay in shape.'' Then he paused. ''Don't know if I should tell you this, but David, the part-Melanesian man back on the beach at Milne Bay, said, Morotai means 'death's head'' in their language when I was asking him about the shrunken heads they had.''

Sorenson grinned. ''I should have guessed that.''

Fineman said, ''I think you did. There can be madness for us off Morotai.''

When Kittredge finished his watch on the signal bridge, he felt the urge to go aft and see how his old friends in mount 53 were getting on. When he arrived, the crew of the mount had just finished their watch and were securing their telephones and the mount. Kittredge climbed up the side of the mount and poked his head in the door. Smith, the mount captain, was climbing down from his elevated seat. He grinned at Kittredge, revealing his gapped front teeth, and waved a muscular arm. Two others of the mount crew were stowing the tattered acey-deucey set, and they looked up and waved.

Big Jackson, hanging up his telephone set, saw Kittredge and said, ''Hey, signals, how's it going up there?''

Kittredge sat on the edge of the door frame. ''Great, but I miss you guys.''

Smith rubbed his blond hair to erase the marks his telephone set had left on it. ''What's the dope? I can't get much out of Jackson.''

Jackson grinned widely. ''Hee! Hee! Chief Williams tol' me to keep mah big mouf shut.''

Kittredge shook his head. ''Aw, come on, Jackson, cut the corn pone accent. You can talk as well as I can.''

Jackson sobered. ''Well, all I know is that the Captain is really down.''

Kittredge nodded in agreement. ''I heard him say the CVEs might have to leave early and maybe the other covering ships, too. Then there was something about the airfields might not be ready soon enough. I didn't get all of that. They were trying to keep their voices down like officers do when they don't want you to hear that important stuff. Then a message started coming in, and I missed the rest.''

''Jesus!'' Smith said. ''We'd be in a helluva shape if that happened! When would we be able to leave Morotai?''

Kittredge shrugged. ''Maybe not soon enough.''

CHAPTER THIRTY-FOUR

The next day the *Carson* got underway and fell in with the five light cruisers, Destroyer Division 24, the *Warramunga,* and the *Arunta.* Kittredge received a message from the *Warramunga* and brought it to Sorenson. Kittredge grinned and said, ''I think the skipper over there opened the bar too soon.''

Sorenson loked at it and laughed. ''He read it to Dubose, ''Listen to this, Forrest, he says not to be alarmed by the smoke on his bridge. It's the first of the cigars I gave him for the day.''

Dubose said, ''Is that one of the cigars he told me you gave him?''

''I guess so.''

Dubose scratched his head. ''He told me you are a rich cattle baron. Is that true?''

''I don't know what that means. All I know is that my brother and I used to ride the range on our ranch eighteen hours a day. I can hardly remember a day off. Sometimes I studied for school sitting on a horse. I'd get so sleepy I'd begin to fall off.''

''You must have done all right. You got into the Naval Academy.''

"Oh, yes, sitting on a horse for a long period is a powerful motivator. I studied like hell just to get off the ranch."

Dubose said, "You managed to avoid my question again. Are you rich?"

"Let's say my brother and I are comfortably well off, and now we can hire all the hands we want to ride the horses out on the range. Also, someday we're going to use light aircraft to move our herds."

Dubose said, "I'm afraid that wouldn't work in Alabama. All the aristocrats would rise in their graves and send in letters to the Selma Times about all the crude noise from the aircraft engines."

The covering force steamed north on the fourteenth and then west during the night. At midnight Admiral Barbey turned southwest and began the approach to the beach off Morotai Island. During the early morning before dawn, Sorenson could hear navy night fighters droning over the covering force, and Bronte sent word up that they were being well defended and that even the *Carson* had been allowed to exercise control over the orbiting fighters.

As dawn broke, the Covering Force dropped that title and became the Fire Support Force, and the cruisers took station off the beach. The scheduled bombardment began shortly afterward. Sorenson plugged his ears with cotton when the *Carson* guns joined in the continuous din. For forty-five minutes the firing continued, then it stopped abruptly. The silence was so unusual that Sorenson continued to shout his commands until he realized that yelling them was no longer necessary.

Bemtley, listening to the Army radio, said, "The first wave is ashore. They had trouble getting over the coral heads."

Sorenson sat back in his chair and wondered how soon he could afford to relax the ship's condition of readiness and feed the crew.

Bentley spoke up. "The Landing Force Commander reports no opposition on the beaches, but they are having trouble getting through mud behind the landing beaches."

That helped Sorenson make up is mind, and he ordered condition III set and the crew fed. He sent for his own breakfast, but by the time Vila brought it up, he had lost his appetite. The slack period had allowed him to think about the problems they might face later.

Bentley continued to receive positive reorts from the Landing Force Commander, and Sorenson wondered if he might have been exaggerating his fears. Then the first report of contact with the Japanese came in, and the situation ashore got worse. Several fire support missions were called for, and all were assigned to the cruisers.

Bt night-fall, Admiral Berkey apparently had decided that the cruisers and Destroyer Squadron 24 and the Australians should depart for their covering assignment, and the *Carson* and *Ransome* were left alone to render fire support ashore. Sorenson muttered under his breath, "There's the first part of what I worried about. If more happens, we're really in trouble."

Just as the cruisers were disappearing around the end of the island, Fineman ran up waving a decoded dispatch. When he saw Sorenson, he said, "Just like you predicted."

Sorenson sagged. "What now?"

"The CVEs have been detached.

Sorenson was so disgusted he could only shake his head. With great reluctance he got back to the problem at hand and assigned the first four hours of fire support to the *Ransome*.

Then he sat in his chair and tried to sleep, but the intermittent firing by the *Ransome* kept him from meaningful sleep, and he finally got out of his chair and began to pace the deck of the bridge wing.

At four o'clock the *Carson* was scheduled to take over the firing, and Sorenson called for reveille at 0300. After a quick breakfast, he had general quarters sounded. The clanging of the alarm sounded ominous to him. He had heard it hundreds of time before, but this time it seemed to grate on his nerves more than usual. He shrugged and decided it was because he was tired, but still he didn't like the odd feeling.

About 0500 the first requests for fire support came in, and the *Carson* commenced firing with one gun. After three shots had established the range, the fire control spotter ashore called for rapid fire with all guns, and the projectiles poured out of the elevated guns.

Sorenson grinned and wondered if the new hot shellman in mount 53 was hitting the hole in the deck instead of the projectile man's stern sheets.

All that day and the next night the *Carson* and the *Ransome* alternated fire support missions. Bentley reported that the Landing Force Commander reported heavy opposition and difficulty moving through muddy regions. The Army Engineers landed and soon reported that the nearly finished airfields would be unusable for the heavier American aircraft because of poor soil. They would have to move inland to new sites.

When Sorenson heard the report he groaned. There went the chance for quick transfer of Fifth Air Force fighters to Morotai,and he felt they were doomed.

When Sorenson relayed the report down to Dubose in CIC, Dubose said, "I see what you meant the other day. Now we have no fighter cover, and we're sitting on the bullseye by ourselves. As soon as the Japs get the airfields on Halmahera repaired and move replacement aircraft in, we're dead ducks. I'll get the word up to Steiner."

By dawn of the third day the Landing Force Commander reported that they could now rely on their artillery and that the fire support ships were no longer needed. Sorenson did a rapid mental calculation and concluded that the Japanese aircraft could attack any minute. If they were lucky, the two ships could get off of the bullseye before that happened.

Sorenson heaved a sigh of relief and set a course for Humboldt Bay. The *Ransome* fell in astern. As they left the fire suppport area, Sorenson looked around at the sky in the breaking dawn. The morning tropical fog was still heavy, and the visibility above five hundred feet was nil. Even the air below five hundred feet was thick with moisture, and it was raining lightly.

He felt that the overcast would give them enough protection so that he could go to condition III, and he had the word pased. Down below he could hear muted conversations as the crew moved down to the mess hall for breakfast. He looked up at the director. Steiner's head protruded out of the gunnery officer's hatch, although he didn't have the watch. He looked down at the forward gun mounts and noted that mount 52, just in front of the bridge, had the watch.

Dubose called up from CIC, "Captain, I'll be in CIC if you want me." Sorenson remembered the conversation he had had with Dubose and Steiner earlier, and he was grateful that they were taking extra precautions. He decided to add his own alertness, and he moved to the bridge wing facing the receding shore of Morotai Island. It was still quite close, and he could hardly wait to leave it behind. Staying there even an extra hour might be disastrous.

The squawkbox sounded. Bronte's voice said, "Bridge, we see something on radar low over Morotai Island, but we can't get a fix on it. Too much weather."

Sorenson swung his binoculars toward the island, now about 2 miles on the starboard quarter. His heart began to pound. It was a flight of eight low-flying aircraft. They had to be Japanese, and they were coming fast."General quarters!" he shouted. Then, without bothering to use the telephone talker, he shouted up to Steiner in the gun director and pointed to the incoming aircraft.Steiner saw them at once and shouted orders to his director crew and gun mount.

Sorenson grabbed the TBS handset. "Condition red!" he shouted and flung the handset back in its holder.

Then Sorenson yelled, "All ahead emergency flank! Right full rudder!" He was trying to bring the ship to starboard so mount 52 could bear on the onrushing aircraft.

The annunciator man crashed the handles forward, and the helmsman spun the wheel. Almost instantly the ship began to heel, but the increase in speed took longer to be felt.

Sorenson looked again at the approaching aircraft. Now he could see them plainly. The four lower ones were in line abreast, and there were big bombs slung under their silver fuselages. They were twin-engined Bettys, fast and dangerous. The four slightly above were escorting Zekes, capable of loosing a deadly stream of machine gun bullets, either at other aircraft or at ships.

In the seconds that remained, Sorenson remembered his foreboding and wondered what he could have done to avoid this impending disaster. Before he could answer himself, two of the Bettys veered astern of the *Carson* and headed for the *Ransome*. The other two lowered their noses and glided toward the *Carson*.

The Zekes peeled off overhead and were obviously preparing for a strafing run.

Mount 52 began to fire, the blast shaking the bridge and all on it. Sorenson peered through the smoke. At first he thought the Bettys were going to come through their attack unscathed, but then a VT fuse burst in front of the cockpit of the left hand Betty. The aircraft wobbled, dropped a wing, and headed for the water. Sorenson, peering through the blast of the next shot, could see the Betty catch a wing in the sea and then cartwheel. He shifted his attention to the remaining Betty. It bored in, headed directly for the bridge, but the violent turn the ship was in made its point of aim shift aft.

Now he could hear the 40-millimeter machine guns joining in, and several of their tracers penetrated the fuselage of the Betty. Soon racing men manned the 20-millimeter guns, and their higher pitched stacatto roar added to the stream of steel hosing the Betty. But it came on, seemingly unaffected.

Sorenson couldn't see how it could survive, but at a hundred yards a large bomb fell free and headed for the *Carson*. The pilot tried to lift the aircraft, but instead it nosed over. It came straight at the *Carson*. Sorenson held his breath, expecting it to hit the bridge, but at the last moment it dropped its nose slightly, veered left, and crashed into the area between mounts 53 and 54. Seconds later, the bomb, slower than the aircraft, hit the side of the *Carson* just abreast of the after engineroom. The ship rolled to port from the force of the detonation. Then it rolled back to starboard and oscillated back and forth. The 40s had stopped firing, and Sorenson knw thay were gone.

Sorenson could feel a periodic up and down motion of the ship beginning, and he knew it must be caused by a propeller shaft that had been damaged by the bomb blast.

Then he was aware that the peculiar motion of the ship had ceased, and he knew it was because the engine driving the damaged shaft had stopped.

Steele poked his head out of the pilothouse and yelled, ''Captain, lost propulsion on both shafts. Also all electrical power.''

Sorenson swore. Now they were almosst helpless. The ship could not maneuver to avoid aircraft attack, and he had only two 5-inch guns left. Without electrical power, the mounts could only be operated slowly and laboriously by hand. He shook his head, took a deep breath, and turned his attention to saving the ship. All guns had stopped firing, and in the sudden silence, Sorenson could hear feet pounding on the deck below as men ran aft to man mounts 53 and 54 and to take care of the damage. Even in the fog of battle, Sorenson was surprised that he could take a second to be thankful that the crews of mounts 53 and 54 had not been in their mounts when the action started.

Then he was conscious that Brophy was shouting. ''Zekes!'' Brophy yelled. ''Get down!''

Sorenson looked around to make sure all hands on the bridge were either on the deck or in the pilothouse. But he forgot to get down himself. Then he heard the stuttering roar of machine guns. Bullets clanged around the bridge structure, and suddenly Sorenson felt a heavy blow to his left arm. He was still conscious, and there was no localized pain,but he knew instinctively that he had been hit by a bullet.

He felt around his arm. It was numb, but the bones seemed to be intact. He could feel blood spurting from a wound, and he clamped his right hand over the artery above the elbow. The spurting stopped. He rolled over and got up slowly.

All around him figures were rising from the deck. He saw Brophy nearby. ''Brophy, see if there are any casualties that need help.''

Brophy left and came back in a moment. He started to say something and then looked closely at Sorenson. ''Nobody was hurt bad, but you need help. You've been bleeding all over my deck.''

Sorenson grinned wearily. ''Sorry.''

Brophy took a rubber tourniquet out of the bridge first aid bag and tied it around Sorenson's upper arm. Sorenson took his right hand off of his left arm and saw that the arterial bleeding had stopped. He felt weak, and he realized he might have been close to unconsciousness for several minutes. He took several deep breaths and felt better.

He staggered over to the talker, who was pale and shaking from shock and fright. ''Tell CIC to have the Executive Officer go back aft and take charge.''

The talker looked surprised. ''Sir, I told you several minutes ago he'd gone aft.''

''Sorry,'' Sorenson said. ''I guess I was out of it for a while.''

Sorenson held his wounded arm and walked slowly aft to the flag bags anbd looked astern. He knew that at least the after engineroom was flooded. He hoped the after magazines had been flooded as a precaution, but then he realized that if the bulkhead between the enginerooms did not hold, both enginerooms might flood, and the ship might not survive. If the keel were damaged, the ship might even break in two.

He looked aft, trying to line up part of the forward structure with a parallel surface on the after structure. He closed one eye and he held his breath as he watched with the other eye. After a minute he let out his breath. So far the after section of the ship was not moving with respect to the forward section. But more flooding could change the situation. He could see that the stern was down in the water by at least three feet, and he remembered that the rudder had been at right full when they had lost power.

He looked back at the green hills of Morotai, still only about 3 miles away, and then he looked for the *Ransome*. She was circling the *Carson*. Now he knew he had a decision to make. He would have a hard choice, the kind commanding officers were paid to make. If he chose to wait near Morotai while his laboring men tried to make temporary repairs to the one engine room and the rudder and find out whether or not the keel was damaged, another Japanese attack might come over those damnable green hills and finish the ship off.

On the other hand, if he had the *Ransome* take the *Carson* in tow, the pull of the towline with the rudder right full and a possibly damaged keel might vibrate the waterlogged stern section right off the ship. Then he might even lose the whole ship if flooding spread.

He looked back again at the threatening shores and thought about his decision. They would all have to live or die by his choice. If they sat there, they might all die ignominiously. If they tried to move out of danger, at least they would be taking the initiative, and if the ship sunk the *Ransome* could pick them up. He grinned. There really wasn't a choice; they would take the offensive.

Brophy was standing nearby looking at him solicitously. Sorenson cleared his throat. ''What's wrong, Brophy?''

''Captain, you ain't thinking about sitting here and letting those damned Japs kick our butts again?''

Sorenson laughed. ''Hell no, Brophy, tell the *Ransome* by semaphore to take us in tow.''

''Aye, aye, sir,'' Brophy answered. ''but please go below and have the Doctor sew you up. You're ruining my deck.''

Sorenson managed a weak smile. ''Not until I know the ship is safe.''

Then he thought about the problem of rigging for towing, and he called the talker over. ''Tell Mister Auerbach on the forecastle to take charge of rigging the towline.''

The talker relayed the order, but in a few minutes said, ''Mister Bentley is in charge. Mister Auerbach has gone aft to take charge of controlling damage aft.''

Sorenson nodded weakly. ''Very well.''

When Bronte had picked up the aircraft on radar in CIC, Dubose knew they were inbound, and he thought they might pass over or be shot down. He was surprised to feel the double shock of the aircraft hitting the ship and the almost simultaneous bomb explosion that knocked him to the deck. He could feel the ship heel over to port from the force of the explosion and then roll back and forth as she tried to regain her equilibrium.

He knew from instinct that the *Carson* had suffered major damage, and he told the CIC talker to inform the Captain that he was going aft.

He bolted out of CIC and ran toward the stern. He could see a towering blast of fire centered around the two 5-inch mounts and the 40-millimeter machine gun platform. He knew the two 5-inch mounts had been empty when the aircraft had hit because only mount 52 had been manned for condition III. But the 40-millimeters had been manned, and he concentrated his attention on their crews.

As he ran aft, he noticed that steam was coming out of a hole in the deck over the forward engineroom, and several men, led by Ensign Lloyd, were piling out of the hatch leading up fom the engineroom. A few yards aft, the crew of the after engineroom was also coming up on deck. He knew he would have to take care of their problems soon, but now he had to concentrate on the fire aft to keep it from getting to the magazines.

As he got closer, he could see that there was no hope for the 40-millimeter crew; the fire was too intense. Now the first priority had to be to control the fire. He remembered his days at fire-fighting school and tried to analyze the color and shape of the flames. He decided that most of the flame was coming from the fuel from the aircraft, but paint and other combustibles were beginning to burn, too. Then a few 40-millimeter rounds exploded. Now the firefighters, who were rapidly deploying hoses behind Dubose, would have to cool the ready ammunition storages and the adjacent depth charges as well as fight the fires, He corralled a man running aft. He turned out to be Kittredge. Dubose said, "Go down below and flood the after magazines"

Kittredge nodded and set off for the ladder that led to the magazines.

Dubose grabbed a man with a hose. "Play it on Kittredge going to the living quarters hatch!"

The hoseman sprayed salt water on Kittredge as he headed for the area of the fires, and he got to the hatch safely and disappeared below.

Chief Bellows pounded up, his heavy shoes thudding on the deck. "Gotta get them depth charges wetted down," he said.

"Good!" Dubose answered. "Go to it."

Now the aviation fuel began to burn itself out, and the hoses washed some over the side. The mounts themselves were burning from the fuel that had sprayed on them, and Dubose could see that their sides were bashed in from the force of the heavy engine and other parts of the aircraft hitting them. Now they had no fighting capacity at all aft.

He continued to direct the firefighting until he was sure Chief Bellows had it under control. As Dubose watched, he heard men approaching, and he turned toward them. Steiner and Auerbach were running toward him.

Steiner said, "What can we do?"

"We've got to get the fires under control first." Dubose said. "I've ordered the magazines aft flooded, and we're making progress."

Auerbach looked at the hole in the deck. "Jesus!" he said. "If both enginerooms flood, all that water will put us in danger of losing the stern."

Dubose nodded. "We're riding okay now. We're down about three feet at the stern."

"Yes, sir, but if I know the old man, he'll want us to get towed out of here. The rudder is over full, and the strain of the towline may break the keel if it's damaged."

Dubose said, "Where did you learn all that?"

Steiner said, "He's a graduate of damage control school. I suggest you put him in charge of controlling the flooding. Let me go aft and try to get the rudder put amidships manually. Then maybe I can get emergency power to it. I think you ought to go up to the bridge and take charge. The old man is in pretty bad shape."

"What?"

"Yes, sir. He took a bullet in the arm,. and he's bleeding pretty good."

"Why hasn't he gone below to see Fineman?"

"You know him. He told Brophy he wasn't going below until he knew the ship was safe."

Dubose gritted his teeth. "Okay, you guys do your best. Send information up by messenger as soon as you can."

Dubose stopped by the small knot of engineers around the hatch to the forward engineroon. Ensign Lloyd was putting temporary bandages on two slightly burned men. ''What's the dope?'' Dubose asked.

Lloyd said, ''The forward engineroom is full of auxiliary steam. I've cut off the steam to the auxiliary line, and as soon as the engineroom clears, I'll take some men down and isolate the damaged portion of the line. I don't think anything else is damaged. If we're lucky, we'll be able to have the negine back in commission in and hour. I've sent a man forward to start the emergenmcy electrical power generator. The after engineroom is completely flooded, and there's a good deal of damage down there.''

Dubose nodded. ''Keep me informed.''

Dubose got to the bridge in time to see the *Ransome* approaching the bow to pass the towline.

Sorenson saw him coming. ''What's the dope, Forrest?''

Dubose said, ''The after magazines have been flooded. Mounts 53 and 54 are out of commission. The 40-millimeters have been destroyed. The depth charges are suspect. All of the crews of the 40-millimeters are dead, and more men may be found when the area aft cools down. Chief Bellows is spraying it to keep more ready ammunition from cooking off. I don't want to send anybody too close until the ammunition stops exploding.

''Both enginerooms are out of commission. From the way the ship was galloping before we lost power, I'd say one shaft is bent. The after engineroom is flooded and unusable, but the forward engineroom may be back in commission soon. Ensign Lloyd should have the emergency diesel electrical generator on soon to furnish electrical power. That should give us lights, communications, and enough power to use the guns forward. I don't know about steering. Steiner is back there now trying to put the rudder amidships by hand and then will try to rig an emergency power line from forward.''

''Damn!'' Sorenson said. ''We really need to get the rudder amidships as soon as possible.''

Dubose nodded. ''If it can be done Steiner will do it.''

Sorenson asked, ''What about flooding? Are we in danger?''

Dubose shrugged. ''The water in the after magazines combined with that in the after engineroom puts us right on the danger line. If the keel is broken or the bulkhead between the enginerooms goes, we can kiss the stern good bye if we go ahead with the towing. I left Auerbach in charge aft. If he can get the water pumped out of the magazines and can send a diver down to look at the keel, we may pull through.''

'A lot of ifs,'' Sorenson said, ''but I've made a decision to be towed. We'll have to live with it.''

Dubose looked aft at Morotai and shuddered, ''I'm with you.''

Then the bridge talker spoke up. ''Forecastle reports we have the towline. They are ready to walk out the anchor chain by hand.''

''Go ahead,'' Sorenson said.

The *Ransome* went ahead slowly and Sorenson and Dubose watched the towline slowly lift out the water, in turn lifting the long bight of anchor chain from the *Carson*. Water dripped off of the straining towline. The *Carson* began to move forward slowly, but then verred to starborad as the rudder took charge, and then shuddered and veered to port.

Dubose looked at Sorenson and shook his head.

Sorenson said to Brophy, ''Tell the *Ransome* to hold at five knots.''

The *Carson* continued to yaw back and forth, and Sorenson held his breath, looking aft to see if the stern section was still firm.

He said to the talker, ''Does CIC have emergency power to the air search radar?''

The talker said, ''Yes, sir, no bogies in the area.''

Sorenson heaved a sigh of relief and looked back toward Morotai.

Jablonski said, "Only eight miles away now."

Then the talker grinned. "Mister Steiner is on the telephone line. He says he has rigged an extra sound powered telephone on an emergency line. You now have comminications with the steering engine room. He's putting the rudder amidships."

"Can we steer by telephone?"

"Yes, sir. He asks that you send a quartermaster back to relieve him so that he can go back to the gun director."

The ship began to steady and follow the *Ransome* with out veering.

Sorenson grinned wealky. "Brophy, tell the *Ransome* to increase speed to ten knots."

Jablonski said, "Another hour and we'll be out of danger from the Japs."

Sorenson said, "Maybe so, but we're still in danger of losing our stern. Forrest, please go aft and see what you can find out about flooding and the keel."

When Dubose reached the area around the hatch above the forward engineroom, he found Ensign Lloyd and Chief Vickers examining a heavy diving rig. Chief Vickers was the ship's qualified deep diver.

Dubose said, "Chief Vickers, you can't use that thing to go down that narrow hatch and travel around the engine room. It's too big and clumsy. Where's our shallow water diving rig?"

Vickers said, "I'll send Smith after it. He's the only one qualified to use it."

In a few minutes Smith came pounding down the deck carrying his equipment. Vickers helped him put it on. It consisted of a mask connected to an oxygen regulator on a single back-pack bottle. Vickers connected a life line to Smith's belt and gave him a large waterproof flashlight. "Take a good look at the fore and aft keel members," He said.

Smith nodded. ''I'll do a good job. I don't want to lose our stern either.'' He looked up at his mount, still smouldering. ''I guess I'll have to get another gun mount, though.''

Smith stepped over the hatch coaming and started down with Vickers carefully tending the safety line. In fifteen minutes he was back up and pulled off his mask just after he reached the top of the hatch. His blond hair was plastered to his head, and he was breathing hard. Through a gap-toothed grin he said, ''She's solid as an Australian whore. Let's go!''

Dubose looked aft toward the after deck house. All fires were out. At the hatch leading down to the living compartment and the magazines below it, Auerbach and two men stood by a small gasoline-powered pump called a handy-billy. One man was wearing a telephone, and the black cord led down the hatch alongside the pulsating hose bringing water up from below. A second short hose ran from the pump overboard. A full stream spouted over the side.

Dubose walked aft to the pump and shouted in order to be heard over the laboring pump. ''How's it going?''

Before Auerbach could answer, the pump coughed, and air begen to come put of the outlet hose.

''Damn!'' Dubose said.

Auerbach laughed. ''I don't think anything is wrong. I'll ask Chief Bellows.'' He turned to the talker, but the talker held up his hand, ''Chief Bellows is reporting.''

In a minute the talker said, ''Chief Bellows said all the water is out of the magazines, and you can turn off the pump.''

Auerbach reached over and turned the on-off switch. The pump sputtered to a stop.

''That's it.'' Auerbach said. ''This is the best we can do until we get in drydock.''

Dubose ran back to the bridge. ''Captain, you can make any speed you want to. The keel's okay, and the magazines are dry.''

Sorenson sighed. "Thank God!"

Before he could tell Brophy to signal the *Ransome* to speed up, Ensign Lloyd came on the telephone line, and the talker reported, "The Chief Engineer reports that the steam has been cleared out of the forward engineroom, the steam leak has been bypassed, and the forward engineroom is ready to answer all bells."

Sorenson said. "Brophy, tell the *Ransome* to cast off the tow."

Sorenson looked back over his shoulder. The green hills of Morotai had disappeared. He shuddered. "Madness! Madness! Madness," he said.

Dubose looked down at the deck under Sorenson. Captain, you're bleeding badly."

Sorenson looked at the deck. "Not so much. I just loosened the tourniquet a little bit."

"Fineman can't do anything for the badly wounded until the after section cools down. We're safe now. Let me take charge up here and you go below to see Fineman."

Sorenson nodded. "I'm getting too weak to argue."

Caruso took his good arm and helped him below.

Fineman was supervising the pharmacist's mates in bandaging a few burns on men who had been fighting the fires. When he saw Sorenson come in, he looked at his arm and groaned. "Get on the table."

He gently cut the sleeve off of Sorenson's shirt without removing the tourniquet. "Why did you wait so long to come down here? A wound like this needs prompt attention."

Sorenson grinned weakly. "So did a lot of other stuff going on topside."

Fineman shook his head. "I'm going to have to tie off this bleeder. Then I'll clean it up as best I can. You'll need more help as soon as we can get to a shore hospital or a hospital ship. I can see two tendons partially severed."

Sorenson said, "Can't you sew them up?"

"Sure. I'll have a go at it, but they may need a more skilled surgeon for permanent repair."

Fineman said to his Chief. "Let's do this with a local and some morphine."

Sorenson was so faint he failed to notice when the chief began to stick needles in his arm, and then the strong light above faded to a soft glow as the morphine took effect.

On the bridge Dubose paced the deck and kept a close watch on the decreasing column of smoke aft. Finally he could stand in no longer and said, "Steele, I'll take the conn. Go aft and see what you can find out. Also let me know about personnel casualties."

Steele came back in fifteen minutes. "Chief Bellows says the ready ammunition is now cool enough so that he has been able to send men into the area. I went with them. There weren't any bodies. The mounts are completely gutted. The 40-milimeters are junk and most of the depth charges, both in the K-guns and the after rack, are charred. I told the men to set them on safe and jettison them."

"How about personnel casualties?"

"Twelve men on the 40-millimeter crew are dead. Also a dozen slight burn casualties. We were lucky the 5-inch mounts aft weren't manned."

Dubose looked around the bridge. "We were also lucky up here. The Captain was the only one who got it. All the others were either in the pilothouse or flat on deck. Look at the holes and dents." He pointed at a dozen bullet holes. "Look at this. A round went right through the mast structure."

Steele said. "Some entered the pilothouse, but the bulkheads took up most of the bullets' energy."

Dubose said. "Have you seen Bentley? I want to get him started on a casualty report."

Steele said, ''I'll send for him.'' He sent the messenger off to look for Bentley. Fifteen minutes later the messenger came back, pale and stammering, ''Sir, Mister Bentley is dead.''

''Where is he?'' Dubose asked.

''In the coding room.''

Dubose ran down to the coding room. Bentley was slumped over the coding machine, his fingers still across the keys.

Dubose lifted his head gently. Then he noticed a red smear on his back. A machine-gun bullet had penetrated the bulkhead behind him and had retained enough force to pierce his back. Dubose felt for a pulse. Then he shook his head an said to the messenger, ''Send down for some stretcher bearers.''

He trudged slowly back to the bridge.

Steele saw him coming. ''Dead?'' he asked.

Dubose nodded. ''Poor bastard. He was just a kid, learning to become a good naval officer.''

Steele said, ''While you were gone a report came in from the *Ransome*. They have six dead and two guns out of commission. I told them to screen us ahead.

Dubose nodded, but he was still thinking of young Bentley's slumped over body and he gripped the bridge bulwark tightly in his hands and put his head down on them. After a few minutes he lifted his head and looked back toward Morotai. There was nothing there but a blank horizon. The nightmare was over for those who had survived the madness. But for thirteen young men lying quietly below decks life was over, and they would fight no more. He wondered if the high-ranking planners who had decreed that two inter-dependent operations would take place within two days of each other would ever know that their decision had killed a score of men on the *Carson* and *Ransome* and had left two ships in a shambles. He blinked his eyes, trying to hold back the tears.

He sighed deeply, took his hands off of the bulwark, and began to pace the bridge wing. Now he had to think about his duties as executive officer. Burying the dead, tending the wounded, feeding the living, and cleaning up and repairing the ship. Color returned to his knuckles as he walked up and down, but he was still deeply troubled. When he thought about the importance of his duties as executive officer to the men below and to the ship, he wondered why he had ever wanted to command a ship.

When Fineman was through patching Sorenson up, he had him carried to his sea cabin.

Dubose came in and sat down. "I'm putting together a message action report for both ships. I think we should ask to go to Manus for temporary repairs. Also I think we will have to go to the States for permanent repairs."

Sorenson said, "Fine. I agree. I'll be up and around before we get to Manus. In the meantime, you're in command until Doc Fineman lets me up."

Dubose nodded. "I think I can handle it, at least temporarily.

I've just had a report that we should be able to make 20 knots using jury-rigged steering. All the water is out of the after magazines and the draft aft has come up to two feet."

Sorenson bit his lip. "I hate to do this, but I must ask about our personnel casualties."

Dubose frowned. "We just found Bentley. A machine gun bullet killed him. We have twelve dead on the 40-millimeters and a dozen burn casualties."

Sorenson sighed. "We'll bury them ashore at Seeadler Harbor with Scorse. We'd have had many more if it hadn't been for your leadership and the good work of Bellows, Vickers, Auerbach, Lloyd, and Steiner."

"And thanks to you most of all." Dubose said. "You got us out of that hell-hole."

Sorenson shrugged. ''I didn't do much but make a decision.''

Dubose said, ''I've heard you say that's waht command is all about.''

''Thanks. By the way, I'm recommending you for command as soon as possible.

CHAPTER THIRTY-FIVE

The next day was a blur for Sorenson. Fineman kept him on pain-killers, but on the second day, Fineman came in and said. ''Stop loafing and get up. We get to Manus in two days.''

Sorenson grinned. ''I was getting tired of all this sleep anyway. I feel pretty good.''

''Any pain?

''Sure. A little, but I can manage with a sling.''

Fineman watched as Sorenson got up. ''You're a little shaky,'' he said.

''I'll be all right out in the fresh air.''

Fineman took him out on the signal bridge. Brophy saw him coming. ''Too late,'' he said, ''I've swabbed up all the blood.''

Sorenson laughed. ''Any doughnuts left?''

''One cinnamon I've been saving for myself, but you can have it.''

Sorenson reached for it, but grimaced as he inadvertently pulled tha stitches on his left arm.''

Fineman said, ''You'll get used to it.''

The day before they were to arrive at Manus, Brophy brought a visual message from the *Ransome* to Sorenson.

Sorenson read, "WILL HAVE BURIAL AT SEA SERVICES FOR SIX MEN AT 1300 TODAY." Sorenson reread the message and wondered if his decision to bury the *Carson* dead at Seeadler Harbor had been right. But then he felt better about it. After all, the *Carson* had a lonely shipmate there already, and he needed company.

Sorenson went back to the signal bridge and wrote a reply. "INTEND BURYING CARSON DEAD AT SEEADLER HARBOR. I WILL CLOSE YOU TO THREE HUNDRED YARDS DURING YOUR CEREMONY."

Shortly before 1300 the *Carson* eased in to three hundred yards and lowered her colors to half mast.

Sorenson, standing on the port wing of the bridge, watched the all-too-familiar scene on the *Ransome's* main deck. On the *Ransome* the breeze fluttered the edges of the flag draped canvas bags lying on tables, and the Commanding Officer had trouble keeping the wind-blown pages of the hymnal steady while he read from them.

Then he stepped back, and Sorenson knew the service had been completed when the men standing on either side of the bodies, raised the tables. The canvas shrouds weighted with projectiles slipped over the side and headed for the blue depths.

Sorenson said to MacIntosh, "Pass the word-attention on deck."

Then, as the as the bodies hit the water, he said, "Pass the word-right hand salute."

Below he could hear the orders coming put of the loud speakers, and he raised his own right hand in salute and in farewell to the men headed for the lonely reaches of the Pacific Ocean.

"Well done, and farewell," he said softly.

The next morning the two ships entered Manus Harbor. Sorenson sat in his chair and watched as Dubose brought the *Carson* alongside a repair ship with only one shaft and help from a growling LCM acting as a tug. The process took a little longer than usual, but Dubose made it without casualty, and Sorenson said, "Congratulations. That wasn't easy. Now that you've done the hard part, I'm ready to assume command again."

Dubose sighed, "This command stuff wasn't as easy as I thought it would be."

Sorenson frowned. "Now the hard part really starts. I've got to arrange for the burial of our dead as soon as possible. If you'll take care of the preliminary arrangements for temporary repairs with the repair officer, I'll go over to see the commanding officer of the repair ship to see if he can help."

Sorenson left Dubose deep in converation with the repair officer, and went over to see the commanding officer of the repair ship. He found he could negotiate the brow between the ships if he was careful, and he gained confidence as he got stronger.

The commanding officer received him sympathetically and asked what he could do besides the temporary repairs.

Sorenson said, "A few weeks ago you helped by arranging transportation to Seeadler Harbor in a PT boat for funeral services. Any chance of doing that again?"

The Captain rubbed his jaw thoughtfully. Then he said, "The PT boats are all up north, but we have an LCM. As you know, it's a big steel landing craft. I can arrange for you to use it. It makes about 10 knots. That means an hour and a half to Seeadler. I'll also have our carpenters get to work. How many coffins do youneed?"

"Thirteen. The LCM sounds fine. Can we have it tomorrow morning?"

"Certainly. Let me know if there's anything else."

"Yes, there is. The officer who conducted the last service is gone. Could we borrow a chaplain?"

"Yes. He'll be in the boat when it comes alongside at 0800 tommorow."

After lunch, Sorenson met with all the officers in the wardroom. The mood was somber. Sorenson said, "First,

I've made arrangements with the repair ship for an LCM to be alongside tomorrow at 0800. We'll bury our dead at Seeadler Harbor cemetery as we did Scorse. Chief Vickers should be ready with his firing squad and Terrill with his clarinet. The repair ship will furnish a chaplain to conduct the services. Anything I haven't covered?''

Dubose said, ''I think that does it. I'll make the arrangements.''

Sorenson said, ''What about our repairs?'

Dubose said, ''The repair officer said of course he couldn't fix us permanently. He'll put us in drydock, patch the side of the after engineroom, and do what he can to put it back in commission. He won't be able to replace the bent propeller shaft, but I think we'll be able to use the engine for emergencies. He's going to recommend that we go back to the San Diego ship yard. The *Ransome* will probably go, too.''

Fineman said, ''We've got some other repair work to do on you, too. There won't be any hospital ship in here for some time, butthe Army has established a fine field hospital. They've even got an orthopedic surgeon.'' He looked at Sorenson. ''You've got an appointment for an operation at 0800 day after tomorrow.''

Sorenson bridled. ''I'm not going to be left in this hell hole!''

Fineman laughed. ''This isn't a hell hole. It's almost a tropical paradise. But you aren't going to be left. You'll be back aboard in two days, and we're scheduled to be here a week.''

Sorenson calmed down. ''Will this fix me up finally?''

Fineman scratched his head, ''Well, that depends on what you mean. If you mean fixed you up like you do to your steers, the answer is no. If you mean no more operations, the answer is yes. But either way, you'll need at least several months of therapy in or near a hospital after you get back.''

The next morning the large steel-hulled LCM came alongside the *Carson's* port side, and the huge diesel engines roared as it backed down and then sputtered to a stop.

Chief Bellows, the carpenter's mate, and Fineman's pharmacist's mates had already prepared the thirteen bodies and placed them in the sturdy wooden coffins that the repair ship had sent over late the night before. The coffins lay in a line on the port side just forward of the fire-blackened deck and equipment. Each one was carefully covered with an American flag.

Vicker's firing squad began to load the heavy boxes into the LCM. By 0830 all the coffins had been loaded and Vickers, his firing squad, and Terrill and his clarinet got in the boat.

Sorenson, Dubose, and Auerbach came aft and climbed down to the boat. Sorenson felt clumsy with his left arm in a sling, but he managed to embark without falling. He greeted the chaplain from the repair ship who had been waiting in the boat, and said to the coxswain, "Shove off and make the pier at Seeadler Harbor."

The coxswain saluted, and said, "Aye, aye, sir." He nodded to the engineer who pressed the starter buttons for the engines. The two engines roared into life, and the coxswain backed away from the *Carson*.

The trip took about an hour and a half, and the engines made so much noise conversation was impracticable. Sorenson stared at the shore of Seeadler Harbor, thinking of Scorse lying by himself in the hot sand, and he was glad he had decided not to bury Scorse's shipmates at sea.

The LCM bumped against the steel pier at Seeadler Harbor, and Sorenson sent Dubose to find the sergeant in charge of the cemetery. Dubose came back followed by two natives pulling a wheeled dolly and the same sergeant they had dealt with before, now dressed in a complete uniform.

Dubose said, "The place has changed a lot."

The sergeant was clearly not happy at the change.

The *Carson* men got out of the boat and loaded the first three coffins on the dolly. As the coffins were being moved up to the grave area, the group walked slowly up the beach toward the cemetery. Sorenson said to the sergeant, ''A few months ago we buried a man in the consecrated part of your cemetery. Today we want to bury a mixed group, some Catholics and some Protestants. We'd like to bury them close to the first man. Will that give you any trouble?''

The sergeant shrugged. ''It won't bother me, and the Catholic Chaplain when he comes over here doesn't seem to mind. He only requires that all Catholics be buried in this sector.''

''Good,'' Sorenson said. ''Please give us graves as close as possible to the one marked Scorse.''

The funeral services went off as planned, with the repair ship chaplain in charge. After the completion of the services, Sorenson, Dubose, and Auerbach remained behind by the graves and watched as the natives began filling them.

Auerbach stared at Bentley's grave. Then he sighed, ''I'm glad he got to live a little in Sydney.''

Sorenson looked at him. ''If I said anything in Sydney that offended you, please forgive me. I am grateful to you for taking care of him.''

Auerbach nodded and started back to the boat.

Dubose remained behind with Sorenson. Sorenson stared down at Scorse's head stone. ''Now he won't be alone,'' he said.

Dubose said, ''As I understand the Catholic religion he never has been alone. They don't mourn death; they celebrate it. They feel he's finally found his parents, even if he didn't know who they were in this life.''

Sorenson said, ''A comforting thought. In any event, all of the bodies of our men will be together.''

Sorenson and Dubose, followed by the others, walked slowly toward the boat, each lost in his own thoughts. The coxswain started the boat engines when he saw them coming, and after they boarded, Sorenson nodded to the coxswain and said, ''Return to the *Carson*, please.''

An hour and a half later they were back. Sorenson thanked the coxwswain and the chaplain and walked slowly up to his cabin. He realized how much the morning had taken out of him, and he slumped in his chair.

Fineman followed him into the cabin without knocking and bent to feel his pulse. ''Will you be all right for tomorrow's operation?'' he asked.

Sorenson said, ''Sure. I want to get it over with.''

Early the next morning the gig left for the landing in Manus Harbor with Sorenson and Fineman, and by 0830 Sorenson was lying prone on a wheeled stretcher outside the operating room of the Army field hospital, wondering if he was doing the right thing.

A bottle of fluid hung above him from a tree-like stand, dripping into his veins through a needle. A green cloth cap covered his head, and he remembered that under the sheet he was naked. If he wanted to get up and leave, he realized he would be in trouble.

He saw Fineman walking down the hall toward him, talking animatedly with a tall man. Both were in hospital gowns. Sorenson watched them come.

Fineman noticed his attention, and said, ''Captain Sorenson, this is Colonel Moore. He's going to work on you this morning. I'll be with him since I did the original job.''

Two hours later Sorenson was back in the corridor that also served as a recovery room. Consciousness came back slowly, and he noticed the sunlight through venetian blinds. Then he heard feminine voices talking and laughing. At first he thought of Ferren, but then he realized they must be the voices of nurses. He enjoyed the musical sound of the voices, and he realized he would be back with Ferren soon.

Then he was aware of a familiar face bending over him. The face blurred and then cleared, and he knew it was Fineman. ''Hello, David, I'm back,'' he said.

Fineman said, ''You're back and in fine shape. The experts opened up your arm and took a look at my work. They declared you'll be as good as new.''

''When?''

''Your tendons will take several weeks to heal. Then you'll need at least four months of physical therapy and rehabilitation of your muscles, nerves, and tendons.''

Sorenson sighed. ''I guess I can live with that. When can I get out of here?''

''You stay here tonight. Some very nice nurses want to take care of you. I'll be back to get you tomorrow morning early.''

The next day Sorenson was back aboard the *Carson*, and by the time the temporary repairs were completed, he was walking a mile a day on the forecastle. The sling hampered him a little, but otherwise he was recovering.

Three days later, temporary repairs on the *Carson* amd *Ransome* were completed, and they left Manus Harbor bound for Majuro Atoll for a fueling stop, two thousand miles away.

Sorenson looked at the palm trees bordering Seeadler Harbor, now less ragged than when they had seen them last. As the trees faded below the horizon, he realized they were leaving behind fourteen shipmates, not just one.

As soon as the ship was secured for sea, Sorenson went to his sea cabin to start composing letters to the next of kin of the dead. He had done it once before when the *O'Leary* had lost a number of men in her battle with the *Sea Wolf* in the Atlantic, and he had hated it. Now it was no better, and he got up and paced up and down. After a few laps, he sighed and sat down again. He had to get at it, and he gritted his teeth and picked up a pen.

Then he looked at the thirteen folded American flags piled on a chair. He would have to send them with the letters, and he wondered if he should have buried his men at sea as the *Ransome* had done. Would it have been better to end the emotional trauma for the next of kin, or to leave them wondering about whether they would want to visit the distant graves after the war? He sighed deeply; it was all over for the dead now, and the next of kin would have to learn to live with it or make arrangements for the bodies of their loved ones to be returned home. In any event, Scorse was where he wanted to be, and Sorenson resolved to see that he stayed there.

CHAPTER THIRTY-SIX

On the second day out of Manus the *Carson* and *Ransome* crossed the equator. The weather was very uniform. ''Every day is hot,'' Jablonski said, wiping the perspiration off of his sextant after taking noon sun sights.

Sorenson spent the time exercising. He realized how much he had let himself go, and he took off three pounds on the voyage.

On the morning of the sixth day the palms of Majuro thrust themselves over the horizon. When the *Carson* entered the lagoon, Sorenson was impressed by the new buoys and navigational aids. The magnificent harbor, once filled by Task Force 58, was now home to a few tankers and station ships. The Fleet had moved westward to Eniwetok and Ulithi, the new fleet anchorages.

Ashore Sorenson could see jeeps and trucks moving about on coral-surfaced roads, and galvanized roofing on new buildings glinted in the hot sun.

Brophy, moving his signal telescope about, said, ''Don't see any mermaids over there. Just a lot of bare-bellied Seabees.''

Fueling was quick, and the two destroyers steamed out of the lagoon entrance and set course for Pearl Harbor, two thousand miles away.

The course to Pearl Harbor led them each day a few miles farther away from the equator, and on the fourth day the trade winds began to blow. The temperature dropped to a comfortable eighty, and the humidity slid to thirty percent.

Kittredge began to stand his watch on the signal bridge in the sunshine instead of the shade, and shirts began to come off on the main deck as sun bathing began to be a pleasure instead of something to avoid.

Flying fish began to appear in abundance, leaping out of wave fronts, jittering their tails, and gliding for a hundred yards. Porpoises increased in numbers, frolicing along the *Carson's* bow wave. The atmosphere became clear, and at night the stars were clear and sparkling instead of the murky glints in the upper blanket of moisture of the tropics.

As they steamed along, Sorenson was aware of a change in attitude of the crew. The somberness of the first few days after the loss of their shipmates turned into a feeling of anticipation as they approached civilization.

Sorenson watched Kittredge laughing with Caruso. He walked over to them. "Do you have any plans for Pearl?"

Kittredge grinned. "Sydney was nice for a few days, and all those New Guinea women didn't do much for me. There will be real women in Pearl."

Caruso nodded. "I didn't like the Australian beer either. The only good beer we had was what we took with us, thanks to you."

On the morning of the seventh day, the *Carson* rounded the southernmost tip of Oahu, and the men watching anxiously on deck could see Diamond Head in the distance. Sorenson turned north short of the Harbor of Honolulu and headed into the entrance to Pearl Harbor. The net was pulled aside, and the *Carson* headed for her assigned berth. The *Ransome* was given a berth astern of her.

Sorenson decided to keep the conn himself in view of the difficulty of handling the ship with only one propeller. He managed to get alongside with out too much difficulty although he scratched some paint on the flare under the bow when a gust of wind caught the bow and blew it against a bollard on the pier.

When the ship was secured, Sorenson started down below to get ready to call on Admiral Nimitz. Halfway down the bridge ladder a messenger intercepted him. "Sir, a Lieutenant Commander wearing them golden ropes is coming up the brow."

Sorenson recognized the messenger as one of the men who had come aboard recently and made a mental note to hold a little school for the new men in naval customs and usage.

Sorenson hurried down to the quarterdeck and met the aide who saluted and said, "Sir, I'm Admiral Nimitz's Flag Lieutenant."

Sorenson said, "Welcome aboard. I was just getting ready to telephone you to make an appointment for me and the commanding officer of the *Ransome* to call on Admiral Nimitz as soon as possible."

The aide said, "That won't be necessary. Admiral Nimitz wants to call on you and inspect the ship and crew at 1300. Then he'll go aft and do the same thing on the *Ransome*."

Sorenson blanched. "But we're not ready for inspection. We've been at sea for a long time."

The Flag Lieutenant said, "You don't know Admiral Nimitz. Inspection for him is another name for a friendly visit. Just have all of your crew on the forecastle in undress whites and the officers and chiefs in khakis. The

Admiral will take it from there. Otherwise, all you have to do is sweep down.''

After the Flag Lieutenant had taken his departure, Sorenson went down to his cabin and sent for Dubose. He told him what had happened.

Dubose laughed. ''I should have warned you. I remember his visit to us when we came back from Guadalcanal. Admiral Nimitz likes to see all of his ships and their crews. He'll talk a while, and unless I miss my guess, those awards we recommended and sent back by air mail will be ready. He likes to present them.''

At a few minutes before 1300, Sorenson was pacing the quarterdeck, wondering whether he should do away with his sling for the occasion or leave it rigged. He finally decided to leave it on. After all, if the ship could be wounded, so could the Captain.

Promptly at 1300 a black sedan drove up and Admiral Nimitz got out, followed by his Flag Lieutenant. He started toward the brow, but then veered aft and stood looking at the burned guns and patched side.

After a few minutes, he headed again for the brow. At the top, he paused and saluted the colors. Then he stepped down and carefully saluted the petty officer of the watch. ''Good afternoon, young man. I request permission to come aboard,'' he said.

The young petty officer of the watch, proud to be noticed, smiled and said, ''Good afternoon, sir. Permission granted, sir.''

The Admiral turned to Sorenson and said, ''You are Commander Sorenson?''

Sorenson saluted and said, ''Yes, sir, commanding USS *Carson*.''

Admiral Nimitz said, ''A fine ship, and I hope you will be fixed up soon. We need you back out here for the final push to Japan. Please take me to your crew. I have something to say to them and a few well-deserved awards to present.''

Sorenson escorted Admiral Nimitz to the forecastle and presented Dubose to him.

The Admiral said, "I'm glad to meet such a fine officer. I read the recommendation for your award and the citation carefully, and the medal and its citation I am about to award you tells it all."

He turned to the Flag Lieutenant and nodded.

The Flag Lieutenant began to read a citation, and in Sorenson's mind he could see the events being recreated. He was startled when the reading stopped, and then Admiral Nimitz reached forward toward him and pinned a second Navy Cross on his khaki shirt.

When Admiral Nimitz had secured the medal, Sorenson stepped back and saluted.

The rest of the ceremony seemed to go by in a daze for Sorenson as the medals were pinned on the recipients and the citations were read. A Silver Star for Dubose, and Bronze Stars for Lieutenant Steele, Lieutenant Steiner, Chief Bellows, and Chief Vickers. Legions of Merit for Brophy, Smith, and Williams, and then Silver Life Saving Medals for Dubose and Williams.

After these medals were presented, Purple Heart Medals for wounds received were presented to Sorenson, Brophy, Wencey, and a dozen other men who had been wounded. When Admiral Nimitz had pinned on the last medal, he handed Sorenson a small box. "These are Purple Heart Medals awarded posthumously for the men you lost. I trust you will get them to their next of kin."

"I will, sir," Sorenson said.

The Admiral said, "Now I have a few words to say to your crew."

He climbed up to the deck above and stood near mount 52. His blue eyes glinted below white eyebrows as he looked at the crew below. "I try to call on all of my ships coming east, particularly those that have been damaged in battle. I saw the damage aft, and I know it cost you the lives of some shipmates. The fact that they died has to make the rest of us try harder to justify their loss.

The reports I have received from Admiral Kinkaid of the *Carson's* contributions to the Seventh Fleet's success have indicated to me how well you have done. I would like to be able to say that you have now done your part, but I will have to say to you that we still need you. The task is not finished, and it won't be until we enter Tokyo Bay."

There was a tentative cheer, and it swelled in volume as Admiral Nimitz smiled. He raised hand his in salute and turned to leave.

Admiral Nimitz climbed down to the forecastle deck and headed aft and down the ladder to the quarterdeck. Sorenson followed him, and the Flag Lieutenant brought up the rear.

When they reached the quarterdeck, the Flag Lieutenant took his departure. Admiral Nimitz saluted the petty officer of the watch, asked for permission to leave the ship, and then turned to Sorenson.

Sorenson said, "Sir, I appreciate that you took time from your busy schedule to visit us."

There was a steely glint in the Admiral's eye that Sorenson hadn't seen there before. "Son," he said, "there are three admirals, a general, and a congressman waiting in my conference room, and they can keep on waiting. I make it a rule to put visiting my ships at the top of my priority list. When you get to be my rank someday---and I think you will---remember that."

All Sorenson could think of was to say, "Aye, aye, sir."

The twinkle was back in the Admiral's eye. He returned Sorenson's salute, smiled, said, "Good luck," and turned on his heel and walked down the accommodation ladder bound for the *Ransome.*

CHAPTER THIRTY-SEVEN

Sorenson slipped ashore that evening to telephone Ferren. The connection was bad, but he managed to tell her without violating security that he was in Hawaii and would be home soon. He also told her he had been wounded slightly but would be in shape by the time he got home. She started to ask questions about his wounds, but he hid behind the difficult telephone connection and didn't answer her directly.

He went back to the ship and walked up to the vacant forecastle. In the fading light he looked at the remains of the battleships rusting near Ford Island. How far the Navy had come, he thought. Soon they would be knocking at Japan's door.

As he paced up and down the forecastle, he thought how Ferren must be feeling. He remembered her reluctance to marry him and the months he had tried to get her to change her decision to put off their marriage until the end of the war. The loss of her first husband had haunted her, and even after she had agreed to marry him, he had almost lost his life in the Atlantic. Now, after they had been married for only a short time, he would have to tell her he had come close to leaving her, off Morotai. He shuddered involuntarily, remembering the Japanese aircraft coming directly at him, and the staccato sounds of the machine gun bullets walking toward him.

They had mutually agreed not to have children until after the war, and he knew how much she wanted to have them. Shepherding a group of second graders might be rewarding, but she had said in a letter that they couldn't take the place of her own child for long.

Now he would be in San Diego for several months, and he resolved to bring up the subject of a child when they got in. He paced in the pleasant air, hearing the hundreds of mynah birds near by settling in the trees for the night. The slight breeze brought the smell of sweet frangipani blossoms to him, and he thought of the gardenia cologne Ferren always wore.

Then he went below and turned in, but sleep was slow in coming as he thought about Ferren.

They were permitted to stay two days so each man could have a night ashore.

On the morning of the second day, the quartet was at breakfast when Sorenson came in to the wardroom. MacIntosh had been substituted for Reifel in the quartet. They were obviously feeling poorly.

Sorenson said slyly, "Too much poi?"

Dubose sighed. "Not enough. That Damned Duke Kalana made us sing for our supper."

"Well, you must have sounded pretty good last time we were here. You got more than poi then."

"That was last time. This time the three of us had to sing extra loud to drown out MacIntosh. You should have heard him trying to sing Aloha Oe with a Scottish burr."

"You could have switched to Scottish songs."

"We tried one, but the Hawaiians couldn't understand Robert Burns."

Sorenson sighed, "I don't either, particularly when sung by a sheepherder."

MacIntosh, silent until then, said, "This was an emergency assignment for me. I'll learn my part better next time."

Sorenson said, "Unless you switch duties, there won't be a next time. We fuel today and leave early tomorrow morning."

At lunch, MacIntosh, now acting as communication officer, brought Sorenson three messages. Sorenson read them. Then he sighed. "I don't know whether to laugh or cry."

"What's the trouble?" MacIntosh asked.

"This first message tells the present Executive Officer to relieve me of my command of the *Carson*. The second tells Mister Steiner to relieve him as Executive Officer. The third tells me that when I'm relieved I'm to proceed to the Naval Hospital at San Diego for treatment. Then, when I'm released from treatment, to proceed to Long Beach, California, and report as prospective commanding officer of a new construction destroyer, as yet unnamed."

"What's a prospective commanding officer?"

"That means I supervise the last stages of construction, and then, when the ship is completed and commissioned, I assume command."

"And right back to sea?"

"No. About two months fitting out of the ship with equipment and stores and a month of refresher training at San Diego."

"We'll miss you," MacIntosh said somberly.

Sorenson turned away to hide the growing moisture in his eyes. "Not half as much as I'll miss this ship and all of you in it."

"Could you get some of us transferred to your new ship?" MacIntosh asked anxiously.

"Sure. Just like I had you ordered to the *Carson*."

MacIntosh brightened. "I'll be waiting. So will a lot of others. I'm sure Commander Dubose will be a good skipper, but somehow this ship has always been special with you in command."

"Yes, it has, but he'll do well."

The next day they left Pearl Harbor with the *Ransome* following and rounded Diamond and Koko Heads before settling on a course for San Diego, five days away.

Sorenson conferred with Dubose and the department heads and decided to have the change of command at sea on the third day out.

On the third day, the morning dawned with a light sea and a following wind, and the crew assembled on the forecastle at 0900.

Sorenson and Dubose came to the deck above in front of mount 52 and looked down at the assembled crew. Sorenson saw familiar faces looking up at him. He remembered how few of them he had known nine months ago when he had assumed command. Now he knew all of them by sight and name. They had all been through a lot together, and he knew he would miss them all.

When all was ready, Steiner, now the Executive Officer, nodded. Sorenson stepped forward and began to speak, summarizing their operations over the last nine months and telling them how much he appreciated their fine performance. He felt himself getting emotional, and he cut his remarks short. When he lifted his orders to read them, he had to pause and blink to clear his eyes. Then he read his orders in a firm voice and turned to Dubose. "Sir, I am ready to be relieved."

Dubose returned his salute, and stepped forward. He read his orders and said, "Sir, I relieve you."

Sorenson could hear Brophy up on the signal bridge give Caruso orders to haul down the commission pennant and break a new one. There was a squeal of the signal halyard blocks, and Sorenson knew he was no longer in command.

Dubose turned to the crew and said, "My remarks will be brief in accordance with custom. All orders of my predecessor will remain in effect. I pledge to maintain the readiness of the *Carson* to fight and to maintain the high reputation this ship has attained. When we return to the fleet we will be ready to continue the fight.''

Dubose turned to Steiner. ''Sir, please dismiss the crew.''

Steiner waited until the two commanding officers were clear of the forecastle before giving the order, ''Crew dismissed.''

Sorenson stopped Dubose at the foot of the ladder, ''Forrest, I'll move out of the lower cabin as soon as I can.''

Dubose said, ''Of course not. Stay there until we get into port. I'll be fine in the sea cabin. But I'd like to have a cup of coffee with you now.''

Dubose led the way to the lower cabin, and they sat down. Dubose ordered coffee from Vila. Then he said, ''I've been thinking all night about how to phrase what I want to say.''

Sorenson said, ''To hell with the phrases. Let it all out.''

Dubose took a deep breath. ''I know you had reservations about me, or even disliked me, when you first came aboard. But I've done my best to meet your requirements and to take your advice. Within those limits, I am what I am, and I can't change completely. I'd like to know what you thought about me when you recomended me for command.''

Sorenson stirred his coffee and looked up at Dubose. ''Frankly, I think you are one hell of a fine person, a very capable Naval officer, and will make a superb commanding officer. The only flaw I found in you that I couldn't stomach was your bigotry, and I think you've overcome that.''

Dubose nodded. ''I think I have. Out here the only thing that counts is what a man is. Color, religion, family background, money---none of it is important. Just what a man is and can do. I don't say I won't have a few problems when I go back to Alabama, but I'm going to work on them. too. Maybe the Alabamians will change one day, too.''

Sorenson nodded, ''I hope so. This bigotry business may tear the country apart.''

Dubose went on. ''I know the Navy needs to change. Maybe it will before the country does.''

''You can do your part.''

''How?''

''Chief Williams?''

Dubose grinned. ''I'm ahead of you. Last night I had Chief Carmody write up a letter recommending that Chief Williams' rate be changed to chief signalman. If he gets it, I intend to keep him and ask that Chief Brophy be sent to new construction.''

Sorenson grinned, ''I could use him.''

Dubose said, ''I hope you'll use the next two days resting and getting ready to meet your charming wife. Use Carmody and Vila for anything you need.''

Sorenson said, ''I want to apologize for the fuss I made about your accent. You've learned to talk so that the officers and crew can understand you. At other times I find your accent very soothing. I've grown to like it. I also want to compliment you on the way you handled Steiner and his grumpiness.''

Dubose laughed. ''I'm glad you said that. Frankly I've gone about as far as I can on the accent. As for Steiner, I've grown to appreciate him too. I think we'll fit fairly well together.''

Sorenson grinned. ''I think you'll find he'll change just as you did.''

On the morning of the fifth day, the 15th of October, Bronte reported a radar contact on land ahead. By 0800 Brophy identified Point Loma on the port bow.

Then Sorenson could see the rising white bulk of the Hotel Del Coronado. He wondered where Ferren's apartment was located and if she knew he was coming in to port this day.

Then the channel buoys appeared, and Sorenson watched idly as the *Carson* threaded between them. He found it hard to realize he no longer had responsibility for the safety of the ship, and he shrugged as they passed an outgoing merchant ship a litle too closely.

At last, when Sorenson was beginning to be impatient, he could see the long piers of the ship yard jutting out into the channel.

From the forecastle he could hear Dubose's quiet commands on the bridge, and the *Carson* swung slowly to port and headed for her berth. Steiner, standing next to Dubose, seemed to be confident and happy in his new role.

He was concentrating so much on the progress of the ship he failed to see Ferren standing on the pier. When he did see her, he was taken by surprise. She was standing in the middle of six second-graders. Two were holding her hands and the others were holding on to each other.

He waved, but Ferren was looking up at the bridge and didn't see him.

He waved again, and she saw him. Even at a hundred yards he could see her beautiful smile clearly. She bent down and spoke to the children at her side, and they waved to him.

Chief Bellows was standing nearby with the forecastle crew, and he said, "Captain, I didn't know you had so many children."

Sorenson laughed. "They aren't mine, or at least I don't think so."

The *Carson* glided on, and then Dubose stopped her a little wide of the pier. Sorenson knew he had to be careful with only one propeller to maneuver with. But in minutes Chief Bellows had the mooring lines over and the bow snugged in with the anchor windlass.

Sorenson walked aft and was the first off the ship when the huge brow was hoisted into place by a yard crane. As he walked up the pier he waved at Dubose, Steiner, and the bridge crew, and they waved back. He could hardly keep the tears back, but he turned to Ferren, and all else left his mind.

She was all that he remembered she had been, but he had a hard time taking her in his arms with six small fry clinging to her.

When he had hugged her as hard as he could with one arm, he whispered in her ear, "What's all this?"

Ferren said, "This is my second grade class, or what's left of it. The rest has mumps. I hope you've already had them."

"Oh, yes."

Ferren said, "Because of the epidemic I couldn't get a substitute teacher to take my class, and I had to bring them with me. If you'll walk down the pier with us and tell them what the ship does, we'll go back to the class room. By the way, why weren't you on the bridge?"

"I've been relieved. I'm no longer in command."

"Then you're mine?"

"As of this moment. I'll have to send back for my baggage tomorrow, and then I'll have to go over to the Hospital in San Diego for some therapy. Other than that, my wound is completley healed."

Ferren grinned mischievously. "I take it your arm won't bother you otherwise."

"No. I can do anything but pick up heavy weights or you."

"I promise to be careful of your arm and the rest of you. Other than that, I'll keep you busy."

Sorenson asked, "What's this about the classroom? That wasn't what I had in mind."

"You have to go there with me and give a short lecture to my kids on the war. After that it will be time for school to let out."

"It had better be. Otherwise we'll be teaching sex education right in the class room."

Ferren drove them all back to school in the green Buick. Sorenson was crowded in back with three children at his side and one on his lap.

Ferren looked back at him and said slyly, ''How does it feel to be a daddy?''

''Fine, but one at a time would be better.''

Ferren said, ''We'll talk about that later.''

After Sorenson had told all the sea stories he could remember about New Guinea, and school was out, Ferren said, ''Now I'm yours. Let's go to our new house.''

''House?''

''Yes. You told me I could buy one, and I did.''

''Where is it?''

''Coronado, of course. On Alameda Boulevard between eighth and ninth. We face the golf course, and we can see Point Loma from the upper bedroom window. We're two blocks from the ocean.''

''It must have cost a fortune.''

''You sent me one.''

The house was all he thought it would be. Two stories of white stucco with adobe walls enclosing a small patio and garden. Furniture filled the patio except for many flower beds. Martha Washington geraniums of all colors filled beds in front of the house.

But Sorenson wasn't interested in details. ''Where's the bedroom?'' he asked.

Ferren arched her brows, ''You want to see Point Loma out of the bedroom window?''

''No, and I'm in a hurry.''

''Not so fast, buster, come over here and sit down.''

''Under protest.''

Ferren asked, ''When will you go back to sea again?''

Sorenson started counting on his fingers. ''Four months physical therapy time in the hospital. One month leave. Two months precommissioning. Three months fitting out. One month refresher training. Eleven months from now.''

Ferren said, ''That's about right. I'm going to resign from teaching this week.''

''I thought you liked teaching.''

''I do, but I've decided to go in for one at a time.''

''You changed your mind about children?''

''Oh, yes. I want one of my own as soon as possible. The way I figure, you get one month's precommissioning time, as you call it, then you get down to keel-laying, and if all goes well, that means you'll have one month to get acquainted with your new family before you leave.''

Sorenson said, ''To hell with the that precommissioning stuff. As I told you, I can't pick you up in my arms yet, but if you'll lead the way, I'll be happy to assist with laying the keel right now.'' She looked at him tenderly and smiled, ''This way,'' she said.

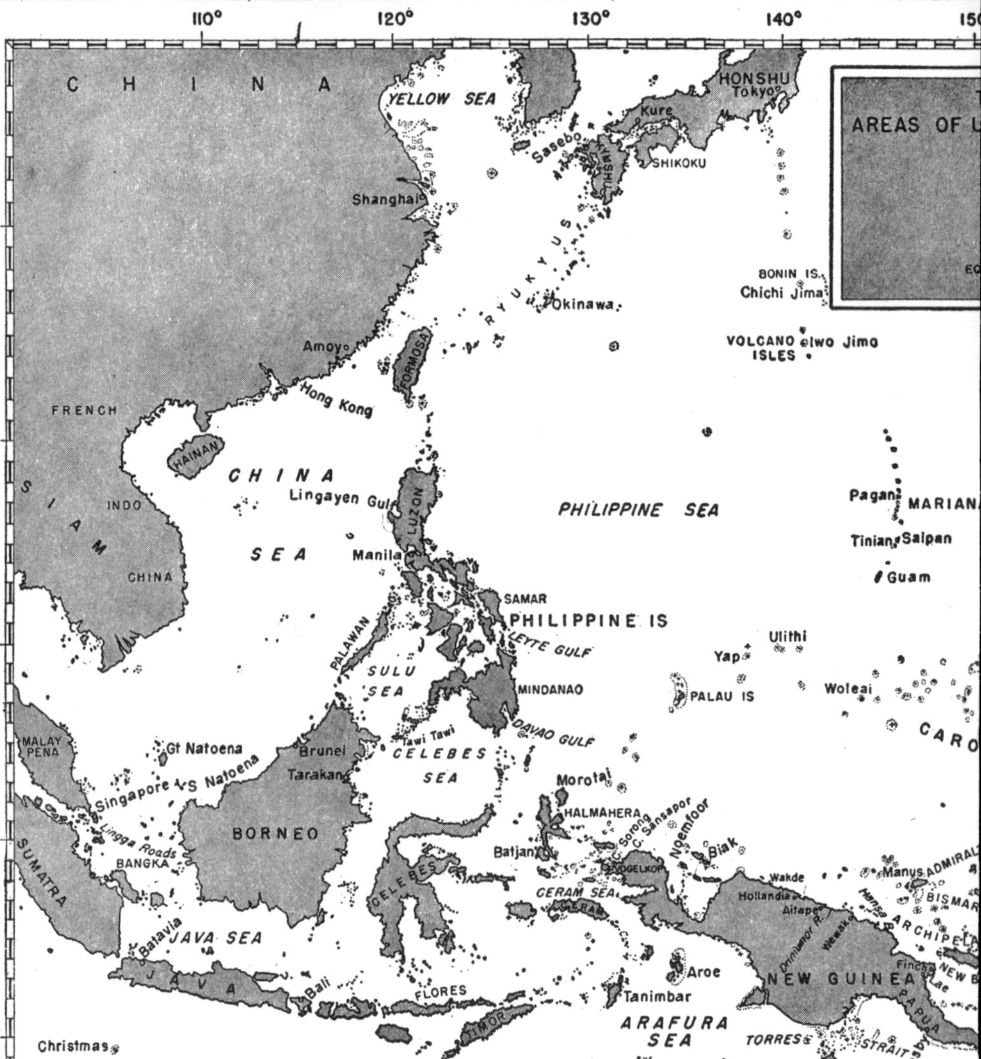
110°
120°
130°
140°
30°
20°
10°
0°
10°
CHINA
YELLOW SEA
HONSHU
Tokyo
Kure
Sasebo
KYUSHU
SHIKOKU
AREAS OF
Shanghai
RYUKYUS
BONIN IS.
Chichi Jima
Okinawa
Amoy
FORMOSA
VOLCANO ISLES
Iwo Jima
Hong Kong
FRENCH
HAINAN
CHINA
SEA
INDO
CHINA
SIAM
Lingayen Gulf
LUZON
PHILIPPINE SEA
Pagan
MARIANA
Tinian
Saipan
Guam
Manila
SAMAR
PHILIPPINE IS
PALAWAN
LEYTE GULF
Ulithi
Yap
SULU SEA
MINDANAO
PALAU IS
Woleai
CARO
MALAY PENA
DAVAO GULF
Tawi Tawi
Gt Natoena
S Natoena
Brunei
Tarakan
CELEBES SEA
Morotai
Singapore
HALMAHERA
Sansapor
Sorong
Noemfoor
Biak
Lingga Roads
BORNEO
Batjan
VOGELKOP
Wakde
Manus
ADMIRALTY
BANGKA
SUMATRA
CELEBES
CERAM SEA
CERAM
Hollandia
Aitape
BISMARCK ARCHIPELAGO
Batavia
JAVA SEA
Wewak
NEW GUINEA
JAVA
Bali
FLORES
Aroe
Tanimbar
Finschhafen
Lae
PAPUA
NEW B
Christmas
TIMOR
ARAFURA SEA
TORRES STRAIT
P Moresby
Darwin
INDIAN OCEAN
AUSTRALIA